The Drug Lord:
A Novel
By

Peter A. Neissa

Floricanto Press

ISBN:0-915745-52-6

FLORICANTO PRESS

650 Castro Street, 120-331

Mountain View, California 94041

(415) 552-1879 (702) 995 1410 Fax

Website: www.floricantopress.com

E-Mail: info@floricantopress.com

The Drug Lord

To John Piccolomini Jr., fellow traveler, friend, and brother on a long and dusty road.

Author's Note

As early as 1988, the American people were not aware of who Gonzalo Rodriguez Gacha was, despite the fact that he was a ranking member of the cocaine cartel and the most wanted criminal in America. A man who had smuggled over 300 tons of cocaine into the United States and blown up a jet-liner in mid-flight. Gacha was a man who had taken part in bribery, extortion, murder and earned an estimated $5 to $8 billion dollars. A startling fact, when compared to the statistics compiled by the Dow Jones News Retrieval Database—Comprehensive Company Reports, which states that General Motors net income in 1988 was slightly less than $4.5 billion.

This biographical novel is based on historical facts. The events portrayed such as drug seizures, cartel meetings, laboratory locations are all now a matter of public record and knowledge. Although some dates have been changed to suit the plot of the story, I have tried to remain within the spirit of the historical facts. Dialogue between characters is construed to fit the events after careful research and how I imagined these events to have happened. Although many will see similarities to living people, I can only say that such comparisons will lead to erroneous conclusions.

I was born in Bogota, Colombia and witnessed the blood spill in the streets. I have written this story from a Colombian perspective, an outlook that comes from seeing loved ones disappear without a trace and of finding friends in the morning paper with their brains blown out. I did not write this novel to give a quick and easy solution to the drug problem, but to show how complex the problem of narcotics is, in view of Colombian history and Colombian society and its relation to the drug expansion.

3

When I first wrote this fictional account, I was forced to use an alias for Gonzalo Rodriguez Gacha in order to protect my family in Colombia. Now that he cannot hurt my family from the grave, I have since changed the name. Although Gacha's life is as murky as the business he dealt in, it is a fact that he was a street kid peddling black market emeralds by the age of ten.

This biographical narrative would have been impossible to write had I not received the help from certain people and government bureaus both in the United States and Colombia. Thanks go to the Bogota F-2 police, DAS Colombia, the Drug Enforcement Administration (DEA) in Boston, Massachusetts for clarifications on the U.S. Narcotics and Dangerous Drugs Bureau, Hans Richter for his counsel, the office of the Honorable Senator Edward M. Kennedy and finally to the United States Department of State.

Colombia is a country under siege by drug lords who would kill their own mothers for money, men who are financial geniuses and sociopathic killers. Thus, I would also like to thank the People of Colombia who are paying a terrible price and to the men and women of the various anti-narcotics branches in the United States who each day put their lives on the line.

4

PROLOGUE

In the year 1957, at dawn on the twenty-fourth day of the twelfth month, the month of the birth of Jesus Christ, the army came to the village of Maraguey. It was in the Colombian rain forest near the snow-capped peak of Tolima beside the Magdalena River, as the first scratch of sunlight fired across the horizon and the Southern Cross began to fade from the sky.

Maraguey, the last rebel outpost of a rag-tag *campesino* brigade that had been involved in the bloody Colombian Civil War known as *La Violencia*. A civil war had begun when the liberal candidate for President Jorge Eliecer Gaitán fell to an assassin's bullet on April 9, 1948. Although it was never proven, it was believed that the assassination was ordered by the conservative party that was opposed to Gaitán's ideas about land reform.

The liberal party, led mostly by reform-minded men who were well-educated and from the oligarchic families, had its broad base of support with the *campesinos*. The conservative party, which wished to see things remain as they were, was also comprised of the oligarchic families, but its base of support rested with the military.

What was a difference of opinion among the Colombian upper classes became a bloody and violent fight between the *campesino* and the military. To the oligarchy, who won or who lost was a matter of no importance; to the *campesino*, it was a matter of life and death. But after nine years of bloody civil war and disorder rampant around the country, the oligarchy handed over the reins of government to a *junta*.

Headed by General Gustavo Rojas Pinilla, the military *junta* in a massive use of force began to systematically wipe out the rebel strongholds. However, before the government was to be handed back to the politicians, General Rojas Pinilla proclaimed himself leader of Colombia and became its dictator.

5

Now, on Christmas Eve as the army drove into Maraguey in trucks, Gonzalo Rodriguez Gacha stood on a small rise watching his village from a kilometer away as he returned from fishing in the mighty Magdalena River. As he stood watching he did not understand what it all meant nor foresaw the catastrophe that was about to ensue from such a military visit.

No, Gonzalo Rodriguez Gacha did not know that his village was a rebel stronghold opposed to the conservative party or that General Rojas Pinilla had a mandate to exterminate the rebel village. Neither did he know of the secret agreement reached between the conservative and liberal parties at the capital, Bogota, in which both parties would run under the banner *Frente Nacional* (National Front). Once in power, however, the conservative and liberal parties would alternate every four years. No, to Gonzalo Rodriguez Gacha that was not within the realm of his imagination. What was possible and very real to him was what he saw with his very own eyes.

The army had rounded up the men, women, and children in the center of town and then searched them one by one. For what reason Gonzalo Rodriguez Gacha could not fathom; he just stood there on the small rise, dumbstruck, as the cries and wails of the women and children reached his ears from the village. He tried to shut his eyes to the horror as the women were stripped and raped on the ground, but some invisible force made them stay open as if he were a camera recording the holocaust. He winced but did not blink when the army fired fifty caliber machine-guns and blew down the citizens of Maraguey, like blades of grass on a windswept plain.

When the village people were all dead, the soldiers set fire to the village, climbed aboard their trucks and drove away. It was all over in less than fifteen minutes and even before the sun had risen from the cordillera beyond.

Gonzalo looked at the dead fish he held in his hand, at the village full of dead bodies, and at the clouds of dust left by the departing army trucks. Somewhere deep inside his mind, something had associated the dead fish with the corpses. Somehow they were all connected but he could not sense the connection. The dead fish, the bodies, and the clouds of dust were all parts of a chain, the links of which he could not see, so that the chain of events appeared haphazard, convoluted and the story of life did not flow.

Suddenly, Gonzalo dropped the fish as if it carried some contagious disease, turned around and walked away. He did not know where he was going, but one place was just as good as another. Yes, his family was dead, he reasoned to himself, but he wasn't frightened, mad or sad. In fact, he didn't feel anything. He tried to force himself to cry, knowing that he should, but no tears came. Maybe later he thought, so he kept on walking.

Where was he to go, he asked himself. He did not know. All he knew was that he had a life to live, a long life, for he was only six years old.

_____*Peter A. Neissa*_____

Part I

HANDS OF THE GODS
(1970-1972)

*Our lives have already been
preordained by some greater
power, the loadstone of
chance, the random fall of
the dice that roll from the
hands of the gods.*

_____*Peter A. Neissa*_____

CHAPTER ONE

Curtis Mathews, United States Ambassador to Colombia, sat back in the black 1970 Chevrolet Impala and suddenly realized he had mucked-up U.S.-Latin American relations for a good long time, maybe even forever.

A short, almost comical looking statesman of forty-seven with a farmer's bearing and enormous political ambitions, Mathews was to be Richard Nixon's 'man' in Latin America. But as the car drove through the streets of Bogota on its way to the American Embassy downtown, he realized that his Latin American studies doctorate from Georgetown University meant absolutely nothing here. He was as lost as a child. The crowded sidewalks hinting of a major metropolis, tri-colored open buses, horse-drawn carts, glass and concrete skyscrapers, and tin and straw shacks had all been facts and statistics. Now they were his life, and trying to reconcile them all made him want to pack up and run.

It was September 1970, the first year of the newly elected, conservative President of Colombia, Misael Pastrana Borrero. Curtis Mathews was to be Nixon's trouble-shooter for Latin America and to make sure everyone kept towing the line. It did not matter what Colombia did as long as it remained pro-democracy and anti-communist, freeing the Nixon administration from added worry while it tried desperately to seek a solution to its Vietnam problem.

Colombia, however, had not been immune to the new cultural and political conscience raising of the 1960s. Protests began in the capital, strikes known as *huelgas* began to occur more frequently, small riots flared up now and then, causing the President to declare a state of siege or martial law, depending on the gravity of the strike. Rock music came in with the Beatles, hemlines went all the way up to places a Catholic nation found shocking but

11

found a way to live with, and the United States became the big bad bully on the block.

Protests were constant around the American embassy, with crowds of people holding up signs saying "America Out Of Vietnam, *Yanqui Imperialista*," and shouting "Yankee go 'ome!" It was a scene that said the times were changing.

Colombia may have looked to be anti-American but it was not. Colombia, after having put an end to *La Violencia* of the 1950s, became the most stable government in all of Latin America. Not only had the government stabilized but it had formed deep political and economic ties with the United States, ties that made Colombia the showcase of Latin America. It had a coffee industry second to none, one of the biggest leather industries in the free world, a new and growing textile industry and a wealth of mineral elements ranging from copper, coal, emeralds, gold, and iron, to oil and salt. It was a country on the move without any 'real' problems or so it seemed, until alarming reports of communist guerrillas stopping the flow of economic production by means of sabotage reached the White House.

Although under General Rojas Pinilla the era of *La Violencia* was put to an end, some of the renegade brigades remained. Most of the brigades that did not die remained without much of a following or as a political power base to threaten the Colombian government. What the brigades could do was slow the economic development of the country by blowing up refineries and disturbing the trade routes around the country.

Out of these outlaw brigades only two seemed to have solidified into terrorist groups whose only aim was to topple the government: the M-19 *(Movimiento 19 de Abril)* and FARC *(Fuerzas Armadas Revolucionarias de Colombia)*. Their methods were brutal, from assassination and kidnapping to throwing bombs into crowded restaurants. Blackmail and murder were the norm, sabotage of oil refineries was sophistication.

A plan developed at the United States Department of State called for a massive infusion of monetary aid into Colombia. The aid was to help Colombia develop low-income housing, better its health system and reinvigorate its stalled economy. Along with the monetary aid was a package to help the Colombian military do away with the 'troublemakers,' the M-19 and the FARC. The man chosen to put the plan into effect was the leading theorist on Latin American studies and career diplomat, Curtis Mathews.

It was all supposed to be very simple, Mathews thought. He was supposed to deliver the plan to high inner staff at the Bogota embassy and then ride on up to the Nariño Presidential Palace and present it to the Colombian President. That was the plan. It was all carefully delineated, with names of people who would favor such a policy in the Colombian government, since they were on the CIA (Central Intelligence Agency) payroll. It was, as President Nixon had put it, "a no lose proposition." But that was before a *gamín* had come up behind him at the El Dorado International Airport and ripped the briefcase out of his hands and run off with it, plan and all.

At first, Mathews stood with mouth agape on the street curb outside the airport terminal, not believing what had happened. Then, as realization set in, he started shouting in English at the top of his lungs, "Get him! He stole my briefcase!"

To those around, Mathews simply looked like another crazy *gringo* complaining about some commonplace occurrence on the streets of Bogota. When a police officer finally made his way to Mathews, who was by then shouting like some hysterical child, the *gamín* had disappeared along with the briefcase.

"*Qué pasa?*" asked the police officer.

"That kid stole my briefcase. I want it back!" Mathews roared in English. "I am the United States Ambassador. Good God, man, that theft is an international crime under the Geneva Convention and rules of international law!"

The police officer was starting to get mad but he decided to keep his cool. "That may be, Mr. Ambassador, but the *gamín* doesn't know that, does he?"

Now, as the black Chevrolet made its way to the American Embassy, Curtis Mathews understood what the police officer had tried to tell him, but he did not like it nonetheless. The *gamines*. Street urchins that lived off of pickpocketing, burglary, auto theft and other crimes. The *gamines* were an unnoticed fact of life in all the major Colombian cities. A group of street urchins estimated to be thirty thousand strong in Bogota alone. The *gamines*, they had the briefcase now.

What do I do, Mathews thought. Should I approach the government anyway? What happens if the M-19 or the FARC get hold of the briefcase? Good God! It would be a bomb. Major political figures would be thrown out of office, not to mention that he too would be thrown out and Colombia would then return to the turmoil of *La Violencia*. Damn it all!

Mathews deliberated with himself. He had been briefed by the CIA and told of the only contact that could get him in touch with the M-19. However, he was told not to use or expose the contact under any circumstances unless the life of the Colombian President were at risk. The problem was that the contact man was also a *gamín*. In fact, the contact man was a leader of *gamines*.

Mathews was revolted by the idea that his own stupidity had forced him and the United States government to deal with a goddamn street kid by the name of Gonzalo Rodriguez Gacha. A leader of a gang of *gamines*.

Jim Harrison, United States Cultural Attaché to Colombia was a tall, handsome Harvard man who had studied business and graduated with honors. He had confounded his right and proper investment banker father by not following in his footsteps. Harrison who was really the CIA's station chief, instead had joined the CIA in the hope of keeping his country one step ahead of those who wished her ill. However, that was 1953, a lifetime ago. Now, all the reasons he had joined the intelligence service for were illusions he had created in his own mind.

Harrison slammed down the telephone so hard that he cracked it. He then cursed so loudly that his old pals from grammar school would have been proud of him, but the fact was that no one heard him. He was in the soundproof and anti-bug room that was known as the bubble, inside the American Embassy in downtown Bogota. The embassy was also known as the fortress because of the high walls that surrounded its perimeter.

Before the telephone had rung inside the bubble room, he had been struggling with information that had been imparted to him via cipher code, information about a new plan to be put into effect by the State Department-- a department which he was convinced had no idea where Colombia was or what it was like to be living there during the era of *La Violencia*. In fact, Harrison remembered when the State Department had printed brochures on Colombia spelling the country's name Columbia. And now, those same people wanted a plan implemented in Colombia as if Colombians would assent to it without a debate.

Even if the plan were good for the Colombians, it would still raise many questions and cause them to look on the gift with an evil eye. Colombians still remembered the United States inciting a rebellion in one of Colombia's western states known as the Darién region or what came to be known as the country of Panama. That had been 1903, and every time they negotiated with the United States, they brought up the point and rubbed it in, as if the event had occurred the day before yesterday. But Jim Harrison was really not worried because of a long and bitter grudge the Colombians had, but because he had been informed that Nixon's advisor, Henry Kissinger, would be flying into Bogota within the next several weeks. In other words, Harrison thought, they had put the responsibility of security squarely on his shoulders.

Providing security in Bogota meant putting every man available on every street corner on every route Henry Kissinger would travel while he stayed in Colombia. In other countries this would be an impossible task, but in Colombia one simply asked the commanding general to put a soldier on every corner with an M-16 rifle for extra insurance. A tank every half mile was the general's idea and it was why the general always responded happily to the request.

Harrison knew that even all that security wouldn't stop one or two characters from lobbing eggs at the entire American entourage. In fact, he remembered when Richard Nixon had come down to Colombia as President

Eisenhower's Vice-President and he had been showered
with eggs.

Now, on top of all the security work, Harrison had to
deal with a self-appointed textbook expert on Colombia, an
appointee to an ambassadorship because the appointee had
in some way contributed to the election of President
Richard Milhous Nixon. To Colombia, the new ambassador
was being billed as a career diplomat because of the
expertise he had developed as a Peace Corps volunteer in
some remote corner of the earth, which someone in the
State Department had equated as being the same as
Colombia.

Appointing an inexperienced person to Colombia
instead of a career civil servant who had spent time there
was, as Colombians would say, "*Una cagada pero bien
verraca*"- a phrase that could only have an equitable
translation as "a massive fuck-up." It was a diplomatic
fact that had been proven over and over again, and it
seemed that Curtis Mathews had just proven it once more.

Usually Jim Harrison would write off anything that
was stolen by the *gamines*, but this time he had to get
that briefcase back. He knew that the *gamín* who had
ripped it off did not know what was in it, but rather seen
the value of the briefcase itself. A two-hundred dollar
American briefcase would sell on the Colombian black
market for only ten American dollars. Harrison cursed out
loud again. He had to find the bloody briefcase before it
started another civil war, before the negotiator Henry
Kissinger arrived, and before the newly arrived goddamn
American Ambassador gave himself a heart attack.

The usual procedure for recovering an item of "value,"
which in CIA terms meant "secret", was to saturate the
area with "friends" and flush out the culprit with the
briefcase. In normal circumstances it would be like
flushing out a rodent from a city sewer. No chance at all.
Now, knowing that he had to concentrate on the security
of Henry Kissinger, he would not have those "friends"
available to look for the briefcase. No, this time he would
need the services of the "Kid," after the Kid had just
returned him a favor too. Damn! That would mean he
would owe the Kid a favor. Damn Gonzalo Rodriguez
Gacha to hell!

16

Carlos Fuentes made seven hundred and ninety-five pesos a week, which he knew in American dollars translated to fifty-three dollars a week. He also knew that in Colombia he was a success story. Born to *campesino* parents in northern Caldas province, he grew up confident in himself and without the fear that those people south of him in Tolima province had grown up with. The northern part of Caldas province had been relatively unaffected by *La Violencia* and General Rojas Pinilla's extermination forays.

Fuentes, an unusually tall man for a Colombian, was strong and well built. He was easily six feet two inches, with fair skin leaning to olive, and a shock of dark hair. He was also ruggedly handsome and was never far from women, who dubbed him the Colombian Omar Shariff after the popular film *Dr. Zhivago* had made its run through Bogota.

Brought up in a solid, Catholic *campesino* community, he was scrupulously honest and relentless in his pursuit of the truth. But in his five years as police lieutenant for *El Centro* (downtown) division, he had learned to compromise certain high-minded qualities in order to achieve goals that pertained to justice. Not that he ever took bribes; he didn't. The compromise took place with contacts, informants. He wouldn't arrest a drunken vagrant if the vagrant had some good information, or he would look the other way on a traffic violation if the violator could in the future provide him with some valuable information. It was unethical, he knew, but sometimes knowing where your enemies were and what they were up to was worth the compromise.

It was a good life, Carlos Fuentes reflected over his bowl of cold *ajiaco*, a soup made of noodles and chicken. It was a good life, or at least it had been until forty minutes before when the telephone had begun to ring and hadn't stopped since. Everyone seemed to be phoning him to declare outrage at the mugging of the United States Ambassador in broad daylight. The President of Colombia called, the Mayor of the City of Bogota had called, the Minister of Mines and Petroleum had called, as every concerned citizen and watchful reporter to blame him personally for the event.

Fuentes looked down at his cold *ajiaco* and his stale *mojicón* (bread roll with a jellied center), wondering if any of the callers knew he made less than a street sweeper in the streets of New York City. True, he said to himself, he had read it in *Time* magazine. He himself was outraged that the rightful citizens of Bogota were appalled that the mugging had taken place in broad daylight when thirty thousand *gamines*, who controlled ninety percent of the city's black market items, roamed the streets!

All the rightful indignation was nonsense, of course, but they still wanted him to recover the damn briefcase, which would be as easy as winning the State-run lottery. A lottery that was fixed so that only the State won, of course. Recovering a briefcase from a *gamín*, Fuentes thought, would be an exercise in futility. And added to what had been whispered to him the night before, it all promised to make the next several weeks a living hell.

It was at the home of Roberto Vásquez, one of the Colombian oligarchic families and one of the original forty, where he had been approached by a member of the Gómez family, another of the forty. The forty families were a group of families who had controlled and owned eighty-five percent of Colombia's industrial and agricultural products. After major reforms at the end of *La Violencia*, the forty group's political power ceased to be effective; however the forty families' individual influence was still as great and was measured in proportion to their wealth. Heriberto Gómez, who had quietly whispered to Fuentes of the upcoming visit of Henry Kissinger, had asked him to prepare the safety measures accorded to such a visit. However, with the whisper had come a veiled warning: no egg throwers, the government of Colombia could not afford to be embarrassed this time. To Fuentes it meant two things: First, something major was in the works; and second, his job was on the line.

So, he was left with trying to find a goddamn briefcase for some stupid *gringo* ambassador, who didn't have the common sense to let the authorities know of his impending arrival and to set up a major safety net to protect a future VIP guest. He knew that he could do one or the other, but not both, and since the safety of the VIP was more important, he would have to delegate the case of the briefcase to someone who could find it. That someone was not in his own police department and that meant asking someone who could find it, a *gamín*. A *gamín* gang lord would do the trick, he thought, and since he was only on a personal level with one of the four *gamín* gang lords, it meant asking the one he most feared. *Qué Carajo!* (Damn it all!).

He would have to ask a favor from Gonzalo Rodriguez Gacha.

_____*Peter A. Neissa*_____

CHAPTER TWO

Gonzalo Rodriguez Gacha, a young man of considerable resource and guile, had no idea he had become the center of so much attention. Not that he would have cared had he known, because at the moment all his mental concentration and physical ability was involved in the pursuit of a man called Bizco (Crosseyed).

Gacha had cancelled a meeting with Cebollo (Onion), a man who resold most of the hot items stolen by the *gamines*. Instead, Gacha had elected to go to the El Dorado International Airport and catch a good view of the incoming American delegation. It always helped him in forming ideas about the character of people by seeing the way they acted in a new environment.

Gacha had bought a copy of *El Tiempo*, Bogota's biggest daily newspaper, and sat in a chair beside the Customs Exit of the international terminal of the *El Dorado* Airport. He did not blend in well. At nineteen years of age, he looked more like a man in his late twenties. He was tall, strong, muscular and carried himself with the grace of a large cat. With fair skin and fashionably cut long dark hair that was parted from left to right, he could have passed for one of the sons of the wealthy families. Dressed in fashionable clothes, white shirt and bell-bottom pants, he did look the part unless you looked at his eyes, wide-set brown eyes that darted every-which way, taking in every detail around him like a sponge. He was a young man whose confidence in himself radiated a strength to those around him, a man who was acknowledged by other men whether he wished to be acknowledged or not.

The American delegation had finally shown their black diplomatic passports to surprised Customs officials who immediately stamped the passports and showed them the way out of the terminal.

21

It was because of Marta, Gonzalo Rodriguez Gacha thought, that he knew the American Ambassador was coming. Marta was a maid at the home of the Consul General of the United States in Bogota, and it was there that she had overheard the conversation between the Consul and Jim Harrison, the Cultural Attaché. Gacha smiled, realizing how far his network of rag-tag kids as informants extended. He also knew that he would have to get a gift for Marta, information like that was never free.

At first, Gacha was relatively unimpressed with the short, funny-looking ambassador, but as he bumped into him by accident, or so he made it appear, he locked eyes with Curtis Mathews. Gacha saw beyond the baldish scalp and the beady looking eyes and found intelligence and ambition.

"Excuse me," said the ambassador, stepping out of the young man's way.

"Please, it is my fault. Excuse me," said Gacha, stepping out of the way.

"You speak English well," said the ambassador.

"Thank you," Gacha said, knowing it was true. The English courses he had taken at the *Centro Colombo Americano* had set him back almost two hundred American dollars, which he had put down as a necessary business expense. Every time an American administration changed, new people came to Bogota, who almost always never knew how to speak Spanish. At first he had taken the English courses to understand certain business words, so he could deal with the *gringo* diplomats-- words like rate of exchange, favor-for-a-favor, deal, cash, meeting place, contact, contract, and a whole slew of other words.

After having completed the first course, he realized that English was an incredibly easy language to learn. That is, if you only meant to speak it and not write it. Written English which required learning grammar was unnecessary for transactions in the dark alleys of Bogota.

"Could you direct me to the pick-up zone?" the ambassador asked.

"Yes, of course. Through those two doors you will come out to a street, the whole street is the pick-up zone." Gacha pointed at the glass doors the ambassador was to go through.

22

"Thank you," said the ambassador and walked away.

The ambassador walked on but Gacha fell in behind him at a discreet distance. When the ambassador walked through the sliding glass doors, Gacha remained inside and watched him from behind the glass doors. The ambassador had stepped to the edge of the street curb, raised his hand and waved.

Looking down towards the area the ambassador had waved at, Gacha caught sight of the black 1970 Chevrolet that was beginning to roll towards the ambassador.

Suddenly, out of the corner of his left eye, Gacha caught the sudden burst of acceleration of a *gamín*. It was going to be the standard *gamín* snatch, the grab of an exposed purse, briefcase or some sort of jewelry, on the run. Alarms tripped deep inside his brain as his eyes zeroed in on the eyes of the *gamín*. Instantly he knew the *gamín*'s target: it was the ambassador's briefcase.

Gacha raced past the sliding glass doors and tried to avert the snatch of the briefcase, but when he reached the ambassador it was already too late. The *gamín* was already turning around the bend and disappearing from sight. Gacha was about to burst out laughing and tell the ambassador, "Welcome to Colombia," when he heard the ambassador mutter under his breath, "My God, the President's proposal."

It wasn't so much the words that the ambassador used, but rather his ram-rod straight, paralyzed shock that made Gacha realize that what was in the briefcase was valuable, very valuable. Gacha took off after the *gamín* even though he had already disappeared from sight.

Now, as he closed in on the *gamín* two hours after the briefcase snatch, he recognized him as Bizco.

Bizco was a member of the Suba *gamín* gang, one of the four *gamín* gangs that ruled the criminal underworld of the city of Bogota. The *Suba* gang was the weakest *gamín* gang in the city, but under the unwritten *gamín* gang law, a fair *robo* (snatch) could not be interfered with by another member of another *gamín* gang. The reason for the unwritten law was three fold, Gacha knew. It set up turf areas and prevented the outbreak of gang violence. It also set up a way of funneling black market items throughout the city.

23

With that in mind, Gonzalo Rodriguez Gacha was still in pursuit of Bizco, mindless of the fact that he was breaking the law of non-interference on a fair snatch. The snatch itself had been fair, committed in a "free zone," an area considered by all gangs to be accessible to all. There were only three "free zones" in Bogota. *El Dorado* Airport, the *Autopista Norte* (Northern Highway) and *El Salitre* amusement park. Bizco had made his "free zone" snatch in the El Dorado zone, and under unwritten law he could do with the hot item what he wished.

Gacha knew where Bizco was going with the item: San Andresito, an area of Bogota between El Centro and *barrio* Jiménez. San Andresito was a market for tax-free goods bought overseas and in Colombia. However, most of the items sold in San Andresito were black market hot items. San Andresito was also controlled by *La Mano Negra* (The Black Hand), the Colombian mafia.

La Mano Negra, through cunning agents, bought all 'hot' items at discount prices. Usually the agent the moment he laid eyes on the item knew what price to pay for it. However, he would still go through the ritual of haggling for a price.

As darkness fell over the city and smells of foods cooking filled the crowded streets of San Andresito, Gacha knew that Bizco would never get a chance to sell the briefcase. Gacha had made up his mind to take it and as gang lord of the *El Centro gamín* gang, he had weighed carefully all the ramifications of such an act.

The moment Gacha took the briefcase, he was committing the *El Centro* gang to a turf war with the *Suba* gang. Although *Suba* was the weakest of all the gangs, a gang war could hurt him financially and personally. If he underestimated his gang's strength he would be killed, not solely because the wars themselves were violent but, because the unwritten law said that the loser gang lord had to be killed. Once a gang leader was on the run he could not obtain sanctuary by joining another gang, as it would jeopardize the other gang.

Small drops of sweat formed on Gacha's forehead as the weight of his future actions fully rested on his mind. The whole history of the Bogota *gamín* system would change with his act, a system that was so institutionalized it seemed unchangeable.

Bogota, the capital of Colombia, is located on a plateau 8,661 feet above sea level, flat as a billiards table and surrounded by massive mountains. The smallest of the two mountains, known as Guadalupe, had a massive statue of the Virgin Mary on its peak. The tallest mountain which loomed over Bogota was called Monserrate and on its peak it had a church and a convent. Both Guadalupe and Monserrate were on the eastern side of the city.

The city plan of Bogota was fashioned after New York City. Avenues (*Carreras*) ran north-south while streets (*calles*) ran east-west. *Carreras* were numbered from 1 at the eastern side of Bogota to 28 at the western edge of the city. *Calles* began with 1 downtown and went up to 116 at the northern edge of Bogota. If you went south of *calle* 1, the furthest street you could reach was 35-south.

The city was further divided by imaginary lines that were even more defined, lines that defined class and wealth. If you lived in the northern suburbs from *calle* 70 to *calle* 100, you lived in a wealthy area. If you lived north of *calle* 100, you were an oligarch. The exceptions were *barrios* Santana and Suba.

Santana was on the eastern slope of the city, while Suba was on the western slope of the plateau. Suba was really an hacienda *barrio*, a neighborhood that still had some farms that were productive.

The *gamín* gangs were divided according to lines set by the city itself. The four gangs, *El Centro* (downtown), *Chapinero* (midtown), *Séptima* (Seventh Avenue) and *Suba* (western Bogota), were all natural partitions of the city. The *El Centro* gang controlled the downtown area from *calle* 20-south to *calle* 35, and from *carrera* 8 to *carrera* 17. The *Chapinero* gang controlled from *calle* 36 to *calle* 62, and from *carrera* 8 to *carrera* 13. The *Séptima* gang controlled from *carrera* 7 to *carrera* 1, which was the highest road on the eastern slope of the city. The *Suba* gang, which was not actually part of the city proper but was rather a suburb, controlled the western area of the city. The underdeveloped area of the city was *Suba*'s domain.

Every gang had a leader. In *Suba* it was Ramón, and he controlled through delegates some eight thousand *gamines*, almost four thousand *gamines* more than any other gang. The ages of the *gamines* ranged from six to twenty, the leader being the oldest and most experienced *gamín*. The chief source of income of the *Suba* gang was the theft of automobiles, some jewelry and the occasional hooker they managed to control.

The *Séptima*'s gang leader was a sixteen year old boy nicknamed *El Loco* (The Crazy One). Their chief source of income was the rip-off of wealthy students going to private schools on the eastern slope of the city, which *Séptima* controlled except for *Santana*.

In *Chapinero*, the leader was a young man of eighteen years called Ernesto Bosco. *Chapinero*'s financial support ranged from stolen jewelry to stolen auto parts and a few black market emeralds.

The *El Centro* gang, which was ruled by Gonzalo Rodriguez Gacha, controlled the wealthiest area of all. It controlled all or at least most of the black market emeralds sold in Bogota. All the emeralds belonged to *La Mano Negra*, but Gacha and his gang were his selling agents. The *El Centro* pulled in five percent commission on each sale made on the streets. Their income also included stolen jewelry, auto parts and the occasional hooker. It was enough of an income to keep Gacha and his three top men in a small two bedroom apartment which Gacha alone had a single room. To a *gamín*, a place to stay was a luxury of the first magnitude. Ninety-seven percent of all the *gamines* in Bogota slept in the streets; to have an apartment was to be a king.

As Gonzalo Rodriguez Gacha followed Bizco, who carried the ambassador's briefcase under his right arm, he knew that his actions would spark an immediate war between *El Centro* and the *Suba* gang. However, he was counting on the fact that with the briefcase he would be able to seek protection by blackmailing the United States Embassy. Of course, he would have to wait until Jim Harrison came asking him to find the briefcase. He would give it to Harrison with certain conditions. Of course, protection from the *Suba* gang would be a start. It was also very probable, Gacha thought, that the police would also ask him to find it. If the police did ask him, he would then have two favors instead of one, if he played his cards right. The only problem was that he would have to wait until they both asked him and that meant he would have to hold his own against the *Suba* gang, at least until he was able to maneuver the favors to his advantage.

Gacha weighed the pros and cons of his possible act, and he came to the same conclusion every time. He would come out even if that briefcase were worthless, but if it were valuable he could come out on top. *Bizco* suddenly turned into a corner and Gacha thought, it's now or never.

Gacha turned into a long, dark alley, following *Bizco* stealthily. Smoothly, he reached into the inside of his leather coat and retrieved a four-inch black switchblade. When he was a foot behind *Bizco*, he snapped the switchblade open.

At the sound of the switchblade *Bizco* turned around violently, just in time to catch the blade in the left kidney. His face contorted in pain as he tried to shout, but the legs buckled under him and he fell face down onto the street. His left hand twitched for a few seconds as he gasped for one last breath that never came.

Gacha wiped the blade on *Bizco*'s brown sweater, secured the blade and put it back into the inside pocket of his own leather coat. He took a deep breath, picked up the ambassador's briefcase and walked away, leaving *Bizco* lying dead in the gutter. Gacha's face showed no emotion, it was ice-cold, worry-free, and that was exactly how he felt, worry-free.

Death to Gonzalo Rodriguez Gacha was just a means of doing business.

Peter A. Neissa

CHAPTER THREE

When Gonzalo Rodriguez Gacha reached his small two bedroom apartment he felt the feeling of claustrophobia. He was glad that he had a room all to himself, but with three other business partners in the same apartment it sometimes became a little crowded. Tonight the apartment felt smaller than a rat hole.

It probably wouldn't have felt so crowded if his other business partners didn't have girlfriends coming in at all hours of the night. Since they had as much right to the apartment as he did, anyone they invited was welcomed. But sometimes those who were invited stayed for days so that the apartment always seemed crowded. Sometimes he would wake up and find close to thirty people lying all about the apartment.

It was not a spacious apartment and it wasn't very nice either. It was a small two bedroom apartment which had seen its day half a century ago. The only good thing about it was the rent was cheap and that more than made up for its faults, which were many, like the plaster falling from the walls, the light bulbs hanging precariously from electrical fixtures not fixed to the ceiling, the leaky plumbing and the wooden floors that had long since rotted out from the damp Bogota air.

When Gacha turned the key in the lock and opened the front door, he was met with a barrage of greetings and a half a dozen hands thrusting bottles of *Aguardiente* into his face. *Aguardiente* was Colombians' favorite alcoholic drink, a mixture of licorice and firewater extremely tasty and powerful. Gacha greeted his colleagues first, their girlfriends second and then he drank from one of the bottles of *aguardiente*. He then locked eyes with his second in command, José 'Chulo' Moncada. José's nickname Chulo meant vulture. Gacha then excused himself and walked into his small bedroom.

Chulo went into Gacha's room a few moments later. He was a small man of five feet three inches whose very size was the most deceiving feature he possessed. Chulo was the "enforcer" for the *El Centro* gang and his loyalty to Gonzalo Rodriguez Gacha was legendary among all Bogota *gamines*. As enforcer he carried out personally all contracts, hits, punishments and other lessons to keep *gamines* and enemies in line.

"Where have you been, *jefe* (boss)?" asked Chulo as he stood beside the small bamboo cot.

"Business," replied Gacha, as he changed into fresh clothes.

"What's wrong?" Chulo asked, eyeing the briefcase on Gacha's bed.

"Nothing's wrong! What the hell makes you think something is wrong?" Gacha shouted and realized those outside his bedroom had ceased partying and were listening in.

"I'm sorry, *jefe*, it's just that it's Friday night, you know?"

Gacha finally smiled. "I'm sorry, José, I didn't mean to snap at you." Gacha had used Chulo's first name, something he did only when they talked as equals, which was rare.

Chulo immediately softened at the mention of his name and at once realized how he loved Gacha like a brother. He would walk to hell over hot coals for Gacha. "It's okay, *jefe*. We are all going out to the *As de Copas* nightclub. You coming?"

"No, I promised Margarita I would take her out to eat at the Salinas restaurant in Chico. I'm already running late as it is."

"Chico, eh?" Chulo said, imitating the voice of a rich snob. "Moving up in the world, eh *jefe*?"

Gacha shook his head in resignation. "Yeah, she's been after me to take her out to a good restaurant. Not only does she want me to take her out to a good restaurant but she wants to be taken in a taxi...women!"

Secretly, Gacha was also excited to be going to the restaurant that had taken him two months to get the reservations.

"I think she has you by the balls," Chulo said. "You

better watch out you don't get her pregnant."

Gacha raised an eyebrow and shook his head slowly conveying the message that it would never happen.

"By the way, *jefe*, before I forget, a *Señor* Mathews called. He said to give him a call at any time. His number is on your dresser, over there by the corner."

Gacha didn't recognize the name except for the fact that it sounded American. "Okay, I'll call what's-his-name tomorrow before our meeting. What time's the meeting?"

"Two in the afternoon, but that's not all, *jefe*. That *tombo* (cop) Carlos Fuentes roused one of our kids today. He gave the kid a message to give to you. He says he wants to see you tomorrow at nine in the morning in his office. The bastard! Someone should knock-off that self-righteous bastard."

"Okay, I'll speak to him, too. Anything else?" Gacha asked as he adjusted his tie in the mirror.

Chulo was taken aback for an instant by how nonchalantly Gacha took the news of a cop calling him into the station. It was one of the reasons why he liked Gacha. Gacha was always so self-assured and unpredictable.

"No, *jefe*, that is it."

Gacha nodded. "Was the boy hurt bad?"

"A black eye and a bruise, a regular roust," Chulo said with a shrug. He was trying to be as off-handed about the matter as was Gacha.

"See to it that the boy gets some business his way, maybe an emerald or two more. Okay, I have to go pick up Margarita. Have someone phone her. By the way, that is our next item on our list, a telephone for this apartment."

Chulo smiled wide and said, "*Sí, jefe!*"

The phone the *El Centro* gang used was a public telephone on *carrera* 13 and *calle* 26. It was manned by a *gamín* twenty-four hours a day. *Gamines* were put on five-hour shifts, three *gamines* to a shift.

"Okay, I'm out for the night," Gacha said slapping Chulo on the back like an old comrade in arms.

Margarita Coro was a sixteen-year-old girl from the city of Cali, a major city one hundred and eighty miles southwest of Bogota. Women from Cali, known as *Caleñas*, had a reputation as being the most beautiful women in Colombia.

Margarita was a petite girl of five feet, with a small delicate face and a smile that could melt the heart of a man six times her age. She had left the city of Cali to become a maid with the Gonzáles family of Bogota. It was a job that paid about eighty *pesos* a month ($6.00). Half her salary was sent back home to help out her family, but since she was one of twelve children, her contribution was almost negligible.

The Gonzáles family, whom Margarita worked for, was rich, so affluent it was hard to tell how wealthy they really were. They were one of the forty families. The Gonzáles family, being in the oligarchy, lived on *calle* 116, which was in the wealthiest area of town. The neighborhood was patrolled by armed guards twenty-four hours a day. Margarita had not been able to find out what exactly made the Gonzáles family so rich, except for the hints that the oldest daughter in the house, who was fifteen, had whispered to her. "Cattle, land and everything else you can grow on a half a million acres."

At the time Margarita had thought the girl had been lying. It wasn't possible to own a half a million acres. Now, she wasn't so sure. After all, her own father owned half an acre outside of Cali and it had cost him a fortune! Yes, her family was poor compared to the Gonzáles family, but in the area around her father's farm, they were a respected family.

Margarita had hung onto that belief of family and to the fact that she was a someone, at least around her father's farm. That all changed, of course, when she met Gonzalo Rodriguez Gacha.

They met the day Margarita came by train to Bogota from Cali. The train station in Bogota, which was on *carrera* 17, fell under the *El Centro* turf. Gacha, who was at the station meeting a man from *La Mano Negra* to make an exchange from cash to emeralds, had heard the shouts of a young woman in the station. He turned to see what the commotion was all about and locked eyes with Margarita Coro.

Margarita, who had just stepped off the train with her

only suitcase in her hand, had become a victim of a *gamín* snatch. Instinctively, she had run after the *gamín* shouting and wailing for someone to help her in detaining the *gamín*, but no one did. Finally she gave up, as the *gamín* seemed to disappear into a crowd of people. Exhausted, she walked over to a bench, sat down and burst into tears.

Gacha, who had witnessed the snatch would have laughed at the scene like he had done in hundreds of other cases similar to it, but this one was different. He had seen the tear-stained faced of Margarita. He hastily concluded the transaction with the agent for *La Mano Negra* and walked over to Margarita.

"Hello, my name is Gonzalo Rodriguez Gacha. I saw what happened. Is there anything I can help you with?" Gacha asked, as he towered over Margarita with a benevolent charisma that was intoxicating and which he could turn on and off like a light switch.

"That...that boy stole my...everything! I...Gonzáles... money...all!" Margarita said in a staccato burst of words that was completely incoherent.

"It's okay, take your time to calm yourself," Gacha said, handing her a clean handkerchief.

Margarita wiped her face and managed a thankful smile. "Thank you," she said lightly, her voice a soothing harmony.

Gacha believed that the smile was meant for him and had touched him like no other woman had done before. At that very moment he had made up his mind to possess her.

"What am I going to do?" Margarita asked, but didn't wait for a reply. "I have a job at the Gonzáles' residence and now I have no money, no clothes, no nothing!"

"Where is the Gonzáles residence?" Gacha asked.

"*Calle* 116, *Señor*," she said adding the *Señor* to be formal. She was hoping the attractive gentleman, God willing, would help her out.

At the mention of the address Gacha raised his eyebrows in surprise. It was the wealthy section of town. More than that, it was the area of the oligarchy and he could use an informant there.

"Well, I can give you some money so you can take a

bus there..."

"Oh, would you?" Margarita said, pleading.

"Yes, I can also lend you some money so you can buy some clothes if you need to."

Margarita almost burst into tears again. "*Dios le ampare y le favorezca.*" May God protect and favor you.

"Oh, he has," Gacha said sarcastically, but quickly added, "I am not without influence in this city, you know, maybe I can even regain the suitcase for you."

"Oh, you are a saint, *Señor*. You must be very important. How can I repay you?" Margarita asked, hoping to strike at the man's vanity.

"Have dinner with me some time. Here is my telephone number. Call me when you have a day off." Gacha removed a piece of paper from his wallet and a pen from the inside pocket of his Brooks Brothers coat. He wrote the telephone number that belonged to the public pay phone at *carrera* 13 and *calle* 26. Then he peeled off a hundred *pesos* from his wallet and gave them to Margarita.

"But *Señor*, I don't even know you, I don't even know what it is that you do. It would not be proper," Margarita said, with the appropriate innocence that said she did not go out with just anyone. Her mind was racing. She had never been out on a date before and even in her wildest dreams she had never thought of going out with such a good looking man. Was he too old for her? He did look like he was in his late twenties.

"I am a businessman," said Gacha smoothly, "but I will tell you more about myself when we meet for our first dinner. I must go now, so I wish you the best of luck in your new job. I'll see you soon."

Margarita felt his hand on her shoulder and had to hold back from leaping at him and kissing him. My God, she thought, what am I thinking? I've just been robbed and I'm thinking of committing a sinful act! Get hold of yourself, girl.

"Thank you, *Señor*. I will return your money as soon as I am able," Margarita said and watched Gacha walk away.

At the Salinas restaurant in Chico, an area for the

nouveau riche, Margarita and Gacha sat at a table eating *arroz con pollo* (chicken with rice), *papa* (potato) and *cerveza* (beer). The meal was tasty and spicy in traditional Colombian fashion.

It was a heaven sent meal, Margarita thought, as she stared with a lusting gaze into Gacha's eyes. She knew she had fallen in love with him the week she had arrived in Bogota, when Gonzalo had said to her that he had been able to obtain the suitcase and all her money. He had even brought it out personally to the Gonzáles house and handed it over to her.

Gacha, who was aware of Margarita's gaze, ate in silence ignoring the look she had for him, women always looked at him that way. Well, at least most of them, he corrected himself. But something wasn't right, he had felt ill at ease from the moment he met Margarita. It wasn't that she didn't excite him, most of the time she could do it with just a smile and the times they had spent together had been wonderful. She had been a virgin when she gave herself wantonly to him. He loved her, but not enough to marry her. He loved her like a friend, which was crazy, he thought, gauging by how many men took second and even third looks at her as she walked by. Even Mario García, his fourth in command, had told him she was one of a kind and still he could not force himself to love her any more than he already did. Tonight he felt something odd, but he couldn't quite pinpoint exactly what that feeling was. Maybe it was because Margarita was distracting him that he wasn't able to concentrate on what exactly was bothering him.

"What's wrong, Gonzalo?" Margarita asked. She was the only person who dared to call him Gonzalo, instead of Gacha. Not even Chulo was able to call him Gonzalo.

"Nothing," Gacha said, "I must be coming down with something. So, go ahead with what you were saying."

"Well, last night the Gonzáles' had a big fancy party. A lot of important people were there, you know, I mean people with a lot of medals on their jackets and all."

Gacha suddenly tuned into what Margarita was saying. "Oh, what was the occasion?"

"I don't know exactly, but the oldest girl of the family, the one I've been telling you about, told me her father

35

was going to run for the Mayor's job..."

"Of Bogota?" Gacha cut in.

"Shush! It's supposed to be some sort of secret or at least that is what Ana-Alicia said to me."

"How old is the girl, what's-her-name? You think she was telling you the truth?" Gacha asked looking as deeply as he could into Margarita's eyes.

Margarita looked at Gacha, puzzled. "Yes, she was speaking the truth. Why do you want to know how old she is?" A tone of jealousy laced her voice.

"I don't know, you talk about her so often," Gacha said, avoiding Margarita's eyes.

"Do I?"

"Forget it!" Gacha said angrily, causing some other diners to look over with disapproving glances.

"I'm sorry, Gonzalo, I just get so jealous. I see how other women look at you and I feel I might lose you." Margarita paused, then continued. "The girl is fifteen, a year younger than I am." Margarita then spoke about what the guests wore at the party and what they talked about. She spoke mostly of the glitter and the ball gowns. She did not know what the men had spoken of because they had retired to another room to talk business.

Gacha, however, was not listening. He was already thinking of how he could put the newly discovered information to use.

After the meal, Gacha paid the bill and left a handsome tip. He did not want to let the manager know that he was just a "visitor." People who came in from the poorer sections of the city to the richer sections to have a good meal or do some window shopping were known as "visitors."

Margarita and Gacha hopped into a taxi and told the driver to take them to the Cordillera Hotel on *carrera* 8. The drive was twenty minutes from Chico to downtown. On the way to the hotel Margarita kissed and nibbled on Gacha's neck as Gacha slid his hand up her skirt and felt her wetness. The driver peered into the rear-view mirror every now and then to catch a look.

The room at the Cordillera Hotel was simple, one bed, one night table, one chair and bathroom with cold running water. There was a telephone, and the gray plaster on the walls was peeling, plaster that was already covering more dilapidated plaster.

It was a room, Gacha thought. All that was necessary was the bed. He looked over at Margarita, who let her skirt and blouse fall to the floor.

Margarita walked over and stood in front of him as Gacha sat at the edge of the bed. She undid her brassiere and removed her panties in front of him. She reached for Gacha's face and drew it to her so that his face nestled in between her breasts.

Gacha kissed her breasts and then kissed her on the mouth, his tongue darting in and out as his hand reached up to the soft dark triangle between her thighs.

She lay down with him and grabbed his maleness and slowly stroked him as he stroked her with the same careless abandon.

Gacha rolled onto his back as Margarita climbed on and began to ride him. As their thrusts met each other with greater force he stood up from the bed with her legs wrapped around his waist and still thrusting against him. As the thrusts became more feverish he put Margarita's back against the wall and pushed. Her soft moans told him not to stop. An eternal moment later, Margarita suddenly went rigid and exploded in climax, but he kept thrusting until she climaxed again and again, until he finally exploded with the force of a bull.

Margarita left the hotel at seven in the morning. She felt odd, as if she had simply been going through the motions. She hopped onto the Centro-Usaquen bus knowing that she would have to walk five blocks and through a field of grass when she stepped off the bus. She wanted it that way, she wanted to walk so she could think.

Bus rides in Bogota were cheap. For eight *pesos* you could go anywhere in Bogota. Catching a bus was not a problem either, since all the routes were covered by a bus every fifteen minutes. Bogota's public transportation system was one of the best in the world. The only problem was that everyone rode the bus, so trying to get a seat was extremely difficult.

The ride from El Centro to Usaquen took about fifty

minutes. Usaquen was a small neighborhood for low-income housing. Most of the housing was made of straw and tin shacks that fell apart with the big rains that came in November.

Margarita sat in the middle of the bus looking out of the window as she passed the homes of the newly rich on the north side of *barrio* Chico. She also thought for the first time whether Gonzalo really loved her. They had, after all, been going out for nine months and he hadn't even mentioned marriage. Last night she had wanted to tell him that she was pregnant, but somehow she could not bring herself to do it. Tears welled up in her eyes and she shut them, not wanting anyone to see that she was crying, but someone did.

When the bus stopped on *calle* 65, three well dressed *gamines* had stepped on and sat two seats across from her. *Calle* 65 was three blocks away from the designated turf of the *Chapinero* gang. The area from *calle* 62 to *calle* 70, where the three *gamines* had boarded the bus, was designated by all gangs as the "buffer zone." The buffer zone was the area that separated Chico from Chapinero, the rich from the poor. The buffer zone was also neutral territory. It had been designated neutral by the police, a sort of warning track. Any *gamín* caught past *calle* 70, which meant Chico and northward, would be picked up by the police and roused. The rich didn't want any *gamines* hanging around their homes. If a *gamín* crossed into Chico, the rules changed. In Chico and northward, the law of the rich existed. No *gamines* allowed. Of course, this also meant that they could not commit any crimes while they were in the rich sections "visiting." Once in a while a *gamín* got greedy and committed a *robo* (theft), and usually before he left the rich neighborhood he was caught. Once caught, the *gamín* would be sentenced to *La Picota* prison and forgotten. *La Picota* was a cold and dangerous prison where insane men were thrown into the same cell with children. The results were always disastrous.

All this was foreign to Margarita. She didn't know that her boyfriend and the father-to-be of her unborn child was a *gamín* himself, a *gamín* gang lord to boot. She still believed he was a respectable businessman and definitely not a leader of thugs. At the Usaquen bus stop, she stepped off the bus and began to walk westward towards the Gonzáles' residence.

Two blocks away from Usaquen she entered a *potrero*, a field that was half a mile long and half a mile wide. It was a *potrero* she had to cross in order to reach the Gonzáles home which was in the neighborhood called La Pepe Sierra. The Pepe Sierra neighborhood extended from *carrera* 15 to *carrera* 19, and *calle* 114 to *calle* 116. The *potrero* Margarita was crossing was merely a divider between the rich and poor. The view of the poor sections was cut off by the large eucalyptus trees that bordered the *potrero*, so that the rich would not have to gaze on the "unhealthy" sections of town.

Margarita, since having her suitcase stolen, always looked behind her. As she turned around this time, a sudden overwhelming fear flooded her, as she watched three young men spreading out around her in a half moon. Without thinking, she broke into an all out run. She looked back once and saw the young men in pursuit.

They caught her halfway through the *potrero* tackling her by the ankles. She fell hard on the spongy green grass that was still moist from the frost of the night. Her skirt had torn at the side and with horror she watched the young savages' eyes bulge with lust. She screamed but the tallest thug punched her in the mouth, silencing her immediately.

"Please don't hurt me," Margarita pleaded, as she wiped her bloodied mouth with the back of her hand. Raw fear was sending uncontrollable spasms through her body making it appear as if she was about to have a seizure.

"Your *maricón* (fagot) boyfriend should have thought of that before he killed *Bizco*," said the ugliest thug, who was pinning Margarita to the ground by the arms.

"What?" Margarita asked in shock. "He is a respectable businessman!"

The three thugs laughed.

"Yeah, well we'll give you some of the business," said the tallest thug as he unzipped his pants.

"NO!" Margarita cried out in terror.

"Oh yes," said the pimple-faced thug, ripping her skirt off.

"Hold her down, Paco," said the tall thug, "while I show the *hija de puta* (whore's daughter) a good time. Show her what a real good fuck is, eh?" The thugs laughed again.

Margarita spit into the thug's face but it didn't stop him from raping her. They all took turns with Margarita as she simply looked upwards into the indigo blue sky of Bogota.

"And this, *querida*," said the tallest thug, "is to remember us by." He pulled out a switchblade and slashed the blade across her face, from the left corner of the eye to the right corner of her lip.

Margarita never felt the pain or the hot liquid seeping over her face as she began to bleed. Her mind had shut down to outside stimuli, the shock being too great to bear. She simply lay in the *potrero* half naked, bleeding and hoping to die.

CHAPTER FOUR

When Gonzalo Rodriguez Gacha sat down for the *El Centro* monthly meeting, he had no idea that how he conducted this meeting would forever change the course of his life. As always, the meeting started by Gacha recounting the business profits of the previous month. Profits were always given in dollar amounts.

"Our total intake for the month of September was $7,045. The breakdown is as follows: $4,030 in emeralds; $2,120 in auto parts; $210 in office burglaries; $150 in apartment burglaries; and the last $535 in purse snatches around Bogota." Gacha took a deep breath before continuing.

"The first thing we do with the money is have a telephone installed in the apartment," Gacha said and paused for the yells and cheers to rise. He was only met with half smiles; something was wrong. However, the rules were that everyone spoke in turn, no matter how urgent. He wondered if they knew why he had met with Jim Harrison and Carlos Fuentes earlier in the day.

The meetings had gone as expected with Harrison and Fuentes. There was a lot of tough talk from Fuentes, but it was still clear enough that he was asking for a favor. Fuentes wanted the briefcase. Harrison had asked for the same thing, but he had been more polite about it.

Gacha himself was still not sure how to work the briefcase deal to his advantage. He needed time to read what was in it. All those papers inside the briefcase were in English and most were in complicated business language.

"Last but not least," said Gacha, "we should expect war with the *Suba* gang."

Gacha's three top men looked at him with mouths open. Then suddenly they all burst out at the same time, "Why?!"

Gacha had to wave them down with his hand to be quiet. "I killed *Bizco* early last night. I cannot tell you why just now, but we are going to have to hang tough for the next several weeks, maybe less or maybe more." There was an awkward silence, so he added, "In three weeks we will have the *Suba* gang under our control. We will then be the biggest gang in the city. We might then be able to consolidate the whole city under our control because we will be the richest and most powerful. But that can only be achieved if we hang tough and watch our backs."

Chulo shook his head gravely. "I don't know, *jefe*."

Gacha looked at Chulo coldly. "Report."

"Things are not good, *jefe*," Chulo said. "*Chapinero* has been muscling in on our turf. At first I thought it was to see if we were on our toes, but I don't think so anymore. They are dealing heavily in emeralds. In fact, they are flooding the market and driving the price down. I think they are going to try and push us out of the market."

"That's impossible! We have *La Mano Negra* and their protection. Who would go against *La Mano Negra?*" Gacha asked as if he'd just heard something completely unbelievable.

"Well, I have a *ratón*, *jefe*, in the *Chapinero* gang." Everyone looked at Chulo in awe. He was the only one who had and controlled spies known as *ratones* in rival gangs. "My rat tells me that *La Mano Negra* is having problems, a territorial dispute of their own."

"Someone in Bogota is trying to force *La Mano Negra* out?" Gacha asked. If that was the case, his own survival, briefcase or not, would be in extreme jeopardy.

"My rat says that the pressure *La Mano Negra* is receiving is not from Bogota, but from Medellin, the Pérez family of Medellín."

There was a long silence, as if the distance between Gacha and his enforcer was as vast as Bogota itself. The Pérez family of Medellín controlled the emerald black market for Medellín and the northern provinces.

Medellín was the "orchid" city. One hundred and sixty miles northwest of Bogota, it was one of the more remarkable cities in Colombia. Medellín was the capital of the province of Antioquia, and the people who populated it were known as *paisas*. The *paisa* way of thinking about business was frontierlike, with a single-mindedness known only to that region. The saying in Medellín was that if a *paisa* wasn't involved in the business deal, the deal wasn't worth it.

The thought of the Pérez family trying to muscle in on *La Mano Negra* sent shivers running through Gacha's body. It meant that he would have to talk immediately to Don Eusebio Corraza, *La Mano Negra*. However bad the situation was, Gacha did not let his emotions be seen by his subordinates. Instead, he nodded as if he had been informed of the matter long ago and he was dealing with it.

The next report was from Rodrigo Vargas, who was *El Centro*'s number three man. Vargas was the least liked by Gacha, but he never let it show. What made Vargas indispensable was his tactical knowledge in carrying out any type of "business" operation. Business operations ranged from gang wars to the distribution of stolen goods. Gacha believed Vargas was a bomb waiting to explode.

"I don't know if this is important," began Vargas, "maybe Mario would know better than myself, since he is the money man. You all know I have a girl who lives in the *Séptima* turf, but what you don't know is that she has a cousin in the *Séptima* gang. Her cousin's name is Guido..."

"The *Séptima* enforcer?" Chulo asked in surprise.

"Yes. She tells me that he told her he was pulling in three thousand dollars a week. He was drunk with *aguardiente* at the time, so he might have been talking shit."

"How would they make three thousand dollars in a week?" Gacha asked evenly.

"*La mala hierba*." The bad weed, said Chulo. "They sell it at the American and German schools up on the hill. You know, the rich kid schools."

"Yes, I've heard it's popular among the rich," Gacha said, nodding his head in agreement, "but I think it's a fad. We all know these crazy Americans and their fads."

"Maybe so, but if Guido is in fact pulling in three thousand a week, it's a fad we cannot afford to pass up," Vargas said with some anger. He hated it when his reports were taken so lightly.

43

"You mean the whole *Séptima*, Vargas," Chulo qualified the point.

"No, I mean Guido alone. My girl said that the ones above Guido make more."

Chulo let out a long whistle.

"Okay, Chulo, you look into it," Gacha said. "Anything else?" Gacha pushed. He wanted the meeting to end quickly. The Pérez family of Medellín meant more trouble than he could handle and he wanted to meet with *La Mano Negra* to find out what the hell was going on.

"Well," Vargas said, taking on airs, "my friends in the M-19 told me that some bigwigs from *gringolandia* are coming to Bogota. The M-19 is going to try and knock them off."

"That's bad for business," Gacha warned Vargas.

"I don't know, *jefe*, they look very committed. I think they might take out a few of the oligarchs for good measure. I, like always, am with them." It was a challenge and everyone knew that.

"No, you are not. Your allegiance is with us first!" Gacha said angrily, but Vargas sneered. "Listen to me, you fool. I have been told that this visit is going to mean money for development, that means contracts for buildings, money for trucks, cars, materials, it can mean a hell of a lot of money for all of us."

"Bullshit!" Vargas exploded. "We will be nothing as long as the oligarchy rules this country. The money you speak about will never reach our pockets, except for a few measly *centavos* that trickle down to us. No, the big money will always go to the oligarchy while the poor get poorer. Hell, we might be better off without the oligarchy, you ever think of that?"

"Shut up!" Gacha's voice was a sound of cold and projected anger. "Next time you mention the M-19 in terms of knocking off someone, you're on your own. Do you understand?"

"Yes, *jefe*," Vargas said, subdued.

Gacha took another deep breath to regain his composure and nodded at Mario to commence his report.

Mario García was the finance man for the *El Centro* gang, a genius for money. "I have bought some municipal bonds because the last ones we bought gave us a very good return. If it's true about a big American visit coming with aid for development, we should invest heavily in municipal and other bonds. A two-year investment period, but I would need to know the extent of the aid package and for how long. In other words, I need to know the terms the United States is going to impose on us. If we know these details we could make a good-sized gain."

"I'll look into it," Gacha said. "What else?"

"I have opened twelve new bank accounts, all with moderate deposits. However, one of the bank representatives thought I might want to invest through the bank. The bank invests in London and New York. I told them I would think about it. As of yesterday our total was $11,045. After payroll, bribes, and other necessary expenses such as attorney fees and bail money, we should have a balance of $8,500 by the end of the month."

"How much could we make if we invested three thousand dollars?" Gacha asked, taking some notes down in a little black book. The black book was the size of a deck of cards and he carried it wherever he went.

"Under normal circumstances, maybe eight or nine hundred dollars above the original investment. If the aid package the Americans give us is good, it might create a bonanza market. If that were to occur, then we could really clean up, maybe quadruple our money."

"Good, I'll let you know tonight," Gacha said as he stood up from his chair. "That's it for today. Chulo, can I speak to you?"

There was a knock on the apartment door. Under *El Centro* rules, the meetings were never disturbed unless it was an emergency.

Gacha walked over to the front of the door and looked through the peephole. It was one of the seven guards who watched the apartment during the monthly meetings. The gang was always at its most vulnerable during its monthly meetings not only because one rival gang could stop by and wipe them out, but the police could also stop by and seize all their illegal profits. The guard outside the door, Gacha could see, was out of breath. Gacha recognized him as one of the best. He opened the door.

"Sorry, *jefe*," the guard said, wheezing. The guard was a sixteen-year-old boy who was cleverly armed with a .38

45

snub nose revolver in the small of his back.

"Yes, what is it?" Gacha asked, bracing himself for the news.

"We just got a call from the Samaritana hospital. The *Señorita* Margarita is there. She's been cut up," said the guard, holding on to the door frame for support.

Gacha felt as if a cannon had blown a hole through his stomach that was wide enough for an army tank to drive through. He forced himself to nod, to make sure the guard knew he had heard him. He then walked away towards his room and called Chulo over. "José, I want you to set up a meeting with Ernesto Bosco in the buffer zone."

"The gang leader of *Chapinero*?" Chulo whispered in shock.

"Yes, make it for next Wednesday. It will give me time to talk to *La Mano Negra*. Once you do it, meet me at the hospital."

"Yes, *jefe*."

Gonzalo Rodriguez Gacha thought events were spinning out of his control. Just a few hours before he had thought of how he was going to consolidate all the *gamín* gangs under his command. Now, his very own existence was teetering on the brink of extinction.

Margarita Coro lay in the intensive care unit at the Samaritana hospital. Her face was completely bandaged and she had intravenous needles sticking into her wrists like some robot.

The Gonzáles family was present except for the oldest daughter, Ana-Alicia, who had gone to the *hacienda* the night before and did not know of the tragedy that had befallen Margarita. The members of the Gonzáles family were in a waiting room waiting for the doctor to give them the news. They were arguing quietly among themselves.

Gacha, who had seen the Gonzáles family in the waiting room, stood outside in the hallway and out of sight, but he could still hear them arguing.

"I don't see why we have to be here," said *Señora* Gonzáles. "We are not her family. We are not responsible. You know who's going to end up paying for this, don't you?"

"Yes, yes," said Emilio Gonzáles, the head of the Gonzáles household. "It's still the decent thing to do."

"So, then why don't you stay and I'll go to the club. We are expected there, you know?"

"Yes, I remember. Go ahead then, go meet your little bitchy friends and gossip to your heart's content."

Señora Gonzáles' face turned scarlet. "Did I not come with you? Why do you treat me as if I were the person responsible for that barbarous act on Margarita, eh?"

"Yes, I'm sorry, you're right. I'm sorry, *querida*. Why don't you go along and represent the family. I'll meet you as soon as I am able," said Emilio turning away from her.

"Are you sure?" Emilio's wife asked with a trace of happiness returning to her voice.

"Yes, go along now."

"All right, *chao querido*." She kissed him on the cheek and left.

A few moments after Emilio's wife left, the doctor walked into the waiting room.

"Ah, Don Emilio," the doctor said expansively.

"Doctor, what a pleasure to see you!" Don Emilio stretched his hand out and shook hands with the doctor. "Tell me, how bad, doctor?" Emilio asked getting straight to the point. He was doing away with the niceties of greeting that were customary among polite people of Colombia. The only time that such things could be done away with were in times of tragedy.

The doctor shook his head slowly. "Bad. She'll have a pretty bad scar across her face, almost six inches long. Plastic surgery might help, but I doubt it. The surgical technique has come a long way but not enough for the kind of damage that Margarita has."

"No plastic surgery is possible?" Don Emilio asked, his voice breaking.

"You could try, but in my opinion you'd be throwing away twenty thousand dollars. The surgical technique needed for that kind of repair is still ten or fifteen years away. I'm sorry."

"Yes, me too. She was such a pretty girl."

"Yes, Don Emilio, but she is alive. It's too bad about the pregnancy."

"She was pregnant?!"

The doctor nodded. "Six weeks. She has miscarried, of course. Will you dismiss her from your employ?"

Don Emilio Gonzáles, a lean aristocratic man in his early fifties, tried to look into the future. "I don't know. If it were up to me, I would let her stay on."

"But your wife would not." The doctor said rather than asked.

"Oh, she'll keep her on for a while, but then later on she will begin to complain. I mean try to imagine how the poor girl is going to react when she has to serve drinks to our house guests and they all recoil in horror because of the scar. Margarita might survive such rejection, but my wife would have a major coronary. The guests would probably be frightened to death. Hell, I couldn't blame them. A six-inch scar across a face is a damned ugly thing."

"Well, don't fire her just yet. I have a friend who is an expert with make-up. Perhaps she will be able to do something with Margarita."

Emilio looked at the doctor skeptically. "You really think so?"

"I don't know. My friend teaches some burn victims how to cover their faces with amazing results. Margarita is young and maybe in ten years when we have the technology she could have the scar taken care of. She will only be twenty-six, and cells at that age still regenerate quite rapidly. Of course, that is assuming she has the money for the surgery. However, she will be okay here for the next few days. Go home, Don Emilio." The doctor guided Emilio out of the waiting room.

"Thank you, doctor," Don Emilio said shaking the doctor's hand in thanks. "By the way, doctor, about the pregnancy, let's keep that between you and me."

The doctor looked at Don Emilio wondering if he had been the father-to-be. A girl like Margarita was powerless against someone like Don Emilio.

"You know who the father is?" the doctor asked.

Don Emilio shook his head. "Well, thanks again, doctor," Don Emilio said and walked down the hallway passing Gonzalo Rodriguez Gacha, who had concealed himself behind a newspaper.

48

Gacha sat in a small bench in the hallway seething with rage. Someone had once again killed his own flesh and blood. A son or a daughter? Margarita would have to learn to live with the scar, she had no option, but their child, his child would not get to live. It was a stab from the thugs at his own heart too. It was a permanent loss and a permanent loss called for vengeance, an eye for an eye, a life for a life.

"*jefe*," said a soft voice from behind Gacha. It was Chulo. "I'm sorry," he said when Gacha faced him.

"Thank you, José. Did you manage things?" Gacha asked, glad for the distraction.

"Yes, the meeting is to take place in the buffer zone. The conditions are one enforcer each and no one else."

"Good. When?" Gacha asked, his voice returning to normal.

"Wednesday at two in the afternoon."

Gacha nodded suddenly exhausted. With his fingers he rubbed the area between his eyebrows as if trying to rub some of the pain away. Did he love Margarita and had he been fooling himself that he didn't all along? No, he was almost sure that he didn't love her, but he did care for her.

"Listen, Chulo," Gacha said suddenly, in a business-like tone. "I'm going to meet *La Mano Negra*. Have *gamines* posted all around the hospital. If she wakes up, ask her who did it and then tell her to keep quiet about it. She's not even to tell the police, got it?"

"Yes, *jefe*, I've already posted some *gamines* around the hospital. She will be okay."

Gacha walked away, thinking about a dead child, a disfigured girlfriend, and the most vile forms of vengeance.

Don Eusebio Corraza, sixty-two years of age and of considerable girth in the middle, was one of the most powerful men in Colombia. As head of *La Mano Negra*, he had a supply of information that was practically unlimited.

La Mano Negra was beyond wealth that could be determined on an accountant's spreadsheet. A man of considerable taste in art, sculpture and music, Corraza could not read the first six letters of the alphabet. Not a surprising fact, considering he had spent the first twenty-eight years of his life digging for emeralds with his bare hands, at ten *pesos* a day. The fact that he had been able to dig himself out of that station in life had made him an almost mythical folk hero around the country.

It began in 1926, when he realized that over sixty percent of Colombia's emeralds were being sold illegally, a fact he readily understood because he was one of the people who smuggled the emeralds out of the mines in plain sight of the guards. It was usually done by swallowing one or two emeralds a week. After having swallowed the rocks, they would go back to their huts and move their bowels until they produced the emerald. What most of them did not know was that the government knew of this practice and had set up fake buyers, who bought the emeralds for less than the market value.

Once Don Eusebio became aware of this practice, he convinced some of the men to give the emeralds to him on consignment. He would sell their emeralds, and with the profit of such a sale, he would pay them for the emeralds at a slightly higher rate than the government would pay legally or illegally. Once they gave him the emeralds, Eusebio Corraza went to Bogota and sold them at an astronomical profit. Within two months he cut out the middlemen in Bogota and started dealing directly with the big fashion houses of London, New York and Paris.

By the age of thirty-six, Eusebio Corraza was one of the wealthiest men in all of South America, a multi-millionaire several times over. Although the government still controlled seventy percent of the market, Eusebio controlled seventy percent of the finest emeralds in that market. When the government caught on to the practice of the black market, there was nothing to be done about it. It had become an institution. Disrupting the market that Eusebio controlled would have had an adverse effect on the government's market. This was because Eusebio controlled the largest foreign market, since he dealt directly with the big fashion houses. In order to control the market, the government began to sell the emeralds to Eusebio. The effect was to give the cloak of respectability to Eusebio, something that every Colombian wants more than money itself.

In Colombia, simply being rich did not mean you would be invited to the social functions at the Presidential Palace or to the homes of the distinguished citizens of Bogota. There were only three ways to become one of the "respected." You were born with a respected name, you became internationally famous as a surgeon, attorney, businessman, writer, or painter, or, you married into one of the "respected" families. The only exceptions to these cases were people who by some twist of fate had made a name for themselves. Don Eusebio Corraza had done it by forcing the country to deal with him since he provided something the world held in high esteem, emeralds.

Gonzalo Rodriguez Gacha knew all of this as he sat across from Don Eusebio in *La Mano Negra's* own plush estate north of Bogota. In fact, Gacha knew a lot more about Eusebio than anyone else. He knew about his control over the gambling industry, the control over the dock workers in all the major ports of the country, and the vast grip he had on the black market items which had earned him the nickname of *La Mano Negra*.

"I am sorry about your girl, Margarita," Don Eusebio said soothingly.

Gacha was not surprised that Eusebio knew already, since he had men everywhere. "Yes, a sad business," Gacha said with the appropriate solemnity in his voice.

"You know who did it?"

"I have an idea, but I will wait until I have the proof," said Gacha.

"Ah, smart. Would you like me to take care of it when you do find the proof?" Eusebio asked. It was no secret that he liked Gacha. Both men were skirting around the real subject to be discussed, like a pair of matadors looking for an opening in which to make the decisive move.

They had met when Gacha was only ten years old and living like a sewer rat. Back then Gacha had only been a soldier for the *El Centro* gang. A soldier was the lowest level in *gamín's* rank. From soldier you progressed to *gerente* (manager), which was a *gamín* in charge of a cadre of sixteen *gamines*. From manager one stepped up to *controlador* (controller), a *gamín* who controlled the managers. There were one hundred controllers in the *El*

Centro gang. Those one hundred were supervised by the leaders, Gacha, Chulo, García and Vargas.

"I appreciate the offer of help, but at the moment I don't need it," said Gacha with a half smile. "I'm here, Don Eusebio, because the *Chapinero* gang is flooding the market with emeralds. Not only are they driving down the price, but they are threatening to take over. At first, I thought the reports were outrageous, but later on I found out that they were being financed by the Pérez family of Medellín."

Don Eusebio was silent for a moment before he spoke, as if considering whether he should tell Gacha some dangerous secret. "It's true," Eusebio said. "The Pérez family controls a new emerald mine, the one they discovered about a year ago. Usually that would not be enough to make a push on me because they would need the capital to do it. A mine takes some time before it starts really producing profits. So, I figured they were being stupid and I decided to let them burn themselves out because they would have to use critical capital in order to do it. The idea was good if they were using the capital for the mine, but they were not. As you know, to make a push on me, you would need to flood the market with emeralds in order to drive down the price. By driving down the price of emeralds, they would catch me with a lot of emeralds that were overpriced, forcing me to take a big loss."

"Then where are they getting the capital from?" Gacha asked excitedly.

"Marijuana. The bad weed. Somehow they are turning a profit on marijuana. Don't ask me how, but they are."

Gacha nodded but made a mental note of it. He would have to look into this business of the marijuana. It was the second time in the same day he had heard someone making a profit by selling it. The fact that the Pérez family was making a profit at it was a good sign that he should start thinking about investing in it.

"So, are they going to push you out?" Gacha asked coldly.

"Pérez is trying but he has made a fatal error. I'm going to need ab   ee weeks for my plan to come to fruition."

"Could you tell me what the plan is?" *La Mano Negra* smiled and shook his head.

Gacha let out a long, soft whistle. "Three weeks. I don't know, Don Eusebio. I got big problems too."

"I can help you out as much as I am able to, but at the moment, that is not much. You're going to have to ride out the storm one way or another. My advice is to drop out of sight and let the *Chapinero* gang take over the market until I solve my problem or until you figure a way out of yours. Can you do that?" Eusebio looked at Gacha, two men discussing their own survival.

"Maybe, but with the *Suba* gang on the war path, *Chapinero* fixing to wipe us out, and no real money coming in..." Gacha let his voice trail off, giving the impression that the odds were not in his favor.

"You don't have any of your own money?" Eusebio asked with a tone of surprise. If Gacha did not have any money, then maybe Gacha wasn't as smart as he had first thought.

"Yes, but most of it is tied up in investments that will take at least two years to mature. If I use those funds in any way, I will have to pay a penalty. The problem is Carlos Fuentes. You know, the cop? If he realizes I'm weak he will go for my throat, because I will be the weak link in the gangs and, therefore, he will have me removed in order to stabilize the city from gang warfare. It would be smart of him if he did. It would stabilize the current troubles even though *Chapinero* will become the strongest gang."

"Yes, that cop Fuentes is smart and honest. An honest man will always keep coming at you until there is no need for him to keep coming because he's got you. I don't know what to tell you, my friend, but these are the times when one must ride out the storm alone. If you are able to hang on for a month, if you have the balls to hang tough against all the sons-of-bitches that will be coming at you, you will become king of Bogota. You will rule all the *gamines*, so keep a low profile and stay out of Fuentes' way."

_____*Peter A. Neissa*_____

CHAPTER FIVE

Carlos Fuentes was rocked by the revelations of the past twelve hours. *Bizco*, the enforcer of the *Suba* gang, had been found dead in the gutter earlier in the morning. Margarita Coro, the girlfriend of Gonzalo Rodriguez Gacha, had been found in the early afternoon by an *obrero* (laborer) gang raped and badly cut, and on top of all that, there was the news that the *Chapinero* gang was muscling in on the *El Centro* turf.

"What the hell is going on?" Fuentes cried out. Out of the twelve months of the year the *gamín* gangs had to choose to have their bloody massacre in, they had to pick the one that coincided with an American VIP that was coming into town. It was a time when his resources were being committed to finding a goddamn briefcase and trying to put together a security net for the incoming American hot-shot.

The news was bad all around, Fuentes thought. One of his own *ratones* had said that Margarita Coro had been revenge for the death of *Bizco*. The *ratón* had also informed him that Gonzalo Rodriguez Gacha had been seen following *Bizco* sometime yesterday in the late afternoon. Of course, all this was supremely bad, but the worst of the news was of *Chapinero*'s encroachment into *El Centro* turf. That meant that sooner or later *La Mano Negra* would be involved.

If *Chapinero* were able to take over the *El Centro* turf, then it would just be a matter of time before it ruled all of the other gangs. A combination of *El Centro* and *Chapinero* would be powerful enough to overtake all the others. The outcome of such a scenario, Fuentes thought rapidly, would mean that a new mafia would take over the city and *La Mano Negra* would be threatened. Fuentes let out a long sigh.

The whole thing was his worst nightmare come true.

Ernesto Bosco, the gang leader of the *Chapinero* gang, certainly had the balls for such a push. He was an organizational man. His control over the *Chapinero* gang was due to his efficiency in re-distributing "lifted" goods with a minimum "hold" time. He was able to change hot items without really ever coming into contact with them, so he was rarely caught with the hot items. Bosco, however, for all the street-smartness, organizational skills, and capacity for violence, did not have the mental ability to plan for the long haul. His ability was only to project in the short run, a week on tactical matters and six months on financial matters.

On the other hand, Gonzalo Rodriguez Gacha lacked organizational skills, even though he seldom revealed it. His personality was that of a quiet loner and he always demanded full control. Delegation of authority had never been one of his strong points; he had to be involved in everything, no matter how trivial the detail. What made Gonzalo Rodriguez Gacha the most important of the *gamín* gang lords was his street-smartness, his propensity to violence almost leaning towards the psychotic, and the almost mythical ability to plan financial long-range goals. When Gacha talked in terms of long range, he talked in terms of years.

If he were a gambling man, Fuentes thought to himself, he would call it a fifty-fifty chance for either Bosco or Gacha to become the next black market king of Bogota. The only problem was that as a police officer upholding the law, he could not hedge his bet, because no matter what the outcome, the police would be the loser. It was not a situation of dealing with the lesser of two evils, because the victor would some day become a monster. But looking at all the indicators and gauging the direction the wind was blowing, it seemed that Bosco would become the new king of Bogota, when it was all said and done. However, Gacha was not the type of person to go down easily and neither would his top men. Gacha's men, dangerous kids really, were fiercely loyal to him. It was the one and only difference that made the *El Centro* gang different from all the others. In *El Centro*, there was loyalty, while in the other gangs there was just a common shared interest.

Fuentes stood up from his chair behind a small desk in his office in downtown Bogota and walked over to his file cabinet. He opened a drawer marked "current" and withdrew a file with a title on it in big black letters: *El Centro*. He closed the drawer, walked behind his desk and sat down, putting his black police shoes on his desk. Lazily, he reached into his suitcoat and retrieved a pack of *Pielroja* cigarettes. He tore the cellophane wrapping off the pack and pulled out a non-filtered cigarette. He lit it and inhaled deeply. The tobacco was harsh and it always made him cough on the first puff, as it did now. He took another drag and this time he released the smoke slowly through his nostrils as he began to read the file.

The first record ever made on José 'Chulo' Moncada was on a birth certificate that was on permanent record with the F-2 police. He was born in 1952 in the township of Libano in northern Tolima province, at the epicenter of *La Violencia*.

Chulo was the son of Tuburio Moncada, also known as *Relámpago* (Lightning), because of the speed in which he could ambush a military convoy. In 1954, on the second wave of violence that shook the country that came to be known as the Second War, Tuburio Moncada was shot dead, betrayed by his own men. His wife, caught in the deadly crossfire, was also shot dead, leaving their only son José an orphan.

For the next eight years no record existed for Chulo and no reports could be confirmed on what he had done during that time. In 1962, Chulo began to leave a trail that the civilized world could follow, a bureaucratic paper trail.

At the age of ten, Chulo was arrested in Bogota, charged with grand theft. He had snatched a $5,000 gold and diamond watch from a high ranking politician's wife as she exited from a beauty salon. Chulo was caught by crazy coincidence. On the public bus in which he had made his flight, he had made the unfortunate error of sitting beside an undercover policeman. He was arrested and charged, but not convicted, because children under the age of twelve could not be convicted of felony crimes in

Colombia. Chulo was sent to the San Gabriel Orphanage in downtown Bogota, where he should have remained until the age of eighteen.

The orphanage for all intents and purposes was a prison. Chulo, taller and stronger than most children his age, was able to hold his own inside the violent and very deadly world of the orphanage. He met many children but did not become friendly with them until he was certain they were loyal to him. Once they were loyal, they came under his protection. It was also the beginning of his vast network of *ratones*.

By the age of twelve he ruled over every kid in the orphanage that was his own age or younger. The only people he could not control were the older mates and the administrators who ran the orphanage. His own subjugation came under two types. The first was in terms of favors that ranged from gambling to prostitution. The gambling subjugation occurred when he had bet more than his share and were unable to pay up. The gambling syndicate, made up of sixteen-year-old kids, would decide the method of repayment. Usually it meant sleeping with someone. The second type of subjugation occurred with the administrators themselves, who forced every kid at some point to have sex with them. Women ran the orphanage except for a few men. And if you refused to have sex with them, it meant the isolation cell. Sometimes they could leave you in the isolation cell for over two weeks and when you came out you were totally crazy.

When Chulo turned fourteen, he was the tallest and most powerful kid in the orphanage, even though he was only five feet three inches. He ruled with an iron hand until the day when a matron ordered him to have sex with her, and he punched her to the brink of death. Charges were never pressed, but he was thrown out nevertheless.

The next two years, according to the F-2, Chulo toughened and developed into a cunning young man. He was reported to have killed with his bare hands a man who had tried to force himself upon him in a dark alley of Bogota. The report could never be confirmed because a body was never found. Not an unusual occurrence, thought Fuentes. The body was probably thrown into the Bogota river. There had been another incident with Chulo, when two cops had overestimated their rousing abilities and found themselves in the hospital soon after. For that, Chulo had been sentenced to one year in jail, but the judge released him after six months. On the day he was released from prison he met Gonzalo Rodriguez Gacha.

Rodrigo Vargas was the distribution man for the *El Centro* gang. Born a bastard in Bogota in 1954, he was an ugly kid with a violent temper. Vargas was not the kind of person Gacha would want in a position of command, Fuentes thought, as he read the file. Gacha always favored the cool, level-headed individual.

The only reason Vargas was still around was due to his tactical ability in gang war. And if war between *El Centro*, *Chapinero* and *Suba* ever broke out, he would be the pivotal man for the *El Centro* gang. The rest of Rodrigo Vargas' file was unimpressive. It was filled with hearsay, gossip and a brief psychiatric profile done on him in 1969, when he had been picked up in a wealthy neighborhood speaking incoherently while not in a state of intoxication. The psychiatrist had noticed some deep emotional wounds that were consuming Vargas. The wounds were in two forms: First, there was the resentment towards the oligarchy for having all that they had. Second was the driving hatred of his mother for having driven his father out of the house. Whether true or not, Vargas believed that was exactly what his mother had done. Given Vargas' violent temper, the psychiatrist had noted, Vargas would vent these feelings through violence someday. Because further testing had showed that Vargas indeed hated women and only wanted them when they screamed in pain, the doctor had concluded that Vargas would commit violence primarily against women.

The only rumor to ever reach Fuentes' ears about Vargas was that Vargas had been seen in the company of some *guerrilleros*. *Guerrilleros* were a band of fugitives who called themselves patriots, but were really nothing more than murdering bastards. Whether the *guerrilleros* were M-19 or FARC could not be proven or confirmed, but it was a rumor that Fuentes had believed from the very first time he heard it. A gang of savages like the M-19

59

and the FARC recruited psychotic killers like Vargas.

As Fuentes turned the page on the Vargas report, a police officer walked into his office. It was one of his most trusted men. The officer took bribes to compliment his measly income of four hundred *pesos* ($30.00) a week. The bribes were not major, they were small. Most of them were 'fees' in lieu of traffic tickets or health and city code violations, but never had he taken a bribe from *La Mano Negra*. By not doing so, the police officer had become one of the trusted ones.

"What's up?" Fuentes asked, looking up from the file.

"I just heard there's going to be a meeting between Gacha and Bosco next Wednesday. It has been arranged to take place in the buffer zone. Only one *pistolero* each," said the officer.

Fuentes grunted as he absorbed the information. "You think *Chapinero* can push Gacha out of *El Centro*?"

The officer laughed. "Not unless *Chapinero* has a death wish. Bosco doesn't have the money or the *cojones* (balls) for a long, drawn out war. *El Centro* also has the tacticians."

"Suppose Bosco had the funds," Fuentes said, lighting up another of his harsh cigarettes.

The officer thought for a moment before responding. "It would be a close one, but I think Gacha would win out in the end. You know how the saying goes, eh? Lose the battle but win the war? Bosco could win a battle but in the long run not the war."

"Suppose *Chapinero* gets the funds and makes a takeover attempt while *Suba* and *El Centro* are going for each other's throats?" Fuentes asked as he brought the cigarette to his lips and inhaled a lungful of smoke.

The officer began to laugh and then turned stone cold when he realized his boss wasn't joking. Then the gravity of the situation hit him like a slap across the face. "My God!" the officer blurted out. "That could change the whole make-up of the city. *La Mano Negra* would be threatened. Oh no! Blood will run in the streets."

"Yes, think about it some more and close the door when you leave," Fuentes said returning to the file. The officer walked out, but his humor had left before he had.

Mario García was the enigma of the *El Centro* gang. He was born in 1953 to *campesino* parents. The parents, unable to feed him and not wanting him, gave him up for adoption. Mario, however, had not ended up as an adopted child of the rich and famous as his parents had hoped. Instead he had ended up as one of the unfortunates of the San Gabriel Orphanage, where, as fate would have it, he met Chulo. They became friends and what was curious about the friendship, Fuentes reflected, was that they were the exact opposites of one another.

Although good looking, Mario was shy and awkward with girls while Chulo was the embodiment of the Latin lover. Mario was a student who graduated at fifteen from the orphanage and had been accepted into La Javeriana University, after Gonzalo Rodriguez Gacha had called in some favors, of course. For the last two years he had been studying business administration at the university and receiving excellent marks. He had also become the financial wizard for the *El Centro gamín* gang. Beneath the sharp and intelligent business acumen, there was an extremely likable character. He was known as the joker in the pack. Always ready with a joke in hand, he became the center of attention at every party.

Mario was sought after by girls, but was very seldom seen with a girl. At first it was rumored he was *marica* (gay), but that rumor was put to an end when he took a string of girl lovers in a single month. At first everyone believed it was only for show, which to a certain extent was true. The reason behind the non-involvement with women was that he was deeply religious. He always believed it to be a sin to sleep with girls unless married in the eyes of the Church, but he thought it worse to be regarded as *marica*.

In a rare face to face talk with Fuentes, Gacha had confided that Mario García was thinking about joining the priesthood, which explained why Mario was so incredibly well liked and respected by all the gangs. In a country where the Spanish Inquisition had played a heavy role in forming the moral character of the nation, the Catholic Church was still thought of as all knowing. It also made it almost impossible to get a divorce, not to mention an abortion. To become a man of the faith was a calling that all Colombians admired. It was the next best thing to becoming a saint. Since Mario was thinking about joining the seminary, he had become an untouchable, meaning he could not be knifed if caught in a rival gang's turf. To knife a possible saint was risking eternal damnation in Colombians' eyes. So Mario walked around the city with a sort of gang immunity.

Carlos Fuentes closed the file and threw it on his desk. There was nothing more to be read and there was no new information on Gacha that he had not memorized already. Hard police records on Gacha could not be found because under the last police lieutenant, the Gacha file had mysteriously been misplaced. So, all he knew about Gacha were the same stories that everybody else knew, which, truth be told, didn't amount to much. He knew that Gacha was liked by *La Mano Negra*, that Gacha had shown up in Bogota sometime in late 1958, and that he had worked his way up to *gamín* gang lord of *El Centro*. Police officers remembered Gacha being at the station many years before, but they could not remember whether it was for a simple visit or if he was there under arrest. It seemed that the previous lieutenant and Gacha were the best of friends or worst of enemies depending on who you talked. Whatever the case, Gacha had outlasted the lieutenant.

Yes, Fuentes thought, if Gacha could weather the onslaught, he would come out extremely powerful. Perhaps powerful enough so that as a police lieutenant he might never get to see Gonzalo Rodriguez Gacha behind bars like a common thug. But then again, he had seen *gamín* gang lords come and go as fast as crap through a goose. Maybe Gacha was really on his way out.

Maybe.

Gonzalo Rodriguez Gacha sat on his bed reading and re-reading the difficult technical pamphlets and reports from the United States Department of State. At first he didn't comprehend the written language, but with the help of a Spanish-English dictionary he slowly began to translate the papers.

The strategy envisioned by the U.S. Department of

State was beneficial to Colombia, but not one that would break the economic ties that kept Colombia in bondage.

There was a light knock on Gacha's bedroom door, causing him to look up from the papers he held in his hands.

"Who is it?" Gacha called out.

"Mario," said a voice on the other side of the bedroom door.

"Come in, Mario," Gacha said, moving some papers out of the way.

The door opened and in walked Mario with a smile on his face. "I heard from Vargas that you wanted to see me," Mario said, standing beside the bed. An honor for any *gamín* in Bogota.

"Yes, I wanted to ask you some things about economics..."

"Economics?" Mario cut Gacha off.

"Yes, sit down please," Gacha said shuffling some papers back into the briefcase.

Mario sat down uneasily on the edge of the bed. People were rarely invited into the *jefe's* bedroom, except for Chulo, who had immediate access.

"Okay, what is it that you want to know about economics?" Mario asked, puzzled but still thrilled that Gacha was interested in such things. He always thought Gacha only concerned himself with being the power and leader of the group.

"How would you characterize Colombia's business arrangement with the Americans?" Gacha asked in an off-handed manner.

Mario laughed but then realized that Gacha was serious. "In theory, it is an arrangement that should work. They lend us the money to industrialize and develop, whereby we use that money to produce a product to sell to them or to others. Once we sell the product we invest half the money from the sale by putting it back into the making of such a product. The rest of the money from the sale goes towards paying off the loan. Once the loan is paid off, the country can re-invest the money it would have used for the repayment of the loan into other areas of the economy. The goal, of course, is to become self sufficient. When that occurs, progress and development occur at an accelerated pace."

"So, why doesn't it work?" Gacha asked, quite interested in the subject, thrilling Mario even more.

"There are many complex reasons, but the two biggest factors are that the United States makes more money by keeping us less developed..."

"How is that?" Gacha cut in with some anger.

"Well, they lend us enough money to buy the machinery, which, by the way, we have to buy from them. Once the machinery is bought, not only are we out of money, but we still owe them the money for the loan. So, we take out another loan to pay the workers to produce the product. Once the product is made, we sell it. The problem, of course, is that the money we make from the product is only enough to pay for the loans we took out to buy the machinery and to pay the workers with. There go your sales profit and your re-investment money. Now, not only are we paying off the loans but the interest as well on the two loans, which is a considerable amount because the loans are into the hundreds of millions of dollars."

"What is the other reason, Mario?" Gacha asked, writing something in his little black book.

"Corruption," said Mario. "The Americans give us three hundred million but two hundred million disappears here in Colombia."

Gacha chuckled. "How?"

"The military takes a bite, the oligarchy with their consulting fees take another bite, and fake companies take another bite. It is grand scale theft," Mario said, shrugging his shoulders.

"If Americans make money off of us, why would they hesitate in giving us the money?"

"They are afraid to lose it, simple as that. They are bankers, not people in the charity business," Mario said with a smile on his face.

"How would they lose?"

"For a bank to make sure they get a fair return on their loan, they must make sure that the person they are going to lend the money to is good for it. Countries are the same way. Anything that could disrupt the return flow of the money makes a loan risky. Latin America in the past ten or twenty years has nationalized industries and companies that rightfully belong to the Americans. In some instances we have stopped paying on some of the loans they have given us."

"What is this word 'nationalized' that you speak of?" Gacha asked. He had remembered reading the word every now and then in the State Department's plan.

"Make the companies 'Colombian,' that means that the Americans lose everything. Therefore, the Americans seek assurances that the government they are about to enter into business with is as stable as a rock."

"But we are stable!" Gacha cried indignantly.

"Maybe," said Mario full of doubt.

"Uh?" Gacha muttered in bewilderment.

"The M-19 and the FARC are raising hell in the oil refineries. I think that is the reason the Americans are sending Kissinger here. They want to see if it's okay to invest." Mario stopped and then winced as if an ugly thought had crossed his mind. "Listen, *jefe*, I shouldn't be telling you this, but I'm worried about Vargas. If Kissinger really is coming, that means the military will make a sweep-up of all guerrilla suspects. Vargas, no matter what he thinks, is going to get caught. If he gets caught, he will implicate us by association. I know he has high ideals and all that, but that hot-head is running around with idiots waving guns. They do not know that the real power comes from the American dollar."

Gacha nodded wisely, as if he had thought out the problem at length and seemed to agree with Mario on the matter. This time he nodded, not out of habit but, because he agreed with Mario completely. "I know, Mario. Okay, that's all I wanted to know about economics except for one last question. If what you say is true about the mechanics of the international loans, how come you would want to invest?"

"Because while the money is in Colombia, there will be a bonanza in the economy. There will be money everywhere in the economy. We can clean up."

"Thanks, Mario, you have my permission to invest the money in what you deem proper."

"Really?" Mario asked, overjoyed. Now he had no doubt that Gacha was indeed a very wise man.

Gacha nodded and once again turned his attention to

the papers in front of him.

As Mario stepped out of the room, Gacha stretched his legs and accidentally knocked the briefcase off the bed. As he picked up the briefcase from the floor, he saw a little sliver of paper under what he now knew was a false bottom. Carefully he felt for the secret catches, wondering why he had not done that before. When he found them he pressed lightly and the false bottom came open. Underneath was a single sheet of paper with the most feared logo in all of South America, if not the world. It was the logo of the United States Central Intelligence Agency. *La CIA* to Colombians.

The sheet of paper was something Gacha had always dreamed of having. It was a list of people on the CIA payroll and how much they made from being informants. All of them were Colombians. It was also a list that if certain people knew he had, they would want him dead before sun-up the next day. Knowing this, Gacha still wanted to jump for joy.

Once Gacha settled down, the wheels in his head began to turn like little cogs in a small wheel, that would in time connect with bigger cogs turning an even bigger wheel, which would finally end up moving a vast and complex machine. And as the machine in his brain turned, a plan for his future began to take shape.

CHAPTER SIX

Gonzalo Rodriguez Gacha ate breakfast at the *El Centro Cafetería* on the day he was to have the meeting with Ernesto Bosco, the *gamín* gang leader for *Chapinero*. He nervously ate his fried eggs with bread and cheese and was washing it all down with coffee.

To others he looked calm, especially to those who knew who he was and what he was up against. The older folk were smiling at him because they had never liked Gacha. They had hated the inbred arrogance about him, as if the reason they themselves had not succeeded in life was because they hadn't handled it like he had. Now they were all laughing behind his back thinking, you stupid kid, don't you know we tried every get-rich quick scheme under the sun? Be content with what you've got. Only a few are chosen to be born into the oligarchy and you're not one of them. Gacha, however, ignored their smiles of satisfaction and continued sipping from his coffee as if he had no worries.

He had been up since before dawn. He had dressed early and hitched a ride to the far northern areas of the city, past the wealthy suburbs of Bogota. He had gone as far as Zipaquira, a small town as far north as one could go on the plateau. It was a routine he had been doing since Sunday. From these far and away areas he was mailing letters to the United States Embassy in downtown Bogota.

It was part of his master plan, a two-fisted plan which he thought would cause a major alarm within the embassy. But Jim Harrison, the CIA man, unexpectedly hadn't even lifted a finger to give him a call. Had they received the letters? The letters were simple and in Spanish.

Dear Mr. Ambassador: Perhaps you would like to

recover these documents...for a price! If you wish to recover the documents, please put a classified advertisement in the *El Tiempo* newspaper. Write international documentation wanted and list a phone number for contact.

It was always signed the same way: The People.

Attached to the letters were five of the twenty State Department pages that he had photocopied. And still there had been no answer, nothing.

The second part of his two-fisted plan was to carefully place small bombs under the vehicles of certain high government officials, then blow them up. He made sure the bombs exploded when no one was in the car. Although the bombs were detonated via remote control, nothing had been written up in any of the newspapers about the demolished cars on the city's streets; even after he had called the major radio and television stations claiming responsibility for the bombs, identifying himself as M-19. But the police had been worse than the embassy, they hadn't even put out a feeler or casually made an approach to see if he had heard anything or who might be involved.

Today was the last straw, Gacha told himself. He had mailed the letter to the U.S. Embassy from *Suba*, but this time he had sent the first five names on the CIA list. He had done that at four-thirty in the morning. Then just before the first scratch of dawn, he had snuck into the car park of the Presidential Palace in a milk truck. While he was inside the compound, he had left a fake bomb in the back seat of the Presidential limousine. Beside the bomb, he had left a small note that read: *THE NEXT TIME IT'S FOR REAL. M-19.*

Gacha knew it was a desperate measure, but he was in desperate straits. He had asked his men to hang low until after he had the meeting with Bosco. After the meeting he would tell them how to proceed. This meant telling them about his plan which so far wasn't working. If it didn't work out, he would have to tell them to merge into the *Chapinero* gang. If a merger occurred, his death by unwritten *gamín* code was required. With this in mind, he stood up and walked over to the counter and paid for his breakfast.

The woman who took his money smiled at him, leaned over the counter and whispered. "Listen, Pachito, I have some money you can use if you need it. Don't think about what those old men in the corner are thinking, they know nothing."

"Thank you, but I have enough money. I won't forget your offer of kindness," Gacha said putting his hand on her shoulder.

The woman smiled again and put her hand on his shoulder. "Good luck, Pachito, I'll pray to the Virgin Mary to protect you." Gacha nodded and walked out of the cafeteria.

The sidewalk was full of people walking to work as Gacha walked on the same sidewalk. He had to alter his step many times or he would have been trampled over by a wall of small businessmen all carrying briefcases and walking in the opposite direction. It was perhaps one of the reasons why he had not seen the two men following him.

As he was about to cross the road on *calle* 24, two men grabbed him by the arms and forced him into a black Chevrolet that had pulled up to the curb. Once inside and flanked by two more men, the car pulled away from the curb quickly.

The man on the passenger seat beside the driver turned around and faced Gacha. "Hello there," said Jim Harrison. "Sorry to have to pick you up like that, but we have been trying to reach you all fucking morning. Where were you?"

"Business," Gacha said in English with a rough Spanish accent so that the word sounded like "beesness".

"A-ha, what kind?" Harrison asked.

"I have problems of my own, you know?"

"So I hear, any predictions?" Gacha shrugged. "I hear Bosco's got it all wrapped up. They say he's been selling emeralds all over downtown this week. Is that true?"

"You know kidnapping is against the law in Colombia?" Gacha asked with a cold smile.

"All right, all right! Enough with the games, I don't

69

have the time to fuck around. Have you heard anything about the briefcase?"

Gacha wanted to shout at the top of his lungs that he did know something about the briefcase, but he knew he had to play this for all it was worth. So he shook his head in response.

"Are you sure?" Harrison asked.

Gacha nodded. "Nothing."

"Damn!" Harrison muttered under his breath.

"Well..." Gacha said, letting his voice trail off and his face take on an expression as if he were reaching way back into his memory bank.

"Well, what?" Harrison asked, looking almost desperate.

"One of my *ratones* said he heard something 'bout it, but he didn't say anything 'bout any briefcase."

"Oh?"

"Something about some *yanqui* papers..." Gacha said looking pained, as if trying to come up with a word from a conversation held long ago. "Something about some United States apartments."

"United States Department of State?" Harrison asked, his tone almost of a supplicant.

Gacha hesitated before he answered. "Maybe, I don't know. It was a *ratón* who told another, who told another and then another until it finally came to me."

"Listen, Gacha, if you can get that briefcase to me intact or point the way to it, I can help you out with some of your problems."

Gacha laughed out loud and then raised his left eyebrow skeptically. "How could you do that?"

"I can put pressure on certain authorities to take certain enemies you have out of circulation. Margarita..."

"What about Margarita?" Gacha cut in angrily.

"We can see that she gets certain doctors."

"But they don't have the capability. That is what the doctors told me."

"True," said Harrison. "But it's just a matter of a few years. We can arrange it. Gacha, we don't forget our own."

Gacha looked on doubtfully. "I'll see what I can do, but I've told you, I have problems of my own, big problems." Jim Harrison nodded in agreement. "Where can I reach you if I do find out something?"

Harrison pulled out a white business card and wrote a number down. "You can call me at this number day or night."

Gacha nodded and took the card as the black Chevrolet pulled up close to the street curb and stopped. "I'll see what I can do," Gacha said as he opened up the door and stepped out.

Harrison rolled down his window and said, "Gacha, we take care of our own."

At nine in the morning Gacha walked into his apartment to find his top three men waiting for him, their faces lined with worry and grief as if they had just been to a funeral.

"*Jefe*, where have you been?" Chulo asked. "They've been calling you all day. One of the kids beside the phone says the phone hasn't stopped ringing.

"I had a meeting with the American," said Gacha in way of an explanation.

"Fuentes came by asking for you," Mario said, his face so white he looked like he was going to throw up. "He started cursing when I told him you were not around."

"Here?" Gacha asked in shock.

"Yes, showed up with a whole army of *tombos*. He asked where you were. I said you were out making the rounds. He said that you were to call him the moment you were told."

"Did he say what he wanted?" Gacha asked, suddenly electrified.

"No," Mario said, his voice almost breaking. "But I have never seen him look so mad in my life. Whatever it is, it has to be bad and not good for us."

"*Jefe*," Chulo said, as if the next couple of words would be the straw that would break the camel's back. "There was

71

another call, a man who said that he wanted to meet with you as arranged. He said his name was *El Palo Grande* (The Big Stick). He said you would understand."

Gacha nodded. He knew that *El Palo Grande* was the codename of the United States Ambassador. It also meant that the ambassador had been informed of the latest M-19 caper: the fake bomb in the Presidential limousine, the same bomb that he had put there himself but had blamed on the M-19.

Vargas cleared his throat trying to force the big lump in his throat back down to the pit of his stomach. "*Jefe*, the hospital called too. Margarita is being released today. Are you still meeting with Bosco?"

Gacha nodded. "I'll call Fuentes and see what he wants. Mario, you pick up Margarita and make sure she gets to the Gonzáles' house with no problems. Vargas, you still hanging around with the M-19?"

"A-ha," Vargas said defiantly.

"I want it to stop from this moment."

"Eh, what? You cannot order me!" Vargas replied more in shock than anger.

"Listen, you and your friends have become targets. The military knows about you. I spent all morning trying to convince people that you were not with the M-19," Gacha lied. He had not discussed it with anyone, but the lie was also intrinsic to his master plan.

"Bullshit! We have always kept the way secret. It's just the oligarchy trying to squeeze you for information. We're going to take down that imperialist dog from America and whoever gets in the way. Nobody knows where we are because we are everywhere! You said, Gacha, that you didn't care if we joined the M-19, that we could do whatever we wanted."

"Yes, but not when our lives become threatened by association with you because you're running around with a bunch of maniacs."

"I won't change! You don't know where we are, so *al Diablo* (to the devil) with you!" Vargas roared, spit flying every which way with every word.

The room became deathly quiet, the tension electric. Chulo and Mario knew at once that Vargas had gone too far, no one talked to the *jefe* that way and got away with it. Nobody.

"We are all very anxious, Vargas, maybe we ought to calm down and think this out," Gacha said calmly, his fingers curled up into tight fists.

"No, I will not change. You know nothing of us," Vargas said with less conviction. "We are more powerful than all the *gamín* gangs put together."

At the mention of those very words, Gacha made up his mind to get rid of Vargas. The bastard just didn't know when to quit. Gacha let out a long sigh of resignation, "Okay, just be careful."

Vargas looked on imperiously, showing off that he had forced the *jefe* to back off. He was full of pride, and deep in his mind he thought that he was the one that should be in control of the *El Centro* gang.

Chulo looked on with a twitch in his eye. He had known the *jefe* a long time. He did not give up that easily. Vargas was a goner. Or was the *jefe* coming undone at the mounting pressure? Did the *jefe* have the balls for war?

"Chulo," said Gacha, cutting into his thoughts. "Are you ready for the meeting?" Chulo nodded. "Who's going to be Bosco's *pistolero* (gunman)?"

"Crater Face Gómez," Chulo answered.

Gacha nodded with hesitation. Crater Face Gómez was the enforcer for the *Chapinero* gang. He was a good pick, thought Gacha. Gómez was calm and wasn't given to making hasty and stupid decisions.

"All right," said Gacha. "I'll be back in one hour. I'm going to meet with Fuentes and then *El Palo Grande*. Chulo, I'll meet you here and together we will go to the buffer zone."

"*Sí, jefe*," Chulo said as Gacha walked out of the apartment without saying another word.

Carlos Fuentes met Gonzalo Rodriguez Gacha outside

El Banco de la República (the National Bank) in downtown Bogota. The bank was the place where all the money the Americans would loan to Colombia would be deposited, at least for a while.

"I wasn't sure you'd call," said Fuentes. He walked beside Gacha in the big *plaza* in front of the bank. It was a terrible day for walking. The wind was gusting, a prelude to a driving rain.

"Why do you say that?" Gacha countered.

"I got problems, major problems," Fuentes said, ignoring Gacha's question. "My job is on the line."

"Why?"

Fuentes hesitated for a moment. "The last week or so, the M-19 has gone around Bogota blowing up cars belonging to the big-shots. Thank God no one has been hurt, but people are nervous, very nervous. They want it cleaned up quick and they don't care how, they just want it done."

Gacha raised an eyebrow. "You know I'm looking for the briefcase you asked me to look for?"

A flash of anger crossed Fuentes' face. "The hell with the briefcase! Someone this morning put a fake bomb inside the President's limousine with a note that was signed by the M-19. The note said nothing really, but the message was clear. They could have killed him."

"And what do you expect me to do about it? I know shit about the M-19. They are just a bunch of loose cannons running around with nothing better to do than kill people," Gacha said in a cold voice.

"We know the M-19 has a branch in Bogota, the problem is that we don't know where in Bogota. I need your help to point the way to those maniacs. If you help me out I can help you out with your current problems."

"Oh, and how is that?"

"Don't be a wise-ass, Gacha. I know you have a meeting with Bosco today. I can get him arrested and put away for a long time."

So, they knew about the meeting, Gacha thought. I

wonder who the informant is? Is it one of Bosco's men or is it one of mine?

"Listen," Fuentes said, "I'm going out on a limb here. The Americans are sending Henry Kissinger and yesterday we received a threat against the man's life. If he cancels his trip, Colombia is out of a three billion dollar aid package. We lose that money and there will be a lot of oligarch *hijos de putas* (sons-of-a-bitch) after my ass for not having caught the crazies in the M-19."

Gacha sighed. "I'll put out some feelers, but you know I have troubles of my own. Not only that, *Suba* is on the warpath."

"Yeah, they said you killed Bizco."

Gacha didn't answer. He simply ignored the comment.

"Listen," said Fuentes, stopping in the center of the *plaza*. "The *Suba* gang knows they made a technical error by cutting up your girl. Everyone knows that the girls are out of everything and, therefore, are neutral. The worst of it is that they cut her up north of the buffer zone. They know they are bird cage lining because of it. I am going to take them out, that should eliminate some of your troubles, eh?"

Gacha looked at Fuentes incredulously. He doubted Fuentes would do it. Would he? After all, the man was between a rock and a hard place. Well, Gacha thought, if the meeting went badly with Bosco this afternoon then he would consider what Fuentes had proposed.

Damn it all! I feel like I'm dancing on a high wire just above a pool of sharks! Gacha thought.

"I'll see what I can do," Gacha said with finality. Fuentes nodded wanting to say something more but he turned and walked away.

El Palo Grande wore a black poncho, leather sandals, faded green pants and a straw hat. The man looked right at home in them, as if he were truly a real *campesino*. The man was not a peasant at all, but he was instead the United States Ambassador to Colombia. He was sitting behind a formica

75

counter in a seedy little bar in downtown Bogota.

"*El Palo Grande?*" Gacha asked with a trace of laughter in the words.

"*Sí,*" said the peasant looking man in a terrible American accent. He felt out of place, like a little league ball player playing in the big leagues.

"I speak English, Mr. Ambassador," Gacha said, taking the bar stool beside him.

The ambassador let out a long sigh of relief and then looked at Gacha with a quizzical look. "Have we met before?"

Gacha shook his head.

"No, of course not," said the ambassador. "Lousy day, eh? I hate when it rains like this, brings a cold that numbs the marrow in the bones." Curtis Mathews fidgeted uneasily in the seat not knowing how to approach the subject. He had never done this and had never envisioned doing something like this. "You follow any sports?"

"What is it you want, Mr. Ambassador?" Gacha asked, looking at his wrist watch.

"Yeah, well, okay. The previous ambassador said you had a contact in the M-19. I want you to find out if they are going to make an attempt on the incoming VIP."

"You mean Henry Kissinger?" The ambassador nodded. "That's easy, they are. I heard about it this morning from the horse's mouth."

"Good God!" The ambassador exclaimed. "So, the bomb scare on the President was no fluke!"

Gacha shrugged.

"God curse these terrorists. Can you convince these M-19 hoodlums not to do it?"

"What?!"

"Can you..."

"I heard, Mr. Ambassador. I am not M-19, I don't know how they plan their operations. Why do you care if Kissinger comes or not?"

"I don't understand," Mathews said puzzled.

"Why would you care if Kissinger comes to Bogota?"

"It has to do with the money he might bring to Colombia." The ambassador paused and then added, "Are you sure we've never met?"

"No, we have never met. So, if he comes we get the money."

"Yes, but there is a lot more to it than just making money."

"What could be more important than making money?" Gacha asked.

"Stability. If the American banks lend the money to Colombia, the United States gets to flaunt the economic aid to other countries who want the same thing but are thinking of going Communist. We are trying to lure those governments, the ones that are leaning towards Fidel's side. A bribe if you will, but the hell of it is that it works. It's a long range plan of stability. We want to stabilize the region. Christ! I'm talking foreign policy to a thug kid! Forget it, Gacha, it's been nice talking to you."

Anger flashed through Gacha's face, an almost livid presence of violence that stilled the ambassador. "Sit down," Gacha hissed like a snake ready to strike at its prey.

"You Americans think we cannot grasp complicated situations, but we can. We were a global power two hundred years before the down and out from Great Britain decided to make a living in America. We are a culture that goes back thousands of years. Your American history goes back the whole of two hundred years. We understand stabilization better than you might think, Mr. Ambassador. What you are trying to do is to stop the further spreading of Communism on the continent, eh?"

The ambassador nodded, shocked that the kid who he gauged was younger than his second oldest daughter understood American foreign policy. Not only that, he knew history as well. He began to re-appraise the kid rapidly. "Yes, what you say is the basic essence of our goal."

"Good, now we can deal."

"Deal?" the ambassador asked, bewildered.

77

"Yes, nothing is for free, Mr. Ambassador. First, I have a friend at a good university here in Bogota. He will be graduating in two years. I want you to make sure that he gets into Harvard University Business School."

"Harvard! Are you joking?"

"No, he has the marks and the money but not the right recommendations.

"Yeah," the ambassador said, impressed. "Two years, eh?" Gacha nodded. "Well, when it's time for him to apply let me know and I'll see what I can do."

"I would also like to obtain a visa to go to the United States whenever I want to," said Gacha.

"It can be done."

"Then I think I can help you, Mr. Ambassador. Yes, my business partners do not like this M-19 either, they cause trouble for everyone."

"How can you help me?" the ambassador asked.

"Once I discover their hideout I will send the police, but I will make sure that you know when that happens so that you know I was the one who told them. That way you will know that I kept my end of the deal. I'll make sure it's in the papers too."

"You'll tip off the papers too?" The ambassador said, smiling. "Here's my private number. Call me when you have something concrete. If you can get it in the papers, you'll solve my problems."

"Yes, I'll make sure there is a lot of publicity, front page stuff," Gacha said with a grin on his face.

"Great, that would be the right stroke of luck we would need to go ahead with the VIP." The ambassador stood up from the bar stool and shook Gacha's hand and then walked out of the bar, unaware he was born to dress like a *campesino*.

Gacha sat on the bar stool looking at the ambassador as he walked away. He had learned some things from the American Ambassador. For example, the ambassador and Jim Harrison did not cooperate on information and therefore were unaware that each of them had offered him a deal. The only thing the idiots cared, thought Gacha, was whether people were Communists or not. They did not know that a peasant in Colombia couldn't grasp what Marxism-Leninism was, even if someone tattooed it on their foreheads. Most *campesinos* wouldn't be able to show someone where Russia was on a map, and much less cared if it existed at all.

Ernesto Bosco, the *gamín* leader of the *Chapinero* gang, was an orphan from birth. The father who had left his seed inside his wife was killed before Ernesto was born in 1952, killed in the Korean Conflict with Colombian troops that were part of the United Nations peacekeeping force. Ernesto's mother, after a complicated delivery, died seconds after Ernesto came into the world.

For the first ten years, Ernesto raised himself at the Soacha *manicomio* (insane asylum). At the age of five, because he was unable to read, he was diagnosed as mentally retarded. Quickly he was condemned to live out the rest of his life in the *manicomio* until the good graces of God would free him from this earth. However, Bosco was not retarded. He suffered from an acute case of dyslexia that made him see letters and words in strange patterns.

Gifted with a shrewd analytical mind, he was able to grasp complex problems at one hearing. He had the capacity to think in logical ways but in short term strategies. At the age of twelve he escaped from the Soacha insane asylum and became a *gamín*. For the next two years he apprenticed in theft, burglary and murder. His mentor was a kid his same age who had taught him all there was to know about being a *gamín*. Both of them were inseparable, almost like brothers. They shared all the booty equally until they came under the eyes of the then *gamín* gang lords of the city. Both of them had rejected the offers to work for the *gamín* gang lords until by sheer force they were convinced otherwise. The problem was that each chose to go with a different gang.

There had been bad blood between Ernesto Bosco and Gonzalo Rodriguez Gacha ever since.

79

The meeting was held in the buffer zone in a small bar called *La Dorada*, which was relatively empty when Gacha walked in with Chulo a step behind him.

At a glance Gacha took in the bar and saw Bosco sitting at a table in the center of the room. Crater Face Gómez sat in the back with his back against the wall. The bulge under the armpit of Crater Face's coat let Gacha know that he was packing *fierro*.

Gacha moved ahead and formally shook hands with Bosco as he rose from his chair. Formality dictated that whenever *gamín* gang lords met, the exchanges should be with the utmost politeness. Chulo nodded formally at Bosco and at Crater Face, as was customary, then walked over towards Crater Face and sat beside him. No words were exchanged between Crater Face and Chulo. None were required.

"How is Lucia doing these days?" Gacha opened the conversation by inquiring about Bosco's girlfriend.

"She is well, thank you," said Bosco. "I am sorry to hear about Margarita. If there is anything I can do, please do not hesitate to ask. Rest assured that the attack did not come from *Chapinero*, but I think you know that already."

Gacha nodded. "I called this meeting to discuss some unclarified boundaries."

"And what boundaries aren't clear?" Bosco asked with a glint of humor in his eyes.

"Well, I have been hearing reports, fabrications I know, since our neighboring colleagues of *Chapinero* would not be stupid enough to encroach on the emerald market of *El Centro*."

Bosco stared coldly at Gacha, anger written all over his face. He was about to lash out in a verbal barrage but remembered Crater Face was with him and he might misinterpret his actions. The last thing he wanted was a shoot out. Bosco glanced over quickly at Crater Face, who already had his hand inside his coat. Crater Face was an enormous kid with an acne complexion that had scarred his face. Someone had once observed that it looked like the lunar landscape and from then on the nickname had stuck.

"I'm afraid those reports are accurate," said Bosco, his facial features softening. "The days of the *El Centro* gang having an exclusivity on the emerald market are past."

Crater Face chuckled from the back of the bar.

Gacha felt like putting an end to it right then and there, but instead drew deep within him the vast reserves of self discipline to keep himself under control. "You know, my supplier is *La Mano Negra*? My ene...competitors are his competitors."

"Yes, but *La Mano Negra* may not be able to control the current national situation, with respect to emeralds. The Pérez family of Medellin will back us up against *La Mano Negra*."

Something did not make sense, Gacha thought. Bosco was talking as if the Pérez family had offered help and he had not taken it. If that was true, where was he getting the money to finance the takeover?

"What if *La Mano Negra* survives and the Pérez family doesn't. You will be made an example of by *La Mano Negra*. A gamble not worth taking, eh?" Gacha asked, as he tapped the table lightly with his fingers like a judge's gavel.

Bosco sat looking at Gacha, almost satisfied to see him squirm. Now, he thought, was the time to lower the boom on Gacha. "You are right, of course, unless the structure of the *gamín* power is altered in the city. Then *La Mano Negra* would be forced to distribute through *Chapinero*..."

"You're dreaming," Gacha said, dismissing Bosco like a professional dismissing an amateur.

Bosco flared up with anger. "As of this moment, *Chapinero* has taken on a limited partnership with the *Séptima gamín* gang. They are financing us. Your days of power are over!"

So, *Chapinero* and *Séptima* had merged, Gacha thought. *Séptima* had the funds from the marijuana, so why hadn't he looked into the marijuana angle yet? Somehow he had not provided for this little twist. Now, there was not only

Suba on the warpath but *Chapinero* and *Séptima* also. It was everyone against Gacha. Things were not good.

Gacha, although burning with anger on the inside, had not let his facial features show it. His surface features were ice-cold and etched in stone.

Gacha stood up. "Then we have nothing more to talk about. Please send my regards to Lucía."

"Yes, of course. My regards to Margarita and may she have a speedy recovery," Bosco said, extending his hand towards the outstretched hand of Gacha and shaking it.

Gacha nodded at Chulo and together they walked out of *La Dorada* bar.

War broke out the following morning between *El Centro, Chapinero, Séptima* and *Suba*.

CHAPTER SEVEN

One week after the meeting in the buffer zone between Bosco and Gacha, *El Centro* had suffered three casualties. Two *gamines* had been stabbed to death near the *Chapinero-Séptima* border while another had lost three fingers in a knife fight during a *Suba* ambush.

The *Chapinero* gang was openly selling black market emeralds in *El Centro* turf and Bosco was said to have been eating in Gacha's favorite restaurant. However, all *gamines* could not conceal their surprise when Gacha and his three top men dropped out of sight.

Although a *gamín* gang war was raging across the city, it appeared as if Henry Kissinger was still going to visit Bogota.

The first article on the rash of M-19 bombings appeared in *El Tiempo* newspaper several days after the outbreak of war. It was in the back pages, the article was brief and stating nothing more than that the police had suspects. On the front page, however, was an article about Don Emilio Gonzáles proclaiming his candidacy for the position of Mayor of Bogota. A picture of him in the right hand corner showed Don Emilio shaking hands with a man identified as a respected industrialist. The respected industrialist was *La Mano Negra*. Gonzalo Gacha chuckled as he threw the newspaper into a corner of the barn.

The *El Centro* gang leadership had been hiding out in a small town in the northwest area of Bogota, known as Facatativa. The barn they were in was damp and cold, grating on everyone's already sore nerves.

"We are a bunch of cowards; we have *gamines* dying for

us while we are out here hiding like chickens," Vargas said as he paced inside the barn. "I for one cannot stay here another night. I have a meeting tonight."

"Nobody moves," Gacha said, as he sat in a corner playing solitaire with a deck of cards.

"Like hell!" Vargas roared. "I have a meeting and that's the end of the discussion."

"All right, all right," Gacha said wearily. "You made your point. Go play guerrilla with your hooligan friends."

"Hooligans?" Vargas asked, almost on the verge of rage. "We fight for the *campesinos*, we fight for what is rightfully ours. Ours is a just cause, we want government for our people, our twenty-two million Colombians! We don't want one more stinking year of white oligarchs telling us what is good for us while we get hungrier. The oligarchy must be overthrown!"

"In your dreams," said Gacha with a wave of his hand.

Chulo and Mario didn't answer. They knew that Vargas was speaking in the tired old clichés, but even in those tired old clichés there was truth.

"No, Gacha. Not this time, we are gaining support daily. Yes, small numbers that don't amount to much, but we know the way now. In ten years we will be bigger and the government will have to recognize it is a fraud. We will make the people see that *El Frente Nacional* is nothing more than a mirage put on by the oligarchy.

"Year after year the poor get poorer, it is not just a lack of housing but of food and of not being treated like a human being. We are people, we have rights! The oligarchs promise year after year that we will be better off, but what do the poor have? Nothing, except we are one year closer to dying. People are starving to death, and nobody seems to care, there are no schools for the poor, disease is rampant, a man cannot speak his mind for fear of being arrested and called a subversive. It's not living, it's torture."

Gacha was silent because he did not want to respond. Vargas had a point, but it was like trying to build a sandcastle as the tide came in. The oligarchy and the military were the tide in this country. Anyway, he had already made up his mind to eliminate Vargas.

"I'm going for a walk," Gacha said. "You can go to the meeting if you like, Vargas. It's your life." Gacha walked out of the barn and carefully made his way to a public telephone in the center of the *pueblo*. He had telephone calls to make and how he played each caller was crucial to his master plan. A plan that would begin with his first telephone call.

Jim Harrison was sitting behind his desk inside the United States Embassy. He had slept sparsely in the last six days. The letters which had been coming in through the mail had him on edge, letters which mentioned three of the top paid CIA informants in Colombia, who had been on the list inside the ambassador's briefcase. The M-19 was still raising hell all over Bogota and his sources inside the police and the military were completely baffled. And still, the Assistant to the United States President for National Security Affairs was intent on visiting.

Today was the worst day. There had been a direct threat to Henry Kissinger's life, something he was directly responsible for. It was a nightmare. It was also the typical don't-give-a-shit attitude by Washington, which had no idea about what kind of security measures had to be called into play for such a visit. So far, he had the regular police, the F-2 which was Colombia's version of the FBI, the military police, the Colombian army and the United States FBI. The FBI had an office inside the embassy in downtown Bogota. So many men were involved in security that he was unable to determine how many men exactly were working for security.

Harrison's private telephone rang, the one that only a handful of people knew the number. At first he thought he had imagined the telephone ringing. How many times in the last couple of days had he stared at it wishing it would ring? Fifty? One hundred?

The telephone rang again.

"Hello?" Harrison said, never letting the caller know

who was answering.

"Harrison?" Gacha said, equally non-committaly.

"Who wants to know?"

"I have a lead Harrison, you want to know about it or do you want to play games?"

"Who is this?"

"Gacha."

"I'm listening."

"I can get the briefcase for you. I know who has it," Gacha said.

"Who? Where?

"Oh, no. You know Harrison, I learned a knew contract word the other day. *Quid pro quo*."

"What do you want for the briefcase?" Harrison said excitedly. It was his first major break in the whole damn sorry mess.

"Well, I don't have it, but I know who does. The problem is they want me dead."

There was a silence and the telephone line seemed to fill with static before Harrison spoke. "How do you want to work it out, Gacha?"

"First, I have to get the briefcase. If I can get it, I will call you. I should tell you that some of the people who have it may be M-19. I cannot confirm that, but that's what I've heard."

"Jeeesus. You just let me know Gacha and I'm sure we can work something out."

"I will. By the way, you tell anyone I'm your source and I'll have you killed."

"No need for threats."

"Good, I'll call you later." Gacha hung up knowing that he wouldn't call him until tomorrow when all the other phases of the plan were in place.

Carlos Fuentes, was in a gym inside the police building in downtown Bogota. He was punching a heavy-bag with lightning fast one-two combinations. The sweat was pouring off him as if he had been standing under a shower.

"Lieutenant!" cried out an officer from the doorway, letting a draft come in as he opened the door. "You got a telephone call."

"Tell'em I'm busy. I've had it up to my neck with no-good politicians. Why don't they try catching the bastards for seven hundred pesos a week." Fuentes finished his point with a flurry of punches that rocked the heavy-bag like a swing.

"It's Gacha," the officer cried out.

"Who?" Fuentes asked, dropping his gloves so that the heavy-bag knocked him to the ground as it returned from its forward swing.

The officer ran over to Fuentes, but he was already getting up. "Put a tracer on it, hurry!" said Fuentes.

"No good, he already hung up. He said he'd be calling in five minutes, which should be in about forty seconds from now."

Fuentes looked at the officer for a moment and then ran out of the gym, the officer trailing in his footsteps.

When the call came, Fuentes picked up the phone before it had a chance to ring out completely. The moment he picked it up, he cursed himself mentally. He had not wanted to let Gacha know he was desperate.

"What do you want Gacha?" Fuentes asked.

"I thought that as a good citizen of Bogota, you would be more receptive to my calls but I guess not. Good day..."

"Wait! I'm sorry. What do you have?" Fuentes asked, his voice conciliatory.

"I have a major problem or haven't you noticed?"

"Yes, I've noticed. Again, what is it you want?"

"I can lead you to the M-19, but there is a problem. They have guns. They are also a little *loco* if you know what I mean."

"So, tell me something I don't know. What do you want for the information, Gacha?"

"I want Ernesto Bosco and Crater Face Gómez removed, permanently." There was a vast silence on the telephone line. "Hello?" Gacha said, thinking the line had been disconnected.

"I heard," Fuentes said, his voice low. "You know he's being backed up by the Pérez family?"

"Not exactly. *Séptima* is bankrolling him initially..."

"What do you mean initially, and where in the hell did *Séptima* get the money?"

"Calm down. Initially means that *Séptima* reserves the right to break off their limited partnership after this trial run. The run being against me. So, they are waiting to see if it's successful for a full partnership. The Pérez family of Medellín said they would back-up *Chapinero* if they got control over Bogota. That means that Medellín and *La Mano Negra* would get involved depending on the outcome of the gang war.

There was another long silence before Fuentes spoke. "Shit!"

"Yes, I agree. However, you must choose between stability now or major instability later. If *Chapinero* takes over the gangs, then *La Mano Negra* will be forced into a war that will mean bigger problems than the ones you got now. Not only that, if you don't seize this opportunity, the war that *La Mano Negra* will run will coincide with Henry Kissinger's visit."

"All right," said Fuentes resignedly. "I'll have Bosco and his enforcer removed. It's going to take several phone calls and certain arrangements."

"I understand. There's just one more thing. Nothing can be connected to the *El Centro* gang."

"Oh?" Fuentes said in surprise.

"I have a loose cannon in my organization. He's not far from going off the deep end. I think he's in it, I just don't have the proof. I'll know by tonight."

"*Madre de Dios!* Vargas!" Fuentes shouted.

It was a nightmare come true, Fuentes thought. If Vargas was in it, it meant that the M-19 faction was going to die before giving up. Fuentes knew that he held the cards to get rid of the *El Centro* gang right now, but that meant a void would be left and it would be filled with *Chapinero*. If that was

the case, he would just be postponing a gang war for a mafia
war which was far worse and which would coincide with
Kissinger's visit. That was bad. How many calls had he taken
from the United States Ambassador today? Six? Seven? The
hell with Kissinger, Fuentes thought. The M-19 running amok
in Bogota was worse.

"I agree to your conditions, Gacha. Give me a call when
you have your end straightened out," Fuentes said and hung
up.

Curtis Mathews was sitting in bed reading one of the
greatest novels he had ever read, *One Hundred Years of
Solitude*, a novel written by a Colombian. He had begun to
read the book after he had met the writer Gabriel García
Márquez, at a social function held at the Presidential Palace.
The copy had been signed by the author, and since the book
was all the rage in Latin America, he figured he'd better read
it.

Mathews cursed when the telephone rang beside his
bed. He marked the page and answered the phone on the
second ring. "Mathews," he barked into the phone.

"*El Palo Grande?*" said a neutral voice over the phone.

"Speaking," said Mathews.

"It is all arranged. You are to do nothing or say nothing
to anyone. All will take care of itself, do you understand?"

"Yes, but how?" Mathews asked, sounding like a little
boy on Christmas eve.

"None of your business. You just stick to the end of
your bargain. It will occur tomorrow night, just so you know it
was me. Remember, Harvard."

"Agreed," said Mathews.

"*Adiós,*" Gacha said and hung up.

Mathews sat on his bed wanting to yell in happiness.
If he could pull this loan off and make sure that Kissinger had
a safe visit, he would go far in his career. Hell, he might even
get to that coveted diplomatic position in London at the Court
of St. James.

Don Emilio Gonzáles was eating a late-night dinner at his home after a long meeting with his campaign strategists. It was a meeting in which they had sung his praises and in low tones told him he needed a certain type of exposure, macho exposure.

All his campaign strategists had said the same thing. "They know who you are, it's just that you have to make them believe that you are one of them." It was impossible to be one of them, Emilio thought, he was caucasian and not mestizo, he was wealthy, had foreign schooling and had never really done any kind of hard labor in his life.

The solution everyone had hinted at but not told him directly was that he had to equate himself with the typical Colombian male. They had to make him into a Colombian *macho*, a masculine tour de force. He needed a common denominator which would transcend political, economic and racial barriers. The denominator was the psychological bonding between males. A *macho*, a man with guts, would defy the odds and take risks, such a man had *cojones* (balls). Colombian men respected males who risked their lives for something they believed in. If a man had *cojones* (balls) the size of dump trucks, he would be viewed as one of them by the voting populace.

Colombia was a nation forged by *macho* men, men like the conquistador Gonzalo Jiménez de Quesada, Sebastián de Belalcázar, Chief Yuldama of the Gualies, who revolted against the Spaniards, Blas de Lezo, who defended the port city of Cartagena against the British pirate Francis Drake, Antonio Nariño, translator of the Rights of Man and of the Citizen and jailed ten years for doing so, and the greatest *macho* of them all Simón Bolívar, The Liberator.

Some men had been able to portray themselves as *macho*, Don Emilio thought, but in the last couple of years no one had really been able to run for mayor on that alone. How was he going to do it? What in this modern day Colombia could possibly make him look like he had the *cojones* of a bull?

Somewhere deep in the back recesses of the house he

heard a phone ring. "Margarita, could you get that please," Emilio cried out.

"Gonzáles residence," Margarita said as she answered the phone.

Gacha was taken aback by Margarita's voice. He had not planned for it, he had forgotten that Margarita worked at that house. How long since he had spoken to her?

"Hello?" Margarita cut into Gacha's thoughts.

"Don Emilio Gonzáles," said Gacha in a deep, throaty, almost whispered voice.

"One moment, please."

Gacha could hear voices in the background until he was sure someone had picked up the phone and covered the mouthpiece with a hand.

Suddenly came a voice. "Hello, this is Don Emilio."

"I am sorry to call you so late..."

"Who is this?" Emilio asked brusquely.

"My name is unimportant. I am a businessman if that makes you more comfortable," Gacha said soothingly.

"I...I don't like to talk business with people I do not know."

"Which is why we should meet."

"What for?" Emilio said, his voice becoming irritated.

"I could get you elected. I can make you look like you have brass balls. I can make you front page news the day after tomorrow."

Gonzáles laughed. "Are you a magician? No, I don't think..."

"I could go to your competitor," Gacha said threateningly.

"Go ahead, he'll tell you the same. I suggest you stop bothering me and please don't call..."

"I am a business partner of Don Eusebio Corraza," Gacha said desperately. The mention of the name had its intended effect, although he had never intended to use his association with *La Mano Negra*.

"I'm listening," said Emilio, his voice suddenly alert.

"Meet me in *La Fuente Azul* bar on 116. You know it?"

"Yes, what time?"

"Midnight," said Gacha regaining control of the conversation.

"I'd like to check on what you have just told me," Emilio said, wanting confirmation of the caller's association with *La Mano Negra*.

"Sure, tell Don Eusebio that it's the man who found the solution to his port problems back in 1961."

"Is that it?" Emilio asked doubtfully.

"It should be more than enough. Midnight," Gacha said and hung up.

Gacha looked at his watch as he stepped away from the telephone booth in Facatativa. It was nearly eight o'clock in the evening. He walked back to the barn and met up with his subordinates. Vargas was on his way out as Gacha walked in. They stared at each other coldly.

"Be careful, Vargas," Gacha said catching Vargas off guard.

"I will," Vargas said, looking at Gacha.

"Listen, here is some money for you to take a taxi. Don't expose yourself on buses, there is no need to run into an enemy on a bus." Gacha handed over a roll of *pesos* to Vargas.

Vargas took the money. "Thank you," he said and then walked away.

Chulo and Mario looked at Gacha skeptically, they knew that their *jefe* would not forget the last couple of outbursts by Vargas. They couldn't either. Vargas was putting them in jeopardy.

"What gives, *jefe*?" Chulo asked.

"Nothing. We're going into *La Fuente Azul* bar. I suggest you get cleaned up and dress well."

Vargas convinced one of the three taxis in the *pueblo* to take him to Bogota. It would cost him a lot of money but what the hell, it wasn't his money. It was that self-appointed superior Gacha's money. Once he was done with the M-19 knockover plan for the incoming American VIP, he would concentrate on removing Gacha from the *El Centro* leadership.

The taxi dropped him off at *calle* twelve and *carrera* eight.From there he walked to *carrera* fourteen, better known as *Avenida* Caracas, and then across to *calle* eleven where he entered an apartment. It was easy to see he'd gone into the second floor apartment.

The taxi driver noted down the address and the apartment number. Then he ran back to his taxi eight blocks away.

La Fuente Azul was a bar-discothéque for the wealthy young adults of Bogota. It was also located in the very wealthy part of town. Gacha felt comfortable with the surroundings, even with very rich young adults. Chulo and Mario, although dressed properly, felt out of place. But that would change, Gacha thought. The music was blaring through the speaker system and the song was one they had heard many times on the radio, it was very popular. The song's name was *Delilah*, and it was sung by a man called Tom Jones.

Gacha had chosen the bar because he knew none of the other *gamín* gang lords would ever come here. He also wanted to impress Chulo and Mario, by showing them that he was still more important than they ever dreamed of. It was a way of bringing up their spirits when things were getting so tense.

"Shit!" Chulo said. "Look who just came in. He's the one in the papers, isn't he?"

"Yes, Emilio Gonzáles," Mario said, as they watched Don Emilio walk up to the bar counter, sit down on a bar stool and order a drink.

"Man, I'm telling you, look at these rich bitches! They are better than anything I've ever seen," Chulo said, admiring a group of young girls. The Tom Jones tune had ended and one by the Beatles began. Chulo liked the Beatles and he began to move in his chair to the beat of the song.

"Stay here," Gacha said. "I have some business to discuss." He stood up from the table and walked over to where

Don Emilio was sitting.

Chulo and Mario watched, bewildered that Gacha had business with such an important figure. A few minutes later they watched Don Emilio smile wide and pat their *jefe* on the back as if they were old friends.

"Are you su— Don Emilio asked Gacha.

"Oh, yes. As sure as the sun will rise tomorrow," Gacha said, wishing the music were not so loud so he wouldn't have to raise his voice so much.

"What do you want in return?" Don Emilio asked unsurely.

"You invite me to the Inaugural Ball and if you see me at a party you simply greet me. Nothing else, just say hello and whatever else you want to say. Just enough so that people know that you know me," Gacha said looking straight into Don Emilio's eyes.

"That's it?"

"That's it, but it is worth more than you know."

"Deal," Don Emilio said and shook hands with Gacha.

Suddenly a voice in the discotheque cried out. "Papa!"

It was a girl of about seventeen, Gacha immediately gauged, as he tried to gasp for breath. She was absolutely stunning. She walked across the dance floor as if she owned it. Her five foot seven inch frame appeared even taller with her long shapely legs that seemed to go all the way down to Argentina. To Gacha she appeared to glide over the floor.

The girl kissed Don Emilio on the cheek. "Papa, what are you doing here?"

"I'm meeting with a young businessman," Don Emilio said.

The young girl turned and faced Gacha. Her hair which tousled down past her shoulders was the color of tiger-eye. She was a stunning beauty with smoky, wide-set, sultry eyes, a wide generous mouth and high cheekbones that made her look like a Paris fashion model.

"Hi," she said. "I'm Ana-Alicia and you must be?"

"Gacha...Gonzalo Gacha," he said, catching a frog in his

throat.

"You're not from Bogota, are you?" Ana-Alicia asked coyly.

"Why do you say that?" Gacha asked puzzled.

"I would have run into you if you were. My girl friends have all been wondering who you are. They think you are handsome." Gacha felt the heat of a flush on his face.

"Ana-Alicia!" Don Emilio said disapprovingly.

"Oh, papa! He knows that already." She kissed her father on the cheek and turned to Gacha. "I've got to go back to my friends. It was nice meeting you...Gonzalo," Ana-Alicia said winking at him as she walked away.

"She is a father's worst nightmare," Don Emilio said, shaking his head. "It's like having a bomb in the house, unpredictable and dangerous. Anyway, give me a call when it is all set to go down. You said you would have a reporter there, right?"

"Yes," Gacha heard himself say, his concentration still swirling around Ana-Alicia.

"Then, until tomorrow night."

"Tomorrow night," Gacha said standing up from the bar stool. He shook hands with Don Emilio and said good-bye.

When Don Emilio left, Chulo and Mario walked up to Gacha and bombarded him with questions. He heard himself answering their questions, but all he could see was the beautiful Ana-Alicia smiling at him from across the dance floor. She winked at him again and he knew right then and there, that somehow their destinies would be interlocked. Of that, he had no doubt.

_____*Peter A. Neissa*_____

CHAPTER EIGHT

Gonzalo Rodriguez Gacha no longer had the feeling that he was in control of events. The events he had set into motion now controlled him. He sat down in a small, run down restaurant known as *El Pollo Asado* in the free zone on the north highway of Bogota. He had chosen this free zone because at dusk *gamines* rarely stopped by, making his rendezvous with Ramón 'Tiburón' Machado even more secretive.

Ramón 'Tiburón' (Shark), was the *gamín* lord for the *Suba* gang. A small, conniving little kid, who had to be violent in order to be who he was, was still out of his league in respect to other gang leaders.

The meeting had been set by Gonzalo Rodriguez Gacha, who made Tiburón believe he was desperate. Gacha named *El Pollo Asado* as a meeting place and asked Tiburón to bring a suitcase with him, because he had official papers that he wanted to turn over before *Chapinero* got a hold of them. He said to Tiburón that he was passing him the papers as a sign of good intentions. Tiburón agreed. However, the agreement had come at a price. Gacha would have to come alone while Tiburón came with his new enforcer, a kid by the name of Santos. The meeting was set for six in the afternoon.

That same morning after Gacha had called Tiburón, he had stashed the ambassador's briefcase behind a broom closet at the Pollo Asado restaurant. That way he would be sure to be seen going in with nothing. Once he stashed the ambassador's briefcase, he called Jim Harrison and told him that he would be obtaining the ambassador's briefcase at the *Pollo Asado* restaurant at six o'clock in the afternoon. He told Harrison that he was to do nothing until he emerged from the restaurant with the briefcase. Harrison agreed readily.

Now, Gacha sat in the *Pollo Asado* restaurant with the briefcase safely in his lap. He waited for Tiburón and his new enforcer to show up with the suitcase, which Harrison would believe contained the ambassador's briefcase. Gacha sensed eyes all around the restaurant. Was it Harrison's men, Tiburón's men, Bosco's men, *Séptima*'s men or Fuentes' men? It was impossible to tell because it could be all of them or none of them. The only thing he trusted was the fact that somewhere out there was Chulo, watching the watchers.

Suddenly, Tiburón walked in, holding the door wide open and taking the place in with a slow and careful look. It was no secret that Tiburón wanted everyone to believe that he had presence like the American actor Clint Eastwood. He had gone as far as imitating the actor's mannerisms and it was why he was lighting up a cigarette as he stood in the doorway.

Ramón was anything but Clint Eastwood. He was a kid of fifteen years of age with acne on his face and half his teeth broken from fistfights on his climb to the top of the *Suba* hierarchy. When he smiled it gave him the appearance of a shark and was why he was known as Tiburón.

Tiburón inhaled the cigarette smoke deeply and let it out slowly. He moved towards Gacha who was sitting at the center table in the restaurant. He sat down at the same table.

Santos, the new enforcer for *Suba*, was inexperienced, and he also sat at the same table. An experienced enforcer would have stood beside the doorway. Tiburón did not shake Gacha's outstretched hand as custom dictated. Gacha shrugged, letting Tiburón know he was displeased.

"Well, Gacha, here we are. What do you want?" El Tiburón said with some distaste.

"Want?" Gacha asked with a bewildered look.

"Yes, you called us, remember?" Santos said unaware that during *gamín* leader meetings, enforcers did not talk.

Tiburón winced as Santos spoke.

"I don't want anything. I was going to offer you a deal.

98

Join the *El Centro* gang or suffer the consequences," Gacha
said with some amusement.

Tiburón laughed. "What *El Centro*? You are a thing of
the past. History. We are the new breed. Now, what about the
papers you were going to hand over?"

"Papers?" Gacha asked innocently.

"Eh?" Tiburón began to squirm in his seat. "The papers,
hand them over!"

"I'm sorry, you must have been misinformed. If you do
not wish to join the *El Centro* gang then we have nothing more
to talk about. Good day."

Tiburón and Santos looked on with wide open mouths
as Gacha stood up, walked out of the restaurant and broke into
an open run.

"Get him!" Tiburón shouted as they ran after Gacha.
"Kill him!"

As Tiburón and Santos emerged from the restaurant,
two powerful looking men collided with them. Then there were
two muted spits that Tiburón and Santos recognized as the
discharge of two pistols with silencers on them. They keeled
over as a van pulled up beside them. The last sound they
heard in the land of the living was the van's door closing like
a steel trap. Clunk. Dead. Lights out.

Two blocks away from *El Pollo Asado* restaurant,
Gacha handed over the briefcase to Harrison.

"The slate's clean, Gacha," said Harrison as he opened
the briefcase. "We're even."

"For the moment," Gacha said. "Next time you ask me
for something it's not going to be this easy."

"Fuck you, Gacha. You're just a little thief who's
making a few bucks, but don't ever fuck with the United
States."

"Have I insulted you, so that you have to use such
vulgar language with me?" Gacha said smiling.

"Get the fuck out of my car!" Harrison roared, his veins
in his temples starting to protrude.

Gacha got out smiling, but peered in before he closed

the door. "Harrison, you will be doing business with me from now on. You just wait and see," Gacha said and slammed the car door before Harrison replied.

Chulo had been waiting for Gacha at *La Cantina* bar in Chico where he was having a beer. When he saw Gacha walk into the bar, he raised his hand and waved to him.

Gacha saw the wave and signalled that he had to make a phone call first. Chulo nodded in understanding.

La Cantina bar was well lit and looked more like a restaurant. The bar counter was made of solid white marble, making it appear cool and detached. It was ugly, almost hospital looking.

Gacha walked up several minutes later and sat on a bar stool beside Chulo. The bartender wandered over and Gacha ordered a hot *canelaso*, a drink of hot rum, water, sugar, lime and cinnamon.

"What's next, *jefe*?" Chulo asked, taking a sip from his mug of beer.

"I just talked to Fuentes. They are taking down the M-19. That means..."

"Vargas," Chulo cut in. He rubbed his forehead as if to alleviate pressure.

"Yes, sooner or later he's bound to get us screwed up in that M-19 shit." Chulo nodded. "There might be another way, but I don't think Vargas is bound to listen to any of us. I'm getting him wasted tonight."

"I agree, the bastard just didn't know his place," Chulo said taking another mugful of beer.

"Did you call your friend?" Gacha asked.

"The one on the newspaper?" Gacha nodded. "Yes, he says he is ready. All he needs is the time."

"Call him then. It's going to take place at *Avenida* Caracas with *calle* eleven. Tell him to be there at eleven. Chulo, tell him if he leaks this to anyone, even if it's his father confessor, he's a dead man.

Chulo nodded, stood up and walked over towards the

telephone.

Gacha sat on the bar stool looking into his empty glass where his hot *canelaso* had once been. He wondered if he should order a brandy. He'd had chills all day even though the day had been warm. A hand then touched him lightly on the right shoulder and he spun around with fists ready to strike. The movement was so rapid and so violent, it was as blinding as the strike of a scorpion.

Ana-Alicia gasped, her face turning white as she closed her eyes, waiting for the blow to come.

"My God, I'm sorry," Gacha said quickly. "Please forgive me. I thought I was going to be robbed."

Ana-Alicia opened her eyes slowly and took a gasp of breath. "I need a drink," she said.

Gacha snapped his fingers and the bartender walked over. "An *aguardiente*."

Ana-Alicia steadied her breathing and quickly downed the shot of hard liquor that the bartender brought her. "Another," she said to the bartender. The bartender refilled the shot glass, but Ana-Alicia only took a small sip from it this time.

"Please, I'm sorry," Gacha said in a tender voice.

"I heard you," Ana-Alicia said haughtily.

"How can I make it up to you?" Gacha asked, looking at her from head to toe, wanting to possess her so badly that he could feel every fiber in his body reaching out for her. "Can I buy you dinner sometime?" Gacha asked, but there was no answer so he added, "A car? Maybe a house?"

Ana-Alicia laughed, the sound of her laughter almost melodic. She brushed her hair away with her right hand, a movement that was incredibly sexy, a movement that Gacha knew was practiced.

"I guess some time you could buy me dinner, but not just yet. I haven't made up my mind about you." Ana-Alicia saw Gacha's eyes wander to where Chulo was sitting. "Your friend frightens me, he's kind of scary looking."

"Who, José?" Gacha asked with a child's innocence.

"Yes, unfortunately he was not born with handsome features, but I guarantee you he's a very loyal friend."

"You make him sound like a dog."

"No, he's a very good friend. So, when shall we go out to dinner?"

Ana-Alicia smiled at him and Gacha realized that he had never been so excited with a woman before, even with Margarita at her most alluring.

"I don't get out of school until December. My family usually spends Christmas in the *hacienda*, so I won't be around until sometime in January," Ana-Alicia said, finishing the rest of her drink.

"That's a few months away, how about Friday night or Saturday?"

Ana-Alicia shook her head. "I cannot go out on dates until my vacation from school starts, unless I go out with a group of friends. It's my parents, they make the rules."

"I thought that schools got out in November?" Gacha asked, his hopes for a date crumbling.

"Yes, Colombian schools do. However, I go to the American school. My parents want me to learn English, so I can go to an American university.

"I speak English," Gacha said proudly. "Not very good, but I can speak it."

"Really!" Ana-Alicia said as if Gacha were kidding her. "Listen, I have to get back to my friends. We usually hang out by *La Fuente Azul*. Maybe I'll see you there some time." She put her hand on his, winked at him and said, "*Chao!*"

Gacha nodded. "See you later," he said, believing that she had turned him down cold.

Chulo walked up immediately after Ana-Alicia left, sat down on the barstool and looked at Gacha curiously. "She's a real woman, *jefe*."

"Yeah, that she is."

"My friend at the newspaper is ready," Chulo said and then added "You like her, *jefe*?"

"Yeah, " Gacha said nodding his head.

"You know, *jefe*, Margarita has been asking about you a lot. She's been calling every day. We figured you had a lot on your mind these past couple of days, so we decided not to bother you with it. Mario has been out her way to see how she is doing, you know? He does it to make sure she knows you are still thinking of her."

"That's good of Mario. I'll have to thank him," Gacha said looking over at Ana-Alicia.

"Yes, he goes there almost every day, takes her something too. Candy or a trinket of some kind. Signs your name to the card."

"He does?" Chulo nodded. "A good man Mario. Does he say how bad it looks?"

"The scar?" Chulo asked. Gacha nodded. "He says that when she uses make-up it's not visible from five feet away, but when she becomes angry or excited it turns purple. He says that's when it's kind of scary. When she doesn't wear make-up, it's positively frightening."

Gacha let out a short soft whistle. "Come on, let's get going. We're going to be late for the show."

Ernesto Bosco was celebrating his victory over the *El Centro gamín* gang. Although Gacha and his subordinates had not been found, he had in effect rendered them useless. There had been Gacha sightings all over Bogota, but none of them had been confirmed.

Now, as he celebrated with Crater Face Gómez and three young girls who could not be older than fourteen, he passed around the bottle of grain alcohol. They were all drunk and half naked or just plain naked. The stereo hi-fi, which had been stolen from a repair shop in the *El Centro* turf two days before, was playing a *merengue*.

It was the perfect music for celebrating. It was also being played at full blast, cutting them off from the noises of the outside world. If the volume hadn't been turned up so high maybe they would have heard the army trucks pulling up beside the apartment complex.

103

The Military Police surrounded the apartment complex and a platoon of men splintered off and stormed in with M-16's at the ready. The sound made by their marching boots caused everyone in the apartment complex to look into the hallway and then quickly shut their doors. They didn't want to hear or witness anything. In fact, most of them turned up the volume of their television sets.

Ernesto Bosco and Crater Face Gómez never heard the storming troops until it was already too late. A soldier kicked down their door and the whole troop moved in pointing rifles at their naked bodies. The soldiers were shocked, but enjoyed the scene nevertheless. A captain moved into the studio apartment and stopped in front of Bosco. He looked at Bosco then at Crater Face and then at the girls. He shook his head as if to convey the message that he did not approve at all.

"Ernesto Bosco and Eduardo Gómez?" the captain asked.

"Yes," Bosco said, finding his voice while trying to cover himself with a *poncho*. Something was wrong he knew, as he tried desperately to fight through the haze of his drunken stupor. "What is it, Captain?"

"Captain Fonseca to you!" the captain bellowed.

"Yes, Captain Fonseca," said Bosco with deferential voice.

Captain Fonseca retrieved two legal documents from his side pocket and read the documents out loud. "*Ernesto Bosco y Eduardo Gómez, en el nombre de la ley, están detenidos.*" You are under arrest.

"What's the charge?" Bosco asked as he fought the feeling of falling into an abyss.

"For being a subversive and trying to undermine the government of Colombia. Your connections with the M-19 have been documented and will be proven later in a military court. Let's go."

Bosco sat paralyzed, as if the wind had been knocked out of him. Crater Face, however, had decided to make a run for it. He got as far as the door, when an M-16 rifle exploded his head like a ripe watermelon.

Bosco was then covered with the *poncho* and taken out
with his hands cuffed behind his back. He walked towards the
army truck as if he were living a nightmare, wondering when
he was going to wake up from it. He was pushed into the back
of a green military truck and promptly kicked by the soldiers
already there. Then the order came. "Take him to *La Picota*."

This can't be true was the last thought Bosco had
before the army truck drove him to Colombia's maximum
security prison.

Carlos Fuentes looked through a pair of binoculars
from the second floor of a business office on *Avenida* Caracas.
He could see clearly the group of young men gathering in the
small duplex across the street. He had already identified six of
the nine young men as M-19. Tonight, he said to himself, was
going to be their last meeting. It was also going to be his best
achievement as a police officer in Bogota.

Gonzalo Rodriguez Gacha and Chulo sat beside Fuentes
as he peered through the field glasses.

"So, where's Vargas?" barked Fuentes, trying to
establish his superiority over Gacha. "You better hold up your
end of the bargain, because I held up mine."

Gacha shrugged. "He should be along. You got any
coffee?"

"Back there somewhere." Fuentes waved his hand
towards the back of the room as he looked through the
binoculars.

Gacha moved calmly towards the end of the room as if
the night was unimportant to him. It was important that he
keep his cool in front of all the policemen. They could sense
fright from ten feet away. The real truth was that out of his
entire master plan, this was the most dangerous part. If just
one member of the M-19 faction escaped the trap, he would be
a marked man.

By midnight Fuentes began to get nervous. The men on
the street kept radioing in saying that they should go for the

ones present before they were spotted. Although, Fuentes kept shouting at them to do nothing of the kind, he was beginning to sense the men's fright.

"Where is he, Gacha?" Fuentes asked, his face lined with exhaustion.

Gacha too was getting on edge because Vargas had not shown up. Had Vargas changed his mind about the M-19? Had he judged Vargas too hastily and condemned him to death too quickly?

"He's coming," cracked the voice over the radio.

Fuentes looked out into the street through the drawn blinders and watched Vargas walk up and into the duplex. His forehead suddenly broke out into a sweat and his right hand began to shake.

"Do we go in, Lieutenant?" asked the voice over the two-way radio. The men inside the office were already loading their weapons and checking their ammo clips.

"Negative," Fuentes responded. "Let him get in and get comfortable."

Through the binoculars Gacha watched Vargas shake hands with all his guerrilla comrades, and watched as someone handed a bottle of *aguardiente* into Vargas' outstretched hand.

Fuentes picked up the microphone on the two-way radio preparing to give the order to move in when suddenly a pistol shot fired in the night. "Damn it!" Fuentes shouted. "Move in, move in, move in! Shit!"

Gacha ran out of the building with Fuentes, only to be confronted by a fierce gun fight in the street as the M-19 began to duel it out. The M-19 knew that the only thing that was waiting for them if they got caught was a brick wall and a firing squad.

The two ends of the block were sealed off but that didn't mean anything. A smart person would be able to hide effectively in the office buildings until an opportunity arose for an escape. However, the M-19 seemed quite contained in the front of the duplex.

Three M-19 members had fallen at the beginning of the

gunfight. Now that they knew where the gunfire was coming from, the police shots were sporadic and ineffective.

Gacha's heart banged against his chest like a soft stone. He realized what Fuentes had to have figured out too, that the M-19 had an informant inside his cadre of police. The initial pistol shot had been no coincidence. It was a warning to the M-19 that they were moving in.

The street suddenly became quiet as the battle came to a stalemate. Fuentes spoke furiously into his radio trying to order some men to get closer to the duplex. It was not an easy order to give to the men, since the avenue was wide and exposed.

It all looked controllable as Fuentes began to think of a plan to resume control, but then the circus came to town. Don Emilio Gonzáles showed up with gun in hand, crouching through the side streets as if he were in combat. Behind him and catching up was a reporter for the *El Tiempo* newspaper. Fuentes was so taken aback that he wasn't sure whether he should cry or laugh. Instead he rushed up to Don Emilio and told him he was not needed and that the situation was too dangerous for him to stay.

Don Emilio Gonzáles grunted and that was the end of Fuentes' objections. Don Emilio asked to be updated on what was happening and from then on Fuentes simply became the second in command. Don Emilio then tried to rally the policemen to storm the duplex, but the policemen looked on with blank stares. So Don Emilio stood up and said, "Let a man do a man's job then." And off he went, firing wildly into the duplex. The policemen wanting to see an oligarch get killed followed, but not too closely. The photographer for the newspaper could not believe what he was actually witnessing as he snapped off rolls of film.

Gacha sat across the street behind an overturned oak desk that had been carried out from the office. He saw Don Emilio give his maniacal speech and then charge towards the duplex like he was some cowboy in an American movie. Everything unfolded as if in slow motion. The pistol shots from the M-19 made bursts of light in the night as they fired; the police weapons did the same as their own M-16 rifles fired. It all seemed unreal to Gacha, because with all the gunfire going on, Don Emilio was still on his feet and charging like a madman.

Then it happened.

It was more like a shadow that stood up from behind a shrub, Gacha thought, but then he realized it was Vargas. Vargas was holding up his .38 snub nose and was aiming it directly at Don Emilio. The little burst of light shot out from the short barreled revolver and Don Emilio fell hard on the pavement of the street.

Gacha looked back towards Vargas who was grinning, his eyes afire with revolution. Suddenly he saw Vargas duck down and in the exchange of gunfire watched him sneak-off into the four story building beside the duplex. He was making his escape!

"Goddamn it, Fuentes!" Gacha shouted. "Your police force is a joke." He then stood up and ran after Vargas zig-zagging across the street so he wouldn't be shot.

When he reached the building Vargas had escaped into, he pulled out his Colt .45 from the small of his back. Once inside the building, Gacha put his back to the wall and listened. He heard quick footsteps and immediately knew Vargas was going for the roof. He began to climb the stairs by two's, his forehead damp with sweat. As he reached the top step, he was panting for breath. He heard movement outside on the roof and peered out through the open door that led out onto the roof.

Vargas was looping some television antennae wire around his belt. He was preparing to rappel onto the roof of the building below and make his escape. All he had to do was get onto the roof of the other building and hop across to the other roofs until he was a block away from the gunfight. Freedom was seconds away.

Gacha walked up behind Vargas and put the gun to his head. Vargas froze and turned around slowly, his eyes widening in shock, then hurt and finally confusion.

"Eh, Gacha, what are you doing here?" Gacha looked at Vargas coldly, without expression. "Come on, help me! We don't have much time!"

"No," said Gacha, his voice hard like granite.

"No? Come on, Gacha, they'll kill us! What's wrong with you? I'm not fighting against you but those rich bastards." Vargas broke into a smile. "Eh, you see the bastard I took down?"

"You just don't learn, do you?" Gacha asked as he cocked the pistol.

"Eh? No Gacha! I'm your friend. I helped you make *El Centro* what it is! For the love of God, no, please, I beg you. Have mercy..." Vargas fell on his hands and knees and began crouching into a fetal position on the ground. "Please, no..."

Gacha fired his weapon and kicked Vargas' dead body over the side of the building. He then stood by the edge of the roof and watched Vargas' body swing from the antennae wire from one side of the building to the other.

Gacha took in a deep breath and looked out over the city lights of Bogota. The whole city was now his to do as he pleased. Suddenly, he felt intoxicated with power as the possibilities spun around in his head. He was now the undisputed King of Bogota.

_____Peter A. Neissa_____

CHAPTER NINE

The morning after the shootout on *Avenida* Caracas, Don Emilio Gonzáles was on the front page of every newspaper in Colombia. Having been shot in the right calf made him a hero in Bogota, but more than that, it made him look macho. His photo plastered on the front page, showing him in full battle charge against the M-19, made him appear all the more heroic. The headlines that ran above the photo were just as bold. One of them called him The Political Enforcer while another called him The Man of the Midnight Hour.

By dusk his hospital room was flooded with flowers and get well cards from every politician wanting to jump on the bandwagon. The President, it had been reported on the radio, had stopped by the hospital to pay his respects. The American Ambassador who also stopped by was quoted as saying that it was further evidence of Colombia's stand against ungodly Communism.

Across town there was another parade of sorts. Gonzalo Rodriguez Gacha sat behind his desk in the *El Centro* apartment with Chulo and Mario standing in the wings. They were receiving guests who were declaring their new allegiance to the new King of Bogota, Gonzalo Rodriguez Gacha.

The hierarchy of *Chapinero* came in and explained its financial set-up. Then *Suba* followed with the same disclosure. Although *Séptima*'s gang leaders did not come in person, they had sent a *consejero* (advisor) to set up a meeting with *Señor* Gacha. *Chapinero, Suba* and *Séptima* were now under the control of *El Centro*. The *gamín* gang system had effectively ceased to exist in favor of another system---Gonzalo Rodriguez

111

Gacha.

One week after Gonzalo Rodriguez Gacha consolidated the *gamín* gang system, Air Force Two of the United States of America landed at *El Dorado* International Airport. Gacha, who had gone out to the airport to catch a look at the famous Henry Kissinger, found himself in the throng of a huge crowd. Two thousand citizens had shown up to welcome this respected man, including the President and most of his cabinet. The American Ambassador stood beside the President of Colombia, as protocol dictated.

As Air Force Two came to a halt, a military marching band struck up the Stars and Stripes and all military personnel present came to rigid attention. The ladder was positioned beside the plane's exit door and the red carpet was unfurled on the tarmac.

The door on Air Force Two opened and a young man stepped into the thin and brisk Bogota air. He waved at the crowds but all he got was a collective gasp. He knew something was wrong, but how could he know what that was? How was he to know that they were not expecting the Under Secretary of State for the Department of Agriculture?

It was not that the Under Secretary was not a competent man. It was more of a case where the United States still believed Colombia to be unimportant enough not to send its most skilled and experienced diplomats. To Colombians it was a sign of disrespect. Protocol and manners are a way of life in Colombia. It was a country where to cut into the main topic of conversation without first establishing a greeting and some small talk was considered almost barbaric.

For all intents and purposes, the moment the Under Secretary stepped out of the jet cabin, the loan would never be accepted. The Americans' brash political tactics had effectively sent the loan where they have been sending every other nation, down the toilet.

Colombia needed money to develop but it could easily get the loans from somewhere else, the French, the Germans or the Japanese who were already standing in line at the Presidential Palace. No apology would change things, and Colombia's support for any venture the United States might take either economically or military washed away like the snow and the rain.

The next day, the President of Colombia announced that the country would agree to a six hundred million dollar loan from the French with a concurrent loan of another six hundred million dollars from the Japanese. Within two hours of the announcement, Air Force Two was on its way back to the United States.

Gonzalo Rodriguez Gacha as a Colombian felt glad that the United States had been taught a lesson. America was hurt where it counted, in the bank. For the rest of the year, Gacha busied himself by working sixteen-hour days, trying to bring under control all the vast resources that generated the black market of a city of three million people.

In late December of 1970, Gacha made a visit to *La Mano Negra* to pay his respects to the man.

The moment he had been shown through the front door he sensed something odd. It was not because the servant now called him *Señor* Gacha, for he was used to that already, but it was rather the deference that was being shown to him. He was led out onto a patio where Don Eusebio met him with a warm embrace.

"What a pleasure!" Don Eusebio almost shouted. Whether it was false or not, Gacha could not tell.

"Ah, the pleasure is mine, Don Eusebio. You look good. Your family is well, eh?" Gacha greeted in typical Colombian fashion, inquiring about all the members of the family.

"Yes, yes. We had some sort of bug going around two weeks ago but my wife decided that the only way to cure it was to get out of Bogota. She's gone to Paris. Every time she gets sick, it seems that the doctor always prescribes some faraway place."

"I hope she doesn't get ill too often," Gacha said, looking over a glass of whiskey and soda that the servant had brought out for him.

Don Eusebio laughed. "Once a month. If it's the flu, it's Paris. If it's arthritis, it's New York. If it's rheumatism, it's Rio de Janeiro."

"And your children?" Gonzalo asked.

"My oldest son graduates from Columbia University in New York this coming June. My daughter also graduates this June from the *Gimnacio Femenino*, an exclusive school here in Bogota. I tell you, I had to pull more strings to get her in there than I did to get her into the University of Miami." Don Eusebio took a sip from his drink and then asked, "How's business?"

"Not bad," Gacha answered. At the mention of Don Eusebio's daughter going to the University of Miami, he thought of Ana-Alicia Gonzáles. He had not seen her since the night he became King of Bogota.

"That doesn't sound too good. What's up?" Eusebio's expression became hawklike.

"Oh, I'm making money, but there is no growth, our business is stagnant. My financial advisor reminds me of it everyday. Our only real expansion of capital occurs under him."

"How?"

"With the investments he makes. He buys bonds, shares and every other thing you can think of. He's smart, real smart. I'm going to send him to the Harvard Business School when he graduates from *la Javeriana* University here in Bogota."

"Harvard?" Don Eusebio asked in surprise. "You know, connections alone don't get people in there, one has to have first rate marks."

"Yes, he has them. Like I said, the guy's a genius with numbers."

"Well, Pachito. I think it's time I also expanded your emerald distribution."

Gacha looked on in surprise. Why all of a sudden had Don Eusebio decided this? Why was Eusebio treating him like an equal rather than a subordinate? Then it hit Gacha like a

114

baseball bat. By taking over Bogota he had eliminated access
to the Pérez family of Medellin, which had aided Don Eusebio
in counteracting their takeover plan. It meant Don Eusebio
'owed' him! *Dios mío! La Mano Negra owes me!*

"If you think it wise, Don Eusebio," Gacha said non-
committally, indirectly letting him know that this was not the
repayment.

"Oh, it's been more than overdue. I am also increasing
your commission to fifteen percent."

"Don Eusebio, you do me too much honor but it is not
necessary." Again Gacha deflected the gift as being a
repayment of the debt owed. However, Gacha also knew that
once a gift was given, it could not be turned down.

Suddenly Don Eusebio looked at Gacha coldly. For the
first time since he had known Gonzalo Rodriguez Gacha, he
realized that Gacha had become a dangerous man. Gacha was
skilled in negotiation and his coup in Bogota showed that he
had the will to hang tough and see his own plans through. Yes,
the kid in front of him was no longer a kid, but a cold and
calculating man.

"Oh, it is necessary, Gacha, and if there is anything
where I can be of help, please do not hesitate to ask."

"Thank you. There is no need to bother you with the
problems of my tiny organization."

Don Eusebio nodded. They talked of politics and the
U.S. embarrassment with the Under Secretary. They also
drank until they were drunk and, yet each one of them had
never let his guard down.

On the third week in January 1971, the reports were
mixed at the third monthly meeting after Gacha had
consolidated three of the four gangs in Bogota.

Gacha began the meeting with the figures. "Our total
intake for the month of December was $57,000. The breakdown
is $18,000 in emeralds, $11,000 in auto parts, $20,000 on
investments made by Mario, $4,000 in burglaries and street
snatches and the last $4,000 was made by the *gamines* on the

east side of *Chapinero* by selling marijuana in *Séptima* territory."

"Four thousand?" Chulo asked in shock.

"Exactly," Gacha said. "*Séptima* is making a bundle. Chulo, how are the negotiations going with the *Séptima* merger?"

"They are stalling," said Chulo.

"Stalling for what?"

"I don't know, but in the last meeting they hinted at breaking off negotiations."

"Yes," Gacha said through clenched teeth. "My feeling is that we have underestimated the money they are making. I think they are buying up the police and some low level politicians. I also think it's time we muscled in on *Séptima*."

"I don't know, *jefe*," Chulo said. "It can get very messy, and I don't think Fuentes would like that. We still don't have Fuentes on our payroll even though we have half or more of his police department."

"The marijuana could still be a fad, *jefe*," said Mario.

"I don't think so," said Gacha. "I have been reading *Time, Newsweek* and all the other American magazines and they all say the same thing: There is a huge demand for marijuana. I think it's also time we get into it too. Do you have a plan, Chulo?"

"I think if we can put the heat on *Séptima*, they might negotiate for a merger much quicker," Chulo said with a ruthless smile.

Gacha nodded. "Why not get one of *Séptima's* biggest customers and kill him, then plant some marijuana on the body. That should turn up the heat on *Séptima*. Make the victim a German. If we make it an American, there will be hell to pay. Fuentes will then put the pressure on *Séptima*, and we will begin the war. It should bring *Séptima* under our fold."

Chulo and Mario began to get up, believing that the meeting was over.

"Wait!" Gacha cried. "I'm not finished. I have a few things left to say. Chulo, we are buying an apartment in Chico.

You are moving in with me to this apartment. I'm going to need a bodyguard at all times, just in case someone wants to take me out. Mario, you will stay in this apartment. Chulo will get a bodyguard for you. The last item is for you Chulo, you will buy yourself a car. Make the car a Renault Four, it's small and it's practical."

"A car, *jefe*?" Chulo asked with a dry throat.

"Yes, if you are across town and either Mario, Margarita or myself need you, you should be able to get across town at a moment's notice. Mario, it is my intention that when you graduate from the university you will go to study at The Harvard School of Business. That is why you need this apartment, you must get top grades!"

"Yes, *jefe*, the best!" Mario said with renewed loyalty, as Chulo congratulated him by patting him on the back.

"Okay, the meeting is over. How about celebrating at the *Fuente Azul* bar?" Gacha asked

"Yes!" Chulo and Mario responded vigorously.

As they grabbed for their coats Mario hesitated.

"What is it Mario?" Gacha asked.

"It's Margarita, she's been asking for you many times. I'm running out of excuses," Mario said sheepishly.

Gacha sighed. "Yes, I've forgotten to thank you, Mario, for taking her out." He paused and that vacuous look came over Gacha's face as if he were looking into the future. "Let's see, today's Friday. Yes, tell her I'll see her tomorrow night."

Mario's smile returned and Chulo led the way out.

La Fuente Azul on a Friday night was filled to capacity with students whose ages ranged from fourteen to twenty-four. Most of them knew each other by name even though they came from a variety of schools. Some came from the German school, others from the American and French schools, and those that didn't came from the rich, private Colombian schools.

The multi-colored lights that flashed on and off in the discothèque made it hard to see, but the moment Gacha walked in, he had spotted Ana-Alicia. He told himself that it

117

didn't make a difference, he would have come anyway. He made his way across the dance floor with Chulo and Mario following in his footsteps.

The bartender looked over at Gacha and recognized him. "Good evening, *Señor* Gacha."

"Three whiskeys, please," Gacha answered.

The bartender nodded, set up the three glasses and poured them very carefully and then told Gacha that they were on the house. Gacha thanked the bartender.

Gacha, Chulo and Mario raised their glasses and swallowed their contents. Then they put them back on the bar counter and asked for a refill. Gacha put five hundred *pesos* on the counter and said, "Just keep them coming. If we run over let me know."

"Absolutely," said the bartender as he pocketed the five hundred *pesos* and poured another three glasses of whiskey.

"Man, look at these women!" Chulo said, looking all around the place. "They make all the women we've ever had look cheap as hell. I mean you can almost smell the money on these girls."

"Yeah," said Gacha. "There is no doubt of that. Money, it's the only game that counts in this or any other town."

"Oh, what would I give to lay one of those American or German blond girls," Chulo said with some rare emotion. "Damn! I'd even lay one of these rich Colombian women, you know, the kind that go to the real fancy schools here in Bogota. Those girls have class coming out of their skin. The only thing is we don't have a chance with Colombians. They'd ask for papers on the family background. If they got wind we were *gamines*, they'd be out the door with the cops on their way in."

"So, don't tell them you are a *gamín*," Gacha said.

"Yeah, well how do you avoid a question like, 'where do you go to school?'"

"Tell them you go to school in Mexico or Venezuela."

"Yeah! That's good, *jefe*. Hey, here comes your friend *jefe*."

Gacha looked over Chulo's shoulder and watched Ana-

118

Alicia coming straight for him. She had her arm around a very tall, blonde, blue-eyed American. Gacha who was tall for a Colombian was shadowed by the American who was easily four inches taller.

"Gonzalo!" Ana-Alicia exclaimed as if she was seeing a long lost friend. She kissed him on both cheeks, the customary greeting by women in Colombia. Gacha had to control the urge of kissing her on the mouth. "What a surprise, Gonzalo. Oh, excuse me. Gonzalo Rodriguez Gacha, let me introduce you to a friend of mine, Harry Fosse."

Gacha extended his hand and felt the strong grip of Harry Fosse. He looked at Harry as Harry looked him over as well. Gacha sensed something odd about Fosse, as if Fosse knew who he was.

"A pleasure to meet you, Harry," Gacha said.

"Gonzalo Rodriguez Gacha, you wouldn't have an office in El Centro, would you?" Fosse asked.

Suddenly the mood was tense, Chulo had instinctively stood up from the bar stool and reached inside his coat for the butt of his gun. Mario had put his glass of whiskey back down on the bar counter.

"Yes, I do," said Gacha. "These are my associates. Mario García and José Moncada." Gacha kept his tone businesslike, aware that Ana-Alicia was looking on with curiosity.

"You must then know a friend of mine, Arturo Jiménez. They call him *El Loco*. He lives in *Séptima*," Fosse asked innocently.

The mood was electric, bordering on the ugly. Ana-Alicia at odds on how to proceed with such turn of events, simply stared at Gacha hoping he would do something.

"Yes, I know of him. He is a business competitor," Gacha said in English.

"Sweet Jesus!" Fosse said. "You speak English?"

"Yes, businessmen of the future must learn the language of business."

"Hot damn!" Fosse said. "Listen, perhaps we could talk

business later. I have some good ideas, but *El Loco*...well, let's just say he's small time. I'm thinking big, expansion, new markets, you get my drift?" Gacha looked at him perplexed. "Supply and demand would be your point of view, I guess," Fosse added.

"And your point of view?" Gacha asked coldly.

"Distribution and expansion," Fosse replied firmly.

Suddenly Gacha understood, in less than ten seconds he saw it all. He nodded and smiled at Fosse.

"I see you understand," Fosse said. "I leave for the United States this July, so we better get together soon. What I have been told, correct me if I'm wrong, *El Loco* is on his way out."

"Come to my office at ten in the morning tomorrow. We will talk business then."

"Great," Fosse said and shook hands with Gacha.

"*Pero qué maravilla!*" Ana-Alicia exclaimed. "Gonzalo, I thought you were joking when you said you could speak English."

Gacha smiled. "Come on, let's have a fiesta."

Ana-Alicia introduced Gonzalo to all her friends who were almost everyone in the discothèque. Most of them were drunk or were getting there and by tomorrow most of them would forget ever having been introduced to him.

During the course of the evening some of Ana-Alicia's friends were smitten with Mario's innocence and charm. Some were even more impressed when he told them he was first in his class at the *Javeriana* University and that he was going to Harvard when he graduated.

Chulo tried hitting on one of the American girls, but she was too high on marijuana to notice he was even around. He then tried hitting on a German girl and was met with success. She flirted with him, and he seemed to be getting somewhere until the girl's boyfriend showed up. Chulo knew the girl's boyfriend was no match for him if he wanted to pick a fight. Gacha ordered Chulo to let it be.

Gacha spent most of his time dancing with Ana-Alicia

on the little dance floor. He could not believe it was his hands around her waist and it was his lips that were just inches away from hers. He took the smell of her femininity in with every breath and wondered how he had been able to control himself. He wanted desperately to melt into her skin and breathe the same air she breathed.

Ana-Alicia was swept into Gacha's strong muscled arms and broad chest that seemed to mold perfectly her body, while his face drew her closer and closer like some powerful magnet. She had known good looking men, she thought, so why did she feel the way she did with this one? Was it her imagination? Was this a girlish crush on an older man? But he was just a year older than she! So what was it about him? Yes, he did have this strange aura around him, a dangerous aura, as if she were playing with fire or a straight edged razor. She loved it, she told herself, and at the same time she was scared.

"These are great times and dangerous times, Gonzalo," Ana-Alicia said as she guided him back to the table.

"How so?" Gonzalo asked as he signalled the waitress to bring over some more drinks.

"The whole world is changing. You've seen the protests downtown, of course. I mean the government can't get away without being accountable to the people. Listen," Ana-Alicia said. A Beatles song about revolution was playing. "It's everywhere, in the music, film, books. The people, Gonzalo, are changing the rules."

"Whose rules?" Gacha asked.

"The establishment's!" Ana-Alicia roared.

"Your father is the establishment."

"No, he's for the people. He's running for mayor because he wants better wages, better hospitals, streets, roads, schools for Bogota..."

"Or he's running to further his political career."

"He's running because he has heard the cry of the people. The government cannot ignore the oppressed much longer."

"Of course they can!" Gacha burst out. "They've done it

121

for one hundred years. Better wages, ha! The only reform worth talking about in this country is land reform. That is the only issue to be discussed. Is your father going to give up a few thousand acres of his hacienda for the good of the people? If not, what ruling families are? Why is it that only one tenth of one percent of the total population of Colombia controls over ninety percent of the country's wealth? You didn't see any *campesinos* in that protest, did you? Hell, no! They are just trying to survive working in the fields. The last time this country talked about land reform we had *La Violencia*. Three protests outside a government building doesn't change the times. Nothing has changed. The only way for the poor to make something out of their god-cursed plight is to take what they can in any way they can!"

The closer tables to Gacha's had gone quiet.

Ana-Alicia had tears streaming down her face as she abruptly stood up and ran out of the discothèque.

"Shit!" Gacha muttered under his breath and then ran after her. He caught up with her in the parking lot sitting on the hood of her mother's Mercedes-Benz.

"Get away from me!" Ana-Alicia shouted when she saw Gacha coming after her.

"Ana-Alicia, I'm sorry. I am truly sorry. I had promised myself long ago that I would never argue about politics, but..."

"You are not from a wealthy family, are you?" Gacha felt as if he'd been called at cards. He was about to answer, but she kept talking. "I mean you have fancy clothes and you know my father and Harry Fosse. Fosse who knows everyone knows about you. So somewhere along the line you came into money. What was it, gold, emeralds?"

"Both," Gacha said. In a manner of speaking he was telling the truth.

"Who are you? Where do you come from Gonzalo Rodriguez Gacha? You know, I haven't seen you in three months and there was not a day that did not pass in which I did not think about you."

"I come from Maraguey," Gacha said calmly.

Ana-Alicia gasped in horror.

"Yes," said Gonzalo, glad that she knew what he was talking about. "I saw my father and mother stripped, raped and murdered all in less than fifteen minutes. I was only six at the time, but from then on I told myself I wouldn't let it happen to me. I made a few business deals here and there and they turned out profitable." Gacha cursed himself deeply for having told her and wondered why in the world he had. He hadn't even told Chulo!

Ana-Alicia leapt off the hood and into Gacha's arms and kissed him passionately on the lips. Later she pried herself apart from him and walked towards the door of the Mercedes. She opened the back door and invited Gacha into the back seat with her. It started off tenderly with slow, exploring kisses, their hands exploring their bodies as their passion built up to a point where their desires overcame their good judgement.

Gonzalo pulled her v-neck sweater off in a single movement and lifted her skirt up to her waist as she lay in the backseat spread-eagled. He reached up and pulled off her panties, feeling her moistness as he cupped her breasts with his free hand. Slowly he kissed his way down from her breasts to the flatness of her stomach until his face was in the soft dark triangle between her thighs.

Ana-Alicia let out soft moans of pleasure as he slowly entered her. She felt him reach her hymen and burst through it softly, so that the pain was only momentary. His thrusts were soft and gentle, but began to build in tempo and strength as she herself lost control. She thought she would burst and would not be able to endure the pleasure much longer, until she exploded into a river of uncontrollable pleasure. She climaxed again and again until they both lay exhausted from their lovemaking. The windows of the Mercedes were all fogged up by then.

As Ana-Alicia sat in the back seat smoking one of her father's cigarettes, a shiver ran through her. She was frightened that a man could actually control her body and emotions like Gonzalo could. She was also scared that she had lost her self-control to him and would never be able to regain it again. She looked at him as he rested with his eyes closed and she shivered again. It was the same type of shiver she got when she visited her grandmother's grave. What was it about Gonzalo Rodriguez Gacha that scared her so, she asked herself. Could she love him and be frightened of him at the same time? Yes, she could and she was! There was just something about him, something dangerous, something...evil.

CHAPTER TEN

Harry Fosse walked into the *El Centro* office and sat down in a chair that had been provided for him as a business guest. If Fosse was unimpressed by the measly furniture or the run down walls of the apartment, he never let it show.

"I've never understood why Colombians go through so many preliminary greetings, so let me come to the point straight away," Fosse said, leaning forward on the edge of his chair.

"If you like," Gacha said, not understanding himself why Americans were always in a hurry. The preliminary greetings were a way of bestowing honor and respect.

"As you already know, *El Loco* supplies me with marijuana which I in turn supply to others who they sell to others. The price is constant, the amount of marijuana sold depends on how much my distributors want. It is a way of calculating demand."

"Yes, I understand," Gacha said, folding his hands on his desk.

"Well, *El Loco* has a good thing, but he cannot see beyond the short range profit. The demand among my distributors has almost quadrupled in the last six months alone..."

"Excuse me, Mr. Fosse, but I don't see the point you are trying to make."

"I'm getting to that. Just cool your jets, man. You know, this is my last year in Bogota?"

Gacha nodded. "Yes, you are returning to the United States."

"Yeah, I'm going to the University of Miami. I was there last summer, nice place, huge campus and a lot of

125

students. It was there that I met certain students who told me that they could not sell enough marijuana. Here in Bogota, the price of marijuana is dirt cheap, unlike in Miami. For example, a bag of marijuana would sell here in Bogota for two hundred *pesos* while that same bag would sell on the streets of Miami for ten thousand *pesos*."

Gacha let out a long, soft whistle.

"Exactly," said Fosse. "What I propose is that you supply me with marijuana in the States so I can distribute it there, for a cut of the take, of course."

"Cut? What is this cut?" Gacha asked.

"Fee, commission," Fosse said with a cold smile.

"This is all hypothetical talk, you know?" Fosse nodded his head. "You know I don't control *Séptima*, so why not propose it to them first?"

"First of all, I have, but the jackass wouldn't know a good deal if you handed it to him on a silver tray." Gacha smiled. "The other problem is that for such an operation there has to be stability. Let's say, hypothetically speaking of course, that I go into business with *Séptima* and they get overrun. My supply line then gets cut off and my customers, distributors and everyone else involved is up the spout."

"Are you asking me to go to war against *Séptima*?" Gacha asked.

"No, I can take care of that," Fosse said. Chulo and Mario looked on in surprise, so far they had not thought much about the idea.

"How?"

"When business quadrupled, I began to look over the *Séptima* organization. I like to know who I'm doing business with. Anyway, what I found out is that they are nothing more than a loose bunch of thugs with no real cohesive bond, except they control from Seventh Avenue to First Avenue. Within that area they can burglarize some houses, steal some cars, rob some old ladies, but that is the extent of their economic base. Amateur hour.

"Marijuana has made them rich. Their burglaries have

dropped, auto thefts are non-existent and most of their *gamines* are now hustling the bad weed. I am *Séptima's* biggest dealer and distributor. Without me, they are nothing. Their selling tactics are based on turnover. I ask for twenty or thirty pounds which they have to buy and then sell to me for a profit. Their mistake is that they do not stockpile or control the demand."

"And you do?" Gacha asked, impressed even though he didn't show it.

"When *El Loco* turned me down for forty pounds, I began stockpiling. I have two months' worth, maybe three. In other words I am going to cut *Séptima* off from their income. I'm going to fire the sons-of-bitches. What do you think is going to happen then?"

Gacha smiled as he saw the plan. "They will have no money, they will be weak and ripe for a takeover. Hell, they'd have to come to us or be wiped off the face of Bogota by their own *gamines* wanting... *Madre de Dios*, they will have to come to us asking for a merger!"

Harry Fosse sat back in his chair with his hands behind his head and a huge grin on his face.

Mario stood up from his chair which was off by the side of the wall and walked over to Gacha's desk. He then leaned over the desk and whispered into Gacha's ear. Gacha nodded.

"There are laws against trafficking marijuana, Mr. Fosse," Gacha said in a statement requiring no response.

"Yes, except the U.S. Customs only searches for marijuana as you come off the plane. Pretty stupid, really. I suggest we send it by ship in huge boxes marked to some fictitious company in America, sent by another fictitious company in Colombia. I suggest we take some old television sets, radios, whatever, and take all the electronic garbage out of them and stuff them with marijuana. The cost of sending it by ship can be figured into the price of the marijuana. We'll just pass the cost of the shipping straight to the consumer." Fosse laughed. "It takes about five weeks for the marijuana to go from a Colombian port to an American port. I know I've already tried it."

"What?" Gacha asked in shock.

"If I send a load now, it will be there by March 15th. I have a break from school at that time and I'll be going to the States. We can make it a trial run, eh?"

"I don't have any connections with the marijuana growers," Gacha said, wondering when the conversation had shifted from the hypothetical to the real.

"Can't help you there, man. As I said, I am distribution not supply. I'm sure you can dig up someone who can point you the way."

"Okay," said Gacha, "If we go ahead with the plan, how much do we start off with?"

"I experimented with two kilos, so I figure we should go for one hundred kilos. Does that sound good?" Fosse asked expectantly.

Gacha put his clasped hands to his mouth as if he were praying. His mind was taking in all the angles of such a venture. He realized that there was really no risk to it except for the initial capital to buy one hundred kilos."

"Okay, let's try it," Gacha said as he stood up and shook hands with Harry Fosse.

Chulo brought out some shot glasses and filled them with *aguardiente*. They all picked up a shot glass and raised them for a toast.

"To success in our marijuana business," Gacha said light-heartedly and toasted to success. The glasses clinked and the liquor was swallowed.

Margarita Coro sat with her hands folded across her lap at the *Salinas* restaurant in Chico. She was there to meet Gonzalo, the first time since she had been released from the hospital a few months ago.

She did not even dare order a drink for herself, because she did not want to give Gonzalo the impression that she had turned to liquor for consolation. She had spent a month's wages on her hair and facial. The salon had done an excellent job in hiding the scar, better than she had ever done herself. Yet, she could still see the little children stare at her and she could see the looks of horror from other women as she walked closer by on the street. Why was it that women were more critical of the scar? With the money she had managed to save since working at the Gonzáles' residence, she had bought herself a new dress and a pair of shoes.

She looked at her watch and saw that Gonzalo was fifteen minutes late, but that was all right. Mario had told her that he was working real hard these past few months, almost twenty hours a day! Poor Gonzalo. She would take care of him, she would distract him from business. Poor man, kind hearted too! Hadn't Mario said that he was paying for his university education? Oh, that Mario, he's been a dear to me. What would I have done without him, she thought. I'll have to tell Gonzalo that if it were not for Mario, I'd have gone insane. Mario had seen to everything. If she needed money, he would give it to her without protest. When Gonzalo had not been able to see her, he had taken her out and managed somehow to make her feel good. Oh, Mario was a saint!

At ten minutes of ten in the evening, Margarita knew that Gonzalo was not coming. She then began to imagine unspeakable horrors that had occurred to him. She shook her head each time she had a vision of a calamity that had befallen her loved one. After ten o'clock the bartender and waitress began to look at her coldly, since she had not ordered anything but mineral water and was taking up the best table in the house. Tears began to well up in her eyes, she looked down towards her lap so that people would not see her cry.

"Margarita?" a low, calm voice said.

Margarita looked up and saw Mario. "I'm sorry. Gacha had a business engagement he could not break-off. He called me and asked me to pick you up and take you to wherever you wished to go," Mario said plainly.

Mario's cool steady voice hid the anger he felt at having been asked by Gacha to apologize for him. He hated the fact that Gacha had discarded Margarita, simply because he could

129

not stand to see her scarred face. It was a beautiful face once you got over the fact that she had a scar slashing across it. The scar had not altered the high cheekbones or the wide set eyes and perfect lips.

At first Mario had reacted to the scar and his insensitivity had hurt Margarita. Later, as he took her to the local city parks, museums and the movies, he had stopped seeing the scar. It was there still, but his mind had already accepted it as fact and began concentrating on something else. It wasn't until a month ago he had decided he had fallen in love with her. At first he had tried to deny it by going out with some of the more beautiful girls at the university, but always ended up comparing them to Margarita. Then for a whole week he had not seen or talked to her and it was the longest week of his collective memory.

Now, he talked to her every day and saw her on the weekends. Gacha still believed he was doing him a favor when in reality he was doing it for himself. As he looked down now at her tear-stained face, his heart broke like glass.

"Oh, come now," Mario said as he handed her his handkerchief. "Gacha was really angry with himself for not being able to tear himself away. But with plans of buying an apartment in Chico, a car for Chulo and sending me to the United States, it's a miracle he hasn't collapsed from exhaustion."

"Chico?" Margarita asked in amazement. "Is he really buying an apartment in Chico?"

"Yes, he's giving me his apartment in El Centro. He's a very busy man, so don't hold it against him because he did not show up," Mario said with a smile as his stomach knotted up in anger. "What do you want to do?"

"I'm really hungry and I don't think it would be nice for me to get up now and leave."

"Good, we'll have a feast!" Mario waved down a waitress and ordered two *tamales* and a bottle of *aguardiente*.

Gonzalo Rodriguez Gacha met Ana-Alicia in a small

expensive, restaurant in a section north of the buffer zone known as *El Lago* (The Lake). They had been there no more than a few minutes when someone who knew Ana-Alicia invited them to a party being held in the Santana neighborhood.

Santana was one of the more exclusive, if not the most exclusive, neighborhood in Bogota. It was on the east side of the city and against one of the mighty mountains that ringed the Bogota plateau. There were no small homes or houses for that matter, here there were only mansions and estates. The party they had been invited to was in a large twelve bedroom brick and stucco mansion. From the street the house was deceiving, since it looked as if it only had one floor, but the house was perched at an angle against the mountain concealing the other three floors in the back of the front entrance.

Inside the mansion were marble floors and carefully painted walls. Some oil paintings hung on the walls, paintings whose artists ranged from Leonel Góngora to Salvador Dalí. However, there was one painting that stopped Gacha cold. It was a painting with wild splashes of color, of pigeons in tortured flight against a background of purple so beautiful yet so nightmarish. Gacha looked closer at the name.

"It's Alejandro Obregón," said Ana-Alicia.

"He's..." Gacha stuttered, trying to find the right words. "I don't think I've ever cared for a painting in my life, but this one...It's the greatest painting I've ever seen."

Ana-Alicia chuckled. "This is not one of his best either. If you ask me, his painting gives me the creeps. He kind of reminds me of Dalí when he was painting the surreal stuff, you know the really weird stage he had a few years back?"

"Dalí who?" Gacha asked innocently.

"Forget it, let's get a drink. After all, it's my last night out. School starts the day after tomorrow." Ana-Alicia pulled Gacha by the arm and dragged him onto the outdoor patio where all her school friends were dancing.

Gacha never understood why they all listened to

American music. Colombian music was far better for dancing. You really couldn't dance to the music that they said was *chévere* (cool). So Gacha said, "How do people dance to words like, 'She came in through the bathroom window.' I mean it doesn't even make sense." Gacha nodded his head towards the speaker.

Ana-Alicia laughed. "Oh, sometimes, Gonzalo, you're so terribly provincial you sound like you just got off the bus. Come, let's dance." Ana-Alicia grabbed him by the hand and led him to the makeshift dance floor.

At three-thirty in the morning, in typical Colombian fashion, the party kicked into high gear. Beer, brandy, scotch, whiskey and all types of liqueurs were being consumed with gusto. Everyone seemed to be in good cheer as the stereo hi-fi blared out a string of Colombian dancing tunes. By five in the morning, Ana-Alicia had stolen away with Gacha to an upstairs bedroom.

They attacked each other, ripping each other's clothes off even before they got the door halfway closed. Instead of tender lovemaking, it was energetic and frenetic, causing them to be spent at the early going.

As Ana-Alicia rested her head on Gacha's chest and he curled with his legs and hands around what he thought was a glorious body, he blurted out, "Marry me, Ana-Alicia."

Ana-Alicia heard the words and chuckled, thinking that he was teasing her. "Sure, let's do it now."

"I'm serious," said Gacha, the mood suddenly changing.

Ana-Alicia suddenly looked up and faced him. "You can't be!"

"I am. Marry me. I don't think I've ever loved a woman, nobody for that matter, as much as I do you."

Ana-Alicia moved off the bed and reached for her clothes. "I can't marry you, you know that!"

"What?"

"*Por Dios*, Gonzalo! Even if you were the richest man in the world I couldn't marry you."

"Why?" Gacha asked, his throat dry and his stomach

feeling as if he were dropping from a great height.

"Because of who you are. You have no family name. You don't have...damn it, you know what I mean!"

"No, what do you mean?"

"You're... Listen, Gonzalo, you're a great lover and a dear friend, but a girl like me doesn't marry someone of your background. I'm going to the United States to study and when I come back I'll marry someone with a name. My father, remember that first night we met? Well, he warned me that you were not the right people."

Every word was like a nail sealing his coffin. Gacha seemed to be drowning and yet he kept blurting out words that seemed to go against the flow of the conversation. "But I love you," he kept saying.

"I do too, but not that way," Ana-Alicia said putting on her knee-high black boots. "Don't go confusing a great fuck for love..."

Gacha didn't hear anymore, didn't want to listen to his love anymore. He was falling back into an endless pit, wondering how he had miscalculated so enormously. God in heaven, what had happened?

They had gone to the movies and then walked under the neon signs of the *Chapinero* district. The night was cold and full of stars, Mario reflected. There would be frost on the ground by morning. He had held Margarita's hand as they walked, and she had not objected. After they had walked, they went to a soft lighted bar and nearly got drunk. They danced on the small dance floor, and then suddenly Mario reached and kissed her.

Margarita was not surprised that he'd try, but she was surprised at the fact that she did not do anything about it. She had noticed how Mario looked at her in the restaurant. Why hadn't she noticed before? She recognized the look. He was totally infatuated with her, or was it love? Was that so bad, she asked herself. Would she ever find someone to love her, as she was now? Hadn't Gonzalo turned away from her? Yes, why else wouldn't he have come to see her in the last four months?

"I need you, Margarita. I think I fell in love with you from the very first day I saw you," Mario said, stroking her scarred cheek with his fingers.

"What... what about Gonzalo?" Margarita asked with fright.

Mario shook his head. "I don't know, all I know is that I need you and that I want you tonight! I haven't had a day where I have not thought about you. Be with me, Margarita, tonight."

Margarita's eyes welled up with tears. "Yes Mario, I'll stay with you tonight."

Chulo dressed quickly and walked out of the room. Outside the room in the hallway a man collected the money for "services rendered." Once Chulo paid, he ran. The woman was dead.

The women were always the same, between the ages of eighteen and twenty, born as natives to one of the countless Amazonian rain forest tribes and having the misfortune to be born with pale skin, which made them attractive to the city pimps. The pimps came from the big city to offer the girls "jobs." The families of the girls, not knowing better, would agree to let a certain child go for a price. To the native Indian it was not a strange custom; they had traded women among the different tribes for thousands of years. To the city pimps, however, it was a cheap way of getting young girls to become prostitutes. From three hundred and ninety-eight tribes to select from, the pimps knew their chances of getting caught were slim to none.

It was easy for Chulo to find prostitutes to degrade and kill. Chulo had been one of them. No one gave a shit about his condition then, he thought, so why should he give a shit himself about these women? And with that thought in mind, Chulo forgot all about the woman he had just killed.

The woman had been Chulo's second victim.

134

CHAPTER ELEVEN

For eleven months Gonzalo Rodriguez Gacha turned all of his energy toward business. It was the only way he knew to wipe Ana-Alicia from his mind, and it appeared to have worked. He had been lucky too. A crisis had popped up every time it seemed that the monotony would free his mind of business and let it wander to that devastating night. His business was going beyond any prediction he had envisioned after taking over as King of Bogota.

His rise began as Harry Fosse had predicted. When *Séptima* ran out of a drug income it had capitulated to the pressures of its own *gamines* and merged with *El Centro*. *El Loco* was taken on as a manager in the *El Centro* organization, but that had only lasted a month. Gacha dispatched him to Vaupes province on the outer limits of the Amazon rain forest. *El Loco* was to contract with some marijuana growers for the *El Centro* marijuana business, but he disappeared and never returned. The fact that Chulo had been with him and returned alone hadn't disturbed anyone enough to ask questions.

The first trial run of the one hundred kilos of marijuana in seven, 20-year-old television sets arrived in Miami, Florida one week earlier than expected. Harry Fosse, who worked on distribution, had not sold all one hundred kilos. He had given away twenty kilos to cement good relations with his new but rather small upstart distributors. The approach had worked wonders, they all came back for more.

In a short time, Harry Fosse began a vast distribution network. Because he had been in Fort Lauderdale and Miami, Florida, when all the major U.S. universities were having their spring break, he was able to meet with a lot of out-of-town people. Those out-of-towners were students who were supplying their own universities with meager amounts of marijuana and were ready to deal with much more.

Stuart Jacobs, a drop-out student of New York University, had kept his ties with his college friends and supplied them with marijuana and some heroin. Paul Smith, a black youth from the tough street gangs of Southeast Los Angeles, had come to Ft. Lauderdale with only one purpose: to deal directly with a supplier from Colombia. John Martinez, a Mexican-American who supplied marijuana to the rich students at the University of Houston, was ready for expansion the moment he was able to procure a steady supplier. In one way or another, all three dealers had begun dealing in order to keep up their own habit. However, once they realized that the business end of it was a better high, they stopped smoking the bad weed.

In a small hotel room in Fort Lauderdale, Harry Fosse, Stuart Jacobs, Paul Smith and John Martinez worked out the distribution. It was decided that sending marijuana through old, gutted out television sets would become too impractical. What would be practical, they decided, were huge crates stuffed with marijuana. If an overzealous customs officer opened one of the crates, all he would find was technical manuals. The top six inches of every crate would carry technical manuals, while underneath the six inches were several hundred kilos of marijuana. It was also decided that there would be a shipment every month that would also increase by one hundred kilos with each shipment. The center of distribution for the United States would be in Miami since it had two direct flights to Bogota every day.

Nine months after the distribution network had been set up, Gacha, through Fosse's distribution network, was selling over eleven hundred kilos a month. The profits were so immense that Gacha himself could not believe it was so easy.

The first thing Gacha did with the profits was to buy a tract of land in the province of Cauca and begin growing his own marijuana. To make sure that nothing went wrong with the harvest, he met with the top provincial officials of the region, and the police chiefs of the region who made less than ten dollars a month. Gacha put them all on the payroll.

On the tenth month, the port authorities in Colombia began to notice the large shipments of crates bound for Miami, Florida. Gacha then decided to invite a select group of high port officials for a weekend in the resort city of Cartagena, where they were provided with nubile young women, lots of drinks and money to spend. After the weekend an understanding had been reached between Gacha and the port authorities. The agreement stipulated that those select officials would receive certain gratuities in exchange for looking the other way when Gacha's crates were on the docks.

In Bogota, major banks began to take notice of the growing supply of money that was being deposited by the company calling itself, *Compañía Exportadora* (Cia., for short). Since the depositor was a wise, young and reputable investor by the name of Mario Garcia, they had not found it unusual. After all, they were acting as intermediaries and stockbrokers for the young man's investments in New York. The banking establishment had also noticed that Cia. Export had an investment portfolio second to none. A portfolio that included stocks from blue chip international corporations such as IBM, GM, AT&T, Texaco, Mobil, and countless other solid businesses that made piles of that coveted currency, the American dollar.

Bank officials acted as front men for the big time politicians because the officials could tell the politicians who made what deposits. It was a way to save time on those political supporters who didn't have a dollar to contribute to those who did have the money to contribute. On the fourth month after beginning the Bogota-Miami marijuana run, the word began to spread around Bogota that there was a new player in town and his name was Gonzalo Rodriguez Gacha.

Gacha's headquarters for Cia. Export were located on the eighth floor of the second highest building in Bogota. His offices were, however, small and unimpressive. A secretary took calls in the outer lobby for the three offices. Gacha, Chulo and Mario all had offices, although only Gacha could ever be found at the office itself. Chulo was always out taking care of the *gamines* and Mario was at the university or studying at his apartment.

To the politicians who began to drop by, Gacha would contribute to their re-election campaigns. Once having done so, he was invited to cocktails and minor social gatherings. At the cocktail parties he met more ambitious politicians who were also eager to meet him. It had become such a routine that he could recognize a politician's line for a contribution to his political fund. "I've heard some good things about you, we need more young men like you in Bogota. The entrepreneurial spirit, good for the country and damn good for the economy."

At the end of 1971, in order to keep up his image, Gacha bought himself a black Mercedes-Benz and began tinkering with the idea of buying a *finca* (farm). However, that idea soon died when Mario walked into his office one morning and told him they were in the red.

"What do you mean we're in the red?" Gacha asked bewildered. "We sold two hundred thousand dollars last month!"

"Yes," said Mario, "but we have so many people on the payroll that we are not selling enough." Mario showed Gacha the figures.

"I don't believe it!" Gacha said, looking at the figures. "We have a turnover of over a million dollars a year and we're losing money." Gacha paused and nodded as if he had seen enough of the disgusting information. "Thanks, Mario, I'll take care of it. I promise you we will be in the black by next week and turning a profit." Gacha changed the subject. "So, you'll be going to Harvard in a few months, eh?"

Mario smiled but it was a strange smile, Gacha thought. "What, you don't want to go?"

"No, I do, *jefe*!" Mario replied strongly. "It's just that I'm going to miss the place."

"You'll be back in no time, it's only two years. By the way, send in Chulo on your way out," Gacha said, dismissing Mario as he reached for a ringing phone.

Mario walked out, quietly closing the door behind him.

A moment later there was a knock on Gacha's door and Chulo walked in without waiting for a reply. Gacha motioned to him to sit down as he said good-bye to someone on the phone.

"You wanted to see me, *jefe*?" Chulo asked.

As Gacha was about to speak the telephone rang and he picked it up."Hello?" Gacha listened for a moment as color drained from his face. "When did it happen, Harry?" Another silence. "Damn! I'll have to get back to you Harry," Gacha said and hung up.

"What's wrong *jefe*?"

"Stuart Jacobs was arrested this morning by the U.S. Narcotics and Dangerous Drugs Bureau. They offered him a deal in return for names. Harry somehow bailed him out and shot him off the coast of the Bahamas. New York has been shut down until Harry can get a new distributor for the area. He said it would take time because New York has a turf thing like we had here in Bogota with the *gamines*. Anyway, that is not why I asked you to come in. Mario says we are in the red, almost bankrupt."

"How can that be?!" Chulo exclaimed in astonishment.

"We have too many people on the payroll, we're greasing too many palms."

"*jefe*, once a person is on the payroll you can't cut him off, the person is likely to blow the whistle or do something stupid."

Gacha nodded. "I know, so I want to take a look at who we got on the payroll to see who we can do without."

"And those we can do without?" Chulo asked in a hesitant voice.

Two months before, when Gacha had discovered their offices had been electronically bugged, he began the practice of writing certain things down on paper. He would hand the paper to Chulo who would then read it, hand it back and he would set it on fire. On the small piece of paper that Gacha handed over there were only two words: **Kill them.**

139

Chulo nodded.

Within forty-eight hours, Cia. Export was back in the black.

At a party given at the residence of Don Eusebio Corraza, *La Mano Negra*, in honor of an up and coming politician recently elected to the Senate of the Colombian Congress, Gonzalo Rodriguez Gacha was introduced as '*el estimado señor*.' It was Gacha's first social ball. Although he had been invited to many important and respected homes, the balls had always eluded him. The people invited to a social event were always the 'who's who' of Colombian society.

Men were dressed in tuxedoes and the women in long Paris couture gowns with a complement of jewelry that would make the Queen of England blush. The women were always divided into two categories, those who were married and those who were not married. It was already taken for granted that you had money and that you were important, one of the players.

Gacha walked around, nodding his head politely at the somewhat familiar faces and making some polite conversation with others. It was hard going since the topics of conversation were always about literature, law, music, art and subjects that required a long exposure to a good education and fine, almost aristocratic breeding. Everywhere he turned he saw a respected family. He saw the Gaviria family who controlled the vast coffee plantations in Antioquia province, the Torres family who controlled eighty percent of the cattle market in the *llanos* (plains), the Morales family who controlled rice and beans, the Ledesma family who controlled the banana plantations on the north coast and, of course, Don Eusebio, who controlled the world emerald market.

"Well, well, well," said a voice in English from behind Gacha. "Look at what the cat dragged in."

Gacha turned around at the sound of the familiar voice. "Hello, Mr. Harrison. How are things with you?"

"Fine," said Jim Harrison, the Cultural Attaché for the

United States. "I can see things are going well with you. A veritable rags to riches story, a one man capitalistic *tour de force*, if you will."

Gacha smiled as if used to the quick ironic humor of the American. "No more a capitalist than an American businessman."

"Yeah, in your dreams. I've heard you've been busy, you don't look so good either. How much weight have you lost?" Gacha shrugged. "You need a vacation or you're going to collapse."

Gacha looked at Harrison as if he'd just lost his mind but then he laughed. "Yes, maybe I'll go to America."

"Hell, why not? Go see how the other half lives, go see for yourself what the big red white and blue is all about."

Gacha smiled then shook his head as if Harrison were a good joker. "I better mingle," Gacha said and walked off.

As Gacha walked around the room he accidentally bumped into Don Emilio Gonzáles, the newest mayor of Bogota and Ana-Alicia's father. His wife who was beside him was a tall, slender, striking woman who took Gacha in with every pore in her body. "Don Emilio, a pleasure to see you. Please allow me to congratulate you on your mayoral victory. You start with the new year, no?"

"With the new year, yes," said Don Emilio. "This is my wife *Doña* Juanita."

"A pleasure, *Señora*," Gonzalo said clicking his heels.

"I do declare, my husband is certainly hanging around a much handsomer crowd these days," said *Doña* Juanita Gonzáles looking at her husband slyly. "Where have you been hiding him, darling?"

"Oh, he is a business acquaintance."

"My husband is much too rude tonight, please forgive him Mr..."

"Gacha, Gonzalo Rodriguez Gacha."

"Why don't you call on us some time this week, *Señor* Gacha?"

"Thank you," Gacha said and then caught a look of

warning from Don Emilio. "If I can tear myself away from
business some day, I'll certainly try."

So, the bastard doesn't want me in his house either.
That will have to change, Gacha thought.

Don Eusebio Corraza, *La Mano Negra* to those who
really knew him, called attention to himself by ringing a
Waterford crystal bell. The room quieted down as he had
expected.

As the bell rang, *Doña* Juanita got in between her
husband and Gonzalo, her left hand around *Don* Emilio's right
arm and her right hand wandering liberally over Gacha's
derrière. She copped a few feels but never made eye contact
with Gacha.

Gacha didn't know whether to laugh or to turn around,
so that she could grab his penis instead. He went along with
it and pretended not to notice as *Don* Eusebio spoke.

"...Now, because our new senator will be taking up his
new duties, he leaves behind the office he so faithfully carried
out as attorney general. Our new Minister of Justice, who took
office just a few days ago, has appointed a new Deputy
Minister of Justice, ladies and gentlemen... Come here Álvaro,"
Don Eusebio said to a small man, not particularly handsome,
Gacha noticed, but behind the dark eyes there was fire of the
pure, the eyes of the righteous, the eyes of a man who thirsts
for justice.

The small man was greeted with applause, many
shouting "*Bravo*, Álvaro!" He was young, Gacha thought, no
more than twenty-five or twenty-six."

"Ladies and gentlemen, our newest Deputy Minister of
Justice, Harvard Law School graduate, doctor Álvaro Para
Reyes." The room broke into another round of applause.

Álvaro nodded, embarrassed by the show of support. He
let his eyes take in the crowd as he nodded and waved to
friends scattered around the room.

When Gacha felt Álvaro's eyes sweep over him, a chill
ran down his spine. It was not that Álvaro knew who he was,
but rather felt the strong force, the sheer presence about the

man that said he was dangerous.

"You look like you've seen a ghost," said a voice from behind Gacha. "Hello, anyone in there?"

Gacha turned around, confused and startled for a moment. "Good evening," Gacha said.

"Hello Gacha," said Carlos Fuentes. "They call him Saint Álvaro down at the station."

"Who?"

Fuentes nodded with his head over at the Deputy Minister of Justice. "Him, Álvaro Para Reyes. One of the brightest and most astute legal minds I have ever met. A hard man to corrupt."

"Who wants to corrupt him?" Gacha asked innocently.

"Just a figure of speech. We miss you downtown. Some officers say that police work has decreased since you left for Chico, wasn't it?"

Gacha was aware of *Doña* Juanita looking on from a few feet away. "I can see why," Gacha said off-handedly, "I used to do most of their work."

A flash of anger crossed Fuentes' face but he let it ease out of him. "Yes, we miss model citizens like you in our building, particularly the west wing."

Gacha smiled coldly. The west wing was where the jail cells were.

Finally Fuentes, who was aware of *Doña* Juanita standing a few feet away from them, turned around and said to her, "Forgive me *Doña* Juanita, how are you doing?"

"Fine, Lieutenant Fuentes. And you?" *Doña* Juanita answered evenly, her eyes sparkling with curiosity at the exchange she had overheard.

"And your daughter Ana-Alicia?"

Gacha looked at Fuentes. Did he know about them? Did he know about their last night? Was he needling him on purpose?

"Oh, Ana-Alicita is the same. Always ready to drive everyone to madness. She wrote to me a few days ago. She likes her studies in the States and has six or seven male friends hanging on her every word. She's the limit," *Doña* Juanita said as she removed a champagne glass off a waiter's tray.

"All that trouble going on there worries me," said *Doña* Juanita, after taking a long sip. "You know, that protesting and the police beating up on the demonstrators." *Doña* Juanita shook her head as if the world were going to the dogs. "You really can't blame the police either. My husband and I were in San Francisco a few weeks ago. Oh, may the Virgin of Fatima protect us. We saw all these long-haired, drug-crazed people. Students, really, all protesting that awful war in Vietnam. Sometimes I worry that she's protesting with those crazies, because you know she protested down here in Bogota. Well, she never knew that we knew, but a good friend of my husband's called him up and told him that she was in it. Oh my Lord! My husband hit the roof on that one. He never told her though, figured she only had half a year before she left for the States. Imagine the family embarrassment if her picture had appeared in one of the papers or God forbid she'd been arrested."

Fuentes and Gacha exchanged looks and realized at once that *Doña* Juanita loved to talk. They were her captive audience, speaking about gossipy tidbits, adding her own melodrama to the uninteresting anecdotes by placing "oh's" and "God forbid's" at the appropriate moments.

Suddenly a low, deep voice boomed over *Doña* Juanita's, breaking her monotonous voice and cutting her off at mid-anecdote.

"Mr. Fuentes," said the United States Ambassador. "Let me thank you for the fine work you did with the capture of those ruffians of the M-19..." Curtis Mathews stopped in mid speech, shocked at the sight of Gonzalo Rodriguez Gacha. He regained composure but not before Fuentes realized that Gacha and the U.S. Ambassador had at one time done "business."

"Thank you, Mr. Ambassador. You know *Doña* Juanita and Gonzalo Rodriguez Gacha, of course," said Fuentes with a sarcastic smile.

"Of course, good to see you both again," said the ambassador.

"And your lovely wife, Mr. Ambassador?" *Doña* Juanita asked.

"Indisposed, I'm afraid. Caught a cold sometime yesterday."

"Again?" *Doña* Juanita asked, the tone of voice stating disbelief. Everyone knew the ambassador's wife held her nose up to Colombian society because she was a Philadelphia girl and on that city's prominent social register.

Curtis Mathews ignored the question with a bitter smile. "Mr. Gacha, and how are you faring in..."

"Industry," Gacha answered, wondering where he had come up with such a word. "Very well, thank you for your concern."

"Not at all. I'm sorry I must talk to *Don* Emilio for a moment. Please, Mr. Gacha, do stop by sometime. You know where the embassy is?"

"Yes, thank you. If I can pull myself away from business I will," Gacha said off-handedly.

"Then with apologies to all, I bid that you excuse me," said Mathews as he politely bowed and walked away.

Doña Juanita made a face. "He's useless! After that fiasco with the Under-Secretary of Agriculture, he's been courting everyone like a desperate whore."

Gacha laughed out loud, taken suddenly by surprise with *Doña* Juanita's private gutter language outburst.

"Oh, Gonzalo," said *Doña* Juanita, "may I call you Gonzalo? Surely, we are friends, are we not? I think you should meet my daughter. God knows she needs a real man instead of those spaced-out kids she's been seeing." Gonzalo flinched at the mention of Ana-Alicia, especially at the fact that she was out seeing other men.

Carlos Fuentes managed to slip away, not wanting to be near *Doña* Juanita. He knew she was as dangerous as the jaguar in the rain forests. Had she not seduced everyone, himself included? Let Gacha deal with her, he thought, and then smiled at the idea.

"Let me tell you something, Gonzalo," *Doña* Juanita said as she moved him by the arm into a hallway and into a study that she locked behind her as she closed the door. Gacha had not noticed she had locked it, since he was looking at the painting on the wall. "All the women have been talking about you. They all want to know if you have a girlfriend. Not that it matters, they'll still try to go to bed with you."

"No," said Gacha, turning around to face *Doña* Juanita. "No, not at the moment..." His voice dropped as he realized his mistake.

"Do you think I'm beautiful, Gonzalo?"

"You are a striking lady, *Doña* Juanita," Gonzalo said, as she walked right up to him and her thighs rubbed against his.

"Do you really think I'm beautiful or are you just saying that to be nice?" *Doña* Juanita's hand fell flat against Gacha's stomach and moved down slowly until it reached his groin and squeezed.

"Uh, eh..."

"*Don't* you want me?" *Doña* Juanita asked.

"For God sakes, someone could walk right in and get the wrong impression."

Doña Juanita let her gown fall to the floor, revealing a white garter belt ensemble that made her look positively erotic and with nothing else on her mind but sin. She pressed her lips against Gacha's, letting her tongue dart in and out of his mouth as her hands massaged his erection. She drew his hands down to her crotch.

Gacha had heard stories about her, stories that said that she was a nymphomaniac. She was a furnace of sex that could not burn fast enough. Her kisses were wet, desperate and passionless and when she drew his hands to her crotch and he felt her wetness, he recoiled like someone who had been burned by fire.

Doña Juanita looked at him coldly, shrugged her shoulders and reached for her gown. She put it on quickly,

146

checked her hairdo, looked at Gacha and said; "Too bad, I could have been the best fuck you ever had, but you'll get no second chances from me!" She grunted, turned her nose up and walked out of the study.

Gacha felt as if he had dodged a bullet. He could not explain why he did not want her. Was it because she was Ana-Alicia's mother? No, it was because he still wanted Ana-Alicia.

Gacha picked up a glass of champagne and smashed it against the floor. Hell, he thought, he never would have Ana-Alicia anyway, he should have laid the old bitch! Damn it, he had to get away.

Suddenly the idea of taking a vacation did not seem so stupid. Maybe I do need one, Gacha thought, but where should I go? America, like Harrison had suggested? What the devil, why not?!

CHAPTER TWELVE

In March of 1972, Gonzalo Rodriguez Gacha landed in Miami, Florida.

Miami. A city gearing up for the 1972 Republican convention. A city that was about to let the rest of the United States know that it had arrived politically. Miami. A city, developers had raped in the name of progress. The capital city of tourism.

Harry Fosse had met Gonzalo Rodriguez Gacha at the Miami airport. He had picked Gacha up in a candy-apple red Porsche 911. At the request of Gacha, he drove him around Miami and the road known as the strip, so that he could get a feel for the place. The strip was a long road with fantastically designed hotels at the foot of the beach. Gacha found himself staring at the young girls walking in and out of hotels dressed in outrageous bikinis.

Fosse, who had followed Gacha's gaze, chuckled. "Hold your horses, we'll be driving to Fort Lauderdale later on tonight. Some friends of mine will be throwing a mad bash, man. It's going to be totally far out."

"Far out?" Gacha asked puzzled.

"Expression, man, like it's cool. Far out, you know, like *chévere* in Bogota. Anyway, that'll be later tonight, but right now we have to talk business." Fosse pulled into the driveway of a massive hotel and came to a stop. A valet rushed out from the front door of the hotel, and he handed him the keys to the Porsche.

Gacha stared at Fosse.

"He's a valet, man. He parks the cars for the guests," Fosse said with laughter.

"And they don't steal the cars?" Gacha asked amazed.

"No."

"How stupid of them, they could make a fortune," Gacha said looking at the valet as he drove away in the Porsche.

"It doesn't work that way here. On a good day those valets can make two to three hundred dollars on tips plus their regular salary. That valet is probably paying his way through medical school, man." Gacha shook his head and followed Harry into the hotel.

Inside the hotel, in a specially reserved hotel conference room, Gonzalo Rodriguez Gacha met his entire distribution network. John Martinez and Paul Smith, whom he had already met in Bogota, when they had come down to visit with him just before Christmas. They greeted him warmly, now that they were in Miami. The one Gacha did not know was the third man, the man who had taken Stuart Jacobs' job in New York.

"Gonzalo Rodriguez Gacha," Fosse said, "this is our new distributor in New York, Ellroy Jonson."

Gacha shook hands with Ellroy, whose hand size made Gacha's look like a puppet's.

"Nice to meet you, man," said Ellroy, a black giant, almost six feet four inches in height, his dark eyes glinting like a double-edged sword in the phosphorescent light of the hotel.

"Ellroy," said Fosse as they all took their seats around a long rectangular table, "is a genius at distribution. As you know, we allot ourselves fifty kilos each which we dispose of in a week. Ellroy here, gets rid of it in an hour." Gacha raised an eyebrow.

"Yeah, man," said Ellroy, his New York accent and way of speaking coming out like a runaway truck. "Fifty keys is bullshit, man. What I need is a constant supply, man, but I got nowhere to stash the motherfuckin' load. I also have a problem with the greenbacks, man, I mean I cannot keep on takin' bundles of it to the bank. Them honky's are lookin' at me funny and shit, man, I need to move grass and a way to stash the cash."

150

"Grass?" Gacha asked.

"Marijuana, *la mala hierba*," Fosse said.

Gacha nodded. "How much grass do you need?" He asked Ellroy.

"Start with one hundred to one hundred and fifty kilos a week," Ellroy said smoothly.

"A week?" Gacha asked in shock.

"Yeah, man, that's what I said."

"Yes," said John Martinez. "I'm doing about ten keys a week, I think I can go up to about twenty-five a week."

"Same with me, I could go up too," said Paul Smith.

Gacha's head spun with numbers and logistics. "That's almost one thousand kilos a month!"

Harry nodded. "I figure we start with five hundred kilos. We send it by regular ship except we send it now to a lot of ports, not just Miami. One month Miami, the next Mobile, Alabama and the next Houston, Texas. The other five hundred kilos have to be brought in by plane. One thousand keys is too much to ship. But it's not too cumbersome to send it by plane. In fact, it's a piece of cake"

"We could sneak sixty or seventy kilos through the airlines, but it is too big a risk," said Gacha.

"No," said Fosse, leaning into the table. "I mean bring the stuff on our own plane. We buy a second-hand single-engine plane and we fly it in every week. I know where I can get one for twenty-five grand."

"Who'll fly it?" Gacha asked.

"I know this guy, he was a fighter pilot in Korea. He's won a whole bunch of medals for flying, man," Fosse said.

"What about the fuel?" Paul Smith asked.

"He says he could attach some long range fuel tanks. However, he would still have to land somewhere between Bogota and Miami."

"There's a whole lot of water between Bogota and Miami," said Paul Smith, as if he were convinced the pilot was an idiot.

"Not really. There is a whole bunch of islands in the

Caribbean that can be used," Fosse said, not in the least put out.

"Cuba?" Gacha asked.

"No, none of the big islands. Our coming and going would attract too much attention and we would have to grease too many palms. The pilot, the one I talked to, said the Caicos Islands and the Turks Islands."

"Never heard of them," John Martinez said skeptically.

"They're spread out southeast of the Bahamas and just north of Haiti. Almost halfway between Miami and Colombia, if the pilot takes off from Rioacha, in the Guajira province of Colombia."

"Okay," Gacha said trying to sound American. "About the money problem, I'll have to ask Mario Garcia what to do about it. Anything else?"

"Yeah, man," said Ellroy. "My customers are asking for the powder, man."

"Powder?" Gacha asked not knowing in the least what Ellroy was talking about.

"Cocaine, man."

"Cocaine? You mean *cocaína*?" Gacha asked with a perplexed look on his face.

"It's a very lucrative business. I only sell an ounce here and there to the very rich, but when I do, it brings me more money than the marijuana."

"I'll tell you about it later," Fosse said to Gacha. "Should we set a date for the trial run on the plane?"

"Three weeks if we have the plane and the pilot. Can the Caicos and Turks be brought into the payroll by then?" Harry nodded. "Then in three weeks we do the first trial run. Is that it?"

The faces around the room nodded. "Then business is concluded," said Gacha standing up. He made some small talk with them and then left for Fort Lauderdale with Harry Fosse.

On their way to Ft. Lauderdale, Gacha voiced his opinions about buying a plane. He asked whether the plane would be subjected to a customs search, but Fosse said no, because they would be landing in private airstrips all around Florida. Not even the air control towers would know where the plane was, because as they neared Florida, they would drop below radar, disappearing from the control tower's screen.

Gacha felt as if he were losing control. He kept thinking that it just couldn't be this simple. *Por Dios!* He was buying planes and officials in different countries now. How much could he expand and not be found out? He just wasn't smuggling a thousand kilos of marijuana anymore, he was now smuggling a ton of it a year. Someone was bound to notice. It was too much bulk!

The party was at the southside of Ft. Lauderdale in a home that was situated beside a stretch of beach. The home looked like a hotel because of its sheer size; it had a wide brick and concrete structure with an east and west wing and a large circular driveway out in the front of it. Its driveway was full of cars that were no less flashy than Harry Fosse's Porsche.

Instead of walking in through the front door, they walked around the house towards the back where they could hear a stereo hi-fi playing. Gacha had heard the song playing many times before, but at the time he hadn't known how to speak English. Now, as he listened to the song, he liked the words. They said something of the times. Music had changed, he realized, it was no longer dancing music but protest music. He began to sing along with the tune without knowing that he could be heard. *"...there's a man with a gun over there, a tellin' me I got to beware..."*

"Yeah, you got it, man," said Fosse. "That's the Buffalo Springfield. They knew what the hell was going down long before anyone knew what was what. Down with the goddamn establishment, man!"

"You're not doing so bad, Harry," said Gacha with some criticism in his tone.

Fosse stopped abruptly and faced Gacha. "I haven't told you this because I didn't want to worry you with more problems. I'm failing history in school and my grade point average isn't too hot either."

Gacha looked at him puzzled. "So, you're not good at history, so what?"

"Man! You don't get it, do you? I flunk history and I'm out of school and do you know what that means?" Gacha shrugged his shoulders. "Nam! That's what it means. I'll be getting a draft card telling me to go kill people halfway round the world for reasons no one seems to be able to explain. Day before yesterday, man, a plane came into Miami International with five hundred body bags. Today, one came in with forty-two coffins. Hell, I get drafted and, man, the only way I'm coming back is in a body bag."

Gacha didn't say anything, he just hoped it wouldn't happen.

They moved again until they reached the back of the house. There was a well landscaped lawn with a pool in the center of it. The shocking thing to Gacha was that everyone was either nude or close to it. Men and women lying on huge black towels, he even saw a couple having sex behind some low shrubs. There were marijuana pound bags lying on tables and chairs as if they had been carelessly thrown there. There were also some hash pipes, but no one seemed to be smoking any hashish.

A skinny kid waved at Fosse and walked over. The kid had a bad acne problem and looked near to starvation. Gacha had seen the look before and when the kid stretched his hand in greeting, he saw the track marks of heroin on the wrist and forearm. Was everyone in America on drugs? Gacha asked himself.

"Dutch, this is my friend Gacha," Fosse said. "He's the one from Colombia, the one I've been tellin' you about."

"Yeah? Well, far out man," Dutch said. "Some damn good grass, you know? Hey, you know if you want some, just grab it."

"Thank you, but no," said Gacha.

A beautiful blonde, blue-eyed girl stumbled towards them, with nothing else other than a towel around her waist.

Her breasts were jiggling as she stumbled like someone who's had too much to drink.

Dutch caught Gacha's stare and grabbed the girl by the waist, the towel dropping to the ground. "Hey, sweety, what's cookin'?"

The blonde girl eyed Gacha carefully and licked her upper lip with her tongue unconsciously. She then looked over at Dutch as if trying to figure out who he was. "Oh, it's you, Dutch," said the blonde.

"Where's everyone else, honey?" Dutch asked pulling the girl closer towards him so that he could cup her breasts with both hands. Gacha and Fosse stood there looking on with embarrassment.

"They're cutting some lines. Who's he? He's kind'a cute," said the girl high on drugs.

Dutch introduced them to each other.

"You can call me Sin," said the blonde girl with laughter. "Get it, Sin for Cindy?" Gacha nodded. "So, where is it you're from again?"

"Bogota," said Gacha, aware of her snobbish tone.

"Wow, far out. Like is it like here?"

"Like what?" Gacha asked perplexed.

"You know, like cars, houses, toilets."

Gacha held down the urge to slap her face. "Yes, except without the protests and violence."

"Yeah, do you have electricity?" Sin asked innocently.

"Yes," Gacha said through clenched teeth.

"Does like everyone grow grass down there, like don't get me wrong but really what are peasants supposed to do?" Cindy said with a trace of condescension.

"We only grow grass when we come out of the jungles every eight months or so," Gacha said with a smile, a cold smile.

Harry and Dutch laughed out loud.

"You makin' fun of me, spic?" Cindy asked angrily.

A flash of anger crossed Gacha's face which Fosse recognized immediately, so he cut into the conversation immediately. "Yeah, man, no need to lose our cool here."

Dutch, who had been watching Gacha closely, felt the sudden ability for violence in Gacha. It was like a storm warning. "*Don't* blame the girl, man," Dutch said, getting in between Cindy and Gacha. "Her old man just got canned from his job. He told her he couldn't afford to send her back to school,"

"Canned?" Gacha asked, unaware of the expression.

"Fired," said Dutch. "They threw him out of his job. He use to be a big financial corporate lawyer. They fired him because the old man was an alcoholic or so they say."

"I'm sorry," Gacha said to Cindy, a wave of pity coming over him.

"*Don't* sweat it," Cindy said, walking away from them.

Fosse whispered something into Dutch's ear and Dutch nodded back.

"Come on, Gacha, we have a surprise for you," Fosse said and led him from the back yard and into the big mansion.

The inside of the house was cool and dry with half dressed people scattered all over the rugs and chairs. Marijuana was scattered all over the place. Some people seemed to be having sex, but it was hard to tell with the lights dimmed as they were. The place also reeked of sex, like some cheap whorehouse in downtown Bogota. In the living room, strobe lights were placed in corners so that you could only see the bodies on the floor at intervals.

To Gacha, Fosse seemed to be leading him into a long, dark tunnel littered with spaced out kids on drugs. Suddenly, they walked through a door and into clear stable light. They were in a dining room and the light from the chandelier hanging from the ceiling was warm and reassuring.

Around the dining room table, men and women were hunched over a mirror snorting some white powder into their noses.

Gacha moved closer and watched. The people scooped a half teaspoon of powder out of a crystal bowl and put it on a mirror that lay flat on the table. Then a young kid broke the little mound of powder on the mirror with a razor blade and separated the powder into lines. The lines were usually all the same, two inches long by an eighth of an inch wide. Once the powder was arranged in a set of lines, everyone would come forward with straws and snort a line up their noses. He looked over at Harry who had been watching him all along. "What is it?" Gacha asked.

"Cocaine," Harry said. "Much more powerful than marijuana. Cocaine blasts into your brain like a rocket, the high is powerful but relatively short. Try it if you want but don't get hooked on it. It will fuck-up your life. I've seen people die from it in the short time I've seen it around."

"How much is it?"

"There is a kilo in that bowl or at least there was. I figure half of it has been snorted."

"How much?" Gacha asked again.

"Thirty-seven thousand dollars a kilo or one hundred dollars a line on the street."

"Where does it come from?"

"Colombia."

"I've never seen it in this form, just in leaves," Gacha said in disbelief.

"Actually the best cocaine comes from Bolivia and Peru. It's grown at five to seven thousand feet on the eastern side of the Andes mountains. The reason for the eastern side is because it gets the rich, warm moisture from the Amazon rain forest below. It all comes from a plant that produces the coca leaf. The coca leaf grows on bushes, bushes that grow to ten feet. Since the coca leaf is part of the Inca diet, it is not illegal to grow it in Bolivia or Peru. The Indian who farms the bushes on terraced plots, is known as a *cocalero*. He plants about half an acre. However, it takes about four years for the bush to produce the coca leaf.

"The *cocalero* harvests the crop three to four times a year. Fifteen people working for a full week on a harvest would yield about two hundred kilos of green leaves. Those green leaves are stuffed into potato sacks and carried down a few

157

thousand feet to an area that is exposed to the sun. The leaves are spread out on this flat area of, oh maybe, one hundred square feet and are then left to dry in the sun. Two hundred kilos of green leaves after they have dried will become eighty kilos."

"Then what?" Gacha asked, his mind taking in every detail Fosse said.

"Some of the dried leaves are sent to Stepan Chemical Company, in Maywood, New Jersey. They do some hocus pocus with chemicals that eventually turns it into cocaine powder. The powder is used for surgical operations in some cases. The residue from the cocaine powder which is not cocaine, goes to a factory in Georgia that makes, guess what?" Gacha shrugged. "Coca-Cola. You've heard of the famous 7X formula, haven't you?"

"So, Stepan Chemical sells this?" Gacha asked.

"No. This cocaine is illegal, but if you find the way that Stepan changes the leaves into powder, you got the key to millions of dollars," said Fosse smiling at Gacha.

"So, who sold this then? They must have the formula, no?"

"The Chileans have the market on Coca farms, who then use Colombians as intermediaries to send it to the U.S. pharmaceutical companies. But as you can see, someone along the way has found a way to produce cocaine powder. Cocaine, Gacha, is the future. The profits are beyond our imagination. When you go back to South America, get in contact with the Chileans and tell them you'll distribute some of the coca leaf for them. They'll grab the opportunity to sell more of it. However, you have to find out what the formula is to make the big bucks."

Gacha stared at the crystal bowl with the white powder, amazed that it cost thirty-seven thousand dollars. If he brought fifty kilos of cocaine to Miami, only once a year, he'd make as much as he would make with one year of smuggling tons of marijuana. *Damn, what was he doing here wasting time.*

"Harry, it cannot be possible," Gacha said in disbelief.

"It is possible. Someone in Colombia is doing it and getting rich at it. From what I hear, this kilo came from Medellin and there is also someone else making it in Cali."

"Really?" Gacha asked in surprise.

"Yes, you better get in on the ground floor before some people stake their claims, know what I mean?"

Gacha was about to answer when he heard a shout from the hallway beyond. It froze him. He had heard the voice before, a voice that was soft but the words being spoken now were not soft. He peered over Harry's shoulder and down the long narrow hallway. His heart began to pound against his chest and his hands became clammy. There was a group of people in the hallway. A young man and a girl with their backs to him were arguing, the woman was trying to push the man out of the way. The man was trying to rip her bikini off. The woman pushed him away, but the young man grabbed the bikini string top and ripped it from her body. Suddenly, the young woman kicked the man in the groin and ran off.

Gacha gasped for breath and excused himself.

"Where are you going?" Fosse asked.

"I'll be back in a moment," Gacha said, walking past Harry and into the hallway. He followed the girl who was making her way up a long flight of stairs. With his eyes fixed on the young woman he increased his pace, oblivious to the fact that he was pushing people out of the way. He climbed the stairs and followed the girl down the hallway, but he lost sight of her when she turned a corner. When he reached the corner she was gone. There was nothing but doors on either side of the hallway. He leaned close to every door, and on the third door on the right he heard movement. His heart skipped a beat before he knocked.

"Leave me alone!" came back the angry voice of a woman from inside the room.

Gacha opened the door and walked in. It was a lavish bedroom, with a queen sized bed and a whirling fan above it. The carpets were deep blue and very plush, the French wallpaper gave the room the appearance of a royal bedroom.

"Get out, can't you see I'm dressing!" said the angry young woman with her back to Gacha. "You're all sick, I've got to get out of here!" The young woman pulled on a white blouse covering up the beautiful back that had Gacha speechless. Then as the woman was about to turn she fell to her knees and began to cry. The young woman trembled with each sob. "Oh God, help me. I am lost," the young woman said, even though she knew someone else was in the room. She didn't care anymore.

"Not anymore," Gacha said. The woman whirled around to face the person who had spoken. "Hello, Ana-Alicia Gonzáles. I don't think your mother would approve of the company you've been keeping."

Ana-Alicia stared dumbfounded at Gacha, then she chuckled and cried at the same time. "How do you know my mother wouldn't approve?" she said in between sobs.

"I met her at a social ball in Bogota," Gacha said, his heart tying itself into a knot. His mind was racing over their last night together and now, as he looked into those brown, beautiful, hungry eyes, his heart went out to her. He had promised himself that he would never let another woman do what Ana-Alicia had done to him and, yet, here he was with Ana-Alicia wanting her more than he ever had before. Her beauty was like a magnet but her vulnerability was like a sponge that soaked love out of him. She was everything he wanted in a woman, beauty, intelligence, class and love. She loved him, he was sure of it. In that moment she had turned around in shock to see him, he knew. She loved him and he loved her, right down to the crack of doom.

Ana-Alicia got up from the floor and ran into Gacha's arms and let out a long crying sob. "Oh Gonzalo, hold me. Please hold me, I don't know how to make sense of anything anymore."

"It's not important, let's just get out of here. You want to go to Miami?" She nodded against his chest. "Then let's go find Harry, I'll ask him to lend me his car."

"Harry is here too, Harry Fosse?" Ana-Alicia asked in surprise.

"Yes, he was the one who brought me here," Gacha said, leading her out of the room by the hand.

"God bless him."

Ana-Alicia drove the Porsche south on interstate 95, because she had an American driver's license. She had also convinced Gacha to forget Miami, and go straight for the Keys of Florida.

Gacha was unsure, since they were one hundred and seventy miles away, but seeing her pleading eyes he agreed. If she had asked him for the world at that moment he reflected, he would have given it to her if it were in his power to do so.

Ana-Alicia's driving, like her personality, was fiery and rapid. She kept the needle of the speedometer at sixty miles an hour while managing a conversation with Gacha. He told her about some of her friends that he had run into in Bogota, about the social ball at *Don* Eusebio Corraza's, his new offices, his new apartment and everything else he could think of. She laughed and giggled with each tidbit of gossip and added her own little anecdotes about each person. She told him that she missed the food, drinking *aguardiente*, and the long hot days beside the pool on her father's farm.

The drive to the Keys was under a full moon which seemed almost magical to Gacha. The moonglow reflected off the water in the Gulf as they made their way across the long bridge system that connected the Keys to the mainland. At times it felt like they were skimming over the water and were not on an actual solid road.

Gacha looked over at Ana-Alicia, her slightly parted lips made him want to grab her and put his lips on them. "You are more beautiful than the last time I saw you Ana-Alicia, and I will tell you what I told you that night, I love you."

Tears welled up in Ana-Alicia's eyes and rolled down her cheeks silently, like a drop of water on marble. She slowed the car down, pulled off into the breakdown lane and stopped.

She looked at Gacha and said, "I know." Gacha was about to speak when she put her fingers on his mouth to silence him. "I love you too, Gonzalo, you've known that from the very first time I saw you, but don't ask me to marry you because it can never be. I know it's breaking your heart, why do you think I ran away from you? Because I couldn't let you love me, knowing that I would have to hurt you the way I did when you asked me to marry you.

"You and I, we come from separate worlds, Gonzalo, even though we were born in Colombia. You have become rich, maybe even powerful, perhaps respected, but you will never become one of us. Oh *querido*, I don't want to hurt you, I love you and I always will, but never will I be able to marry you. My family would disown me, I would become a pariah in Colombian society. Yes, it is superficial, I know, but it's my family and it is the only one I have and, even though they may be monsters, I still love them. If we married, you would have your business friends and I would have nobody. I wouldn't even be able to get a decent job. Who would hire me knowing I'd been disowned? Nobody. I wouldn't even have friends, not one!

"Oh *querido*," she said brushing the tears from his face with her fingers. "I will be your lover, your friend and your confidant, but will never be your wife. If I married you, I would lose everything and if, God forbid, you died young, I would be left completely alone. Just know that I love you and always will and don't ever doubt it.

"After I left Colombia to come to school, sometimes I use to cry all night in my room wondering who loved who more, you towards me or me towards you? Let's just love each other while we have the time and if you can't *querido*, you might as well go back to Colombia and think I was dead."

"Why?" Gacha asked, his face moist with tears and his voice shaky for the first time in his life.

"Because one day you will have to see me walk down the aisle with another man. I am not saying this to hurt you, my love. Colombia is not like here, where the rich marry the poor everyday."

Gacha put his hand to his face and let out a long wail.

Ana-Alicia crossed her hands over her stomach as if her soul was imploding and leaving behind a big empty space. She cried, but she did not touch Gonzalo. The decision was now his to make.

After a few minutes, he managed to get up enough courage to look at her, his heart breaking into a thousand pieces and those thousand pieces into a thousand more. He spoke but no sound came forth, so he tried clearing his throat that was as dry as sandpaper. He had to force himself to talk. Finally, he managed to speak. "I understand and I still love you. I will also be with you for as long as it is possible or as long as you want me."

The tears rolled down her face and she leaned over and kissed him softly on the lips. "You are my first and my only true love, Gonzalo Rodriguez Gacha, as God is my witness."

Key West became a place of this world and not of this world. It was time out of mind. It was an island of love that existed only for them. Every nuance, every gesture they made became engraved into their minds. Laying down on the white sandy beach became a way of sharing the sun that only shone for them.

At the end of the afternoon they would walk out towards the point and watch the sun tint the sea red as it fell below the horizon. Then together they would walk around Key West, holding hands as they carried a bottle of wine with them. They would stop to have seafood at some outdoor restaurant and nibble on each other's food and, when finished, walk back to the cabana they had rented alongside the beach. The first night they had made love inside the cabana, but the following days they carried the mattress out onto the beach and made love under the glow of the moon.

With the wine, the rolling surf, the glow of the moon and Gonzalo pleasing her, she never would have thought that such pleasure existed. They lived on three to four hours of sleep a day because the nights were spent making love. Seven days and eight nights they had been together, loving, needing and wanting each other. Time had become irrelevant, day and night were simply changes of color against the sky.

"Gonzalo?" Ana-Alicia said as her head rested on his chest. Tonight they had made love in the cabana, because the rain had begun to fall shortly after sunset. Now, one hour before sunrise there was still a driving rain outside and thunder echoing off in the gulf, flashes of lightning acting like God's own strobe light over Key West.

Gacha was about to answer, he had simply been taking in her voice and rhythmic breathing like an enjoyable wine. Smiling, he was about to say "Yes," when he felt the moist drop fall on his chest. Suddenly the world closed in on him. She was leaving, he knew. Why hadn't he thought of that before? He should have known it would come to this. He panicked, wanting to find a solution to a problem that had no solution, not in his life anyway, he thought sadly. Thunder seemed to explode above the cabana and roll out to sea, and when it passed he said, "I know." He wrapped his arms around her, feeling the soft body tremors of her silent wail.

As the night turned from black to violet and the cool light from the last windshaken star faded from the sky, Ana-Alicia spoke. "Do you remember you told me you loved me, *querido*? Will you stop once I'm gone?"

"No," Gacha said, his voice hoarse. I know that I will never be able to marry you, but I can live on these last seven days forever."

"I love you so much, Gonzalo, that just saying your name makes me feel alive. Our lives are going to change, you will be what you will be and I will be condemned to a life and a man I don't want. How am I to live like this?"

"I don't know," Gacha said. "Perhaps God is trying to punish us by breaking us apart."

Ana-Alicia let out a soft cry. "You know, we think that we all control our lives but we really don't. Our lives have already been preordained by some greater power, the loadstone of chance... God! I wish I could change it!"

"You can't, it's the random fall of the dice that roll from the hands of the gods."

Gacha stood in the terminal at Miami International Airport waving at Ana-Alicia, his eyes full of tears as she waved one last time before she entered the jetway to board her flight. He stood transfixed, watching the jet roll down the runway and take flight as the wings caught the last rays of a blood-red sun. He knew he would see her again, maybe even make love to her several more times, but never again would they have what they had shared together in Key West. She was planning to attend Wellesley University in Massachusetts, then go back home to Bogota and enjoy a year or two of being an adult single woman. And then... then the stake would be driven through his heart, the day she married the "right and respected" man.

As the jetliner disappeared into a bank of clouds, Gacha dried the tears from his eyes. He had nothing left, his wealth meant nothing to him, because no matter how much money he had, it would never be enough to get Ana-Alicia to marry him. He was alone now, really alone. So, he squared his shoulders, straightened out his tie and now realized that the whole wide world was left open for him to take, because he had nothing left to lose. If he lost it all, he would be no worse off than when he had started, broke, alone and starving to death.

_____*Peter A. Neissa*_____

PART TWO

RIDING THE TIGER

(1972-1975)

He who rides a tiger is afraid to dismount.
--William Scarborough,
Chinese Proverbs, No. 2082

_____*Peter A. Neissa*_____

CHAPTER THIRTEEN

The moment Gonzalo Rodriguez Gacha walked into his downtown office in Bogota, he reached for the telephone and made flight reservations for Santiago, Chile. For the return flight however, he asked the travel agent for a two-day layover in both Bolivia and Peru.

As he hung up the telephone, Chulo walked into his office with a big wide grin. "*Jefe*, how are you? You look great, all well and tanned. Harry Fosse okay?"

"How are you, José? Yes, Harry is fine and things are going well for him. How are things here?" Gacha asked as he shook Chulo's hand.

"Things here went as smooth as silk," Chulo said, noticing the look of melancholy on Gacha. "So, how did you like America? Is it the way they say it is?"

"It's nice, but people are really messed up, you know, like they don't know what to do anymore. They've lost perspective. I think Vietnam has them all messed up." Gacha shook his head and added, "I saw some stuff on television on Vietnam, it's a big mess. They can't win and I think they know it. The whole thing worries me, Fosse thinks he might be getting drafted. When I left Miami, I saw this plane with its rear end open like a truck, you know? They were taking silver coffins out of it. I never saw anything like it, the whole plane was full of coffins from Vietnam."

"And is there no end in sight?" Chulo asked.

"Big talk but no action. They are still killing and dying by the hundreds every day. Forget about it, tell me what is going on?"

Chulo sat down on leather chair and rubbed his chin with his fingers. "Well, the M-19 is on the warpath again. They kidnapped some minister's son or something. They asked for ransom but the family called the police instead. The next day a car rolled up to the minister's house and dumped the dead minister's son on the front lawn."

"So, the M-19 have people in the police now. We better watch what we say to the cops from now on. What else?" Gacha asked, looking at the stack of mail on his desk.

There was a big deal visit from an American two days after you left. His name was John Morgan," Chulo had to get a piece of paper out of his coat and read what he had written down. "From the U.S. Narcotics and Dangerous Drugs Bureau."

"What did he want?" Gacha asked, his eyes glinting like stainless steel.

"The marijuana. Wanted Colombia to do more about stopping it. Most of the politicians that met with him gave him assurances that they would the moment the United States would allow more Colombian products to be sold on their market." Chulo laughed. "From what I hear, *jefe*, Morgan almost had a fit."

"That should teach the self-righteous American. Those Americans just don't get it, do they? They think they can come down and tell us what to do," Gacha said it as if he were tired of explaining an old problem.

"I know, but there were a few people who agreed with Morgan."

"Oh?" Gacha looked up from his mail.

"Fuentes, as I knew he would, but there was someone else I never heard of." Chulo looked back down at the piece of paper he held in his hand and read out the name. "Álvaro Para Reyes."

"Yes, an assistant in the Minister of Justice's office," said Gacha shaking his head. "He's trouble, maybe not now but down the road he's going to give us a lot of trouble, take my word for it. We better start working on the Minister of Justice's office. What else?"

"Mario's graduation is in four weeks, *jefe*. Are we going to throw a party?"

"Yes."

170

"By the way, he got his letter of acceptance into Harvard. I wanted to take him out to celebrate but he had already promised Margarita to take her out."

"You know, Mario doesn't have to take her out. I'll tell him later on that his obligation to Margarita is over. I'll let him know before I leave in any event."

"Leave?" Chulo asked surprised.

"Yes, we are going to expand into the cocaine market. The problem is that the Chileans own the market. Some people in Medellin and Cali are beginning to get into it as well."

"But there is no profit in *bazuco*," Chulo said.

"*Bazuco?*" Gacha asked.

"Yes, what the Indians roll up and smoke. They dry their own coca leaf and then refine it into paste, some snort it, some smoke it."

Gacha suddenly became very excited. "Are you saying that the Indians know how to refine it?"

"Of course, it's pretty simple. I think anyone can do it. If you want I'll set up a demonstration for when you get back."

"Yes, yes!" Gacha said, getting up from his chair looking at his watch. "Can you give me a ride to the airport?"

"Sure, *jefe*, but there is one more thing. Ernesto Bosco is out of jail."

"What?"

"He was released last week, but he's not in Bogota, he's gone to Cali. He knows he'd be done here," Chulo said softly. "I went looking for him to do it myself, but that is when I found out he'd gone to Cali."

"Cali, uh?" Gacha asked, his face relaxing. "Well, at least he's out of our hair. Come on, my flight leaves in an hour. Where's Mario?" Chulo shook his head. "I guess I'll talk to him when I get back."

Alberto Saavedra was a fat bellied man with a ruddy complexion that spoke of long bouts with alcohol. Saavedra lived on the outskirts of Santiago, Chile. He was a prominent man and was in with the government. He was also a man who controlled almost ninety percent of the world's coca crops.

At first, Saavedra did not want to make another deal with another Colombian. He already had people in Medellin and Cali doing distribution for him. Minor, of course, but he didn't feel like expanding either. He had all the money he needed. Well, almost.

Gacha was convinced that Saavedra did not know that the Colombians who distributed his dried coca leaves to American pharmaceutical companies were also skimming some of the dried coca leafs. Those Colombians from Cali were also turning those skimmed leaves into coca paste and finally into cocaine powder. Gacha managed, however, to convince Saavedra to let him handle one hundred kilos of dried coca leaves for each crop that was harvested, three times a year. If Fosse were accurate, Gacha thought, he would yield about forty kilos of coca paste with each crop or one hundred kilos a year. A conservative guess of what he could make on the one hundred kilos was three million seven-hundred thousand dollars!

Saavedra believed Gacha was going to make money by buying from him and reselling it for a higher price to the American pharmaceutical companies. It was hustling business, squeezing every possible dollar out of a product that didn't have much of a future. Gacha, Saavedra thought, was just another two-bit businessman from Colombia.

In Bolivia, Gacha toured the Saavedra plantations and found them all strangely the same. The bushes were grown on terraced plots that were from one to two acres in size. They were also high up on the eastern slope of the Andes mountain range. To the east he could see the luscious fluorescent green of the Amazon rain forest, to the north all he saw was the snow-capped peaks of Bolivia and Peru.

Gacha talked to a few Indians who he knew were direct descendants of the Incas. Their annual income was less than fifty dollars a year and were fated to live and die in these wild unspoiled highlands. Many of these Indians had migrated to the capital cities, but only one in a hundred thousand truly ever found wealth. Their lives had already been preordained, hadn't Ana-Alicia said that, he asked himself. Why had he thought of it? Was she okay? Did she still think of him? Gacha shook his head to free himself of the pattern of thought he was falling into. He'd also decided that he didn't need to go to Peru, he'd seen enough and wanted to get back to Bogota, to get back into the swing of things. Business, that's what his life was.

Mario García picked up Gonzalo Rodriguez Gacha at the airport. It was nearly midnight when Gacha arrived and since Mario had a class at eight in the morning the next day, Gacha knew something was wrong. He knew that Mario would never go against him, but deep within Mario, he knew, there was a war going on. That war had to do with whether Mario liked or disliked Gacha. He had seen it in Mario's movements, in the cold half-hearted way that Mario introduced him to his friends at the university. It was a mystery to Gacha why Mario kept hanging around him when he was ashamed of it.

On the ride to Gacha's apartment in Chico, Mario spoke up. "We got financial problems, *jefe*."

The statement almost took the wind out of Gacha. "How bad?"

Mario chuckled and said, "We are making too much money." Gacha laughed but Mario suddenly became serious. "It's a problem, *jefe*."

"How can too much money be a problem?" Gacha asked lightly.

"We need places to put it."

"Put it in the bank," Gacha said, not understanding in the least what was the big problem.

"Yes, but we can only put so much in without attracting attention from the government. The government is going to want to put a tax on our money and once they realize it was made illegally, they can confiscate it."

"So, spread it out all over. Put it in a hundred different banks," Gacha said.

"We already have, I deposit one more dollar into a bank and someone is bound to tell a tax collector."

Gacha looked out the window of his Mercedes as Mario drove around *La Plaza de los Héroes*. "So let's store it."

"Can't," said Mario looking over at Gacha for a moment. "We already have one of the offices full of cash. Every two weeks we are getting a dozen suitcases filled with American dollars. In a few months we will have to rent a warehouse."

"So, what do we do?" Gacha asked.

"We have to make the money look legal," said Mario as he turned onto *carrera* fifteen. "We have to somehow wash it through some financial arrangement so it becomes legal money."

"Money is money, I don't understand?" Gacha said, frustration setting in.

"No, big money can be legal and illegal. We have illegal money. What we have to do is to give the appearance that it is legal. Once we have done that, we can move it into the big banking markets and move it around with the billions of dollars that go from bank to bank. We need an attorney, someone who knows how to set up corporations and knows his way around international banking laws."

"There are hundreds of unemployed attorneys in Bogota, pick one!" Gacha said angrily.

"No, the attorney is going to have to be an American," Mario said unequivocally.

"Why?"

"Because to clean the money, we will have to do it by working it into the global money movements, where regulators have no chance of spotting it. Once in the global movement we can use it without fear of someone saying it's illegal money." Mario looked over at Gacha's contorted face. "I know it sounds confusing but actually it is very simple. A corporate financial attorney could explain it to you quite easily. Meanwhile, we can wash this money by buying assets here in Colombia. Houses, cars, paintings, stuff like that."

Gacha nodded. "Okay, start buying up cars, houses, farms, whatever you want. By the way, we need a plane." Mario pulled up beside Gacha's apartment. "Listen Mario," Gacha said. "I wanted to tell you that you don't have to take Margarita out any longer. You have no obligation to her or to me."

Mario felt his world caving in, he couldn't allow Gacha to have Margarita again. Why would he want Margarita again? Why would he need Margarita when he had Ana-Alicia Gonzáles? Did he love Ana-Alicia? If Ana-Alicia and Gacha were in love, oh God, it could only mean a tragedy in the making. They were playing with fire.

"*Jefe*, Margarita is no problem, I find that taking her out clears my mind from financial work. By the way, before I forget, Chulo told me to tell you that Ana-Alicia called this morning."

"She did! What did she want? Where was she?"

"Boston. Said if you could call her, left her number with the secretary. It's at the office. You want to stop by the office and pick it up?"

Gacha's soul leapt as if on wings, but he was aware of Mario's intent gaze. He knew Mario was wondering what Ana-Alicia was all about. It took all his willpower just to say, "No, it's okay. I'll look at it tomorrow. I need some sleep first." Gacha stepped out of the car.

Had Ana-Alicia changed her mind, Gacha thought. She was still thinking of him! God, do I love her.

Mario honked the horn and drove away.

Gonzalo Rodriguez Gacha woke up feeling old, maybe it was the jet lag, he told himself. How old was he anyway? Twenty? Twenty-one? If he was born in 1951, he thought, that made him twenty-one. When did he get so old? Suddenly, he remembered that he had to call Ana-Alicia and he leapt out of his bed and into the shower.

Within twenty minutes, Gacha was ready and waiting for Chulo to pick him up. When he heard Chulo lean on the horn he practically sprinted to the car. Even Chulo looked on in surprise.

Stupid, stupid, stupid! Gacha said to himself. He didn't want anyone to think that he was head over heels for Ana-Alicia. They'd see his weakness.

"Is something wrong, *jefe*?" Chulo asked as Gacha stepped into the car.

"No, nothing's wrong. Any news?" Gacha asked, as he looked out of the window.

"They kidnapped another oligarch's son," Chulo said.

"I didn't hear anything on the radio, are you sure?"

"Yeah," said Chulo as he turned onto *carrera* fifteen. "They paid Quintero to take the money to them. He called me last night to tell me. He's on the payroll, by the way. I know we can't afford more people on the payroll, but Quintero has many connections."

"How much did the oligarch family pay?"

"A little under fifty thousand dollars," said Chulo, stepping on the gas pedal.

"How long did they have the hostage for, the M-19, I assume?"

"Six hours. They cut off the little finger as proof. The kid was only fourteen."

"I think," Gacha said, "the kidnapping business is going to boom."

Chulo laughed. "Yeah, it looks that way. I have a demonstration of refining cocaine set up. Do you want to see it?"

Gacha thought it would be a good idea to pretend he wasn't in a hurry to go to the office and make a call, so he agreed to see the cocaine set-up. Why was it every time he wanted to do something for himself he had to clear the way? God, he wanted to hear Ana-Alicia's voice more than anything in the world. Images flowed across his mind's eye. He could see her lying naked on the bed, the soft gentle swell of her breasts, the long shapely legs walking along the sand of Key West, her long tiger-eye looking hair blowing in the wind, the soft

176

innocent look that was devastatingly sensual, her generous mouth...

"*Jefe, jefe, jefe,* are you all right?" Chulo asked with alarm in his voice.

"What?" Gacha asked as if he'd just been jolted out of a happy dream.

"Are you okay?" Chulo asked. "We've been parked here for a few minutes."

"Yes, jet-lag, that's what it is," Gacha said, cursing himself inwardly.

"Well, we're here," said Chulo. "Come out and I'll show you how the coca leaf is turned into powder."

Chulo and Gacha got out of Chulo's small car and walked up to a front door. It was a small two-story brick house with a small front yard. The house was in a semi-respectable neighborhood, but it certainly wasn't anywhere near the well-to-do. It was in one of the neighborhoods of the growing but still very small middle class.

A woman of about forty-five years of age opened the front door. Chulo and Gacha walked where they were led, to an outside patio. In the patio there were two *gamines*, whom neither Chulo or Gacha recognized.

The woman spoke first. "Do you want me to explain?" Chulo nodded.

The woman cleared her throat and began. "The dried leaves are treated with an alkaline solution, in our case lime. This is done because the coca leaf has fourteen alkaloids..."

"Alkaloids?" Gacha asked, looking at the small bucket filled with lime.

"Bitter organic bases found in plants. The coca leaf has fourteen alkaloids of which only one has cocaine. The leaves are soaked in this oil drum which is filled with kerosene, which extracts the alkaloids from the leaves. The leaves are then removed and thrown away when the alkaloids have mixed in with the kerosene. Sulfuric acid is added into the new kerosene mix. This makes the alkaloids in the kerosene barrel turn into a collection of small rock salts. One of those alkaloids that turns into a rock is cocaine sulfate. The kerosene is removed or strained out and then an alkaline solution is added to neutralize the sulfuric acid. What is left is a paste at the bottom of the barrel.

"To refine the paste you put it through another round of kerosene, causing the alkaloid crystals to settle at the bottom of the barrel. The ones on the top layer are fifty percent pure cocaine. The crystals are washed out in alcohol and the alcohol is strained out through a filter. The crystals are dried and then dissolved again into sulfuric acid which mixes once again with the alkaloids. Then you add potassium permanganate, which destroys all the alkaloids except for the cocaine alkaloids. Everything but the cocaine alkaloid is filtered out. You add ammonium hydroxide which is eventually filtered out and what is left is a cocaine base.

"The cocaine base is then dissolved in ether and hydrochloric acid is added with acetone which is then filtered. What remains is cocaine hydrochloride. Cocaine hydrochloride is the fine white powder that people put up their noses." The woman finished the explanation and looked at Gacha.

Gacha looked at all the vats and made a schematic diagram in his brain so that he would not forget it. The procedure was relatively simple, all needed were the right mixes. "How can we set it up for large quantities?" Gacha asked the woman directly.

"Instead of vats we use oil barrels and the right chemicals. The problem is that some of those chemicals we cannot get in Colombia. One of those chemicals is ether."

"How much ether is needed?"

"Seventeen liters of ether are needed to make one kilo of cocaine," said the woman.

"If you had to rig one of these things to produce cocaine in large quantities, where would you do it?"

"As close to the coca fields as possible. We could set up a fairly large laboratory in the south of Colombia. It would also be practical because no one would be able to see it in the jungle. The provinces of Putumayo and Amazonas in the rain

178

forest are perfect."

Gacha thought for a moment. He looked at the woman as if he were looking for flaws. She lowered her gaze to the floor when she realized what he was doing.

"Can you set up...what do you call this?" Gacha asked, pointing at all the vats and straining devices.

"A laboratory," the woman said with humor in her voice.

"Can you set up one of these laboratories and get the product to places where Chulo tells you to?"

"Yes!" said the woman excitedly. "I'll make sure nothing goes wrong."

"How much for your services?" Gacha asked coldly.

"Six percent for each kilo sold at street value."

"A half of one percent," Gacha countered. The woman's outburst had given her away. She wanted to deal no matter what.

"Two percent. I have children."

"One percent," Gacha said with finality.

The woman nodded. "When will the first shipment of coca leaves be ready?"

"Next week," said Gacha.

"Good," said the woman. "It will give me time to set up."

Gacha nodded and walked towards the front door with Chulo behind him. He shook hands with the woman and walked out the door and into Chulo's Renault Four. As they drove away, it began to rain.

The rain reminded Gacha of the rainstorm during his last night with Ana-Alicia. He remembered her soft smooth body against his and their legs intertwined around each other's and how wonderful it had felt. The feeling was still so vivid he could feel his stomach going hollow. Was she doing well without him? Did she want him? Had she changed her mind and decided to marry him? Damn! Why couldn't he stop thinking of her?

_____*Peter A. Neissa*_____

CHAPTER FOURTEEN

For the fourth time in the last hour, the telephone operator told Gonzalo Rodriguez Gacha that she still hadn't been able to get a line through to the United States. However, she told him that she would ring him the moment she got through.

Gacha paced his office like a cornered animal and every time he sat down to look at the sheets of paper on his desk, he would suddenly crumple them up and throw them into the waist bin.

The phone rang.

Gacha practically dove for the phone before it had a chance to complete its ring. "Ana-Alicia..."

"Mr. Gacha, this is Jim Harrison," said the CIA station chief in Bogota.

"Oh," said Gonzalo, his voice trailing off in disappointment.

"Sorry, I know I don't generate the same interest that you have for Ana-Alicia, whoever she is. Oh Lord, she's not the Gonzáles daughter, is she?"

"What do you want, Harrison?" Gacha asked angrily.

"I was wondering if I could speak to you for a moment sometime before this day is out."

"Yes, meet me in *El Lago*. You know the restaurant-bar there?"

"Yes, the one with the small restaurant out back?"

"That's the one," said Gacha. "How about four o'clock this afternoon?"

"Fine, I'll be there," said Harrison.

Gacha didn't say good-bye, he simply hung up. What would Harrison want this time?

The phone rang.

This time Gacha picked it up slowly and answered in a casual manner. "Hello?" he said.

"Gonzalo!" Ana-Alicia's voice came in garbled with static.

"Is everything okay, are you all right?" Gacha asked, concern and panic in his voice.

" Y e s . . . n o t   c o m i n g . . . t r y i n g to...complete...studies...early...staying through...Christmas."

"What?" Gonzalo asked. "I cannot hear you that well."

The line was bad. All he managed to hear was a garbled sentence. "Not...home...Christmas...see me?"

"Why aren't you coming home until Christmas?" Gacha asked desperately, his voice shouting through the telephone mouthpiece.

"I..." The telephone line went dead.

"Hello?" Gacha shouted, but then the signal tone came on. "Damn!" he said and ripped the phone line out of its wall plug and then smashed the phone against the wall.

Gacha walked out of the office with Chulo and the secretary looking at him in shock. They had never heard the *jefe* lose his temper or shout so loudly.

"I'm going to get a drink," was all Gacha offered as an explanation.

"I'll come with you," said Chulo.

"No! I want to be alone."

Chulo stopped in mid-stride and looked at the secretary who was just as perplexed.

Gacha stormed out of the office building and walked ten blocks to his old hangout, the cafeteria for El Centro. On the walk there he thought of what Ana-Alicia had said. Why wasn't she coming home until Christmas? What was the difference? They didn't have a future together. Damn it all! He still wanted her. Could he really see someone else walk down the aisle with her and not have that man killed? What choice would he have, Ana-Alicia would know he'd done it.

When he walked into the cafeteria the woman who had served him breakfast before he had become King of Bogota, greeted him with a kiss on the cheek.

"Gachito, what a pleasure!" the woman said, clapping her hands in joy.

"Hi Rosa, how's business?" Gacha asked smiling.

"Much better, now that you walked in."

Gacha looked around the cafeteria, sitting down by the same old men who had once smirked at him when he was almost down and out. Now, they looked at him with hatred and envy. They envied him because he had done what he had set out to do. He had done the impossible; he had broken out of poverty and sky-rocketed to wealth.

"What can I get you, Gachito?" Rosa asked.

"*Pericos y café con leche.*" Scrambled eggs and coffee with milk. "How's business, really?" Gacha asked.

"Not too good," said Rosa, as she poured him a cup of coffee. "I can't compete with the cafeteria across the street. It's new and most of the working businessmen go there for lunch. I'm just getting obreros , not that I mind, but when the *obreros* go to work in another part of town I shall go bankrupt."

"I'm sorry, Rosa," said Gacha, meaning it.

"It's not your fault, you are my most loyal customer. In fact you brought me business."

"You want me to send business your way?" Gacha asked. "I could give you some money to modernize if you want."

The woman looked at Gacha carefully, but shook her head. "I'm trying to sell this place. I want to go live out the rest of my life in the warm climates. I had an offer from a big corporation to buy the place. They want to demolish the restaurant so they can put up another skyscraper. Hell, I don't know why anyone would want to put up another skyscraper, there is no room left up there. There are two, sometimes three skyscrapers to every city block, have you noticed?"

Gacha suddenly began to look the place over. Had not Mario said to change money into assets? Could a restaurant be an asset, especially if he modernized it, maybe even made it part of a chain?

"Listen, Rosa, don't sell the place until I talk it over

with Mario. I'm interested. Just don't sell it until you've talked it over with me. Agreed?"

"Agreed, Gachito," Rosa said.

After he ate breakfast, Gacha left Rosa a handsome tip and his office phone number. When he walked out into the crowded street he stopped by the curbside. He deliberated whether he should go back to the office and get some work done or do something totally unrelated to work. He weighed each choice under the glorious Bogota sun in a crisp indigo sky. When had the rain cleared, he asked himself. Chulo and his secretary were probably worried about him, but what the hell, it probably kept them on their toes. He'd give them a call later and tell them things were fine. Suddenly, as if he'd had a brilliant idea, he decided to go visit Margarita and take her out to lunch.

The two men on the motorcycle, two blocks away from the El Centro cafeteria, watched Gacha emerge from the restaurant. The men on the motorcycle then put on their helmets and slowly pulled out onto the street where they began to gather speed.

It was almost too good to believe, thought the man sitting behind the motorcycle driver. Gacha had positioned himself right beside the street curb. The motorcycle increased its speed. The man sitting behind the driver retrieved a small Israeli sub-machine gun from the inside of his leather coat. Forty yards away from Gacha, a young woman on the sidewalk saw the weapon and screamed.

Gacha saw the woman looking at the motorcycle in terror, then he saw the weapon and the little spits of fire emanating from it. He dove to the ground as a bullet caught him on the upper right side of his chest.

From the moment the ice-like stab of the bullet plunged deep into his chest, everything seemed to have slowed down. It was as if he were watching himself in a slow-motion picture reel. He saw the helmeted men riding away, the shooter still with his fingers curled around the trigger of the sub-machine gun, fingers that were tattooed.

Suddenly everything speeded up and then crowds of people formed around him, touching him, speaking, shouting, screaming. What the hell were they saying? Why couldn't he hear them, Gacha asked himself. His mind changed pictures, as if some inner mechanism had decided that what it was watching was not good enough and therefore replaced it with a picture of Ana-Alicia's face, just before it went completely black.

Voices pierced into the void, strange voices, detached voices and then they faded into the nothing. He felt himself falling into oblivion. Was he dying? Was he in purgatory? Was he in hell?

Blackness.

A whimper rose from the depths. He was no longer in the blackness but in a grayness like a great fog bank. Was he awake?

"Gonzalo..." The words floated as if they were traveling a great distance.

Oh God! It's Ana-Alicia. "Where are you?" Gacha screamed into the fog but he heard no sound. He shouted again, but nothing. Suddenly he was overcome with terror. Was he deaf or was he blind? Or both!

"Gonzalo..." The voice came again like an echo.

The gray turned into a duller gray until it faded completely into black.

CHAPTER FIFTEEN

It was the cold that stirred him awake and then the smell, the smell of disinfectant. He tried to move, but pain rifled through him like an electric current. Light parted the darkness, shadows formed into shapes and sounds took on substance.

Gonzalo Rodriguez Gacha awoke at the Samaritana Hospital in Bogota.

Sleeping in a corner chair was Chulo, his hair rumpled and his face unshaven. In another corner chair Margarita was sleeping, too. Gacha looked at her serene face, the ugly scar slashing across it. She was still pretty, wasn't she? He couldn't say. He felt something for her but not love. Where was Ana-Alicia? Had he dreamed her voice? Probably.

"Chulo," Gacha said, but it came out as a whisper, his throat and mouth tasting brackish and foul. He looked beside his bed and found a glass of water which he drained quickly.

"Chulo," Gacha said again, this time the voice broke in mid-word but Chulo sat bolt upright.

"*jefe!*" Chulo said and crossed himself religiously.

Margarita stirred awake and suddenly her mouth fell wide open. "You're awake!" she muttered.

They hugged each other and then did it all over again.

"Where's Mario?" Gacha asked.

"Harvard," said Chulo. "Almost five days now."

"What?" Gacha asked in shock.

"He left last week," Margarita said with sadness.

"Last week... what day is it?"

"May 11, 1972. You've been unconscious for over nine days, the doctors were starting to think you had slipped into a coma. But you are awake now and that is all that matters," said Chulo.

187

The rest of the day and night, the hospital room was visited by friends who wanted to wish Gacha a hearty welcome back. La Mano Negra was first. Jim Harrison was second and was then followed by the Mayor of Bogota, Don Emilio Gonzáles. Every guest Gacha saw was by order of their importance. By the time Gacha had seen the last guest, it was nearly three in the morning and fifty visitors later.

Exhausted, Gacha took a deep breath and released it slowly. He felt good but he could not hide his disappointment that Ana-Alicia had not called. Don Emilio had said that she was still at Wellesley College in Massachusetts and that she would not be returning until Christmas. He had said that she wanted to finish her studies early and was taking on an extra semester during the summer break.

Chulo saw the expression on Gacha's face and knew what it was about. He knew many things now about his _jefe_, like why his temper had flared that fateful day of the shooting. He had found out who he had been with when he was in Florida. Yes, he knew it all. And now he knew what was obvious only to him, that his _jefe_ was in love with Ana-Alicia Gonzáles. How could he blame his _jefe_? She was almost magical. She was beautiful, intelligent, courageous and loved his _jefe_. But didn't they know it could never be? Yes, they knew. It was in their eyes and yet they continued to love each other, coming together like moths to a flame.

"She was here, _jefe_," said Chulo.

Gacha looked at him and knew that Chulo knew about them. "When?" Gacha asked.

"The second day. She found out the day you got shot. She called that same afternoon. I told her what had happened. She asked me if I could buy her a plane ticket from Boston to Bogota, she didn't want her family to know she had flown back to Bogota. The problem was that I had to get her another visa, so I had to ask a favor from Jim Harrison."

"Where did she stay at night?" Gacha asked.

"Right here," Chulo said. "I said she could stay at your apartment or I could get her a room at the Tequendama Hotel.

188

She didn't want either. She only used the apartment to take a shower before she left. I saw her onto the plane. She left you this." Chulo retrieved an envelope from his coat pocket and gave it to Gacha.

Gacha nodded and took the envelope but didn't open it. "Thank you, José. Thank you for everything." Chulo nodded. "Anything on the two hoods that shot me?"

"Nothing," Chulo answered, angered that he hadn't been able to find out who they were. "All I know is that the contract was put out by Ernesto Bosco in Cali."

"Bosco, old Chapinero Bosco," Gacha said with a chuckle. "Should have known he'd try something like this. The two hoods on the motorcycle, the one who carried the gun had tattoos on his fingers. I think they were crosses, but I'm not sure."

"Yeah?" Chulo said with a huge grin. "Shouldn't be too hard to find someone with tattoos on his fingers. What do you want done with them when they are caught?"

"Kill them and send them in a garbage bag to Bosco."

"Sure, *jefe*."

"How's business?" Gacha asked, half interested.

"We've been shipping the marijuana, but we have been waiting for you on the cocaine. I didn't know how to go about it," said Chulo as if accusing himself.

"Good. Tell Fosse and his men that I will meet them in New York one month from today. Let Mario know I'm going to New York, but don't tell him the exact dates. I'll let him know a few days before I leave." Chulo nodded. "Does Ana-Alicia know I've woken up?"

"No," said Chulo. "She calls every morning at seven thirty. She called today but you were not awake."

"Good, I'll give her a call. Chulo, go home and get some sleep."

"Yes, *jefe*. By the way, there are two cops outside this door for security," Chulo said as he walked out of the room.

Gacha looked at Ana-Alicia's envelope. It shook slightly in his hands. He tore the side of the envelope open and retrieved the folded letter.

> *My love:*
>
> *I am with you as I write this letter, in this cold and ugly hospital. But I look at your face and I return to the walks we took together in Key West, to a sandy beach under a moonlit night, and I fall into a deeper love than I have ever known. Now that two years have passed between us and I see you lying here, the night has become a desolate place and the fire of the sun doesn't burn so hot anymore. I love you even though it can never be.*
>
> *I love you even though we are doomed.*
>
> *From my heart's heart, I love you.*
>
> *Ana-Alicia.*

Gonzalo reached for a phone and asked the operator to place a call to Wellesley, Massachusetts. The operator informed him that she would call him back when she had a line through. He put the phone back down and began to think of what to say to Ana-Alicia, figuring he had an hour before the operator got a line through.

The phone rang.

Gacha lifted the phone to his ear and his throat and mouth went dry.

"Hello, hello?" said the desperate voice of Ana-Alicia.

"Ana-Alicia it's me, Gonzalo."

"Gonzalo, really is it you?" Ana-Alicia's voice screamed over the telephone wire.

"Yes, and I love you."

Ana-Alicia cried for minutes, every time she tried to talk she would break out in more sobs. Finally she managed to blurt out, "I'll come see you tomorrow."

"No, I am going to be in New York in a month, do you want to meet me there or in Boston?"

"New York!" she said excitedly. "I love you, Gonzalo."

They talked lovers' talk for an hour, exchanging sweet nothings that meant nothing, but to them it was all there was. They ended the conversation by promising each other to call at least twice a week. Love and crime were back on track.

Jim Harrison walked in the moment a nurse removed a breakfast tray from Gacha's lap. Harrison looked troubled. He didn't appear to have slept well in the last few days.

"You want some coffee?" Gacha asked as Harrison took one of the corner chairs.

"No, thank you," Harrison said, wanting to cut the small talk. He was here to collect his debt, of that Gacha was certain.

"If you have an in with the M-19," said Harrison, "I want you to tell them to cool it down. The kidnappings have the ambassador and every other American resident here in Bogota worried that they might be next. The White House is furious because they've got more problems than they can deal with. They are getting flack that they are not doing anything to protect American citizens over here. Vietnam has become a gangrenous leg and they want to sever it. The problem is they can't do it until they get the mess down here and every where else in the world under control. The Egyptians are threatening the Israelis, the Arab countries are thinking of raising the price of oil and in Chile Allende is raising hell. The White House doesn't want to deal with this Colombian shit called the

M-19, they just want it cleaned up any way, any how."

"I don't think I can help you," said Gacha.

"What do you mean you can't help me? You owe me!" Harrison shouted, getting out of his seat.

"Yes, I am aware of that. The problem is that the M-19 is not apt to listen. You have hit them where it hurts."

"What?" Harrison asked bewildered.

"Some members of the M-19 sell a certain product that your government finds undesirable..."

"Marijuana?" Harrison cut in.

"Yes, and because of the loss of that income they have resorted to kidnapping," Gacha said, amazed at how easily the lies came to him. "It's all very logical. They were making money, the money filled their bellies and they were happy. You cut their money and now they are hungry. And all for what I ask? So some young hippies in America don't smoke marijuana. I mean what is more important to your government Harrison, marijuana or Communism?"

"Who in particular is doing the cutting off in my government?" asked Harrison.

"John Morgan, of the U.S. Narcotics Bureau," Gacha said easily. It was almost inspirational how he was about to neutralize his enemy in the United States.

"Gacha," said Harrison with a hard stare. "You just fix the M-19 and I'll fix Morgan." Harrison said, then turned around and left.

Chulo walked in as Harrison stepped out. "What's eating him?" Chulo said.

"Nothing," Gacha answered. "You arrange things with Fosse?"

"Yes, he said he was glad you were back in the saddle. Mario is also looking forward to your visit."

Gacha nodded and then said, "Chulo, how can I get in contact with the M-19?"

Chulo looked on with surprise. "I don't know exactly. You cannot trust those people. They are *loco*. They say they kill for the freedom of the people, but we all know that's a load of *mierda*.

"I need to get in contact with someone in the M-19 who is high up in the organization, someone with influence."

Chulo let out a soft whistle. "It's going to take time, *jefe*, but it is not a good idea to get involved with them. They will stab you in the back the first chance they get."

"Yes, I know but we are also susceptible to their blackmail. We could be kidnapped, although that is highly unlikely, but they could intercept our coke shipments or burn our marijuana fields."

Chulo nodded. "Yes, I never thought of that. If they did, they could ruin us."

"Yes, so we might as well know who our enemies are and take them out first."

Two days before Gacha was to leave for New York, he met with one of the leaders of the M-19 known only as *El Fantasma*.

Fantasma had earned his reputation for his ability to walk into military compounds near the Magdalena River and steal heavy supplies of weapons without being seen. After he had done this several times, the soldiers thought the burglar had to be a ghost.

The moment *Fantasma* took a seat opposite Gacha in a small pueblo north of Bogota called Zipaquira, he knew *El Fantasma* was dangerous.

El Fantasma was an intelligent man. He had come to the meeting wearing a *balaclava* helmet, so no one could recognize his face.

"I hear you wanted to see me," said *El Fantasma* with laughter in his words.

They were in a small empty restaurant, a site that had been pre-arranged by Chulo.

"I want you to stop the kidnappings," said Gacha, watching the dark brown eyes inside the helmet go hard. "How much do you make from the kidnappings?" Gacha asked, wanting to keep the man off balance.

"In a good ear?" *El Fantasma* asked, unsure how to proceed. He had heard about Gacha and his connections to *La Mano Negra*.

"Yes, in a good year."

"Sixty, maybe seventy thousand dollars. I think this year we might make a hundred."

"I will pay your group two hundred thousand dollars a year to stop. No more kidnappings with cut fingers, ears or noses in the mail," Gacha said hard.

"And if we don't?"

"You are out two hundred thousand. However, I could raise it if certain things are agreed to."

"Such as?" *El Fantasma* asked.

"I have certain crops that must not be harmed and certain shipments that must be allowed to continue on their route."

"Ah, Cia. Export, no?"

Gacha's blood ran cold. So, they knew. Good, now he had to play tough. "Yes, can it be done? I am willing to go up another seventy thousand for a total of two hundred and seventy thousand."

"I don't see how the committee would look at a proposal that is less than half a million," *El Fantasma* said smoothly.

"Well, maybe three hundred thousand, but I would also like to see who I am dealing with."

"I'll put it to the committee and let you know."

"I'm leaving for New York the day after tomorrow. I have latitude to go up to two hundred and eighty thousand from certain like minded colleagues, who I'm sure will go up to three hundred thousand. My added deal of seventy thousand is for my 'crop' protection." Gacha had him, he knew. He could see *El Fantasma*'s eyes spinning with delight at all the money being offered to him for doing absolutely nothing.

"As I said, we will contact you before you leave," said *El Fantasma* as he stood up and walked away.

Chulo came out of the back room looking unsurely at Gacha. "*Jefe*, we don't have a half million dollars to throw away just like that."

"We are not going to spend a dime of our money," said Gacha with a smirk on his face. "We'll have the major families of Bogota contribute to the fund. They'll be happy to do it once a year. They'll just see it as a cost of doing business in this great country of ours." Gacha laughed. "Not only that Chulo, but they'll probably write it off on their next tax statement. Who knows, the M-19 might just suck the money out of the government indirectly."

Chulo and Gacha laughed out loud, but Chulo knew better. He believed Gacha had opened up a Pandora's box. Sooner or later, the evils he had unloosed by dealing with the M-19 would come back to haunt him.

Don Emilio Gonzáles had listened to Gacha's proposition in silence. It was not so much that he was shocked by the proposition, but that it had taken so long to arrange. It was so simple! When Gacha had finished speaking, he told him that he would get back to him. He would have to propose it to others, but as for him he was ready to go with the plan.

Don Emilio knew it was a contract that the families would make even if the M-19 did not go through with their end of the deal. If the M-19 didn't hold up their end of the bargain, they could say that they had tried to "negotiate," but that the M-19 wouldn't hear of it. Politically and economically, it was a no-lose proposition. A trust fund could be created and the interest from such a trust fund would pay the yearly payments.

So, it was no surprise when he actually phoned Gacha two hours later and told him that the families had agreed. They had given Gacha a latitude of negotiation of up to one million dollars.

The M-19 had not called by eleven at night, one full day after Gacha and *El Fantasma* had met. Gacha began to worry that maybe *El Fantasma* didn't have quite the control he thought he had. Restless, Gacha picked up the phone and dialed the operator to connect him with Cambridge,

Massachusetts. After several minutes, Gacha reached Mario García.

After the preliminary greetings were exchanged, Gacha got to the point. "Mario, I'm sorry to call you so late, but I wanted to ask you a business question."

"Sure, what is it?" Mario asked, the sound of loneliness in his voice.

"I'm thinking of buying some restaurants, you know as assets?"

"Yes, absolutely! How many?" Mario said excitedly.

"Five, maybe six," said Gacha.

"Yes, remodel them and make their value go up. When you open them up, only have one restaurant that takes credit cards. That way you can pass some of our marijuana money into the bank by saying that it is from the restaurant. Find out what a good restaurant deposits in a bank a day in cash and then you can put a little more than that into the bank."

"Good," said Gacha. "I'll be in New York soon. I'll call you when I'm there. Good-bye Mario."

"Yes, I'm looking forward to your visit. By the way, say hello to Margarita and Chulo, goodbye."

Gacha hung up but he was bothered. Every time he talked to Mario, something said or not said made him uncomfortable and each time he tried to think of what that was it seemed to slip away. It was in Mario's voice, it sounded resentful, no, embarrassed? No, it was something else.

The telephone rang and Gacha picked it up. "Gacha," he said.

"The committee agrees with the proposition," said *El Fantasma*. "There is just one little catch. The deal will not work unless it is four hundred thousand and one hundred thousand for crop protection."

Gacha let a silence fall. If he spoke, he thought, he might laugh. "Well uh, maybe four hundred thousand can be arranged, but it will be coming out of my pocket! So, what I'm saying is don't say something if you are not going to do it."

"Take it or leave it, Gacha," said *El Fantasma*.

"Agreed."

"Good. As a sign of our goodwill we have left a package for you in the lobby. We will be in touch with you when you get back from New York." The line went dead.

Gacha ran down the stairs of the office building to the front lobby. When he reached the lobby he was panting for breath. In the middle of the lobby there was a wooden crate with a guard standing beside it curiously. The crate was sealed with rope. The security guard gave Gacha a knife to cut the rope.

Gacha cut the ropes and the crate fell apart on its own as the smell of death wafted out of it. Inside the crate were the body limbs of at least two people. Arms and legs all thrown into a pile, with dried blood caking on the already putrefying skin. As he turned away, he saw a hand with tattoos on the fingers. The tattoos were little crosses. Suddenly he knew whose body parts they were: the men who had gunned him down in broad daylight.

Peter A. Neissa

CHAPTER SIXTEEN

To Gonzalo Rodriguez Gacha New York was just a bigger Bogota. Avenues, streets and buildings were all numbered like in Bogota. It was easy to find out where you were in relation to the city landscape by the number of the street you happened to be on.

The crowds of people walking in almost an open run reminded Gacha of downtown Bogota during business hours. The only thing he hadn't prepared for was the sweltering humidity of the summer season choking the city.

On Seventh Avenue, Gacha stopped in a small tailor shop and ordered twelve suits. Yes, he told the tailor that he would pay extra for them to be delivered early. The old tailor had almost fainted. On Fifth Avenue, he walked into Bergdorf Goodman and browsed. At Saks Fifth Avenue he bought a dozen shirts and had them delivered to his hotel. In the same block he bought Gucci shoes (five pairs), and even further down the Avenue he bought three Rolex watches and four long winter coats. Then he walked back uptown to Tiffany's.

"May I help you, sir," said a young woman, who Gonzalo guessed to be twenty-five years of age. The woman eyed Gacha suspiciously.

"Yes," said Gacha. "I'm looking for something special," Gacha said, taking in the store at a glance.

"I see," said the young woman. "Anything in particular you have in mind?"

"Diamonds."

The woman nodded and walked behind a glass counter that encased a whole range of diamonds. "This one here is a rather nice diamond, small yes, but it's a half a carat and has a magnificent clarity."

Gacha shook his head. He was not impressed. After having stolen diamonds and jewelry for a living in Bogota, he had become an expert on gemstones. He knew he could hold his own with the best dealers in the world. "No, I want something more, with more *fuerza!*"

"*Fuerza?*" asked the young woman.

"Power, glitter, umph. This is nice, but I wouldn't give it to anyone. I want something in a D-flawless one carat. Excellent clarity, no carbon and no flaws."

The woman's eyes opened and suddenly she began to re-appraise the young man in front of her. Wasn't that a Rolex watch he was wearing? Aren't those Gucci shoes on his feet? "Perhaps you ought to speak with Mr..."

"No," Gacha cut in. He put his hand on her arm lightly. "It's for my girlfriend. You are close to her age, you must know what women of your age like, no?"

The woman smiled at him, aware of his energy. A picture of him in bed with her suddenly flashed in her mind. How old was he? she thought. Thirty? Thirty-two?

"Perhaps Mr..." the woman let her voice trail, a trace of flirtatiousness in it.

"Gacha, Gonzalo Rodriguez Gacha."

"Nice to meet you, Mr. Gacha, my name is Mary Lou. Perhaps you could give me a range of what we are talking about?"

"Ten, maybe fifteen thousand dollars."

The young woman smiled wide and led him off to a special area, where she showed him a collection, Gacha agreed on immediately.

"How would you like to pay for them, sir. Check or charge?"

"Cash," Gacha answered.

The woman's eyes widened in shock, she stared at Gacha until he asked her if anything was wrong. There was nothing wrong, she said. How many times had she seen people come in and buy a half a million dollars worth of diamonds? A thousand times. Yes, but how many times had people come in and purchased something over two thousand dollars in cash? Crazy world, she thought, but she sold him the diamonds anyway.

Gacha thanked the woman and walked out with fifteen thousand dollars worth of diamonds on a mounted piece. Gacha knew that now everything he bought was not just articles and trinkets, but assets. Whether they were assets, he really didn't care. The diamond collection was going to be a gift. Gacha then walked to his hotel, The Plaza facing Central Park.

They met in Gacha's suite. Harry Fosse's distribution network, which had once been comprised of three major players, now included fifteen. Around the suite in carefully placed trays, there was Russian caviar and smoked salmon. On the right side of the front door, there was a trolley stocked with champagne, scotch, whiskey and a full range of liqueurs.

Paul Smith from Los Angeles controlled five other men who distributed the "product." The word product had replaced the word marijuana since Stuart Jacobs had gotten himself arrested. Paranoia about wire taps had changed their attitudes about security and secrecy. Smith's men controlled distribution from San Francisco to San Diego, but Smith controlled Los Angeles alone.

John Martinez was the most conservative of the group. He had two men working distribution for him. One of them controlled San Antonio, while the other controlled Dallas. Martinez controlled Houston by himself.

Ellroy Johnson had the most elaborate distribution network of all. He had eight men directly under him. Five of them controlled the five major boroughs in New York City. Those five controlled five kids each, who eventually sold to even more dealers. The other three men under Ellroy's control distributed the product in Newark, Atlantic City and Trenton, New Jersey.

Ellroy's next expansion would include Philadelphia, Baltimore and Washington, D.C. But first he had to solidify the ties. It meant making sure the people he was going to take under his wing were not the kind to give in when the heat was turned up on them by the police. He also wanted to make sure they were not undercover police officers.

Harry Fosse controlled them all. It was Fosse who decided who got how much, when and where. His people didn't mind. They were all making money faster than they could spend it.

"You know," said Fosse, "I picked up a shipment the other day at New York's shipping port. Do you know what the control manager of the port said to me?" Everyone shook his head. "Hey buddy, get those crates out of here. I don't like having CIA shit on my dock.'"

"CIA?" Gacha asked. "As in Central Intelligence?

"Yes, we mark the crates CIA Export which stands for *Compañía Exportadora*, but they don't know that. They think it's the CIA!" The whole room exploded into laughter, even Gacha had to hold his stomach.

"They think," Fosse said, trying to control his laughter, "I'm with the CIA!" They erupted once again into laughter.

"Hell," said Paul Smith. "I bet the CIA thinks it's theirs, too!"

After they settled down, Gacha spoke business. He steered the conversation from camaraderie to business and the mood swung from joviality to that of sharp-edged business.

"The fact is marijuana makes money, lots of money, but cocaine makes more with less," Fosse said, looking at his men. "There is also competition from other Colombians in the marijuana business and the Mexicans have thrown their hat into the ring too. We have to make our position clear in the cocaine field, right now Medellin and Cali have very strong holds on those markets. Things are also getting tense. We're fighting for distribution in the major American cities and things are getting ugly. What we are inadvertently doing is setting up drug turfs."

"How?" Gacha asked.

"Fort Lauderdale is tighter than a frigid virgin. Medellin has that town sealed up all for themselves.

"So, we got Miami?" Gacha said, not impressed.

"Yes," said Fosse without enthusiasm. "But sooner or later we are going to have to fight for the rest of Florida. The person who controls Florida controls the States. Almost all marijuana and cocaine comes in through Florida. Cali controls Pittsburgh, Chicago and most of Detroit. To overcome these problems we need two things: First, we need to expand and that means more product. Second, we need to be able to make quicker deals and have faster distribution. Hell, that plane we bought is already in need of retirement. We need more planes and more pilots. If we can bring the coke in with small aircraft at night, the better for us. For the grass we need a bigger plane in order to see some real profit. The light planes can't carry much grass but can carry enough coke. I think we could pick up some cheap DC-3 aircraft for less than fifty grand. The problem with the DC-3 is landing areas. If they are coming in below radar, they are not going to be able to land at a regular airport."

"We can get some makeshift runways built," said John Martinez. "There's a lot of places you can carve out a landing area in south Florida. Georgia is not bad either, they have lots of woods and very remote areas that are close enough to major highways."

"Yeah," said Paul Smith. "Why not buy some land in the middle of nowhere and have a plane land on it. No one will ever come around asking what the hell a plane is landing on it for, not if the place is big enough."

"Yes," said Fosse. "They are all good ideas, but we cannot put them to work unless we have the money and we can't get the money unless we sell more coke. In a nutshell, Gacha, we need all the coke you can send. One hundred keys every four months will not do, not if we want to stay ahead of Medellin and Cali."

Gacha nodded, and thought where the hell he was going to get more coca leaves? "What else?" Gacha asked.

"Money dude," Ellroy snapped. "I got too much of it." The whole room laughed except Ellroy. "I have a bedroom

203

stacked from floor to ceiling with dollar bills. I'm sending two
people a week to Bogota with suitcases full of bills, and I can't
keep up. I cannot put it into the banks because the IRS will
ask questions."

"I'll be taking care of that problem within the next few
days," said Gacha." What else?"

"Heat," said Paul Smith. "They're sticking their noses
where it don't belong. It's costing me about ten grand a
month."

"Cost of doing business," Gacha said.

"Maybe," Fosse said with doubt. "This John Morgan has
a crack group. I lost one of my distributors last week, got three
hard."

"Three hard?" asked Gacha.

"Three years hard time, jail. He didn't snitch, I told
him I'd take care of him when he got out. He was one of the
men who showed me how to get the product in, in big bulk."

"Oh?" Gacha said intrigued.

"Boat. We have a fishing trawler stacked with ten,
fifteen tons and then have small recreational boats meet it
beyond the twelve mile limit. Fast boats can cost four to five
thousand each. With one bale of grass they're paid for. I've
bought seven of them. Within a few years, I figure the
technology on these boats will make them faster than any
government boat, maybe even a helicopter. The problem is I
need some reliable people to sail them."

Gacha smiled. "I'll have Chulo send some Colombians
up here to Florida to sail the boats. About the police, from now
on we keep records with the ones we deal. Those who will not
come to our side, we keep records on them too. Find out where
they live, whether they are married, single, everything. I think
it's time we start looking at making some friends with
politicians, see if we can compromise a few and then tighten
the screws on them. Our very first priority is to get someone
inside the Narcotics Bureau."

"Fine," said Fosse, "I'll work on it tomorrow morning.
"There's one last thing, it concerns a rumor I've heard. I have

been hearing that Medellin has bought a big chunk of real estate..."

"Yeah," said Ellroy Johnson cutting in. "I hear that too. I heard it was in the negotiating end, I didn't know it went down. If Medellin really has that area locked up, we can kiss Florida good-bye."

"What real estate?" Gacha asked.

"The rumor has it that they bought a chunk of real estate in Norman's Cay in the Bahamas. The deal is they can sail in or fly in with no questions asked. Man, you can swim to the States from Norman's Cay."

The news unsettled Gacha. "I'll look into it tonight. This meeting is concluded. Gentlemen, I have a previous engagement but you can stay here as long as you like," Gacha said, shaking everyone's hand. He left the room immediately after Fosse.

As they reached the lobby of The Plaza Hotel, Gacha turned to Fosse. "Harry, you remember that blonde girl in Ft. Lauderdale a few months back?"

Fosse thought for a moment. "The blonde girl who called you a spic? Yeah, sure I remember her. Sin city, right?"

"Can you put me in touch with her father, the one who got fired from that law firm in Florida?"

"Might be difficult. Last time I talked to Sin, she said her parents had split and her father had packed up and left."

Gacha put his arm around Fosse and said, "See what you can do, Harry. By the way, where the hell is Norman's Cay exactly?"

"A few minutes off of the Florida coast."

"Damn! Where can I reach you later?"

"I'm at the Lennox," said Fosse.

"Good," Gacha said as they walked out onto the street curb and hailed a taxi.

Gonzalo Rodriguez Gacha caught sight of Ana-Alicia as she deplaned and walked into the terminal at La Guardia Airport. She had not spotted him yet, so he was able to see the men around her take two and three glances as she walked on by. If she knew they were looking at her she never showed it. In truth, she simply acted ignorant of the fact that she was beautiful. Even when she toned down the way she dressed, she still looked sultry.

Ana-Alicia suddenly locked eyes with Gacha and broke into a wide smile, a smile that was to Gacha as powerful as a lighthouse for a sailor lost at sea. Gacha's world narrowed like a tunnel causing the rest of life to be blotted out. Ana-Alicia broke into an open run and crashed into Gacha's arms causing Gacha to think that it was just like in the movies. They kissed passionately on the lips, aware that people were looking at them.

From the airport they returned briefly to The Plaza Hotel and dropped off Ana-Alicia's luggage. Then they walked over to Seventh Avenue and down 57th, until they reached Fifth Avenue, where they hailed a cab and went to Greenwich Village. From Christopher Street in the Village, they walked past the hippies selling tye-dyed T-shirts and sunflowers into a small cafe. They laughed at each other's anecdotes and both secretly wondered if life could be this good. After they finished their coffee they walked out of the coffee shop and hailed another cab and went to Broadway.

No matter where they went music assaulted them, sometimes when they both knew the words to the song, they sang together. In Times Square, they sang: 'We are stardust, we are golden and we've got to get ourselves back to the garden.' In Soho they sang: 'Freedom's just another word for nothing left to lose, and nothin' ain't worth nothin' but it's free.' They both knew that they were doing more than just singing, they were verbalizing the feeling of the times.

They had easily walked ten miles by sunset, which came at 8.48 p.m., something which Gacha could not get used to. He had lived in a land where things like sunrise and sunset were constant. Sunrise at 6 a.m., and sunset was always at 6 p.m.

At sunset they returned to The Plaza Hotel, where they

showered, changed and quickly were back out the door to eat dinner. They ate *paella* in a Spanish restaurant on West 52nd. After dinner, they went dancing until two in the morning, when Ana-Alicia gave Gacha a look that said that she too could no longer hold back the sexual energy that needed release.

In the elevator at the Plaza Hotel, Ana-Alicia began unbuttoning Gonzalo's shirt. By the time they made it through their suite's door, she had him half-stripped.

Gonzalo unzipped her strapless gown and let it fall to the floor as he cupped her breasts in his hands. Suddenly he crouched down and picked her up and carried her to the bedroom where he pulled her sheer black panties off. He could see the effect he was having on her as he watched how her wonderful breasts rose and fell with each excited breath.

Ana-Alicia turned him around so that he was on his back and she on top of him. She looked at him deliberately with sin in her eyes, knowing the effect that just such a look of lust had on him.

"*Querido*," Ana-Alicia said. "You must know by now that we are doomed. With that in mind do you still love me?"

"Now, more than ever my love," said Gacha.

"I love you Gonzalo," she said as her hands roamed over his body doing devastating things. Her touch on his skin as light as a baby's touch when grasping objects for the first time.

Gacha felt the world open up and explode with love, and somewhere deep in the recesses of his mind a single thought emerged, should he give the business up? The thought quickly buried itself again but not before a sense of unease flooded him.

They stayed in bed until after sunset the next day when Gacha managed to uncoil himself from Ana-Alicia's wonderful body. He dragged her out of bed and into the shower where they had another passionate session of lovemaking.

They went out to eat at a beautiful candlelit restaurant on the upper East Side of Manhattan, at which time seemed to have stopped for them. They stared into each other's eyes until finally Gacha reached into his pocket and retrieved a small aquamarine package.

"It's for you," Gonzalo said, one of the few words spoken in the entire evening. Words had become superfluous.

Tears welled up in Ana-Alicia's eyes as she reached for the aquamarine box. She knew it was a Tiffany box by the color. As she opened the box and retrieved a jewelry case, a tear rolled down her face. She opened the case. The solid diamond necklace and earrings caught the light of the candle and they gleamed like shooting stars. Slowly she raised her eyes to Gonzalo...

He saw it! Inside his head emotions exploded like thunder. He saw the terrible sadness in her eyes moments before she stood up and bolted for the door.

What happened? Gonzalo asked himself.

A waiter seemed to materialize immediately and asked if anything was wrong. The waiter couldn't keep his eyes off the diamond ensemble.

"I don't know," said Gacha meaning it. "Here, this should cover everything. Keep the change."

The waiter nodded immediately. It was going to be for him a five hundred dollar tip. "I hope the lady feels better," the waiter said lamely.

Gacha nodded, scooped the diamonds off the table and went after Ana-Alicia. Damn! What the hell happened, Gacha thought as he walked out.

Ana-Alicia was just outside the front entrance of the restaurant, sitting on the side of the street curb with her face in her hands. The valets looked on, wondering what was wrong and lusting after the exposed thigh that her short dress revealed.

Gacha walked up behind her and put his hand on her shoulder. Ana-Alicia sprang up off the curb and buried her face in his chest.

"Oh, I'm sorry Gonzalo," Ana-Alicia said. "I'm really sorry. I spoiled the whole evening with that awful scene. I just... I can't bear to love you more when we can never be together. It's tearing me apart, it's killing me!"

Gacha held her close and motioned the valet to flag a taxi.

At the hotel's suite, Ana-Alicia let go with cries. When she finally got herself under control, she spoke calmly, as if tranquilized by medication. "Gonzalo, what is to become of us?"

Gacha could only shake his head because he himself did not know. Together they fell into an embrace and held each other.

"Not being able to see you for another year will seem like an eternity," Ana-Alicia said.

"A year?" Gacha asked in shock.

"I'm trying to finish my studies early, that is why I'm using vacation time for school time. I will only have a week off for Christmas, but my parents and I have been invited to spend it in Monte Carlo."

"You won't be in Colombia until next summer?" Gacha asked, the words coming out of him from a reserve he didn't know existed.

"Yes, and even next summer it will only be for one week," she said stroking his cheek lightly with her fingers. "I really won't be back in Colombia until early 1974."

"I'll work something out," Gacha said. "I'll come visit you even if I have to go all the way to Monte Carlo to see you."

Ana-Alicia looked at Gacha mischievously and then buried him in kisses. "Can I still keep your gift?" she asked lightly between kisses.

Gacha laughed. "Of course, I bought it just for you."

Ana-Alicia stood up from the couch and slowly undressed herself for him. "*Para vuestro cuerpo y ojos solamente, mi amor.*" For thy body and eyes only, my love.

As the jet airplane rumbled off the runway carrying Ana-Alicia back to Boston, the world for Gacha became cold and lonely. What was to become of them? he asked himself, echoing the same question Ana-Alicia had asked the night before. The thought frightened him. He himself had no idea only that he was heading on an apocalyptic course unless he was able to change the rules. The rules. Rich shall not marry poor and the respected families shall not marry into Gacha's kind, no matter how much wealth was involved. It was the way of the oligarchy.

But he would show them, Gacha thought, these lesser men who had less money but also less power. Yes, he would show the oligarchy what real power was. Power to buy and sell anything he wanted, the power that only comes from the American dollar, just like Don Eusebio Corraza had done with emeralds. He would force the oligarchy to deal with him, to give him the most coveted of all things, respect. If he had respect, he could marry into the oligarchy, he could marry into the respected families, he could marry Ana-Alicia. His children could grow up with a respected name and marry with others in the oligarchy who were respected. The only way to do this was to gain power through the money he made and that meant selling cocaine in larger quantities. Respect, Gacha thought, was proportional to the amount of money and power you wielded.

CHAPTER SEVENTEEN

Stephen Goldman was the quintessential Philadelphia lawyer. No matter how bad things got, he still acted as if things were going right according to schedule. It was why no one would have ever guessed that he had been living at the YMCA in Toledo, Ohio, for the last several months.

After having been fired by his old firm, Sheldon & Waterson of West Palm Beach, Florida, at the age of fifty-six, Stephen Goldman might as well have retired. No legal firm would hire someone with only a few years left before retirement. After three weeks of interviewing with legal firms across the country, he came to realize that very somber conclusion.

In the fourth week after having been fired by Sheldon & Waterson, as he came out of the Deputy Minister of Justice's Office for the State of Florida, he was served with divorce papers. A quick divorce left him without a home and without a family. With three thousand dollars left in his bank, Stephen Goldman went on the road looking for a job, any job.

Three and a half months later, as he looked down the one-eyed stare of a Smith & Wesson .38, a man by the name of Harry Fosse telephoned him. That call had led him to New York. He had been put up at the Waldorf, given five thousand dollars for expenses and told that an industrialist by the name of Gonzalo Gacha wanted to have a word with him.

Now, as Goldman waited in the lobby of The Plaza Hotel, he played a game with himself by trying to see if he could tell who the industrialist would be before he made his approach. In any event, he had already made up his mind to do whatever it took to get a job, of that he was certain. As he sat in the lobby, Goldman spotted two of his former clients who looked at him but did not acknowledge his presence. He watched the big players from around the world come and go. Aristotle Onassis, the rich designer Valentino and a whole bevy of beautiful women.

"Mr. Goldman," said a voice from behind Goldman. He turned around to see an extremely well dressed man. Probably the son of the tycoon who wanted to speak to him, he thought.

"Yes, sir. I'm Mr. Goldman." Stephen Goldman rose from his seat and locked eyes with the young man. Suddenly, without warning as he looked into those two eyes he knew he was talking to the industrialist.

"My name is Gonzalo Gacha," Gacha said shaking the man's hand. "Do you mind talking to me over by the bar?"

"Not at all," said Goldman with some amusement in his voice.

Goldman watched the young man walk in front of him. He was without question what people called movie star handsome, but more than that he had presence, which was more than just magnetism and that overused word charisma. The young man walking in front of him, Goldman thought, was a *tour de force*.

At a small table by the corner of the bar, they ordered two scotches. They did not speak but rather appraised each other at first. Once the waitress brought over their drinks they spoke.

"Are you working, Mr. Goldman?" Gacha asked.

"Eh, uh...No, can't seem to get a job anywhere," Goldman said lowering his gaze to his drink.

"Can you still work legally?" Gacha asked looking straight into Goldman's eyes.

"You mean am I still a member of the bar?" Gacha looked perplexed. "Licensed to practice, that is what you are asking, is it not?"

"Yes," Gacha said plainly.

Goldman looked at Gacha with embarrassment and anger. "Yes," he finally said through clenched teeth.

Gacha ignored the anger and continued. "I am told that

you are a financial attorney, is this not true?"

"Yes, Mr. Gacha, I am a financial attorney and I don't have to explain myself to you or anyone else, but I'll tell you what you want to know. I was fired from Sheldon & Waterson because I stopped bringing in clients or, in other words, money. I'm fifty seven years old as of two weeks ago and, well, before I was fired I began to wonder why I was not taken on as a partner. Thirty one years of working my ass off for them when I realized they had no intention of giving me a partnership. I wasn't one of them. They knew I drank too much and capitalized on that. Fired me because of my alcohol problem. Never had a single drink while I was on the job. The only reason they got rid of me was because I started to make waves. You see I wasn't one of them."

"Them?" Gacha asked not understanding.

"One of the filthy rich. I was someone who had worked through law school and come from a lower class family. To them, I was an outsider." Gacha chuckled. "You find that funny?" Goldman said, standing up.

"Please, sit down," said Gacha. "I wasn't laughing at you but at the system. I too know what it's like." Goldman sat down tentatively. "Do you know what a *campesino* is Mr. Goldman?"

"A peasant, I think."

"Yes, my parents were peasants. I have made a lot of money, I have made politicians, solved political crises and still I cannot marry the woman I love, because I do not come from the right family."

Goldman nodded and then took a sip from his drink. When he put the glass back down on the table he muttered, "You're the *nouveau riche*."

"The new money?" Gacha asked.

"Yes," said Goldman. "New money doesn't mix with old money or blue blood with new blood. That is how we refer to it stateside. Tell me, the woman you want to marry, does she want to marry you?" Gacha nodded. "If she does, then what's the problem?"

"Disowned, alienated from her family and friends. She would have no friends because those in her family's circle would make her an outcast and treat her like the plague. The rules set up by the circle apply to all of them and there are no deviations from the rules."

Goldman raised his glass in a toast. "To the bastards!" he said and drained the contents of his glass.

Gacha smiled, with that single comment from Goldman, he had decided to hire him. "Mr. Goldman, I need to deposit a large quantity of bills into a bank. My financial advisor tells me that I need a financial attorney. He spoke of getting it into a New York bank and global money movements."

"So, do it," Goldman said.

"I can't, I would have to pay taxes and that would mean a lot of questions which I am not predisposed to answer..." Gacha let his voice trail off, his meaning clear.

Goldman looked at Gacha and said, "I see. The money is gray, I assume?"

"Gray?"

"Illegal?" Goldman asked, his voice a whisper.

Gacha hesitated but answered anyway. "Yes."

"How much?"

"If it remains in its present state without any growth which is unlikely, about eight million dollars."

"Jesus Christ!" Goldman said loudly. He then snapped his fingers at the waitress asking her to bring him another drink. "Eight million dollars a year?"

"Yes," said Gacha.

"What is your projected net for next year, 1973?"

"Fifteen to twenty million."

A silence dropped between them as Goldman looked at Gacha. After several moments Goldman spoke. "I'm an old man Mr. Gacha. I've worked long and hard all of my life and I would like to enjoy what I got left. I wouldn't want to do what you propose forever."

"I understand," said Gacha, nodding his head in agreement. "I have someone who will take over in three years.

He needs two more years of specialized schooling. He's at Harvard Business School. I figure that one year after he graduates and having apprenticed the business with you, you would be free to leave. Retire at fifty-nine or sixty and life will not be so bad until then either."

"And if I do as you say, what shall be my reward," said Goldman with a smile. "I think I am now ready for a numerical figure, if you will."

"One percent of all washed money," Gacha said evenly.

"Four percent."

"Two percent," counter-offered Gacha.

"Three percent with one condition. I want two hundred thousand in a Swiss bank account number of my choosing, so if I find myself in jail I'll have a nice nest egg when I get out. This two hundred thousand you can deduct from any future earnings, call it an advance."

"Agreed," said Gacha, lifting his drink which had gone untouched throughout the whole conversation.

"I'll need another two hundred thousand to set up," said Goldman.

"Agreed."

"Then Mr. Gacha, we're in business."

"Excellent," Gacha said, raising his drink for a toast. "Here's to making millions. *Salud*!" They clinked their glasses together and drained them of their contents.

"Could you give me a brief overview of how you will wash the money?" Gacha asked.

"The legal aspect is quite cumbersome, but in layman's terms, this is how it works. First, we talk to reputable banker like the Deutschen Bavarian Bank in the Cayman Islands. We tell them we want to deposit money into a bank in the States but want to evade taxes. What the banker will suggest is the following: The Munich branch of the Deutschen Bavarian bank will set up a corporation in Luxembourg where we deposit our cash. You would control this Luxembourg corporation through a Cayman Island trust company, but your identity will be protected, kept secret because of the Island's banking secrecy laws. The Cayman Islands branch of the Deutschen Bavarian bank will then lend you your own money.

"Once you have loaned yourself your own money, you can send it by wire transfer to any bank in the world. Preferably to one of the major financial centers in the world, London, Tokyo, or, best of all, New York City. When New York asks you where you got the money, you just show them a paper that says you borrowed it from the Deutschen Bavarian bank, a reputable bank.

"The ultimate goal, Mr. Gacha, is to get the money into the world's global money movements. It is there where one can no longer tell what is legal and what is not legal in terms of money. Once the money has gone through the clearinghouses, you can put it into secret bank accounts all over the world and let it rot there. Of course, by then the money is as legal as the money coming out of the U.S. Treasury."

"What is a clearinghouse?" asked Gacha.

"An average day, Mr. Gacha, for money moving in and out of New York banks is about one hundred and fifty billion dollars. A clearinghouse sorts how much each bank gets, because the numbers are so vast that all the money gets mixed up into this one pile. The clearinghouse merely sorts it, ten billion for the Chase Manhattan bank, twenty billion for the Bank of America and so on. The problem is that no one really knows where the money comes from or where it's going. You keep that money moving and no one on God's green earth will ever find out which millions of dollars in those billions are yours. After it has been back and forth across the ocean a few times, you have more papers saying how legal it is. Banks all over the world will have touched that money and nobody will be able to say how exactly that money got into the banking system in the first place."

"When can you start?" Gacha asked.

"This afternoon?" Goldman said, unsure.

"Good, I'll have half a million dollars in your suite by this afternoon," Gacha said and stood up. "I think it is going to be a pleasure to work with you, Mr. Goldman."

216

"Call me Steve. By the way, how did you select me?"

"I met your daughter the day you were fired. She told me you were a financial attorney. I never forgot. I have another appointment, Mr. Goldman. I'll be in touch." Gacha extended his hand and shook Stephen Goldman's hand. Gacha then nodded and walked away.

Stephen Goldman felt as if he'd been swept up by a hurricane and was on the ride of his life.

The suite Gacha was using at the Plaza still smelled of Ana-Alicia. It was a smell that he wished to keep only for himself and not have to share with Mario García, who sat opposite him on a plush seat. Mentally, Gacha cursed himself for such an oversight. Outside of Chulo, he did not want anyone else to know he was in love with Ana-Alicia.

After they had greeted each other and caught up with the gossip from Bogota, they settled into a discussion about business. Gacha informed him of the expansion of his business into the restaurant business and the hiring of Stephen Goldman.

"I'm not sure how the legal intricacies work," Gacha said, "but I do know how the money is washed." Gacha stood up from his chair and walked over to the drinks trolley.

"What would you like, Mario?" Gacha asked pointing at the drinks trolley.

"*Aguardiente,*" Mario said jokingly.

"Fine," Gacha said.

"You have it?" Mario asked in surprise.

"Yes, I asked the manager to have it brought up from Colombia. It was in my room within the hour. How they found a case of it in New York, I don't know." Gacha handed Mario a glass of *aguardiente*.

"Mario, the reason I asked you to come to New York is because I sense that you dislike something that I have been doing or..."

"No, *jefe!*" Mario said immediately.

Gacha, however, raised a hand to silence him. "Maybe it's because I have made you work the hardest and stuck you

217

with Margarita..."

"It's not that, *jefe*," Mario mumbled, cutting into the conversation.

"Then what is it? You are half alive when you are with Chulo or myself. You are treating us badly and you know that we would do anything for you, we would give our lives for you. Are you embarrassed by us? If that is what it is, we understand. You are an intelligent university graduate. Do you want us to let you go your own way? Let you make your own future with what you have, is that what you want?"

"I'm-in-love-with-Margarita," said Mario so fast it was almost all one word.

Gacha froze. He stood beside the drinks trolley like a marble statue. Did he say he was in love with Margarita or Maria? It couldn't be Margarita. Officially she was still his girl.

"Excuse me?" Gacha asked.

Mario's eyes moved guiltily up from the floor and looked into Gacha's cold stare. "I'm in love with Margarita. I did not mean to fall in love with her, it just happened. I don't know how but it just did, I tried to fight it but..."

"SHUT UP!"

A silence fell in the room.

Gacha stared at Mario viciously. He looked down at the shot glass he held in his hand and then threw it at the wall. The glass shattered into a hundred fragments. He felt like choking Mario to death, so why couldn't he move his legs toward him?

"Get out," Gacha said softly.

"It just happened, I didn't mean for it to happen..."

"GET OUT!"

Mario averted his eyes from Gacha and walked quickly towards the door. "I'm staying at the Waldorf," Mario said before he left.

Gacha walked into the suite's bedroom and slammed the door behind him, Ana-Alicia's perfume lingering heavily in the air. The smell of her crushed whatever anger he had in him. A memory flash-flooded his mind and he saw Ana-Alicia's face. She was laughing. Where was that?

Gacha walked out of the bedroom and into the living area. He needed a place to go and think. Hadn't he always wanted to see the Statue of Liberty? He looked at his watch. Yes, he decided he would see it.

The ferry pulled away from the dock and the coolness of the breeze felt good against his skin. Gacha had decided that he liked New York, he just didn't like it during the summer. It turned it into a sweatbox.

What should he do about Mario and Margarita? He needed Mario, he couldn't afford to lose him. Margarita, on the other hand, was expendable, but if she went how would that affect Mario? Damn! Did he love Margarita or was it something else? No, he didn't love her, he was sure of it. If he did love her he would feel the way he felt for Ana-Alicia. Mario must really love Margarita, because that scar across her face is hideous. What would Ana-Alicia say about all this? Let them be happy? Yes, it was in her nature. Wasn't he doing what society was doing to him and Ana-Alicia? They loved each other and greater forces kept them apart? Couldn't he just alter those forces in respect to Mario and Margarita? Yes, Ana-Alicia would want him to.

It shall be done, he decided.

Things were so clear when he put them in perspective with Ana-Alicia as a point of reference. Only Ana-Alicia had witnessed his ascension in life, how he had stood on that small rise a lifetime ago, to the masterstroke he had played to become the King of Bogota and finally become the multimillionaire that he was.

"How long can you continue to operate illegally?" Ana-Alicia had asked suddenly one afternoon.

"I don't know," he had answered.

How long could he? Could he always operate illegally? No, he didn't think so. Sooner or later the pressure to stop the flow of the product would come, but when? Next year? Two years or five? Who could tell? The fact was that right now it

was easier than taking candy from a baby. All he needed was
enough money to make himself so powerful that respect would
be automatic. But how much was enough? Ten million dollars?
Twenty? fifty?

What he needed was to convert his illegal business into
legitimate business, but that in itself cost money. However, it
could be done. Hadn't he bought a chain of restaurants
already? Yes, that was the ultimate plan, from illegality to
legality, which in turn would lead to respect. Had not the
robber barons done the same thing as well as the big whiskey
runners here in the United States? Yes, the only thing was
that they ran liquor instead of cocaine!

The ferry docked on the tiny island and Gacha walked
around the massive green statue. He stopped and read the
inscription by Emma Lazarus:

> 'Give me your tired, your poor, your huddled
> masses yearning to breathe free, the wretched
> refuse of your teeming shore, send these, the
> homeless, the tempest-tossed, to me: I lift my
> lamp beside the golden door.'

Gacha laughed out loud, people looked at him as if he
were a blasphemer. Didn't the Grand Lady know? The huddled
masses and the wretched refuse didn't know she existed and if
they did they knew they couldn't afford to come! Gacha walked
away thinking about the naïveté of the American people.

The first time he had ever heard the story about the
Statue of liberty was in the first class cabin of a jet, in a small
pamphlet that had a list of places a tourist should see while in
New York. The statue made no sense to him, the only reason
he stood in front of Lady Liberty was because he had five
million dollars in the bank that had allowed him to go see her.
But where was Lady Liberty when he saw his family wiped out
and he had become one of the teeming millions yearning to be
free? Nowhere! Lady Liberty was supplying weapons to the
government of Colombia to stop the ungodly spread of

Communism. And some of that Communism had been deemed to be in his family, and they had been removed like a cancer.

Gonzalo Gacha returned to his suite at The Plaza and found two messages waiting for him. One was from Chulo and the other from Jim Harrison. Something had gone wrong in Bogota.

Gacha dialed for Chulo and got him on the first ring. That was something else Gacha had noticed, the Americans had a great telephone system.

"What's happening, Chulo?" Gacha asked calmly.

"*Un mierdero pero bien verraco, tamaño familiar.*" A family sized-fuck-up, said Chulo.

"What happened?"

"The M-19 kidnapped a kid, sixteen years old," Chulo said gravely over the phone.

"The bastards! I expected them to break off the agreement but not this soon."

"It wasn't one of ours, *jefe.*"

"What do you mean, Chulo?" Gacha asked his voice sharp, deadly.

"It's the son of some American consular."

"Those assholes just don't learn, do they? How many times must they learn the lesson that you don't fuck with the United States, eh?"

"What shall I tell Harrison, *jefe*? He's been calling every half hour?"

"I'll be on the next flight to Colombia. Arrange a meeting with *El Fantasma*. See you soon." Gacha hung up and then dialed the airline and booked himself on the next flight. The flight was in one hour out of Kennedy International.

As Gacha walked out of the room he hesitated and then walked back to the phone and called Mario. He would pick him up in ten minutes, he told Mario. He wanted to talk to him before he left for Bogota on an emergency.

Mario was nervous as he rode in the same taxi as Gacha. He kept his gaze on the floor as Gacha looked out of the moving taxi.

"You really love Margarita?" Gacha asked suddenly. Mario nodded. "Enough to marry her?"

Mario looked on bewildered. "Yes...yes!"

"Then after you have graduated from Harvard, you can marry her," Gacha said. "But you will have to graduate first."

"Yes! Of course, yes!" Mario said.

"I'm glad you had the balls to tell me, Mario. Had I found out through someone else, I would have been terribly disappointed," Gacha said, looking on like a good parent. If the bastard doesn't marry her, I'll kill him!

A chill ran down Mario's spine as the taxi pulled alongside the curb in front of Avianca Airlines. When Gacha spoke of disappointments, Mario thought, it was in terms of elimination. Something that had to be wiped out, an infection that had to be isolated and removed before it contaminated anything else.

They said some hasty good-byes and promised to call each other. Mario breathed a sigh of relief as Gacha walked into the airport terminal. In his fright he realized he had forgotten to ask Gacha what the big emergency was all about.

Gacha buckled himself into the first class seat and began to think what his plan would be when he got to Colombia. It was clear to him that a lesson had to be taught, maybe several lessons. The M-19 unknowingly had once been an ally. Now, it was a thorn in his side that had to be removed.

CHAPTER EIGHTEEN

The moment Gonzalo Rodriguez Gacha sat down in his downtown Bogota office and took his first sip of coffee, Jim Harrison stormed through the door shouting. "Get him the fuck back!"

"Always a pleasure to see you, Mr. Harrison," Gacha said.

Harrison didn't hear him, he simply walked up to Gacha and grabbed him by the shirt collar. "Listen and listen good. I want the boy and don't give me any of this negotiating crap."

Gacha felt the man's grip around the shirt collar. "You must be distraught, so I will forgive this breach of manners," Gacha said with a raspy voice.

"I don't give a..."

"If you do not let go," said Gacha cutting Harrison off, "I'll have you killed."

Harrison did not hear Chulo walk up behind him. All he heard was the cocking of a Colt .45 right beside his right ear. "*Siéntese o le doy el plomo.*" Sit down or I'll give you the lead, Chulo said.

Harrison released his grip and backed away slowly and sat down in one of the office chairs. Finally he let out a long sigh that seemed to drain the life out of him. He hadn't had more than forty minutes of sleep in the last seventy-two hours. "They took the kid's ear off and sent it to his parents," he said with his eyes looking at the floor.

Gacha looked at him and then at Chulo. "Bring a bottle of *Aguardiente*, Chulo. I think we all need a drink."

Chulo left the office for a moment and returned a few moments later. He placed three glasses on Gacha's desk. They all reached for one and drained it. Chulo refilled them immediately.

"Who is he?" Gacha asked Harrison.

"The consul's son," said Harrison. "We have tried to keep it out of the papers for as long as possible but they know something's up. I got a call from one of the major television networks in New York today."

"That's not good, not good at all," Gacha said.

"I heard you made a deal with the M-19. Can you get the kid back?"

"Our deal was that we would pay a fee every year, and they would not kidnap any one of us."

"Well, they bloody well did!" Harrison said, his anger rising again.

"No, they didn't. We did not include Americans; we didn't think they'd be stupid enough to try it. The leader is a guy who calls himself *El Fantasma*, says he has power among the M-19. I don't think that any more unless he was the one who decided to do it. If he did, the guy is stupid and crazy. You can't do business with crazy people, they're a parasite on economic progress."

"I shouldn't be saying this, but my career is hanging on a wire. The telephone lines between Bogota and Washington are burning up. They're goddamn furious. Every time they think they can count on this place becoming stable, someone or something always happens to make it not so."

"Yes," said Gacha. "Frankly, Mr. Harrison, speaking for most Colombians, we are getting sick and tired of the violence too."

"No, you don't understand Gacha, one of our non-clients south of Colombia is getting out of control. As you say, instability is not good for business and one of the biggest businesses in the world is about to lose a major chunk of their business. They are not happy at all. You know what happens then? The business corporation pressures certain officials who then pressure people like us to take care of it."

"Non-clients as opposed to clients and by clients you

mean pro-democracy?" Gacha asked, tiny drops of sweat began
to collect just below the hairline. This could be his big break in
business. He could almost taste it.

"Yes, non-client meaning Communist," Harrison
answered.

"This non-client wanting to take away this
corporation's business wouldn't happen to be..."

"I'm not saying what client, we have many clients as
well as non-clients. I'm just saying that there is trouble
brewing in a non-client country."

"Strange," Gacha said resting his hand on the
telephone. "I haven't been able to reach certain business
colleagues south of Colombia." It was true, Gacha thought. He
had been trying to reach Alberto Saavedra for the last couple
of days.

"Any international business you have is at best tenuous
with non-client countries," Harrison said, looking at his empty
glass.

Gacha stared at him in shock. The Chilean
government, under the Marxist-Leninist leader Salvador
Allende, was trying to nationalize all foreign owned industries.
The most vociferous industry against nationalization was the
American owned telephone company, International Telephone
and Telegraph (ITT), a company who had invested seventy-two
million dollars into modernizing Chile's phone system. To any
corporation, the loss of seventy-two million dollars was an
untenable proposition; something had to be done. Not to do
something about it was to allow one's own stock in the
corporation to fall. Gacha thought, he wouldn't allow it even if
it were Colombia trying to do it. Didn't he in fact own stock in
ITT? There was only one thing for ITT to hope for and at the
moment it looked like it would be possible.

Coup d'etat.

Gacha realized the enormity of it all and how it could
personally affect him. It never ceased to amaze him how things
several thousands of miles away and in different countries now
affected his life. If the Chilean hold on the cocaine market was

cut, he could march in and contract with every coca crop producer in Bolivia and Peru. He could have an unlimited supply of cocaine! Oh, he had to be very careful how he phrased his next lines. If the room were bugged, it could be all over the *New York Times* by tomorrow morning. He had the office swept electronically every day, but with maids and janitors, an electronic bug could still be planted easily.

"Yes, I don't like international business," said Gacha, "it's too complicated. I've been thinking of breaking all of my international ties and concentrating solely on Colombia, giving myself a time-table of course."

"A good strategy, leave with maximum profits."

"Yes, but when those profits are at maximum is hard to guess," Gacha said softly.

"Well, what I dabble in at the New York Stock Exchange, I have a feeling that the market will peak out in a year."

So, a coup might occur in a year if things have not changed, interesting, Gacha thought.

"I see, well I have heard that it might not peak out for another five years."

"Speculative. A year seems to be correct, maybe sooner." Harrison was sure that Gacha was getting the drift.

"I will have a response for you at midday," said Gacha. "I promise."

"Good enough," Harrison said as he stood up. He was going to say something but decided against it.

Gacha looked at Chulo. "Were you able to arrange a meeting with *El Fantasma*?" Gacha asked.

"Yes, *jefe*, it is set for ten in the morning in Girardot."

Gacha looked at his watch, it was almost five in the morning and Girardot was three hours away by car. "Then let's get on the road," Gacha said, getting up from his seat and heading for the door.

Girardot. To get to Girardot from Bogota, one descended the Andes Mountains, a range known as the

Cordillera Oriental. One descended from twelve thousand feet above sea level to three hundred and twenty feet above sea level, and it was done by a car in a matter of two hours. The roads carved alongside the mountains, although paved, were still extremely treacherous. One swerve too far and you would fall ten thousand feet to the bottom of a canyon.

There was a Colombian custom of marking a spot where people had gone over with a small white concrete cross. And at the top of each mountain, just before one descended down the mountain road there was a small prayer area. These prayer areas were clearly marked with huge statues of the Virgin Mary. Drivers would always stop and say a prayer to the Virgin in return for safety, then they would leave a token of gratitude in the form of a tail light, a car horn, an old tire or part of the front headlight.

The road Chulo and Gacha were on was the second most treacherous road in all of Colombia. The first and most treacherous was the road to Villavicencio, the gateway to the *Llanos Orientales* (The Plains), a road known to be especially treacherous around the river known as Quebradablanca. The road Chulo and Gacha were on was known as *El Boquerón* (The Big Mouth). *El Boquerón*, as the name indicated, was the mouth into a canyon that had been carved out over millions of years by a myriad of rivers that eventually flowed into the mighty Magdalena River.

The descent into *El Boquerón* was a six thousand foot descent done by car in eight minutes. To those who had never been down it before, it was worse than any rollercoaster ride in the world. The only way you knew you had reached relative safety was when you passed the landmark known as *La Nariz del Diablo* (The Devil's Nose). *La Nariz del Diablo* was a huge outcrop of rock that stuck out of the side of the mountain like a huge ominous nose.

It wasn't until they cleared *La Nariz del Diablo* that the passengers inside the cars began to resume their conversations again. In Gacha's Mercedes, which Chulo had been driving, had been no different.

"What do you think we should do?" Gacha asked Chulo.

"I think *El Fantasma* has gotten too big for himself, which is not good for clear thinking. I think he's going to want too much for this kid," said Chulo, blaring his horn as a big touring bus tried to overtake him.

"What's too much?"

"He wants the M-19 in the papers, he wants recognition, he wants the people of Colombia to know that they do in fact exist."

"That is something they can never have," said Gacha, rolling down his window and letting a mass of hot air enter into the car. They were in the hot climates now, where temperatures could range from 90 degrees to 125.

"You are right, of course," said Chulo. "Maybe they only want more money.

"Damn these little guerilla groups!" Gacha said.

The Colombian guerrilla problem had emerged as a direct result of the agreement reached by the oligarchy in the late 1950s. The difference between the conservative and liberal parties today was minimal considering their long existence. But for ten years, between 1948 and 1958, their differences about land reform caused a civil war, a period in Colombian history that came to be referred to as *La Violencia* (The Violence).

La Violencia, was a civil war that left two hundred thousand dead and over one million people homeless. It was a war that came to an end when the liberal and conservative parties, which were run by the oligarchy, agreed to run together under the name of Frente Nacional (United Front). To Colombians at the time it seemed as if the two parties were merging, but it was not so. The agreement was to get elected as the Frente Nacional, but once in, the liberals would change power with the conservatives and vice-versa. The major problem that had led to the civil war, the change for land reform, went unsolved. The unresolved issue led directly to the rise of the armed left, and although unrecognized, it became an institution of violence.

El Fantasma walked up to Gonzalo Rodriguez Gacha's table beside the pool and sat down. He wore the traditional garb that a rich person would wear in Bogota. Linen shirt, linen pants, expensive straw hat and very expensive loafers on his feet.

The first thought that ran across Gacha's mind was that the man sitting in front of him was silly, a silly man playing children's games.

"You wanted to meet me, here I am. I materialize myself," said *El Fantasma* with sarcasm.

"I want the American released," Gacha said, the voice hard and humorless.

"He is not your concern, he is not on the list."

"Americans are untouchable, you know that!" Gacha said strongly.

"Well, we touched one. What did they think of the ear, did they faint?"

"Release him!"

"You son-of-a-bitch, you cannot give orders to the M-19. We are not to be pushed around. The papers know that we have taken the kid, soon the people will be behind us and against the *Yanqui imperialista*."

Gacha smoothly reached under his shirt and took out a small .38 caliber gun and put it under *El Fantasma*'s chin. "What I'm going to say I'm not going to repeat. You release that kid by six o'clock this afternoon or I will have a contract taken out on you. I will offer twenty thousand dollars to the person who will serve your head up on a dish. With that kind of money *pedazo de mierda*, you'll be dead before sunset tomorrow. No, don't say anything, just shut up and listen. I am giving you an option. You can leave and then turn it down and get killed, or you can flat out reject it now and have your brains splattered into that pool behind you. What's it to be?"

"You've signed your death warrant with the M-19!"

"Deal or no deal, *maricón*?" Gacha said cocking the

229

gun.

El Fantasma sat with impotent rage, his fists curled and ready to strike. "You will have your answer by six...dead man!" *El Fantasma* said and stormed off like a bull.

Chulo walked up to Gacha's table grinning from ear to ear. "He has no balls at all."

"Yeah, the dumb idiot," Gacha said shaking his head. "You never come to a business meeting without being prepared to back up your position right then and there."

"What's next, *jefe*?" Chulo asked.

"He will release the kid, the others will force him to do it. They almost have their hands on half a million dollars a year, they would be stupid to give it up for one kid. For *El Fantasma* it's too late; put a contract out on him. After six o'clock tonight, no matter what happens with the kid, I want the bastard dead. That should let the M-19 know not to back out on a deal with me and it will also show them that they are not invulnerable."

"Yes, *jefe*."

In Colombia, guerrilla ideals were all well and good Gacha thought, if only they had balls and guns to back them up and not psychotic killers running the show. That was the mistake they always kept making, the establishment was always ready to use force while they debated, talked and argued about their ideals. For the guerrilla to win, they'd have to beat the army, and in Colombia there was no chance of that. His own parents had learned that the hard way. The fools! Money and guns were the answer for the guerrilla.

Gacha had slept in the car on his way back to Bogota. As he sat in his downtown office waiting for *El Fantasma* to call, he dozed off now and then. The heavy rain falling against the window pane had a soothing effect, almost hypnotic. His hair felt greasy, his clothes soiled and his mouth was starting to taste foul. He had not bathed or washed his mouth in...Damn! How long had it been? He knew he was still wearing the same clothes he had seen Ana-Alicia off in at the airport in New York.

Gacha, didn't care. He was too exhausted. He put his head back down on the table gently wanting to catch another nap, but the intrusion of the ringing phone made his heart skip a beat. Suddenly, he was as awake as he had ever been.

"Gacha," he said into the mouthpiece.

"You can find him in *La Plaza de los Héroes*," said *El Fantasma* angrily. "Just remember, Gacha, I'm going to kill you."

"You won't let me forget," said Gacha with amusement and hung up. He then dialed Jim Harrison's telephone number.

"Harrison," said the Cultural Attache.

"It's Gacha, you can find the kid at *La Plaza de los Héroes.*"

"You're kidding?" Harrison said in disbelief.

"No! Get him before some *gamín* knifes him," said Gacha angrily. Why was it that the Americans had to be so sarcastic at the most inopportune moments?

"I won't forget this, Gacha, trust me. I owe you a big one. Thanks a lot," Harrison said and hung up, leaving the dial tone in Gacha's ear.

Gacha looked up at Chulo with an amused grin as he held the phone in his hand. "You know, Chulo, the *yanquis* have no manners at all."

The M-19 never saw itself written up in the newspapers. The only thing that ever came close to being recognized as a terrorist group was when the name of Antonio Herrera, also known as *El Fantasma*, appeared in the obituary column twenty-four hours after the consul's son had been returned.

El Fantasma was a young man of twenty three years of age who had been born in the province of Huila. He had no surviving relatives since they had been killed during the *Bogotazo*, the riot that occurred shortly after the assassination of the popular candidate Jorge Eliecer Gaitán, in the main Plaza of Bogota. Herrera, however, as it was stated in the obituary column, had no surviving relatives and therefore his half a million dollar estate would revert back to the government. It would be the ultimate twist of fate and the final irony in Herrera's life.

The rest of 1972 progressed with no difficulties. The M-19 had dropped out of sight but had not forgotten to pick up their half million dollars at the end of the year, as per the initial Gacha agreement. The man who had come by to collect the cash, always cash, was a man by the name of Augusto Rojas. He was a young man of twenty-six with a very keen business mind. Gacha told Rojas that *El Fantasma* had simply violated the spirit of their initial agreement. Having violated it, Gacha was forced to give *El Fantasma* an option where no options existed.

By the end of 1972, Gacha had been invited to the Nariño Presidential Palace. He had attended the Christmas Ball, the most important festive event in Bogota. At the gathering, the President of Colombia and other dignitaries had taken the time to tell him that his secretive handling of the M-19 kidnapping had not been overlooked.

Two days after the Ball, Gacha flew to Paris, where he spent his four days and four nights with Ana-Alicia. In Paris, Gacha had gone on another mammoth shopping spree, this time buying three Citröen automobiles for no apparent reason except that they looked funny. He bought lavish gowns for Ana-Alicia at the best *haute couture* houses and jewelry in the best jewelry stores. On Christmas they had exchanged gifts. He gave her a quarter of a million dollar diamond and sapphire bracelet and she gave him a solid gold wrist band with an inscription that read: To my beloved Gonzalo. A-A.

By 1973, the marijuana and cocaine business had expanded so rapidly that Stephen Goldman had to fly to Bogota and inform Gacha that he had taken on a partner to handle the workload. Their projected figures for that year had originally been planned to be fifteen to twenty million and not the current forty-two million. It was a wild and crazy time for business, but the world again seemed to slip into a new gear and settled in for a more relaxed pace. The mood of the world, Gacha had noticed, begun to change in earnest the year before, and the change had not been that clear. The radicalism of the people had changed, people were sick of protests, an easing of tensions seemed to have taken root. It could be noticed even in the music, the sharp edged lyrics of revolution had been replaced by softer songs, more appealing to brotherhood. Singers with a new perspective emerged as superstars, Cat Stevens, Lobo, Neil Diamond and his personal favorite, a blonde goddess by the name of Olivia Newton-John.

The year 1973, was also marked by the American troops leaving Vietnam, in some complicated plan that no one had much faith in. They called the plan "Vietnamization." Americans in their own country seemed to be making a mess of it, a scandal that had occurred in the Watergate Hotel began to rock the United States. Gacha wasn't quite able to grasp what exactly it was that Nixon had done wrong, but whatever it was he seemed to have been caught doing it.

Henry Kissinger, the man who had indirectly started Gacha's rise to wealth and power, appeared to be everywhere. He seemed to be bringing peace where none had existed before. Gacha, like most Colombians and the rest of the world, admired Kissinger. He was a thinking man's thinking man. A realist on the grand scale, no effort was too minimal or too great to bring peace.

However, the peace did not seem to last long.

Chile decided to test the resolve of the world and American corporations. The President of Chile, Salvador Allende, had become an outlaw government. The government had defaulted on its debts to American banks and nationalized American companies.

On June 15, 1973, Chile, due to their copper mine strikes was forced to suspend its foreign shipments of copper to the rest of the world, therefore, cutting off its major source of income. Six days later, the Chilean government closed down

233

the *El Mercurio* newspaper on the charges of subversive activities. On June 25, *The New York Times* warned that Chile was on the brink of civil war and that Allende was to blame. Four days later the first coup attempt was repulsed by Allende's loyalist forces, and the country was put under a state of emergency.

Gonzalo Rodriguez Gacha had hung onto every word coming out of Chile for three months. He'd call the Chilean Ambassador in Bogota to see if he could figure out which way the prevailing wind was blowing. Every day, Gacha read the *El Tiempo*, *The New York Times*, *The Washington Post*, *The Los Angeles Times* and a half a dozen other newspapers. At different times of the day he would tune into VOA (Voice of America), the BBC (British Broadcasting Company) and Cuba Free Radio. His goal was to determine exactly when he should send Chulo down to Bolivia and Peru to contract with the Chilean backed coca growers who would soon be left out in the cold. Bolivia and Peru were contractually bound to Chile. Unless a new government were installed in Chile, the coca growers would not be able to break the contract.

On September 9, 1973, Gacha received a telephone call, a call that would change his life forever.

"Hello?" said Gacha.

"Gacha, consider this a return favor," said a voice Gacha immediately recognized.

"What is that?" Gacha asked.

"You have forty-eight hours to re-arrange you economic ties with Chile," said the voice and hung up.

For the first time since he had become King of Bogota, Gacha had been caught speechless.

A few minutes later, Gacha and Chulo were on their way to the airport to catch a flight to La Paz, Bolivia. Gacha had put his private aircraft on standby since the Chilean crisis had broken, so when he and Chulo arrived at the airport, the pilots already had their engines turning and ready for take-off.

El golpe de estado (overthrow) in Chile occurred at 6.30 a.m. on September 11, 1973. Salvador Allende, surrounded by tanks of the Chilean army, refused to resign from the office of *El Presidente*. But, a few minutes before noon on the same day, the high staff of the Chilean military called in an air-strike to bomb the Presidential Palace. At 12.01 p.m. Salvador Allende Gossens, the President of Chile, was found dead in the midst of the rubble of the palace.

One thousand two hundred miles north of Chile, in an obscure Bolivian province by the name of Cochabamba, at exactly 12:02 p.m. Gonzalo Rodriguez Gacha in the name of Cia. Export., entered into contract with two hundred *cocaleros*, (coca growers), to become the largest producer of cocaine in the free world. In one fell swoop, Gonzalo Rodriguez Gacha had become the Lord of Cocaine.

Although Gacha by the end of 1973 controlled eighty percent of the world's cocaine output, Cali and Medellin controlled the rest. It appeared they too had moved swiftly, but Gacha didn't mind; there was enough to go around.

When the fiscal year of 1973 came to an end, the company owned and controlled solely by Gonzalo Rodriguez Gacha posted a profit of $130 million. Outside of Saudi Arabia's royal family, a handful of business entrepreneurs and outlaw dictators, Gonzalo Rodriguez Gacha was one of the wealthiest human beings in the world.

Gonzalo Rodriguez Gacha had indeed climbed on top of the tiger.

Peter A. Neissa

CHAPTER NINETEEN

The week before Christmas 1974, at his new estate north of Bogota, Gonzalo Rodriguez Gacha threw a social party. The house was a case study of trying to overdo that which was obvious, that he was wealthy.

In the driveway people would see the three Rolls-Royces, the two Mercedes, the two Jeeps and the half dozen motorcycles. Then they would realize he had no use for them.

The grounds around the estate were also meant to impress, with an Olympic-sized swimming pool, a dozen fountains and four golf holes just in case someone wanted to practice some golf putting.

The inside of the house would have made three or four different house magazines. The floors were made of Italian marble, all the walls were decorated with oil paintings from Obregón to Picasso. The furniture was original Louis XVI and every bedroom was equipped with a fireplace and a private bathroom. The doorknobs were fourteen karat gold plated as well as the faucets in the bathrooms, right down to the lever on the toilet. There was a sauna, jaccuzi, gym and, at the rear of the mansion an indoor pool.

The guests began arriving at ten in the evening, fashionable Colombian time. Once they stepped inside the house they were immediately approached by white-coated waiters carrying champagne on silver trays.

A live band playing traditional Colombian music filled the estate with sound and saucy rhythms. Dom Perignon Champagne insured that the guests would be in a good mood. No guest was ever seen without a drink for long, and rooms had been prepared for any guest who'd had too much to drink.

At first, the guests were quiet which alarmed Gacha,

who wanted everything to be perfect. They had all been awed into silence by the unfashionable way that Gacha had displayed his wealth. However, after a few drinks, they went along with the brashness and the evening moved along.

Gacha was standing close to the front foyer talking to two men of the Colombian House of Representatives when she walked in. Perhaps, it was only he that felt the room hush as she stood poised in the doorway. Gacha's heart began to pound against his chest like a warring drum.

Ana-Alicia was a vision, Gacha decided. The black, almost skin-tight dress showed her figure to perfection. He could almost feel the collective intake of breath from every man in the room, as she carelessly ran her hand across her mahogany colored hair. The dress, cut low at the cleavage, was a magnet for every man's eyes. Ana-Alicia's eyes covered the room lazily, her eyelashes seeming to open and close in slow motion as if she were sweeping the floor with them.

They locked eyes.

Ana-Alicia's eyes spoke volumes of panic, as if she were trying to warn Gacha of something. To Gacha it made no sense, so he put his drink down and began to walk across the large foyer to meet her. It was at that precise moment when the Minister of Development and Technology, walked in and took Ana-Alicia's hand.

Gacha froze in mid-stride, his insides feeling like they had been ripped open wide for the whole world to see. Could it be possible? Hadn't she told him that she would eventually marry someone else? Why had she not mentioned him? Why was everything so far away?

"Mr. Minister," Gacha said, unaware of how he got to the center of the foyer. "It is an honor you bestow upon me, please, *mi casa es su casa.*" Was he really saying those things? Where the hell was his voice coming from? Why hadn't Ana-Alicia told him she was coming back from the States?

"Good evening, *Señor* Gacha," Ana-Alicia said with tears welling up in her eyes.

"Good evening, *Señorita* Gonzáles, there is no woman

238

more beautiful than you here tonight."

"Thank you," Ana-Alicia said.

The Minister looked at Ana-Alicia and saw a tear running down her cheek. "Are you alright, *querida*?" The Minister asked, as he dried her cheek with his handkerchief.

The Minister's words and movements were like daggers into Gacha's heart.

"Yes, it must be the flowers," Ana-Alicia said half heartedly.

"I'll have them removed immediately," said Gacha. "Please, enjoy your evening." Gacha bowed politely and walked off as he heard the minister say, "Come, darling."

Gacha went to his bedroom, a place where he could be out of everyone's sight. In the bedroom he gasped for breath as if he had been hit in the solar plexus. His knees buckled and wobbled. My God, have I lost her? Gacha asked himself.

There was a knock on the door and someone walked in uninvited. Gacha turned to scold the person who had invaded his privacy, only to see Stephen Goldman holding two massive sized drinks. Gacha reached out for one of the drinks and drained it like a man dying of thirst.

"So, she's the one," Goldman said rather than asked. "She is without a doubt one of the most beautiful women I have ever seen."

"Who?" Gacha asked, pretending ignorance.

"Oh, come off it!" Goldman said irritated. "That devastating young woman in the black dress, hell, I saw your reaction. You damn nearly fainted in the middle of the foyer."

"*Mierda!* That obvious?"

"No, it was such a slight hesitation I doubt if anyone noticed. However, those who really know you, know that you never hesitate. Hell, to have seen you hesitate was like a physical blow."

"Who else?" Gacha asked, taking Goldman's drink out of his hand and draining the glass.

"No one except for her, of course. She knew, and I suspect she still loves you, that was quite obvious. Did you know she was coming tonight with that overpretentious bastard?"

"I didn't even know she was in Colombia," Gacha said, his tone softening as the liquor began to take effect.

Goldman walked over to the far wall of Gacha's master bedroom where there was a drinks trolley. He refilled the two glasses with scotch and walked back to where Gacha was sitting.

"Funny thing," said Goldman handing a drink over to Gacha. "Men always consider themselves wise in the ways of the world when in truth we're not. It's the women who are wise, goddamn realistic about things. Maybe she did it for your own good. Hell, who am I to talk? My wife ran out on me after twenty some years of marriage. Women!"

Gacha chuckled. "Is that why you came down here with that little blonde number?" Gacha asked, remembering that Goldman had shown up to the estate with a good looking blonde girl draped all over his arm.

Goldman laughed. "Hell, the girl is younger than my daughter. You know, we ran into my wife Carmen a month ago. She said I looked different. I told her it was the money, it agrees with me." Goldman and Gacha laughed and swallowed their drinks and walked back to the drinks trolley and refilled them.

"Steve," said Gacha, "you are out of our agreement by the end of next year, have you decided what you are going to do?"

"No, I guess I'm going to retire somewhere in Monte Carlo. Funny thing is, now that I have millions of dollars, the trappings of the rich bore me. You know what I mean?" Gacha nodded. "It's like you live with this dream of wealth all your life, but once you're there you're not quite sure if someone has pulled a joke on you. Everything comes too easy now. I remember when I bought my first Mercedes, it was two weeks after I started working for you, boy it felt great. Now, I have a Rolls and two Mercedes and I'm hardly ever in them. It's like we have exceeded our dreams, crossed some invisible threshold and for doing so we must pay the price in boredom. We got to get out of this business, Gonzalo, or it will eat at our souls a little each day. I mean how much money do we want to make? Two, three, four or five hundred million? How much is enough?"

"One billion dollars a year would be nice," said Gacha with a slight grin.

"Yeah, but will you be human by then?"

"The game, my friend, is not money anymore, but power. The power to change the course of events at your own whim."

"And once you achieve that, what? Demi-god status or immortality? Gacha, you are playing a game that you cannot possibly win. The only salvation we've got is to get out while we can. The girl you're so fond of might be your last hope, your salvation from falling into some godless money making machine. Remember, in the end we'll all sit before God's judgment seat."

Gacha looked at Goldman puzzled.

"Yes," Goldman said, "perhaps it is age that brings on these thoughts about the human condition. I've blown it, it's already too late for me."

"What do you mean late?" Gacha asked.

"Figure of speech." There was a light knock on the door. "That's my cue," Goldman said, walking towards the door and opening it to see Chulo.

Chulo looked into the room with a worried expression.

"I'm alright, Chulo," said Gacha. "I'll be with the guests shortly." Chulo nodded and walked away.

"Remember what I said Gonzalo," Goldman said from the doorway. "Get out while you can." Goldman walked out and closed the door behind him.

At 4.30 a.m. the party was still going strong. Fifty cases of champagne had been drunk. The food had been consumed and the band was playing its final chords. Outside on the lawns, the servants walked around still serving drinks. There was no reason to worry about the neighbors, because the closest neighbor lived half a mile away and he was at the party.

Gacha had stayed away from Ana-Alicia all night long even though he could feel her gaze on him. He had caught her once looking at him or was it the other way around? It didn't matter, the sight of the drunken Minister holding Ana-Alicia by the waist made him look instantly away. It also made him want to crush the man's skull with his bare hands.

At six in the morning, all the remaining guests walked out to the outside portico to watch the sun rise. Gonzalo who was standing seven feet behind Ana-Alicia and the Minister kept his eyes trained solely on Ana-Alicia. The drunken Minister had his hand around her waist.

As the sun rose from the eastern cordillera everyone clapped except for the drunken Minister and Gacha. The Minister's hand was busy feeling up Ana-Alicia's backside. Gacha simply looked on with a mounting rage, accidentally crushing his glass in his hand, startling the guests.

"Excuse me," Gacha said with his hand beginning to bleed. "I'm done in, I think I will retire now. Please, enjoy yourselves for as long as you want, good night."

Everyone laughed and came back in a chorus, "Good morning."

Gacha smiled and let his eyes sweep over everyone, but as he passed over Ana-Alicia's he saw the tears running down her face. He wanted to run to her but somehow he found the strength not to do so and walked away.

Gacha had been asleep for a few hours he knew, but he had still felt the presence in the room causing him to open up his eyes. He didn't see anything but he could feel someone in the shadows. He faked a toss as his hand reached for a gun under his pillow.

"It's me, Gonzalo," said Ana-Alicia sitting beside the bed.

Gacha took in her perfume, revelling in the bouquet of it. He turned on a small night lamp. He saw her still dressed

242

in the same black dress she'd worn to the party. Her eyes were swollen and her hair tangled and unruly and still it looked wonderful to him.

"I'm sorry," Ana-Alicia blurted out as she sat down beside Gacha on the bed.

Gacha put his fingers to her mouth to silence her and she kissed them.

"Did you do it on purpose?" Gacha asked.

"No! I wanted to surprise you, I had been thinking about nothing else but the party for the last week." Ana-Alicia let out a sob. "I didn't tell you because I wanted to show up alone and surprise you."

"What happened?" Gacha said propping himself up on a pillow, aware of her strong grasp on his hands.

"When I came home yesterday, my parents said that they had arranged for a Minister to take me to the party. I argued with them, and I told them that I did not want to go. My father became angry. He said he had let me go to the United States to educate myself, but now it was time to find a husband and settle down. After all, he said, I was twenty-one years old and in the prime of my life, like I was some side of beef or something. I told him I wanted to work for a few years because I had a business degree. He laughed, he said and I quote, 'You could be Albert Einstein, but you still won't be working. This is Colombia not some liberated place where women get to do what they want. Here the rules are different, young lady, here your job is in the home.' Then he said he thanked God that I had come home before I was infected by the fast and loose ideas of American women. Oh, Gonzalo what am I to do?"

Gacha reached out for her and they hugged, cheek to cheek and then their mouths searched each other out in desperate want, their tongues flicking in and out of each other's mouths, probing, feeling and tasting desire at the very edge of passion.

Suddenly Ana-Alicia fell back onto the bed laughing.

"What is so funny?" Gacha asked, his hand falling over

her left breast.

"When you walked across the foyer, I thought you were going to have a heart attack," she said.

"I thought I did," Gacha looked at her perplexed.

"I love you, Gonzalo, so deeply it scares me. Sometimes I look at you and I wish I could read your mind, to see if you love me as much as I do you.

"*Querida*, I love you so much I have to wonder what is that you see in me. It scares me when you are away because I feel that you may find someone else and leave me. And yet, that is precisely what will happen some day because the rules have not changed."

"I know," whispered Ana-Alicia, "and I am afraid of what it will do to us."

"My love for you is greater than any mountain and still I fear that when the day comes I will be destroyed."

"The fact that we can love so much that it can destroy us is frightening. The worst thing of all is that we are powerless to change it."

"You must keep away from me when you are out with another man. Tonight I almost killed the Minister when he felt you up. It was a torture I do not wish to go through again," Gacha said.

"I promise. Now, make love to me my love."

Gacha slipped her black dress off and kissed her breast. She cooed softly at his feel, his touch always surprised her. Gacha was such a strong man and yet he had the touch of the angels.

Something had changed for both of them, they had crossed a line, a point of no return. Ana-Alicia knew instinctively, although she couldn't quite put it into words or into a clear single thought, she knew that Gonzalo Rodriguez Gacha would be the only man she would ever love, in this or any other life. Gacha, on the other hand, knew that his destiny would somehow be interlocked with hers. Then, like an ominous shadow, a memory crept into his mind, it was the voice of Stephen Goldman, a voice that was like a warning sign on a short and dangerous road. "Get out of this business Gonzalo or it will eat at your soul a little each day...That girl you're so fond off might be your last hope..."

Ana-Alicia and Gonzalo saw each other as often as they could plan it. Ana-Alicia never told him whom she had gone out with and he never asked, but on weekends they were together and they lived only for each other.

The year of 1974 came in with a bang and went out like a whimper. It was a year in which the people learned that governments were not angels. A new President of Colombia took office, a liberal, as agreed by the agreement reached in 1957 that ended *La Violencia*. The embittered United States was still trying to get their last soldier out of Vietnam, as their own U.S. President fell from grace.

On August 8th, 1974, on worldwide television, the world watched in shock as the United States President, Richard Milhous Nixon, resigned from office. The next day, those same viewers tuned in to see the President give his last wave from the stairs of Marine One. For the Americans, what was left was a gargantuan public mistrust, nobody in America it seemed, wanted to hear about another scandal, Americans shut out the forces of government. What the CIA, FBI, Coast Guard or police had to say fell on deaf ears. The public didn't want to hear anything from them, and what they did hear was heard with mistrust and disbelief. The people of the United States for all intents and purposes withdrew into themselves and looked out with blind eyes.

In October of 1975, Gonzalo Rodriguez Gacha was working late. He was studying charts that told him that thirty percent of his business was now legitimate. His goal for that year was to make over fifty percent of his business legitimate. Then and only then he would give up the drug business.

As Gacha stood back to look at the chart, the telephone rang. He looked and the phone rang again, so he walked over and picked it up.

"Hello?" Gacha said.

"Gacha?" asked a voice, it was a bad connection.

"Yes."

"It's Mario..."

"Mario, how are you? When are you coming home?" Gacha asked happily.

"Gacha, I got some bad news."

"What?" Gonzalo said, suddenly alarmed, his pulse beginning to race.

"Stephen Goldman is dead."

Silence.

"How?" was all Gacha managed to ask.

"Cancer, the doctor told me he had known for quite some time."

Words spoken long ago flowered in Gacha's mind. Words that had once puzzled him but now made all the sense in the world. "...In the end, we all sit before God's judgment seat...I've blown it, it's already too late for me." Goldman, Gacha realized, had known then and told him.

Gacha thanked Mario for the call and hung up. He grabbed his coat, he needed to get away, run. He ran into the hallway and pressed the elevator button. When the elevator doors opened Ana-Alicia was standing in the elevator and he ran into her arms.

They fled to Cartagena.

It was time out of mind.

Cartagena. A city of history and of heroes. Cartagena, the warehouse port for all the gold that flowed out of the New World towards Spain. Cartagena, the old walled city founded in 1533-- a city whose walls and fortresses were built to withstand attacks from pirates, men like Francis Drake, walls that were forty feet high and fifty-five feet thick. A city that had six gates, which in the fifteenth and sixteenth century had restricted the entrance to the world. Gates that would close at ten in the evening with a set of keys that belonged to the *Adelantado* (governor). A city that had contained *Adelantados*, ViceRoy's, Inquisitors and noblemen. A city that still retained the old charm of that age gone by, a city that still had streets

246

named after their original purpose, Street of the Inquisition,
Avenue Blas de Lezo, defender of Cartagena against pirates.
Cartagena, a city which would have scared a bloodied pirate
three hundred years before back to the side of the righteous. It
was now a city of grace and romance.

It was Gacha's first time off in three years. At first the
inactivity made him restless, which according to Ana-Alicia
had made him a Latin lover of the first magnitude. Gacha had
responded by saying that it was the woman who made it so.

He had been in Cartagena for three weeks, Gacha had
delegated responsibility to Chulo and then forgot about the
business which practically ran itself. Ana-Alicia would only
stay for the weekends, although she told her parents she was
staying at friends' homes in Bogota. She resented the fact that
her parents still asked her where she was going and what she
could and could not do, even though she was turning twenty-
three in a few months.

Ana-Alicia had told Gonzalo on one of the Cartagena
weekends that her parents were really beginning to pressure
her into marriage. She told him too that she no longer had an
idea of how long she could hold out against her parents
pressure. When he asked her why she was holding out, she had
responded that it was not for a lack of proposals. She told him
in a moment of insight that she doubted if she could marry
anyone beside him. To do so would kill her. And they had left
it at that.

Cartagena had become a reaffirmation of their love, a
love whose rules had been made clear on a lonesome road to
Key West a long time ago. Rules that neither had made, and
yet were powerless to change.

On November 22, 1975, Gacha took a call from Chulo.

"*Jefe*, we have trouble," Chulo said plainly.

"What's wrong?" Gacha asked alarmed.

"Six hundred kilos of cocaine were seized in Cali by the
F-2 police. I'm trying to find out whose cocaine it was."

"Impossible!" Gacha shouted in disbelief.

"It's true, the police were tipped off. *Jefe*, I'm

247

frightened. Everyone is in Cali, F-2, regular police, military police, the army and even the Americans. They've all gone crazy with this seizure. The Americans have some special agents they call DEA, it stands for Drug Enforcement Agency."

"Who tipped them off?" Gacha said evenly.

"Medellin."

Two days after the six hundred kilo seizure in a massive retaliation by Cali, whose cocaine had been seized, killed forty of Medellin's top people in the city of Medellin. It was a killing that came to be known as the Medellin Massacre.

Cali, which was controlled by that long ago deposed *gamín* gang lord of Chapinero, Ernesto Bosco, had set down the rules and picked up the gauntlet. An eye for and eye and blood for blood.

The drug war of 1975 exploded!

PART THREE
(1975-1981)

THE CARTEL

They have sown the wind,
and they shall reap the whirlwind.
---Hosea 8:7

_____*Peter A. Neissa*_____

CHAPTER TWENTY

The drug war raged into 1976; it was bloody, ruthless and violent. No one was immune. Twelve of Gacha's men had been murdered, brutally. They were killed slowly with the fabled Medellin necktie.

A Medellin necktie was a cut across the throat that was done very slowly causing maximum pain and a slow death. Although the cut was called the Medellin necktie, it had originated from the era of *La Violencia*, when it was known as the *corte de franela* (the flannel cut).

No matter where he went, Gacha was forced to take along with him a minimum of half a dozen bodyguards. The worst part about the war was that it had done the one thing they could not afford. It brought them publicity. So far, Gacha had been relatively undetected and now he was making page one.

Every morning, Gacha's carefully cultivated sources called him up to tell him that a man by the name of Álvaro Para Reyes was digging hard and deep into Cia. Export. The news forced Gacha to call in two big favors to have the young Deputy Minister of Justice re-assigned. Carlos Fuentes, however, had turned out to be an entirely different problem. Fuentes was now part of the unchangeable establishment by the sheer fact that he knew too much about too many people. Since the war's breakout, Fuentes had also begun to dig, except that he was immune from re-assignment. Fuentes was at the top of his profession, Police Commander of Bogota and, because of it, he was untouchable.

Cocaine production, although at its highest rate of export ever, had reached a plateau. The increased surveillance, police pressure and the war itself had caused the production to stagnate.

In the United States, the DEA, the successor of a merger between the Narcotics and Dangerous Drugs Bureau and the U.S. Customs, was making its fair share of arrests and, although minor, they were now becoming bothersome. Twelve of Harry Fosse's men had been arrested and sent to jail.

The battle for control of the United States cocaine market reached a stalemate. Gacha controlled the cocaine fields and some highly organized distribution networks in the States. Medellin, however, controlled the best distribution system and network in the United States. Medellin had developed a distribution network that would make even the greatest cargo fleets of the world look on with envy. Cali, for all its lack of cocaine fields and distribution and delivery methods, had developed the best money laundering connections in the world. Cali had a system which could insert money into the banking world and launder it within forty eight hours. They all needed a part of each other's assets, and the method each had sought to acquire them was through war.

Cali and Medellin had killed nearly four hundred people in the year since the war broke out. Each attack was met with a more brutal reprisal, until finally a killing invited a massacre.

Medellin, the once tranquil, peaceful city had become murder central. It was said that the police of Medellin did not respond to the citizens' calls for fear of getting caught in an ambush. So, while the police stayed in the station, outside the guns blazed throughout the night. The following morning, dead bodies were found all across the city. The citizens had at first been horrified, but it had become such a common occurrence it became a way of life.

The newspapers began to print the worsening way of life in Medellin, the politicians of that city hung onto the belief that it was the work of a bunch of renegade hoodlums. The truth was the politicians were all bought and paid for by the

Medellin cocaine group.

However, the rest of the country still had clean and upstanding politicians who called for major investigations. But when the government seemed on the verge of acting its attention was diverted.

To Gonzalo Rodriguez Gacha, the diversion was a godsend.

Deep in the heart of Colombia, near the Magdalena River port called Puerto Boyaca, the M-19 with new and well supplied troops, attacked a military outpost in their drive for legitimacy. Fueled by blackmail, kidnapping, extortion and fees paid by the drug czars so that they wouldn't burn or intercept their crops, the M-19 and the FARC became heavily armed with well- equipped guerrillas. The guerrillas had also found out that they could get money by growing and producing their own marijuana. The end result was the ability to buy armaments for their struggle.

Within a week of the guerrilla drive, the country had forgotten about the drug problem and begun to worry about the guerrilla problem. To Gacha and the rest of the cocaine traffickers, business regained a new momentum even though the war between them still raged on.

Outside pressure from the United States also dropped off when a peanut farmer by the name of James Earl Carter got himself elected to the office of President of the United States. Usually the change of administrations in the States did not affect personnel in Colombia, except this time the change was deeper than just a change of parties. It was also the reason why it had brought Jim Harrison to Gacha's office in downtown Bogota.

"I'll be moving on soon," Harrison said.

"Why?" Gacha asked, concern written all over his face.

"I came in with a Republican Administration and so did the present ambassador. We will be relieved soon, and you will have bumbling amateurs, people who will think that Colombia's problems can be fixed within four years."

"But you're CI...you came in with Eisenhower, you

know Colombia!"

"Yes, but the new President Carter is more than just a change of administration. The country wants to wash itself of the old, it feels soiled with past administrations. Everyone tied to an old administration will be looked upon as part of the problem."

Gacha chuckled. "Americans are not that naïve, are they?"

Harrison spread his hands in doubt. "I don't know, maybe in the end it's a good thing. We will know in a few years time. Good luck, Gacha, you're going to need it. You saved my ass once and I repaid you, but let me say this, I think you should get out of the business that you are in. Once America discovers that you are a threat to it, they will seek your elimination." Harrison stood up and walked to the door. "If my country ever wises up and finds out that you are killing them with the white powder, you will become my enemy."

"Harrison, you have lived in Colombia half your life, can you just pack up and leave like that?" Gacha asked, not put out in the least by Harrison's warning.

Harrison sighed. "I don't know, I've gone back to the States, but I haven't liked what I have seen. It's as if..."

"They've lost perspective," Gacha said solemnly. Harrison nodded, waved and walked away. Gacha looked out over the Bogota skyline, reflecting how much it had changed since the days he had met Harrison in Bogota back alleys. Fifty story skyscrapers were non-existent back then, now they were so common he almost couldn't remember a Bogota without them.

There was a light knock on Gacha's office door.

"Yes," Gacha said, turning from the window. Suddenly he was face to face with Jaime Saenz, Medellin's chief *pistolero*. Gacha's heart began to race as he imagined a bloody carnage outside the office, how else could he have come in?

"I come on behalf of my *jefe* in Medellin. He has asked me to invite you to a meeting to be held at his house one month from now. Security and safety will be provided,

254

however, if you wish to bring your own security you are welcome. My *jefe* also wishes you to know that he will adhere to any rules you wish to impose on him." Saenz stood in the doorway waiting for an answer.

"What's the meeting for?" Gacha asked trying to calm himself down.

"To negotiate an equitable way of ending the war. Cali has already accepted"

It could be a trap, Gacha thought, but what if it were not a trap? What if Cali and Medellin joined forces? They could wipe him out! If he did not accept, he could be done away with, and if he did accept he could be killed.

"I accept," said Gacha.

The *pistolero* moved slowly and calmly, making sure he made no sudden moves that could be interpreted as an attack. He carefully placed a small white envelope on Gacha's desk and walked out of the office.

Gacha looked at the envelope for a long time. He wondered if it were a letter bomb. With curiosity getting the better part of him, he opened the letter. It did not blow up. Instead he retrieved two pieces of paper. One was a letter, and the other was a map of an *hacienda* outside of the city of Medellin. The *hacienda* had flight coordinates and the measurements of the length of its runway. Gacha turned his attention to the letter and began to read it.

> *Don Gonzalo Rodriguez Gacha:*
>
> *The time has come when war has become a waste of valuable resources. It is my intention to seek a solution to our mutual problem. However, our primary concern must first deal with the blackmailing and the kidnapping tactics of the guerrillas upon our*

own families. Although I am told you have been relatively untouched, ourselves and Cali have been greatly affected. Members of my own family have been kidnapped several times, and two have been killed. In Cali, Ernesto Bosco saw his wife kidnapped and murdered. Our crops and our lands are constantly raided and burned if their outrageous fees are not paid. Since we have, through no fault of our own, become members of the landowning class, we are now at cross purposes with the guerrilla. A twist of fate, eh? Well, we must now cooperate or fall to the kidnappers. Enclosed is a route to my hacienda outside of Medellin. Please come by plane, it will keep people from guessing who is at the meeting.

Sincerely, Francisco Torres.
Medellin, Colombia.

Gacha stared at the letter and remained quiet for a few minutes. He realized instantly how big the M-19 problem had become. One of those problems was the exorbitant fees they demanded for crop and transport protection. At first he had laughed it off, but the fact that he was unable to control what he owned, later made him mad.

When Gonzalo was a young upstart *gamín*, he had empathized with the guerrilla; he had even allowed one of his subordinates to become a member. Now, they were against him for the simple reason that he made a lot of money and bought land with the money.

Gacha put the envelope in his desk drawer as his senior secretary entered, her face in shock.

"Don Gacha," said the secretary. "I am sorry to disturb you, but you have another unscheduled visitor. I told him you were busy, but he has insisted on waiting."

"Who is it?" Gacha asked.

"He says his name is Álvaro Para Reyes, Deputy Minister of Justice."

Gacha felt the shivers of danger and warning shoot into his brain like exploding Roman candles. If there was one man he truly feared, it was Reyes. Reyes had become his nemesis.

"Show him in," said Gacha, reaching for his suit coat.

The secretary stepped out and a few moments later the Deputy Minister of Justice walked in. Gacha was always struck by the size of the man. The Deputy Minister of Justice was just five feet tall. The face was also uglier than Gacha had remembered it, but the eyes were still the same, as if they were set in stone.

"Good evening Mr. Para Reyes," said Gacha. "This is a surprise. Please, sit down. Would you like something to drink?"

"No thank you," Para Reyes said. "I am here unofficially, and I won't be long."

"You make it sound ominous, please have a seat."

"No, I don't want to sit down. I'm here to tell you Gacha, that I know who you are or better yet what you are..."

"What's that?" Gacha asked, his face still jovial but his voice sharp like a steel-edged razor.

"You're a parasite. You're the scum that sticks to the bottom of a toilet seat and I am here to wash you out and flush you down. I know it was you who had me reassigned, but I'm here to tell you that I have my eye on you and your days are numbered. Don't think that your money is always going to save you. I've got allies and they too see the scum you are."

Gacha's jovial face had altogether disappeared. The room was so full of tension it seemed ready to discharge in the form of electrical bolts.

"Just how much money do you think I have?" Gacha asked off-handedly.

"Millions, maybe ten, but not enough to save you."

Gacha stood up. "Listen to me good, Para Reyes. You are a mid-level government official who earns in a year what I tip a waiter at a fashionable restaurant. I don't doubt you have allies, I do too..."

"Scum," Para Reyes interrupted.

"You know who called me this morning? Wanted to know if I'd spend some time at his *finca* this weekend." Para Reyes remained silent. "I told the President I couldn't, I had a previous engagement with the Chief Justice of the Supreme Court. Let me give you some advice Para Reyes: Don't go to war against an enemy you cannot beat."

"Do what you like with your money, Gacha, and I'll show you the power of the law."

"So the rules are set, eh? There you stand with your law, and here I stand with my millions. Let history record the victor."

"The law falls hard on people like you Gacha. It doesn't make distinctions."

"Since when?" Gacha asked with a smirk on his face.

"Forever!"

"Then, my friend, the law has never worked. In this country the law only works for the oligarchy."

"Don't make twisted statements to justify your own criminal behavior."

"There are twenty-four million Colombians, three quarters of them live in poverty and half of them are slowly starving to death. I do not twist statements, I speak the truth as I see it. Go back to that fairy tale land you came from, that land where they told you the law was blind. Go back and tell them that indeed the law is blind, but that it can smell money and it smells in favor of the rich."

The attorney general stood in rage and managed to blurt out: "You are evil Gacha."

"No, I'm a survivor."

The *hacienda* of Francisco Torres was north of Medellin and was big enough to accommodate several planes on its own private airstrip. The *hacienda* produced coffee which was then sold to a syndicate team who in turn sold it to the United States.

The ranch style *hacienda* accommodated forty people easily in the most luxurious manner. Oil paintings hung on the walls, Persian rugs were on the floor, sculptures of famous artists adorned the hallways and every other wealthy ornament one could imagine.

When Gacha came face to face with Francisco Torres, he recognized part of himself in the man. They shook hands and greeted each other in typical fashion. They made small talk on world politics, the price of jet fuel, boat fuel and how money couldn't buy what it used to.

Francisco Torres was a man of average height but of considerable girth in the middle. It was pure fat, the kind that comes from too much food and alcohol. Even his fingers were fat and his hands pudgy. He was also a man who liked to ride high-stepping horses. Now, as Gacha looked at Torres, he wondered if the horses shared the same enthusiasm.

One hour after Gacha had talked to Torres, Ernesto Bosco walked in. They greeted each other as if no bad blood had ever occurred between them. It had been over a year since the outbreak of the war, a war that Medellin had begun in Cali, and it was four years since Bosco had tried to assassinate Gacha.

And, now, here they were in a *hacienda* outside Medellin, laughing and joking as if they were the best of friends. They were competitors in a business, and yet they had more in common with each other than they had with anyone else. Here they were, the Three Kings. Bogota, Cali and Medellin. They were kings who had started life off with one foot in the grave; it should have been two had it not been for their ruthless cunning.

259

"When do we get down to business?" Gacha asked. "I'm a little tired."

"Tomorrow," said Torres. "Tonight is for us."

"Us?" Bosco asked puzzled.

"Yes, the rest of the businessmen will arrive tomorrow," said Torres.

"How many businessmen are we talking about?" Gacha asked.

"Two hundred. Why don't we retire for a little *siesta* and talk about business later, eh?"

Gacha nodded and headed off towards the room he had been given. The fact that there were two hundred people in the same business as he was unsettling.

At four in the afternoon, they met again. This time it was by the side of the swimming pool. They sat around a table under a huge sun umbrella, shading them from the powerful sun. At first, the conversation was awkward and slow almost like they were learning how to speak. Then Torres came straight out and said what was on his mind.

"We cannot compete against each other. Each of us controls a vital interest to our business, and because of our control, we run the risk of stagnating."

"I agree," said Gacha.

"So do I," remarked Bosco, "so what?"

"We have to come to an understanding, set limits and boundaries so we don't usurp others' territory and wind up killing ourselves." Torres lifted his drink from the table and let what he had said hang in the air.

"Eventually one of us will have to make a move on the others to expand," Bosco said casually as if testing the waters.

"The other two may join and crush the one making the move," Torres replied not put out in the least. "That is why it is necessary to make the rules now."

"No," Gacha said as Bosco and Torres looked at him with surprise. "No rules, no nothing. You all agree that there is enough money for all of us?" Both Bosco and Torres nodded. "Then I propose we merge."

They all looked at each other as if the idea could never happen but had certain possibilities.

Gacha this time was not lacking in confidence. "I say we all put in eighty percent of our coke together and sell it. The profits are then divided among us; we hire someone to overlook the books to make sure we are all playing fair. We set a standard price for a kilo, so there is no underselling one another. If we control the output, we can name the price on coke. Figures will go through the roof."

"Why only eighty percent?" Torres asked.

"That way we have some autonomy to make our own little side deals," said Gacha with a conniving smile.

"You stand to lose more," Bosco said to Gacha suspiciously. "You have more coke than all of us put together, why do you give us this gift?"

"I'm not giving you a gift. Yes, I supply more coke, but Torres has the better distribution network, and you have the better laundering system. We all have something that the other does not, but together we could..."

"By God!" Torres said loudly, causing a body guard to look over a hedge. Torres waved the guard away. "It cannot be that easy, can it?"

"You know," said Gacha, "I keep saying that all the time, and it turns out to be even easier than that."

Bosco laughed. "It's so simple it sounds ridiculous. We could force the other two hundred businessmen out of the market. All we would have to do is sit back and let the system work itself. It's kind of what the Arabs did in '73."

Gacha smiled. "Yes, they were killing themselves with competition, but then they came together to form OPEC. Today we all know it as the Oil Cartel."

Torres laughed this time in an expansive belly laugh. Finally when he managed to get himself under control, he spoke. "We will be the Cocaine Cartel."

The afternoon progressed. A proposal that at one time had seemed outrageous began to take shape, as if it were the initial plans of incorporation for a new conglomerate.

"We should agree that all policy on cocaine emanates from us three. The word will officially be spoken from right here in Medellin, no matter where the problem may be," said Gacha.

"Agreed," said Bosco and Torres.

"I propose that we meet here every three months to discuss problems we might encounter along the way. In essence, all policy matters related to cocaine come from Medellin, us." Gacha paused for effect before he added, "The Cartel."

They all smiled at each other and shook hands. The deal was sealed. Although they thought in terms of product, numbers, distribution, not one of them ever thought that what they were agreeing on was the mass market distribution of death. Instead Torres stood up and raised his glass for a toast. Gacha and Bosco followed suit.

"To the Cocaine Cartel," said Torres.

"*Salud!*" they chorused and clinked their glasses together.

For the next six hours they exchanged information on banks, bankers, tonnage in coke, distribution, names of DEA agents, people on the take and everyone else they had come into contact with in the business. Late in the evening, just before ten, the workings of the Cartel were put into effect.

At the end of the next day, when all businessmen were present, a policy against kidnappers was fashioned out. The policy was simple and was called MAS (*Muerte a los secuestradores*). Death to the kidnappers.

Moments before Gacha was about to enter his private Gulfstream III executive jet, Bosco and Torres called him over for an impromptu meeting.

"What is it?" asked Gacha.

"You agree that all information and potential dangers to the Cartel should be discussed?" Bosco asked.

"Absolutely," replied Gacha.

"Are you aware that your *pistolero*, Chulo, has killed five women?" asked Torres.

"What?!" Gacha recoiled.

Bosco nodded. "Chulo is the best *pistolero* there is, Francisco and I agree on that. However, he has problems. If he gets caught by the police, he might spill his beans. You know how efficient certain members of the police can be. They have ways of making one talk and that includes truth serums."

"Girls?" Gacha asked, his mind still locked onto that fact.

"Yes," Bosco replied. "He...abuses them. Sometimes they survive. They are very young, really young. Maybe eighteen or twenty years old."

"No," said Gacha in a whisper. "How do you know?"

"Surveillance," said Torres. "When the war broke out we put everyone under surveillance. The first time we caught him was in a small town called Medina, the second was in Guateque. We have pictures..."

Gacha nodded and walked away.

"Hey!" Bosco shouted angrily. "What are you going to do?"

Torres put a hand on Bosco's shoulder. "He will handle it, Ernesto."

Gacha felt the weight of the world on his shoulders. Could he face Chulo knowing what he knew? Was Bosco getting back at him indirectly for what he had done to Crater Face Gómez, in what was now another life? Could he kill Chulo, the only friend he had been able to count on? Could he kill his best friend? Had he come down to that? No! The business has to be protected. If I do not achieve power because he is killing young women, I will never have my respect. The Cartel has to be protected, doesn't it? Yes! No! I don't know! Damn!

CHAPTER TWENTY-ONE

Chulo was already strapped into a seat aboard the Gulfstream III, when Gacha walked in and took the seat beside him.

"Hey, *jefe*!" Chulo said jovially. "We have the world by the tail, eh? Nothing can stop us now..." Chulo's voice trailed off, like someone had let out the air in his balloon.

Chulo and Gacha locked eyes. Chulo shifted uncomfortably in his seat as Gacha's gaze full of pity, anger and loss enveloped him.

"What's wrong, *jefe*?"

"Let's go," said Gacha to the pilot.

The pilot saluted Gacha and returned into the cockpit, closing the door behind him. Moments later the slow whine of the engines beginning to turn could be heard. The aircraft began to move.

Gacha didn't answer Chulo's question, he just kept his eyes fixed on the ground. Chulo knew something was wrong as the plane raced down the runway and took to the air.

The jet landed at the El Dorado International Airport in Bogota, forty minutes later. When the pilot and co-pilot had disembarked, Chulo and Gacha were still strapped into their seats. Neither had looked at each other since the flight had taken off from Medellin.

"What should be done if something threatens the Cartel?" Gacha asked cryptically, his eyes still on the floor.

"Eliminate the threat," Chulo answered at once.

"If Medellin or Cali had something that could jeopardize us, what should we do about it?"

Chulo looked at Gacha puzzled but answered anyway. "Tell them and let them handle it, I suppose."

"And if they don't?" whispered Gacha.

There was a silence before Chulo spoke. "You'd have to take care of it yourself, your survival depends on it. It's business."

"You have been a good friend Chulo, almost like a brother. Medellin and Cali, have told me that you have become a liability..."

"Me?!" Chulo shouted back in disbelief.

"Yes, they told me that you have killed women." Gacha unbuckled his seat belt, stood up and faced Chulo. "They have pictures. If you want to regain respect, you will know what to do."

Chulo his face drained of color, looked at Gacha. "I understand...Gonzalo. I am not afraid, but your day of reckoning is approaching, and you will not be able to cheat it. You are not the same person I once knew. When I killed, I knew it was wrong, but when you kill you don't know the difference."

"So be it," said Gacha walking away.

"Wait!" Chulo shouted angrily stopping Gacha in his tracks. "You owe it to me to hear me out. You're lost Gacha, you don't know what you want. Money? You have enough of that already. Power? You will never get the power you want. Love? Ana-Alicia will some day see the real you. You are not lost to the devil yet, but he's running with you and soon he will trip you."

Gacha nodded and walked away.

At the home of the German industrialist Johann Herzog, there was a party to celebrate a new Colombian-German venture. Since the Herzog corporation was creating thousands of new jobs in Colombia, everyone from the lowest cabinet members to the President himself was in attendance.

Gacha stood in the corner of the room drinking a scotch and soda discussing the possible events that might befall the economic community in 1977. As he explained his feeling for a slump market, he caught a watchful eye on him. It was from

Carlos Fuentes.

Fuentes moved across the room towards Gacha. Gacha excused himself from the crowd and met Fuentes halfway. Gacha extended his hand, but Fuentes did not take it.

"The Chief of Police has become discreet?" Gacha asked with an amused voice.

"You had a visit from Álvaro Para Reyes, did you not?" Fuentes asked.

Gacha sighed. "Yes, a most unpleasant man. His rudeness was not becoming of an Attorney General."

Fuentes chuckled. "Good, I am of the same opinion as Para Reyes. I think you're a danger to Colombia, and I'm going to bring you down. About rudeness, learn to live with it."

As Gacha was about to respond, he saw Ana-Alicia walk into the salon with a young good looking man on her arm. Gonzalo had been meeting with Ana-Alicia once a week, and never did he suspect she had been seeing another man.

Fuentes, who had known about Ana-Alicia and Gacha's romance, smiled inwardly. "Yes, she is the loveliest woman in all of Bogota. She looks positively radiant and so does he, and with good reason I might add."

"Oh?" Gacha asked, trying to sound casual as his heart hammered inside his chest.

"Oh yes, last night at the residence of Don Emilio they made the formal announcement. It was in all the newspapers this morning."

"Announcement?" Gacha's voice slipped a notch, his drink becoming unsteady in his hand.

"Yes, they are engaged to be married. Quite sudden I'm told, but you know the young, full of wild and reckless impulses."

"Who...who is he?" Gacha asked his throat dry.

"You don't recognize him? Of course not, you've never been to Yale University. That's the son of the Colombian President, they say that someday he will run for the office. He's young, so he's got a while to go politically."

"When...when...married?"

Fuentes could not help but enjoy Gacha squirming. "A week from today, he's going back to Yale to finish his last semester. His dissertation in Engineering. Intelligent, very intelligent young man."

"Excuse me," Gacha said and walked away passing Ana-Alicia. They had locked eyes momentarily, but all he could see was her betrayal in her face.

Ana-Alicia saw Gonzalo's eyes and a shiver ran through her. It was as if she had seen him for the first time. Had she not told him that one day this would happen? Yes, some if not half of that fault was her own. She had made up her mind not to marry long ago, if she couldn't have Gonzalo she would have no one. But that was before she had been informed.

She was told on Monday. No warning about it, just a regular visit. No sign that impending doom or catastrophe was ready to befall on her. It simply came like an earthquake, suddenly and with devastating effect. The man in the white frock had simply said three words. "You are pregnant."

She had thought a full twenty-four hours about her predicament. If Gonzalo knew she was carrying his child, he would insist on marrying her and her family would be scandalized. If she married someone else, she would have to pretend the child was his and nobody would know the truth. It also meant that she would never be able to see Gonzalo again. She would be reduced to seeing him at parties, balls and other social events. She could live with that, she had his child in her, she had part of Gonzalo and she could live with that for the rest of her life. She would have something that no one would ever be able to take away.

The same night that Ana-Alicia decided her future course of action, she went out on a date with Luis and slept with him. The whole process made her skin crawl. Luis was a lousy lover and the buffoon had fallen for the line, "I don't think I've ever loved anyone quite like you." Ana-Alicia much later decided that it was the truth, because she didn't love him at all. Luis however, had taken it as a declaration of undying love and a testament to his virility, whereupon he immediately asked her to marry him. Ana-Alicia immediately accepted.

Mario García woke Gacha up at mid-morning. Gacha's eyes were red and swollen. Why couldn't they leave him alone, thought Gacha.

"Come on, get up, *jefe*!" Mario said, propping him up on his chair.

Somehow, Gacha realized, he had fallen asleep on the floor in the midst of a glass frame that had been smashed against the floor. What had happened to the picture? Then he saw the ashes and he remembered lighting on fire a photograph of Ana-Alicia's face. His head was pounding like a sledgehammer and his bloody fingers were shooting messages of pain into his brain. What was pain to him now? His soul had been kicked inside out by Ana-Alicia.

"Leave me alone!" Gacha shouted.

"Sorry, *jefe*," Mario said, "but the police want to talk to you."

"Fuentes?" Gacha asked, forcing his mind to work.

"Yes, they want to know what happened with Chulo."

"What do you mean 'happened' with Chulo?"

"*jefe*," Mario said with shock. "They found him this morning. He blew his brains out."

Gonzalo felt nauseous, he was going to be sick. "Excuse me," Gacha said as he ran for the bathroom.

They buried José 'Chulo' Moncada in the exclusive cemetery to the north of Bogota. It was a cemetery to which plots had been sold years before to those who wished to be buried there. The price of course, always depended on the size of the plot and whether one wanted a simple headstone or a massive mausoleum. To Gacha, this was a macabre practice. He could not understand why people would want to know where they would be buried. He felt that buying a plot was the ultimate act of a pessimist or was it the conclusive act of a realist?

It had been a private service, only Mario, Margarita, and Gacha were in attendance. There was a taxi beside the hearse with a woman in it. Gacha thought it was probably Chulo's mistress or some unknown relative come to pay her last respects. At least, Gacha thought, she had decided to wait and not bother them with empty phrases. Only Chulo knew what he had done and that was the way it was going to remain.

Mario and Margarita crossed themselves when the priest finished the prayer. The act of crossing oneself struck Gacha as funny, he himself no longer believed in God. To him the whole idea of religion and God had become a joke. Religion and hope for an afterlife were for those who had given up on this world, the quitters. After all, where was God when they massacred his village? Where were the Jesuits and the priests who had taught his parents to fight for land reform? Where was the aid from the Church for the starving poor? It was in the Vatican with all the other precious treasures accumulating dust on them. No, Gacha thought, God was an image created by the upper classes to keep the poor content with their lot in life by promising them a reward, heaven. To him, it was the swindle of humanity or maybe Chulo had been right, maybe he was the devil and that is why he did not see any God.

It was all stuff and nonsense.

Gacha turned and began to walk towards the car and saw the woman step out of the taxi. She was wearing a black veil covering her face. Her steps were long and graceful and the swing of her hips almost erotic.

The woman came directly at him, so Gacha stepped aside to let her by, but the woman stopped in front of him.

"I'm sorry about José," said the woman.

"Ana-Alicia?" Gacha asked in shock.

"Yes," Ana-Alicia responded in a whisper. "Please, walk beside me and keep quiet. I will explain much of what hás happened."

They walked along the paths of the carefully landscaped cemetery. She told him of the pressure she had been under to marry, how rumors had been flying all about town. Then she told him how one night her parents had forced

270

her into marriage by threatening to disown her. She told him about how she had tried to reach him but had been unable.

It all made perfect sense, but not once did Ana-Alicia tell the truth. The truth was she was carrying his child and that she had become engaged for that reason.

"I still love you Gonzalo and I always will," Ana-Alicia said, holding onto his arm with a good grip.

"But..." Gacha said letting his voice trail off, he knew what was coming.

"But, we can never go on seeing each other like we have."

Seas of emptiness flowed between them until Gacha spoke. "I love you, Ana-Alicia and I always will, remember that. I will give my life for you if the chance ever arises."

They stood awkwardly in the cemetery, neither wanting to say the next few words but Gacha did so anyway. "Good-bye, Ana-Alicia, my true love."

"Good-bye," Ana-Alicia said, her voice cracking.

Gacha looked at her one last time and walked away. Dust seemed to invade his nostrils and the smell of death exhaling from open graves fell over the cemetery like an unseen weight.

At that very moment Gonzalo Rodriguez Gacha shed his last scrap of humanity, all he had left was his business. From now on nothing would come between him and his business. He would become the ultimate capitalist, he told himself.

The baby was born prematurely according to the Gonzáles family, even if the doctor had said it was right on time. Ana-Alicia named him Antonio, born on August 12, 1977.

Gonzalo was informed of the birth via *El Tiempo* newspaper, which had devoted a paragraph of the happening in the social page. He sent her a dozen roses and a congratulations card and then forgot all about it. He was too involved in his business to care otherwise. His business, unrecognized by the Fortune 500, was among the biggest in the world. He had already cleared his first billion dollars, and now he wanted to clear ten. He seemed to feel he could fool authorities at will, nothing they could bring against him worked. After all, he had better planes, boats, lawyers, politicians, police, than those who sought to stop him, especially that small outfit that called itself DEA.

The call came in November of 1977, when things seemed to be going on automatic pilot. It was late in the evening, rain splattering against the windows of his new penthouse offices in the tallest building of Bogota.

"Hello?" Gacha said into the mouthpiece of the telephone.

"Gonzalo?" said a voice on a long distance line.

"Yes, this is Gonzalo."

"This is John Morgan. I was with the U.S. Narcotics Bureau, remember me?"

Gacha was caught off guard, finding himself near shock was more like it. "Uh, eh, yes," Gacha managed to blurt out.

"Thought you would," said Morgan with a chuckle. "We've got your man up here. I just wanted to let you know that I'm coming after you like a freight train and, I'm going to run you down, so if I were you I'd start running."

"And what man is it that you think you have caught?" Gacha said, composing himself, some humor in the voice now.

"Oh, an old chum of yours, you remember Harry Fosse, don't you?" There was no answer from Gacha. "Well, buddy, he sure does remember you, can't seem to stop talking about you. I thought you ought to know. Now, you have a good-night, ol' buddy," Morgan said with a chuckle and hung up.

CHAPTER TWENTY-TWO

At seven in the morning, Harry Fosse, while on his way to the Greater Miami Superior Court to be arraigned on two counts of first degree murder before Judge Duncan Highsmith, also known as the Hanging Judge, was blown apart by a bazooka as he travelled in a DEA Chrysler automobile.

As Harry Fosse's body burned with the other three DEA agents in the wreckage, so did the evidence on the Cocaine Cartel. For the Cartel, business continued without interruption.

When Gacha was informed of the news, he called up his partners and laughed about it. "You know business is too good, I think we're in a boom town. Big season in Cartel city."

By the end of 1977, the Cocaine Cartel was pulling in from the United States three billion dollars a year on a wasted generation.

Every time the Cartel seemed on the verge of a setback, it dealt with the potential crisis swiftly and decisively. Usually the response meant death. Fosse, however much he might have contributed to Gacha's organization in the beginning, had become useless after the formation of the Cartel. He had become obsolete because Francisco Torres' distribution network had taken over Harry Fosse's job.

Francisco Torres, the chief of the Medellin branch of the Cartel, would ship in cocaine from private airstrips in the Guajira, Colombia. The Guajira province was desert region at the most northern point of Colombia, a peninsula that jutted out into the Caribbean Sea. From the town of Riohacha in the Guajira, a small single engine plane loaded with marijuana and cocaine would take off and fly to the Turks and Caicos

Islands. Once the plane reached one of these islands, it would refuel and take off again for Norman's Cay, Bahamas. Norman's Cay, had been leased to the Cartel by the Bahamian Government. When the pilot landed and refueled in Norman's Cay, it would receive orders for its ultimate destination into the United States. These orders were usually in the form of landing coordinates directing them to fields all over the southeastern United States. The method was effective and incredibly efficient.

In August of 1978, the Cocaine Cartel was at full operation. Production could not keep up with distribution and the DEA was arresting teenagers on the streets for an ounce of cocaine. The American authorities were concerned about busting kids on street corners while the Cartel flew in three hundred kilos of cocaine a week to the tune of twelve million three hundred thousand dollars. The money was almost unbelievable had it not been for the fact that it was all true.

By the end of 1978, Gonzalo Rodriguez Gacha was no longer aware of how much money he really had, whether it was legitimate or illegitimate. He knew the amount of money he had was somewhere in the vicinity of three billion dollars, but it was impossible to tell anymore. The legitimate money that was in the banks now made as much in interest as he made in a week of smuggling. His personal assets included four Lear-jets, forty-two speed boats, sixteen condominium complexes, one of which was in Miami, a hotel by the shores of the Mediterranean Sea, twenty-three apartment buildings housing fifteen thousand people and seven shopping malls in the United States. He also had twelve homes scattered randomly around the globe and a collection of cars which he had never seen.

Nothing could touch Gonzalo Rodriguez Gacha. He was the King.

In a small makeshift office in what used to be the janitors' coffee room, a group of sixteen men and women met. Their purpose for meeting was to bring about the destruction of the Cocaine Cartel.

"What we need is a concerted effort on all fronts," said one of the men. "We need helicopters to spot the planes coming in, we need fast boats to catch the boats and we need someone to infiltrate the Cartel."

"I agree," said John Morgan.

"We also need to make a political issue out of this mess," said an attractive woman. "We need to put pressure on Colombia to bring these drug lords under close scrutiny. We need to find out who our allies really are other than the Police Chief and the new Colombian Minister of Justice. I mean, is this man Para Reyes really strong enough to take the heat and go all the way?"

"There's no way of knowing that," Morgan said, drinking coffee from his paper cup.

"I think we should keep the political issue alone for the time being," said a young man in his early thirties. "Right now, the Cartel is a very loose outfit, sure of themselves. Political heat might make them close up ranks and infiltration might be impossible."

"What are you suggesting?" Morgan asked.

"Are you aware that we have no extradition treaty with Colombia?" the young man asked.

"No," said Morgan in surprise.

"Well, I think we should make our politicians get a treaty signed with Colombia, make it a low profile thing. Politicians love to sign treaties. That way when we get something concrete on the Cartel Drug Lords, we can ask Colombia to arrest them for us."

Morgan nodded. "If we've got the evidence for it. In the last ten years we have not reached the outer perimeter of one of these organizations, those who have tried have ended up dead. To get evidence for a conviction, we need to infiltrate them and who has the balls for that?"

"I do," said the young attractive woman.

"You are new here, eh?" asked Morgan. The woman nodded. "I'm sure you are a brave young woman but there is a difference between being brave and committing suicide. There isn't one person here who wouldn't jump at the chance of infiltration if there were a way in. This is worse than war. They won't take prisoners. If they catch you, they will torture you slowly to find out anything you know. They use a drug called *burundanga* that renders a person susceptible to hypnosis. They use it to extract information and then easy as you please they tell you to jump off the tallest building in the city. No, I'm sorry this is no place to be a heroine Ms. Goldstein."

"Goldman," said the young woman. "Cindy Goldman. I am not being a heroine, Mr. Morgan, but I do have a way into the Cartel."

"Oh?" Morgan said. All fifteen people in the room turned around to face her.

"My father was Gonzalo Rodriguez Gacha's launderer," said Cindy as the whole room gasped. "My father was Stephen Goldman. I have met Gacha. I met him in Ft. Lauderdale. It was during college and during a time of my life which I am sorry to say was not my best. However, I do know Mario García very well. My father trained him, and I have talked to him many times. At first I thought he was one of my father's clients, but yesterday I saw an FBI picture of him with Gacha. I then looked up the relationship between Gacha and García and found out that García was the Cartel's money man."

There was a collective silence in the room.

"Excuse me," said a young man at the opposite end of the room from Cindy. "My field is analysis, and I have some questions."

"Such as?" Morgan asked.

"It takes seventeen liters of ether to make one kilo of cocaine. Making cocaine also involves using chemicals such as acetone and kerosene. The point is where are they getting these precursors? If the rumors are true that the Cartel is bringing in fifty kilos a week, they must have some huge labs and holding areas in which to keep these precursors."

Everyone in the room looked at each other. Morgan

actually chuckled before he said, "Young man, we are not rocket scientists, perhaps you could tell us what you mean in plain English."

The young man stood up and walked to the center of the room and asked Morgan to move out of the way. Once he faced the whole group, he spoke. "If the Cartel is smuggling fifty kilos a week that means they need 3,400 liters of ether to make those fifty kilos, not to mention the other precursors of acetone and kerosene. That, my non-fellow rocket scientists, is a hell of a lot of precursors."

Morgan shook his head in confusion. "Perhaps, young man, this is not where you should be but at the lab..."

"No!" the young man's anger erupted, causing Morgan's face to turn scarlet. "I'm not the fucking idiot here. Three thousand four hundred liters of ether a week!"

"So fucking what?" Morgan shouted back angrily.

"Ether is not made in Colombia, it's made in the United States. Without ether, there is no cocaine!"

"Good God!" said Morgan vocalizing everyone's thoughts.

"Yes," said the young man. "We trace the ether and we get their labs, their coke, we got the evidence." The room broke into applause.

"Okay!" said Morgan as if he were at a basketball game and the home team had just shifted the momentum of the game in their favor. "We will divide into groups. One group will push for the extradition treaty, the second group on the precursor aspect of the trade, the third group on infiltration and the fourth group on distribution. The fourth group will concentrate on closing down the Norman's Cay area in the Bahamas. Let us also get evidence on the Bahamian officials allowing the Cartel to operate there." Morgan paused and looked at each man and woman in the force. "It is going to be a long painful process and we won't see any results for a long time. However, when we've got the evidence we will bring down the bastards for good."

"Yes sir!" came back a chorus of voices.

The old, matronly looking secretary walked into Gonzalo Rodriguez Gacha's office, closing the door behind her. "I'm sorry to disturb you," the secretary said to Gacha.

"Yes, what is it?" Gacha asked, looking up from the papers on his desk.

"There is a *norteamericana* outside asking for *Señor* García, but he is in Paris this week and she seems to be upset about it."

Gacha looked at the secretary curiously. "What does she look like?"

"*Divina!*" Gorgeous, the secretary said. "If Margarita knew about her, I believe her husband would be in a lot of trouble."

Gacha smiled, the thought of his reserved and always proper Mario having an affair was something extraordinary. "Show her in, please." The secretary nodded.

The woman strode confidently into the office, but she seemed confused. The man she had asked to see was not the one she had been shown in to see.

"I'm sorry," said the woman, "I asked to see Mario García. Good-day," the woman said and turned around.

Gacha recognized her the moment she stepped through the door, and she hadn't even recognized him! "Wait!" Gacha shouted, stopping the woman in mid-stride.

The woman turned to face him. She was a tall, good looking, blonde, blue-eyed woman. She had a model's figure and the face of an angel. It was the first woman in almost two years who had excited Gacha in a sexual way. Not since he had last seen Ana-Alicia, had any woman been able to catch his attention long enough to get him excited. This one had done it in a few seconds.

"Yes?" the woman said, there was snobbishness in the voice.

"You don't recognize me?" Gacha asked, feigning hurt.

The woman narrowed her eyes slightly but shook her head. Of course she knew the bloody bastard, his face was on the most wanted list in the FBI and DEA offices. Good God!

278

you bloody well killed my little brother with your goddamn drugs! "No, should I?" she said.

"Well, the last time I saw you, you were... Shall we say *al aire libre*," said Gacha. The woman blushed. "Fort Lauderdale?"

"I don't recall. Those days were spent in a drug-induced haze. It was typical of the time, not to say that it was okay to do it."

Gacha ignored the social comment. "You were a cheerleader for the University of Miami or at least that is what I was told. You called yourself...Sin, you made a big joke of it."

"Oh God! Don't hold that against me," the woman said with a flirtatious look.

"Yes, you are Cindy Goldman. Your father and I were business acquaintances. I'm sorry about his death."

"You knew my father?" Cindy asked in shock.

"Yes, very well. Can I ask you how you know Mario García? He works for me, you know?"

"No, I didn't know that. I assumed you worked for him or...forget it. I knew Mario because he spent a lot of time with my father, he was one of my father's clients or...oh, it's not important. I'm sorry he's not here, I just wanted to say hello. I'm on my way back to the United States, I was to have a modeling shoot in Cartagena, but it fell through."

"Would you like to have dinner with me tonight?" Gacha blurted out.

The woman looked at him curiously. "I don't think so, my plane leaves very early in the morning."

"Come on, I'll show you Bogota. If you miss your flight I'll let you take my jet."

"Jet, is it now?"

Gacha smiled. "The trappings of wealth."

"I guess so," the woman said, eyeing him carefully. "Okay, I'm staying at the Hilton. You can pick me up at seven thirty."

"Excellent!" Gacha said.

"Good," Cindy said and winked at him as she walked

out of the office.

They ate in a small restaurant in Cartagena. Gonzalo had ordered his pilots to take him to Cartagena. Cindy had reacted in an almost fawning way.

At dinner she had teased him, letting him know that she was interested, but not desperate. The flirting covered up her nervousness and the fact that her radio microphone was chaffing the skin above her stomach. Not that the microphone was doing much use, since she was out of range from anyone who might be listening. Her DEA partners were stuck back in Bogota, none of them had anticipated he'd fly her out of the city.

"Are you all right, Cindy? Is the food okay?" Gacha asked.

"I didn't want to ruin your evening by saying anything. Excuse me while I go to the ladies room for a moment?"

"Please, go ahead," Gacha said standing up from the table.

Cindy stood up and moved away towards the bathroom. Inside the bathroom she opened her blouse and ripped the radio microphone that was taped to her belly. The microphone had chaffed the whole area of skin it had been on. She covered up, cursing at her bad luck and then returned to Gacha's table.

"So, Gonzalo, tell me what it was that my father did for you?" Cindy asked with feigned innocence.

"Oh, he handled various transactions for me. He was an expert on international banking laws."

"I guess so, he did very well after...well, you know, after he was fired by Sheldon & Waterson."

"Yes, he made a mistake, but it was to the detriment of Sheldon & Waterson," Gacha said easily.

A waiter appeared at Gacha's table with a telephone. "It's for you, Don Gonzalo," said the waiter.

Gonzalo looked at the man in surprise but took the phone anyway. "Hello?"

"Gonzalo?" said Ernesto Bosco.

"Yes, it's me. What's up, I'm at a restaurant in Cartagena, you know?"

"I know, and I'm sorry, but I have some personal news that cannot wait. I have not confirmed the report but the source is reliable," said Bosco, his voice sounding grave.

Gacha's heart began to accelerate, his expression changing from easy going self-made billionaire, to cold calculating mass murderer.

Cindy saw the change and felt a chill shake her. My God, he knows! she thought, as Gacha's eyes fell on her.

"I'm listening." said Gacha into the telephone.

"A source of mine in Bogota says that Ana-Alicia's child has been kidnapped."

"No, don't tell me!"

"As I said, it is not confirmed, but this is a reliable source."

"What about her?" Gacha asked as Cindy looked on, small shivers shaking her body. Poor woman, he thought, she must be ill and has pretended to be well so that I might enjoy this evening. What a woman!

"A little bruised up," said Bosco. "However, my source says that she will be fine. I've put people onto it, I thought you'd want to know."

"I do. Thank you, Ernesto, more than you may think possible."

"I lost a wife, I know what Ana-Alicia means to you. If you need any help, let me know."

"Thank you again," Gacha said and hung up. He then motioned at the waiter to come over. "The bill, please."

"What's wrong?" Cindy asked, her heart thumping like cannon fire inside her chest.

"Do you remember Ana-Alicia Gonzáles?" Gacha asked.

"The brunette, the Latin goddess?"

Gacha smiled. "Yes, her child has been kidnapped. I'm going back to Bogota, I'm sorry."

"Oh, don't be silly. I'll go with you, that is if you don't mind?" Cindy said coquettishly.

"Not at all."

"Can you help her?"

"Yes, I know more about this country than the leaders who run it. The people who kidnap do it for money although they say it's for the Great Cause. That might have worked thirty years ago, but not today. Today they are simply in it for the money."

The waiter came with the bill. Gacha paid in cash. The waiter smiled when Gacha told him to keep the change. It was half a year's salary for the waiter. To Gacha it was pocket change.

Gacha walked into his downtown office at two in the morning after having dropped Cindy off at the Hilton Hotel. As he walked into the building, Gacha waved at the security guard and told him everything was okay. When he reached his office floor, he saw Herman. Herman was Gacha's latest *pistolero*, and as Gacha walked in he stood up from the chair he was in.

"*Jefe...*" Herman cried out.

"Not now, Herman, give me a few minutes," Gacha said waving Herman back into his seat.

"But, *jefe...*"

Gacha walked into his office and froze.

"Hello Gonzalo," said Ana-Alicia from the center of the office and then ran into his arms. "Oh, Gonzalo, they've got my baby!"

"Everything is going to be fine, I'll find your baby," Gacha said and he held onto her as Ana-Alicia broke down completely. After a few minutes, Gacha calmed her down and saw the black and blue marks on her face. He asked her what had happened and she told him.

"I was coming out of the supermarket with Antonio, that's my baby's name. Anyway, a van pulled up beside us and the door opened...Oh God, it happened so fast..."

"Take your time," Gacha said soothingly. "What color was the van?"

"Blue with a white stripe, but that's all I saw because three men with masks jumped out of the van and punched me in the face. I think one of them was a woman, but I'm not sure."

"A woman, eh?" Gacha said intrigued. His mind was already turning, he would have the *gamines* comb the city. The color of the van would be good, but a woman guerrilla was like a red flag. "What else?"

"Nothing!" Ana-Alicia said sobbing. "I was punched in the face and the next thing I know there was a bunch of people standing around me." Ana-Alicia let go with tears again.

Gacha consoled her as best he could. He was trying to decipher a course of action to take but the scent of Ana-Alicia in his nostrils brought back memories flooding into his brain.

"Oh Gonzalo! they want ten million dollars and we don't have ten million dollars."

"Ten million!" Gacha said in disbelief.

"My husband says that with a figure that size, it means they are going to kill the child. He says they know how much everyone can afford, and he says they know we cannot afford ten million dollars. For God sakes! We don't have ten million!"

"I'll give you the money," Gacha said.

Ana-Alicia looked into Gacha's eyes with astonishment. "Ten million?"

"Yes, however they want it. The only problem is, I think your husband is right. When a figure is that exorbitant, it means they're making an example, but I'll give you the money just in case."

Ana-Alicia looked at Gonzalo, and even though she knew now what he was, she still loved him. Should she tell him that her husband didn't care whether the child lived or died, because he knew the child wasn't his? How could she have known when she had agreed to marry him that he was sterile? Did she dare tell Gonzalo that Antonio was really his son and not her husband's? Her life couldn't get any worse. Her last year with her husband had been a living nightmare. How many times had he beaten her, trying to force her to say

283

who the father of the child was. She had remained silent even when the beatings were severe. Now, she was back in Gonzalo's arms, lost like a child in the wilderness.

Gacha told her that he would be working on it all night and that he would find her baby. When she seemed to believe him, he sent her home.

With the dawn came a new day, but the day brought nothing but bad news. No one had seen a blue van with a white stripe on it. Ana-Alicia's baby, even though he was from an important family, did not even merit a line in the newspapers. Kidnapping in Colombia had become so commonplace that it was said to have been elevated into an art form.

The only good news was that the Iranians had taken Americans as hostages in the American embassy in Teheran, Iran. The captors wanted the Shah of Iran returned in exchange for the hostages. It would help the Cartel: the Americans' attention would shift once again to another area of the world.

The call came at midday from Francisco Torres. "I'm sorry to hear about Ana-Alicia's child. Ernesto told me about the group of *guerrilleros* who took the child. However, I have a lead on a woman guerrilla. They say that she is with a group of cohorts up by Barranca-Bermeja..."

"The oil refinery place?" Gacha cut Torres off. "In the middle of all that military?" Barranca-Bermeja was the biggest oil refinery area in all of Colombia. Because of the constant threats to blow it up by the M-19, the military had stationed a few military divisions in the area.

"Yes Gonzalo, right smack in the belly of the beast, as they say. By the way, you heard anything about this treaty Colombia signed with the Americans?" Torres asked with some concern in his voice.

"Yeah, it's some stupid Mickey Mouse treaty. Makes the politicians look good. I wouldn't worry about it." They exchanged a few more business tidbits and then Torres gave him the location of the woman guerrilla. Gacha then thanked him and hung up.

Gacha then called up his contacts in Barranca-Bermeja and told them what he wanted done. No survivors except for the child, each man on the job would be guaranteed fifty thousand dollars. If the baby was killed while the rescue took place, the rescuers need not return. They too would be killed.

The wait began. Gacha busied himself with office business. He hoped that it would work out.

The call came ten minutes after midnight. The woman guerrilla had been verified and she was dead with her four companions. The baby was well and doing fine. Gonzalo guaranteed payment within the next twelve hours to those involved in the rescue. He then hung up the telephone and dialed Ana-Alicia's home phone.

The moment the telephone was lifted, Gacha knew someone else was on the line. Fuentes? Gacha smiled. Again he had ended up doing what Fuentes had been unable to do. It would drive the man mad.

"Hello?"

"Ana-Alicia?" Gacha asked.

"Gonzalo?" Ana-Alicia responded instantly. "What have you found out?"

"I have found your baby. He'll be in Bogota in an hour or so. He's alive and he's fine."

Ana-Alicia didn't say anything. She simply began to cry.

Gacha could hear her crying in the background, as she put the phone down and cried. He hung up. He knew she wouldn't be able to speak for a long while. As he grabbed his coat to leave the office, his phone rang again. He picked it up on the second ring.

"Thank you, Gonzalo, I love you," said Ana-Alicia and hung up.

Gacha knew that he would have to explain the death of the guerrillas, but he had no idea how the country would react to such an act. The reaction would completely take him by surprise.

CHAPTER TWENTY-THREE

Gonzalo Rodriguez Gacha found himself on the front page of every newspaper in Colombia. He had become a hero overnight. The Colombian people had had enough of the guerrillas and the terrorism. The realization that someone could strike back at the guerrillas so savagely gave the people hope that the M-19 and the FARC were not invincible.

Gacha had taken all the notoriety in stride. Instead of exploiting the publicity he elected to fly to Medellin and Cali to give personal thanks to Francisco Torres and Ernesto Bosco. The other reason was to discuss the serious problem of the ether scarcity that the Cartel was undergoing. The ether problem was bad enough, but at a production rate of five hundred kilos of cocaine a week they were beginning to backlog cocaine.

Francisco Torres received Gacha warmly. They soon retired to a soundproof room to discuss the ether problem. The soundproof room had been created specifically to deter the ability of directional microphones to record random pieces of conversation. Gacha had thought it logical that the authorities would keep such close tabs, but when Torres had found two microphones on his property, he had taken the invasion of privacy very badly. A siege mentality had come over him. He had his men trained by Israelis against terrorist attacks by the M-19. He also had experts sweeping the *hacienda* electronically.

As they sat down drinking *aguardiente*, they began to discuss distribution. It wasn't until an hour later that the conversation turned to the ether issue.

"The ether problem is getting serious," said Gacha. "At

8,500 liters a week, we will run out of ether in a few months."

Torres greeted this information by nodding his head. "I'll send one of my men to buy some in the United States. We will buy a few metric tons."

"Good. The other thing that bothers me is, why isn't Ernesto Bosco ever at these meetings?"

Francisco looked at Gacha with mouth agape, but then said, "Gonzalo, Ernesto hasn't been in the Cartel in almost three years."

"What do you mean, who runs Cali?"

"Ernesto went legitimate three months after we began the Cartel. He bought into that chain of department stores called Casa De Ropa (House of Clothes). After that, he diversified into a hundred other businesses, not a single dollar he has is connected with the coca."

"Good God!" Gacha exclaimed in disbelief.

"Yes, he's as legitimate as you can get. No government on earth will catch him, no prosecutor can throw him in jail. He's the real thing, one of the respected. I have begun to do the same. I began construction on a large low-income housing complex here in Medellin. It will be ready in a year they tell me. It's costing me three hundred million."

Gacha heard Torres speaking but the news of Ernesto Bosco going totally legitimate had been a blow. Now, he knew why Ernesto had been talked about in a circle that he himself had always been excluded from. Why hadn't he done that? Gacha thought about his position. *I could have been legitimate by now. Damn!*

"So, tell me, Gonzalo, are you sure there is nothing to this treaty with the Americans?" Torres asked.

"No, it's just another political showing, but I'll look into it more carefully and let you know. How is the Norman's Cay system working?"

"Like a Swiss watch. What about the labs in the Amazon and Putumayo provinces?" Torres asked.

"Hell, even with proper coordinates my helicopter pilot couldn't find the damn place. The lab technicians on the ground had to fire flares into the sky to tell him where to land."

Torres laughed and said, "I was in the States last week."

"You!" Gacha said incredibly.

"Yes, smuggled myself into Miami in one of your fast-boats. I'm worried Gacha, things are changing. The Americans are getting themselves together. These drug clowns in Miami, fighting over an ounce of cocaine, have made the city into a war zone. The violence has brought a lot of attention toward us. It's like a wave building against us. A lot of our men are getting caught, the Americans are throwing everything they have at us. They have the Coast Guard, the Customs, FBI, Fort Lauderdale Police, Greater Miami Police, New York Police, Los Angeles Police and, of course, those perky little bastards, the DEA. They are now using high technology. Planes and boats that are just as fast as ours, radar. I'm telling you we're fighting a war now."

"The DEA has been quiet since Fosse's death," Gacha said, sitting back down on a chair. He had known Torres long enough to know that the man was worried.

"Yeah," said Torres. "The fact that the DEA has been so silent worries me. They make some stupid mistakes, but they don't make them twice. They are not the same outfit they were a few years back. These bastards are tough, and they are going to keep on coming."

They talked about other matters, but it was Torres' worried face that had somehow rubbed off on Gacha. The siege mentality had taken hold. When Gacha left the *hacienda*, for the first time he really felt there was an enemy out there. He tried to shrug the feeling off, but the feeling stayed with him.

One week after Gacha and Torres had met in Medellin to discuss the ether problem, a *pistolero* by the name of Gustavio "El Roto" Paladinos, calling himself John Roberts, walked into the Gordon Company in eastern New Jersey. Roberts ordered 1,500 fifty-five gallon drums of high-grade ethyl ether.

The attendant winced then told Mr. Roberts that he could not fill such a large order. However, if Mr. Roberts cared to wait, he could make a few calls on his behalf. Mr. Roberts promptly agreed. The attendant smiled and walked back into his office where he picked up the telephone and called the DEA.

A few minutes after the attendant had made the phone call to the DEA, he told the customer that the National Company for International Chemicals in Chicago would be happy to take his order. A happy Mr. Roberts thanked the attendant profusely, unaware that the company's name was an inside joke in the DEA. The initials of the National Company for International Chemicals (NCIC) really stood for the National Crime Information Center.

John Morgan who supplied the ethyl ether to "El Roto" Paladinos, made sure that the ethyl ether was put on the freighter that "El Roto" Paladinos had stipulated. However, John Morgan had some of his workers install radio transmitters in each and every barrel of ether.

For one month, the DEA watched the freighter sail south to Colombia where the barrels were quickly loaded into trucks and then helicopters. The helicopters took the barrels even further south, to the biggest cocaine lab in the world. The DEA had struck the motherlode.

The call came shortly after dawn. Herman, Gacha's number one *pistolero*, had woken Gacha up and handed him the phone. At first the incoherent voice speaking on the other end of the line made no sense.

"Calm down, for Christ's sakes!" Gacha shouted.

The man on the other end of the line took three long breaths and then spoke. "The army, police and the DEA busted the laboratory at dawn and set fire to the place," said the panicked man on the telephone.

"What laboratory?" Gacha asked. The Cartel had

several around Colombia and Peru.

"The big one!"

Gonzalo Rodriguez Gacha dropped the phone, his head spinning with the bad news. Maybe he was still asleep, he thought. Yes, that was it, he would wake up soon.

"What is it, *jefe?*" Herman asked.

Gacha looked at him and then realized it was no dream. "Get my plane ready. Put all the money I have in the house into suitcases. We're going to Brazil. Call Torres and tell him our big lab was busted, and I'm heading for Brazil."

Gacha then jumped out of bed and ran for the shower. How? His mind kept repeating the same question, how were they able to find it? When he emerged from the shower, Herman stood in the doorway, his face drained of color. "They've seized the jets," said Herman, his voice dry.

"Who?"

"Carlos Fuentes. He has an order from the new Minister of Justice Álvaro Para Reyes. The same has happened in Medellin. Don Francisco Torres is on the phone."

Gacha walked over to the phone. "What the hell happened?"

"The ether barrels, they had radio transmitters in them. Gonzalo, they are going to take us to the States! That Mickey Mouse treaty Colombia and the United States signed a few months back was an extradition treaty."

"So?" Gacha asked perplexed.

"That means the Americans can tell Colombia to arrest us and send us over to them. They could put us on trial in the United States."

Gacha gasped. "What the hell do we do?"

"We play tough," said Torres, his voice sharp as a razor's edged. "This Fuentes has become a problem. He is the one who has cooperated with the DEA. Let's get rid of him to show the rest of the bastards what they are up against. It will at least make them think twice about cooperating again and it will make them think twice about sending us to the States for trial. I also have a friend who is a judge. I will make him look at the extradition treaty and see if we can get it invalidated somehow."

"What about the new Minister of Justice?" Gacha asked.

"Para Reyes?" Torres asked. "He's untouchable for now, but I swear that by the end of this week there won't be a fucking attorney who will have us arrested."

"I agree, I'm not handing over what is mine without a fight!"

Carlos Fuentes reached for the telephone that had not stopped ringing since the drug bust. After the raid he had become more than just a Police Chief, he had become the enforcer of the law. Congressmen, senators, governors and mayors were calling him all wanting advice on how to handle the drug problem. It was the first time something concrete was going to happen, he thought.

"Hello, Fuentes speaking," he said, wondering what politician it was this time.

"If you know what's good for you and your family, forget about the drug problem," said the voice and hung up.

A chill ran down Fuentes' spine. Then he smiled and thought, my God, we've got them on the run and they're desperate. Immediately he dialed downstairs and ordered a contingent of police officers to protect his family. He then picked up his coat and walked out of his office in downtown Bogota.

"I'm going to the office of our new Minister of Justice, Álvaro Para Reyes," Fuentes said to his secretary.

As Fuentes walked out into the street and stood on the sidewalk, he looked up at the indigo sky of Bogota. He felt that he was on the side of the good and on the side of the righteous hand. Unfortunately because he had looked up to wonder at the beautiful blue sky, he never saw the motorcycle speeding down the street towards him.

Carlos Fuentes' last thought before the bullet entered his cerebral cortex was of taking a family vacation, perhaps to

Cartagena. One second later, his brains were splattered all over the front entrance to Colombia's toughest investigative agency.

The message was clear: Death to those against the Cartel.

Within a month of the shooting of Carlos Fuentes, every major civil servant in Colombia had been threatened. Álvaro Para Reyes, Colombia's Minister of Justice could then only watch the prosecution of the drug lords go up in smoke. The most humiliating fact for him was to see the high judge of Colombia invalidate the extradition treaty with the United States.

The result was clear. The Cartel had won the first major battle.

Under extreme political pressure in 1981, the United States forced the ratification of the extradition treaty in Colombia. Gacha and Torres immediately had a whole slew of attorneys challenge the validity of the treaty on several different grounds. The Supreme Court of Colombia took it under consideration.

Francisco Torres, who had become a hero in Medellin since the opening of his low-income housing project, played his most masterful stroke yet. He got himself elected to the Colombian Congress. As a congressman he came under the protection of a Colombian law, a law that stated that no congressman could be charged for crimes while in office. The law gave the congressmen an immunity in Colombia, but also international diplomatic immunity too. Since Torres' business came under this protection and Gacha and Torres' company were one and the same, the Cartel began to operate under a government immunity. Gacha and Torres began to operate with carte blanche from the Colombian government.

The result was again made clear. Even with a treaty in effect, because of Torres' immunity status he could not be touched even after he had long resigned from office. No one in Colombia or the United States could touch him without directly violating the Colombian Constitution. The second battle between the law and the Cartel was again won by the Cartel.

As Torres travelled around the country accusing the Minister of Justice of becoming an American puppet, Gonzalo Rodriguez Gacha modernized the Cocaine Cartel. State of the art computers kept track of all business dealings and kept an up-to-date log on everything that was vital to the Cartel, from hit lists, DEA agents, politicians, attorneys, banks, to assassins for hire. Gacha had also set up a long range navigational and communications system in Choco province, which borders Panama. The long range navigational system would allow the Cartel to direct their own aircraft into the United States and evade the American authorities.

In Washington D.C. John Morgan had spent all morning at the United States Capitol. He had just shown to certain United States senators for the Intelligence Committee, incontrovertible evidence that high Bahamian officials were allowing the Cocaine Cartel to smuggle drugs into the United States. He showed that the island being used was Norman's Cay. Some of the senators gasped when they heard the name.

Norman's Cay had been a favorite international yacht club for the rich and famous. It closed when it was sold to a private corporation, whose board of directors could not be divulged because of the Bahamian banking secrecy laws. However, after intense surveillance on the island, the DEA had evidence that the owner was none other than Francisco Torres of Medellin.

During the next several months under intense American pressure, the lease on Norman's Cay was canceled by the Bahamian government. Gonzalo Rodriguez Gacha, however, had been watching the signposts all along the way and was able to see the storm coming. Before Norman's Cay closed down, Gacha had shifted the main distribution point to Mexico. The route turned out to be easier than through the Bahamas. The success of the route earned Gacha the nickname of the Mexican.

_____*The Drug Lord*_____

John Morgan was beside himself. Every time he made
a positive step towards Gacha and Torres, they had foreseen it
and kept a step ahead of him, sometimes two. He had tried
everything, better agents, planes, tighter cases in court and
still Gacha and Torres smuggled even more coke into the
country. How? The Cartel wasn't just lucky. Luck didn't last a
decade. No, they were realists. They planned for every possible
contingency before it happened. They knew their weak spots
better than anyone else, and they didn't have many.

Morgan pounded his fist against his desk, looking at
ten years' work, trying to figure out where was the weak spot
to Gacha and Torres. He couldn't find one, they were
invincible, they were better protected than the highest general
in the Pentagon; The Cartel had better security measures than
the President of The United States. Good God, there had to be
something he could do!

He looked over the major laboratory bust, the DEA's
greatest victory and how close they had come to closing them
down. So why hadn't they? What had stopped the momentum?

The death of Carlos Fuentes.

Suddenly Morgan realized what Gacha and Torres most
feared. Extradition. If you extradited the traffickers, the
cocaine supply would drop dramatically. The only problem was
that Francisco Torres had become un-extraditable. The only
way to extradite Gacha and Torres was for Colombia to allow
them to extradite them. It would have to be a Colombian
initiative, since it would mean a repeal of the immunity law
against senators which many would be against. Not only would
legitimate senators be against it, but Colombians were getting
tired of having to pay in blood for what they considered to be
an American problem. It was the Americans who consumed the
drugs. Only Americans, after all, were the one's creating a
demand for cocaine.

Morgan knew that the Colombian President did not
consider drugs to be a major problem for Colombians, and
therefore, the cocaine problem was not on his agenda. The
Colombian President was besieged by many more problems

such as poverty, inflation and a fierce guerrilla war that was heating up with each passing year. The only person in Colombia who understood what Gacha and Torres were doing to Colombia was Álvaro Para Reyes, the Minister of Justice.

Para Reyes had become powerful. He had allied himself with the Colombian newspapers who were strongly against the Cartel. However, they were only a small group who understood what the Cartel meant. The problem was too complex for a Colombian or an American for that matter. The average person could not assimilate facts such as international banking sandwiches, inflation, corruption, murder, precursors, treaties, navigational treaties and the whole range of laws that intertwined and created civilized society. And this had to be understood in minute detail in order to be able to present it to a jury.

Everyone knew what drugs did to the body, but nobody understood how they undermined the financial world and decayed society. What Colombia needed was a movement against drugs, a groundswell of support that would alter the people's views on the Cartel. And there was as much chance of that happening as Gacha or Torres had of dying from a major heart attack.

The way to begin a groundswell would mean exposing Gacha or Torres. The problem was that the evidence against Gacha was almost non-existent and Torres, well, they had a lot of it but were unable to touch him. The way to bring Torres to justice would mean reversing a Colombian law that would cut off his immunity. The only way to do that meant Álvaro Para Reyes, the Minister of Justice of Colombia would have to do the job. He would have to get the people behind the idea of repealing the immunity law. It was up to Para Reyes. If he did not come through, the Cartel would go unchecked forever.

May God protect Para Reyes, Morgan thought. He's going to need all the help he can get.

PART FOUR

(1981-1986)

FAREWELL TO THE KING

*"...The road lies long and straight
and dusty to the grave."
---Robert Louis Stevenson.*

_____*Peter A. Neissa*_____

CHAPTER TWENTY-FOUR

The attack on the Cocaine Cartel began when the first newspaper hit the street on a cold and rainy Monday morning. In a front page exposé, Francisco Torres' dealings with cocaine, murder, bribery and the Bahamian distribution network were printed for all to read.

The public and governmental outcry forced Gacha and Torres to keep an extremely low profile. When the papers did not cease their front page attacks even months after they had gone underground, Torres was forced to resign from the Office of Congressman.

In Gonzalo Rodriguez Gacha's estate north of Bogota, Gacha and Torres sat solemnly trying to figure a way to end the pressure within Colombia. Everywhere they went, a joke was made about them and worst of all was that they could not travel freely anymore to other countries. The other countries would have them arrested except for Brazil, Cuba and Panama.

"We have to end it, Gacha," Torres said, nodding his head as if the decision were final. The man seemed to have aged ten years in the last six months.

"I know," Gacha said as he stood up from the chair. They had been sitting in the living room for the last hour. "The problem is that no matter what we try, Para Reyes is right behind us. How the hell does he know so much? And that goddamn American Ambassador, he's coming up with little words like *narcoguerrillas*. The idiot, doesn't he know that we have never controlled the M-19?"

"I'm worried, Gacha. There is talk about revoking my immunity."

"Can they do that?" Gacha asked alarmed.

"Yes, the Congress can. It looks very possible too, especially if the papers keep up the pressure. The only way to stop them now is to kill them."

"Damn! Once we kill there is no going back, you know that?"

"I know," Torres said in an almost whisper. "You know, I think it's time we talk about getting rid of the Minister of Justice."

"No, not yet. We will wait a while. Let's take out a few of his major supporters first."

"Like who?" Torres asked.

"Who's the person who owns the newspaper, the one who made the first exposé? the one who has printed something about us every day of the week."

"Yeah, I know which paper you mean," Torres said with anger as he remembered the first exposé.

"Except let's make it look like the M-19 and the FARC did it and I suggest we stay out of town. Let's go to Brazil or something while the contractors take care of business."

Torres nodded and said, "Yes, it sounds like a reasonable thing to do. It makes sense and while we are at it why not start up another round of threats. That should cool the fires of the righteous. The outcry is going to be massive at first, but people will get the message in the long run, eh?"

Gacha nodded and they laughed. They retired to the dining room where they ate a meal. After dinner they had brandies and walked into a library to smoke Havana cigars.

"She's a looker, that woman of yours, Gonzalo," said Torres as he lighted his cigar.

"Yes," said Gacha with a smile. "Her name is Cindy Goldman."

"*Yanqui?*"

"Yes, met her at a party about ten years ago. Her father was the one who set up my laundering system. He was a good man, she's quite upset right now, you know? She gets upset when I don't let her sit in these meetings. She said and I quote, 'I'm not a second-class citizen'."

"Yeah? She said that?" Gacha nodded. "Crazy, these American women are something, eh? How the men get anything done up there is beyond me."

They laughed again.

"Listen, Francisco, you're welcome to stay, you know there is enough room. I have been neglecting Cindy these past few days, so I am going to retire to bed or there will be hell to pay."

"Thanks a lot for the offer, but I'm going to go back to Medellin tonight. Why don't we say three days as a date for leaving?"

"Good, I'll see you in Rio in three days. Good night, Francisco," Gacha said and shook his hand.

When Gacha reached the master bedroom, Cindy was on the master bed wearing a satin teddy. Although the outfit looked erotic she didn't, her face was drained of color as if she had seen the devil himself.

"What's the matter" Gonzalo asked Cindy, as he stripped off his own clothes.

"Nothing," Cindy answered with a pout, trying to hide her nervousness as best she could. She had just heard Gacha and Torres' entire conversation. They conversed about a killing spree that they would handle as if they were executives in a large corporation laying off workers. Killing was just a business decision, nothing personal.

"Oh come on, you're not mad, eh?" Gacha asked slipping into bed.

"Maybe," Cindy answered, wondering if her nervousness were really visible.

Gacha smiled and reached for her breasts. He slipped the satin teddy off Cindy and let his mouth roam over her white creamy flesh. Although she was not as beautiful as Ana-Alicia, Cindy's allure rested on the alabaster colored skin, the flaming golden hair and the tall well shaped body.

Cindy stifled her repulsion of Gacha, biting her lower lip every time he thrust deep inside her. She would bring the bastard down from the high horse he rode, she alone would

301

bring the man right down to the hot seat at the Florida State Penitentiary. She would avenge her brother's death, a death that had been without dignity. Gacha's coke had been responsible, it was his business that was killing teenagers by the thousands every year. Yes, she would bring him down.

The highway to Medellin was dark as the Mercedes-Benz Torres was in made its way out of Bogota, towards Medellin. They were driving the outer suburbs of Bogota, the ones that ringed the city. These suburbs were the slums and hovels that contained most of the poor of Colombia.

As the highway turned around a bend, the chauffeur driving the Mercedes had to slam on his brakes to avoid colliding with another car. There was a car wreck blocking the highway. It was a bad one, Torres thought. A man was hanging through the front windshield of one of the cars. A few feet ahead of the car wreck by the side of the road, there was a woman and she looked alive.

"Stop!" Torres ordered the chauffeur.

The chauffeur pulled the Mercedes off to the side of the road and parked it. Torres jumped out of the car and ran towards the woman as his driver ran towards the man hanging out of the windshield.

Then the dead awoke.

The man hanging out of the windshield brought up his hand which held a pistol with a grotesque and bulbous silencer. He shot the chauffeur through the head with the first shot. The woman by the side of the road sat up and put the barrel of the gun she held in her hand to Torres' head. Two men ran out of the bushes by the side of the road and knocked Francisco Torres out.

Two tow trucks appeared and hitched up the two small cars and towed them away. Torres was put in the back seat of his Mercedes and then driven to Bogota's El Dorado International Airport. At the airport he was moved into a military transport plane and flown out of Colombia.

Three hours and fifty-five minutes later, the military

transport arrived in Miami, Florida. A few minutes before five in the morning he was booked on 217 counts of murder, drug trafficking, failure to declare taxes, arms trafficking, kidnapping, blackmail, extortion and bribery. The law had indeed caught up with Francisco Torres.

Gacha came awake from a deep sleep, the pounding and the shouting making their way through the fog. What was the matter with him?

"What?" Gacha shouted, but the words came out slurred. Was he dreaming?

Suddenly he felt himself being picked up and carried. Ice-cold fingers seemed to rake his body and then the fog started to clear. A flash of pain seared through his brain. He could see Herman, why was he holding him under the shower? Then Gacha knew, something had gone terribly wrong, another assassination attempt?

"*Jefe*, can you hear me?" said Herman.

"Yes," Gacha replied as if his voice were traveling a long distance. "What's happening?"

"The Americans got Don Francisco," said Herman, as he picked Gacha up and put him over his shoulders when he realized his boss would be unable to walk towards the waiting helicopter. Herman then began descending the staircase of the mansion moving with speed and dexterity. They moved outside onto the grounds.

Gonzalo Rodriguez Gacha's private helicopter had its rotor blades moving already, kicking up gusts of wind.

"I need clothes!" Gacha shouted. "I'm freezing to death!"

"They are already inside the helicopter," Herman answered back loudly so he could be heard.

Gacha was thrown into the rear seat of his helicopter still naked. Herman climbed in after him and the helicopter took to the air even before the hatch had closed.

Once the helicopter leveled out, it made its way over the mountains and flew south towards the Amazon rain forest. Gonzalo then dressed with the clothes that the pilot had managed to get for him before their hasty departure from the estate. It was madness!

"Tell me what happened?" Gacha said as he began to dress himself.

"Don Francisco fell into a trap on the way to Medellin. A contingent of F-2 police shot his *pistolero* and arrested Don Francisco. They drove him to the airport where he was put aboard a U.S. military transport and taken to America. He was arraigned in Miami. He's looking at the electric chair."

"Shit!"

"There is no way to get him out," said Herman. "The *yanquis* have him good."

"Who fixed the papers in Colombia?"

"Para Reyes, the Minister of Justice."

Gacha's face contorted in anger. He had played his hand too diplomatically with Para Reyes, he thought. What he should have done was put him in his grave last year. "Where are we going?" Gacha asked

"Our hideout in the rain forest."

"Good," Gacha said and turned silent as he began to think. Suddenly he blurted out. "What happened to me back at the house?"

"Sleeping gas," said Herman.

"Sleeping gas...My God, where's Cindy?"

"She left the compound at three in the morning. We thought it was okay. I'm sorry, *jefe*, I didn't think there was anything wrong with it."

"The bitch! That bitch was in on it! That is how they knew so much! The bitch!" Gacha couldn't stop from cursing, his face was so red with anger that blood vessels were popping out.

Herman didn't say anything; he simply kept his eyes looking out of the helicopter as they cleared the last mountain range on their way to the Amazon rain forest.

Gacha leaned over and whispered in Herman's ear, "Kill her. I want her dead before the end of the day and make sure she knows that I know she did it." Herman nodded.

The ambassador looked into the car in the American Embassy. "You've done something wonderful, a marvelous job. My God! Cindy, you are the first person to bring in a drug lord.

Cindy tried to smile but she couldn't, she was still shaking. All she wanted to do was to climb aboard the plane that would fly her away from the lion's den.

"It's going to be okay," said the ambassador reassuringly. "You're protected. There will be two police cars in front of you and two behind you. Juan, your driver, is a weapons expert, isn't that so, Juan?"

Juan turned around in the drivers seat. "Yes, I will get you to the airport with no problems. You just calm yourself. Juan will take care of you like a baby." Juan had an accent. He was a Colombian.

Cindy smiled and said, "Thank you." The ambassador nodded and shut the door.

Juan waved at the ambassador and the convoy began to roll out of the embassy. Within a few minutes the convoy was on the southern road to the airport and moving swiftly.

Cindy could see the jets taking off in the distance, the knowledge of an airport close by calmed her down. She was actually getting out of here, she thought. The convoy then took a sudden right where a sign said *Parque La Florida*.

"This is not the way to the airport!" Cindy shouted in alarm.

"This goes around the airport. We are going in the back way. No passport control, you know, to avoid hit men in the terminal. You see!" Juan pointed as they drove parallel to the main airport's runway.

"Yes," said Cindy, "I'm just jumpy as hell."

The police cars then suddenly pulled off by the side of the road and Juan pulled off as well.

"Why the hell are we stopping?" Cindy's voice again a river of panic.

"We are meeting a service truck that will take you to the plane." A big yellow truck came down the road and pulled up beside them. "You see, here it is. Let's go!"

Juan got out of the car and opened Cindy's door. They walked towards the back of the truck as the police opened up the truck's cargo doors.

"Climb up," Juan said. Cindy was too nervous to climb up, so two officers gave her a boost. "Thank you, gentlemen," she said with half a smile.

"I have a message for you lady," Juan said, as he retrieved a gun from his coat. "It's from Gonzalo Rodriguez Gacha. He says that you are nothing more than a whore for the U.S. Government."

Cindy gasped.

"Yes," Juan smiled. "We all work for Gacha, you naïve woman. He pays us two hundred thousand dollars a year while the government only pays us eight hundred dollars a year. Now I ask you, who in his right mind is going to risk his life every day and the ones of his family for fifteen dollars a week?"

"Oh, God, No!...Please!" Cindy cried, her voice cracking with every syllable.

Juan shrugged. "It's the way it is down here in Colombia. You ever read Wu Ch'i?" Cindy shook her head. "He said that the field of battle is a land of standing corpses; those determined to die will live; those who hope to escape with their lives will die. Why did you do it, bitch?"

"Gacha killed my brother," Cindy said standing up straight inside the truck.

"Ah, revenge!" Juan said nodding his head. "There is a Sicilian proverb that says revenge is a season in hell."

"I'm partial to Francis Bacon. He said that revenge was a kind of wild justice."

Juan smiled and said "So be it." Juan raised his weapon and shot her through the head.

Cindy Goldman's body arrived in Miami International Airport in the cargo section of a 707 jetliner. Attached to the body was a note addressed to John Morgan, DEA. The note was pinned to her chest with staples under the horrific

Medellin necktie. The note simply said: *Venganza!* Vengeance.

The United States Ambassador's wife fainted when she heard the news. Their own staff had pulled off a murder of one of their own! When the Ambassador's wife came to, she went into a hysterical fit. "Fuck this country, fuck'em all, fuck the President on down, we stay here much longer and we'll be dead soon enough. How long? Goddam it, answer me Mr. Ambassador? How long before that son-of-a-bitch Gacha puts a bullet in one of us or our children, uh? Fuck'em! Let's get out of here!"

The embassy doctor put a syringe into the arm of the ambassador's wife. "A sedative," he said as he did it. "She should sleep until noon tomorrow."

The ambassador hadn't heard the doctor; his wife was right. How long before he was targeted or had he been targeted already? He feared for the lives of his family. Gacha was not going to give up. Blood, madness and murder were coming to Colombia on a grand scale.

Two days later during the middle of the night, a group of twelve men assembled at Gonzalo Rodriguez Gacha's hold out. They were all on the DEA's list for extradition to the United States. A man in his early thirties, however, was speaking about the extradition treaty when Gacha walked in.

"The Supreme Court will not be looking at the legality of the extradition treaty this year," said the young man.

"No." Gacha cut in. "Francisco and I tried everything and the only thing left is blood. I have targeted several different people. Two of them are newspaper men, one is a Supreme Court Judge, one is an Assistant Attorney General, one is a General of the Police, one Governor and lastly...Álvaro Para Reyes, the Minister of Justice. Along with these killings, we make a series of bombings of newspaper buildings, government buildings and cars belonging to the really important families. Every time a job is carried out, we will send in a communiqué to a radio station claiming responsibility. We will call ourselves The *Extraditables*. It's

307

time to get tough."

The men looked at each other and nodded.

The first bomb exploded inside the Mercedes-Benz belonging to the Minister of Mines and Petroleum. Although the Minister was not in the car at the time the explosion took place, there were, however, several children playing street hockey nearby- they were all burned by the killed by the flying debris.

The communiqué was read over the National Radio. "We find the actions of extraditing Colombian citizens to the United States contrary to the civil laws of Colombia. We have therefore instituted action until said treaty is revoked. The *Extraditables*."

Two days later, the publisher of the third largest daily in the country, an active supporter of the extradition treaty, was shot as he was leaving his downtown office. Two days following the shooting of the publisher, the governor for a northern province of Colombia was ambushed as he returned home from work.

The Colombian government retaliated by extraditing three more suspected drug traffickers setting off a wave of bombings not seen in Colombia since the time of *La Violencia*.

When the death toll had reached four hundred people a week, a huge outcry from the citizens of Colombia erupted. The chant that had been taken up was the exact opposite of what government had expected. "Why are we fighting and dying for an American problem? Why doesn't America cut its demand for cocaine? Why are we paying the price? Why doesn't the United States give us the money to fight the Drug Lords?"

The government had no answer for the people. For the first time, Americans were appraised of the facts. To fight the Drug Lords, one needed a lot of capital and the United States was sending pittance. The momentum was beginning to change in favor of the Cartel once again.

On a Monday morning, a Colombian Judge looked at the extradition treaty to make sure it was unbreakable, and, to his surprise, he saw that the treaty was not valid. Someone in the Department of External Relations had signed the treaty and not the President of the Country. The judge, conforming with the letter of the law, said that because the treaty was not signed by the President of Colombia, the treaty was not valid.

The shock-waves were immediate. America woke up to the fact that they could not ask Colombians to pay for a war whose major cause had been the American demand for cocaine. The Americans, instead of sending money, began to squabble about how much money they should send to fight the drug epidemic. Meanwhile, in Colombia, Gonzalo Rodriguez Gacha came out of hiding.

The Cocaine Cartel was back on its feet, again.

CHAPTER TWENTY-FIVE

The Medellin-Rioacha-Fort Lauderdale coca shuttle was back on course and on time. Things were running smoothly and all systems were green. At twenty million a week, the coca shuttle was breaking records. The United States worried about giving money to Colombia, and the Cartel worried about the coke for cash daily express. The Cartel was indeed back on track. Gonzalo Rodriguez Gacha was still master of all he surveyed, for he had won the third battle, perhaps the war.

The President of Colombia, after much pressure by the media and the United States government, signed the extradition treaty. However, the President announced that no more extraditions would take place.

In the midst of all the bloodshed, the accusations, the threats, the international pressures from the United States, Colombia had failed to notice the increasing activity of the M-19 and the FARC.

On November 6, 1985, the M-19 mounted a major offensive, taking by storm the Colombian Supreme Court. The guerrillas laid siege while the Court was in session debating by coincidence the validity of the Colombia-United States extradition treaty.

After a long, drawn out negotiation, the government was unable to persuade the guerrillas to release their hostages. The M-19 went on a killing spree by assassinating all the members of the Supreme Court and everyone else who happened to be in the building at the time. The army, left with no choice, stormed the building which had been set on fire. The M-19 did not surrender, and they were not taken alive.

Eight days after the bloody carnage, while the country was still mourning for its dead, *El Nevado del Ruiz*, the third highest snow capped peak in all of Colombia, a volcano that had been dormant for thousands of years, blew its top. Armero, the town of twenty thousand people twenty miles away from the volcano was wiped out of existence.

Suddenly the drug war became meaningless to Colombia. The United States was told that Colombia had more pressing matters than the drug epidemic the United States was undergoing.

Gonzalo Rodriguez Gacha, however, did not forget. While the country was pre-occupied with the multiple disasters, he quietly and systematically began to eliminate his enemies. In just a few months Gacha had done away with all of his enemies except one. Álvaro Para Reyes.

Para Reyes had not forgotten about Gacha. With the sympathy of the Colombian people, since the Colombian people realized he was a prime target for the M-19, he decided to capitalize on that empathy. It was with this realization and sympathy that he played his one sure master stroke, while at the same time signing his own death warrant. Indirectly, Para Reyes had connected the M-19 storming of the *Palacio de Justicia* to the Cocaine Cartel. However, the public reaction he expected to form in the wake of such news did not materialize. The public had had enough. Nobody believed the government could take a Drug Lord to court and survive scrutiny into its own ties with the Cartel. What made it worse for Para Reyes was that he knew the public was right. Álvaro Para Reyes for the fist time, began to question whether going after the Cartel was worth it.

Gonzalo Rodriguez Gacha, fearing a massive outcry from the public, made his first grave miscalculation. Gacha took out a contract on Álvaro Para Reyes, the Colombian Minister of Justice. The hiring of an assassin was a fatal error for Gacha.

For seven months the Minister of Justice's Mercedes came under the watchful eye of four men. The men knew the car's capability on a hill, on a flat straightaway and from a dead stop to full speed. The men knew that the Minister liked to drive fast and that the windows on the Mercedes were bullet proof. They saw that Para Reyes drove home by different routes each day. They also saw that Para Reyes left work a little early to avoid the rush hour traffic.

It was all quite methodical. For half a million dollars, a group of hit men would know a person to be killed better than they knew their own mother. Álvaro Para Reyes was no exception, the hit would be made.

On a hot, tranquil day Álvaro Para Reyes left work a little early. He had promised his wife that he would take her on a long vacation to the island of San Andres in the Caribbean Sea. He was happy as he drove down the two lane road. He looked into his rear view mirror and saw nothing unusual, just two teenagers on a motorcycle. He watched them pull up beside him. He didn't think much of them, just two kids running wild on a bike. He wanted to roll down the windows but he knew that they were sealed. He was sweating. It was a hot day, and the air-conditioner was not working in the car. Thank God he wasn't wearing that bullet proof vest the DEA gave him, he would've had a heat stroke by now. He looked out of the window again, the kids on the motorcycle were keeping up with him, even though he was almost doing eighty miles an hour. He accelerated and the motorcycle accelerated too.

Suddenly a dark foreboding dread came over Álvaro, and he looked out towards the kids again, just in time to see the spits of fire coming from the barrel of a gun.

The first bullet caught him in the thigh, the second bullet caught him in the kidney, causing him to veer the car sharply into a ditch where it came to a stop. The kids on the motorcycle pulled up beside the Mercedes and walked over to it. They opened the driver's door and fired a bullet into the Minister of Justice's brain. The kids then calmly walked back towards the motorcycle and rode off.

Fifty people in the surrounding neighborhood witnessed

313

the execution, but when the police arrived there was no one to be found. An execution had taken place in broad daylight and no witnesses had come forward. To come forward was madness. If the government couldn't stop a Minister of Justice from being killed, how could they count on the government to protect a witness?

The death of the Minister of Justice made the front page of every major newspaper in the free world. In the United States, the assassination was also the lead story in every news network. The American people finally would begin to see the terrible price the citizens of Colombia were paying for a drug problem that was primarily American.

In Colombia, a line had been crossed. The unwritten rules had been broken, and what Gacha most feared became reality. A groundswell of support took momentum among the people. The Cocaine Cartel had to be brought down at all costs. Congressional investigations were ordered, politicians talked in earnest of solutions, but, most important of all, the military began to hunt down Gonzalo Rodriguez Gacha.

Gonzalo Rodriguez Gacha was on the run.

The military raided homes, *haciendas*, suspected hideouts, combed the countryside and flew aircraft over the rain forest trying to find Gonzalo Rodriguez Gacha. They tried but came up with nothing.

In the DEA office in Bogota, which was located inside the United States Embassy and was just down the hall from the FBI and CIA office, a meeting took place. The Ambassador for the United States, twelve DEA agents, two FBI agents, a Colombian general and two high ranking cabinet members representing the President of Colombia met in the room. The meeting was about how to bring Gonzalo Rodriguez Gacha to justice.

In two hours they had gotten nowhere, all they had managed to talk about was hearsay and gossip. The men could recall a hundred tall stories to be spoken at bars and not at tactical meetings. It was useless, they thought to themselves.

Gonzalo Rodriguez Gacha had insulated and protected himself so well that there seemed to be no way to find his weak spot.

There was a light knock on the door.

"Come in," said the ambassador.

The door opened and a tall, handsome man with snowy white hair entered the room. The Ambassador and the DEA agents had no idea who he was and wondered how he had obtained access. The Colombians however, seemed to recognize him. The Colombians greeted the man like an old friend and the man did likewise.

"Excuse me," said the ambassador as he closed the door to the meeting room. "Who are you?"

The man with the snowy white hair smiled sardonically. "My name is Jim Harrison. I was the United States Cultural Attache in Colombia for twenty-three years." The Colombians guffawed. Harrison let out a chuckle himself.

"That's very nice, Mr. Harrison, we will look forward to hearing from you at dinner," said the ambassador. "I'm sure you will have some good stories to tell."

"Oh, save it, Mr. Ambassador," said Harrison.

"Mr. Harrison!" the ambassador said in outrage.

"Do you know a contract has been taken out on you, Mr. Ambassador?" Harrison asked as he took a seat.

The ambassador stood silent for a moment. "Well, I'm sure it's not the first time," he said with some bravado but he was rocked.

"No, I'm sure it isn't, but when the contract has been taken out by Gonzalo Rodriguez Gacha it usually means that you are not long for this world."

The ambassador went pale and reached out for his seat as his legs buckled under him. "How...how did you find out?" the ambassador mumbled.

"In Panama, a contact approached me and told me people were looking for a contractor. They said it was on behalf of Gonzalo Rodriguez Gacha."

"Good God!"

"After I left Colombia, I kept myself informed of the

315

going on here. You know, it was like keeping in touch with home. I went back to the States, yes, but it had changed to much. So I transferred to Panama. I spent my long weekends in Cartagena..."

"Sounds nice," said the ambassador expectantly, "but what does that have to do with you coming to Bogota? Don't get me wrong, we welcome people here, but you could have called and informed me of the news."

"True," said Harrison. "Except I was ordered here by my employers. They want me to help catch Gonzalo Rodriguez Gacha, they thought I could do it."

"Why is that?" The ambassador asked echoing the thoughts of all the DEA agents present.

"Mr. Ambassador, I have known Gonzalo Rodriguez Gacha since he was eight years old. I saw him go from *gamín* to King of Bogota. I don't think he's ever seen the inside of a classroom, and yet he is an incredibly intelligent man. When we think of future plans, we usually think of what is ahead for us in a month; Gacha has thought in terms of decades. Everything he does he has calculated and tested in fifteen different ways. He will kill anyone, and I mean anyone, who stands in his way. He'd kill you and me with the same amount of indifference he would use to crush a bug.

"Gonzalo Rodriguez Gacha's mind is warped, it's out of whack. He's brilliant, he can mix with people and make them feel comfortable around him. He could make the Pope believe he was incapable of murder. He has a high degree of intelligence and an ability to kill second to none. Gonzalo Rodriguez Gacha is a genius psychopath, but he is just as bad as any Nazi that hunted down Jews."

"So, how do you propose to catch him and bring him to justice, Mr. Harrison?" the ambassador asked, clasping his hands as if he were in prayer.

Harrison laughed. "Oh, I don't propose such nonsense. We will never take Gacha, he will put a bullet in his brain first, and if we do catch him by some miracle he would be killed off quite promptly."

316

"Who would do such a thing?" asked the ambassador in outrage.

"My employers for one; hell, I think everyone in this room. The fact is the government cannot survive the rigors of a trial. I think Álvaro Para Reyes knew that a little too late, but I still believed he figured it out."

"Good God! Mr. Harrison, you're talking about government's condoning · assassination. State sanctioned murder!" the ambassador shouted as he shook his head.

"No. These drug lords are beyond our system of justice. We need a different standard of justice to deal with this kind of crime."

"I won't do it. I will not be a part of it."

"Then Mr. Ambassador, your usefulness here has ceased. The contract on you and your family is still out there. I suggest you pack up and leave Colombia."

"How dare you speak to me that way! I have been the toughest ambassador on drugs from the United States. I'll have the President know about this...this murder!" The ambassador stood up.

"Mr. Ambassador," said Harrison calmly. "People are dying at the rate of four hundred people a week here in Colombia, how many more in the States? In two years Colombia will have as many dead as the United States suffered during the entire Vietnam War. This is a war, Mr. Ambassador, the sooner you realize it the better off you will be. Colombia is turning into a land of dead people and the United States is not far behind. War, Mr. Ambassador, and people die in wars."

The ambassador shook his head and stormed out of the meeting room. No one else did. After a few moments of silence the Colombian general spoke.

"How do you propose to find him?" the general asked.

"By flushing him out," said Harrison.

"How?" asked a DEA agent.

"With the help of the one person he loves in this world, Ana-Alicia Gonzáles."

"Impossible!" said the cabinet member. "What does she have to do with this?"

"What I say will forever remain among us. If it got out, it would destroy one of the most important families in Colombia. Do I have everyone's word?" Harrison asked looking at everyone.

"Yes," came back a chorus of voices.

"I have long had a suspicion of something related to our friend Gacha, but at the time I just jotted it down to the craziness of the young," said Harrison.

"Come on, what is it?" said the general with impatience.

"Gonzalo Rodriguez Gacha and Ana-Alicia Gonzáles were lovers."

"I have heard worse," said a cabinet member.

"So have I, but I didn't think much of it until Gacha rescued Ana-Alicia's child, remember?" The men in the room nodded. "Well, my employers investigated some people and came up with a crucial fact."

"*Oh? Dios mío*, what could that be?" asked the general.

"Ana-Alicia's husband is sterile," said Harrison spreading his hands with a huge grin on his face.

Some men frowned in confusion, while others reacted by gasping.

"Will someone please clue us in?" asked one of the DEA agents.

"Simple," said the Colombian general. "Ana-Alicia's son is Gonzalo Rodriguez Gacha's son."

A silence fell in the room.

"What if she says no to helping us?" asked a cabinet member.

"She will help," Harrison said. "We will give her an option she doesn't have."

The servant brought him a soft drink that was at room temperature. The temperature was ninety-two degrees Fahrenheit. To drink anything colder would cause the stomach to cramp. Gonzalo Rodriguez Gacha knew this, as he sat back in a bamboo chair in his rain forest hideout.

"Don Gonzalo?" said the servant.

"Yes?" Gacha asked without opening his eyes.

"There is a call for you on the short wave radio."

Gacha opened his eyes and said, "Who is it?"

"Don Ernesto," said the servant. The sound of thunder rolled above the jungle canopy.

Gacha walked back into the house he had constructed in 1981, when he had been forced into hiding for the first time. The house itself was made of cement. There was no plumbing in the house, so bottled water was shipped in daily for showering and drinking. Inside the house however, existed every modern convenience. Electricity was supplied by a twenty-year-old, six hundred horsepower diesel engine. Television was made possible by satellite dish, and fans were interspaced around the house to keep a nice breeze blowing throughout.

The short-wave ham radio was located in the dining room. The radio rested on the dining table. Gacha picked up the microphone to the radio and spoke into it. "Hello, over?"

"Gonzalo, it's Ernesto, can you hear me? Over."

"Yes, what's wrong? Over."

"They've got Ana-Alicia. Over."

A rage filled Gonzalo Rodriguez Gacha like he had never known. He could actually feel the blood streaming into his face, the result of tiny blood vessels exploding under pressure. "How much do they want? Over."

"It's not the M-19, it's the Americans. She's under arrest at the F-2 precinct in downtown Bogota. She's being charged under complicity. It looks bad for her. Over."

"But she doesn't know anything! Over." Gacha was beside himself.

"She knew what you did, that seems to be enough. They also got Margarita, but Mario García asked for a deal and he's spilling his beans for freedom. Over."

Gacha picked up the radio and was about to smash it

319

against the wall but changed his mind at the last moment. What have I done? I never involved her in any of it for this single reason. My God, what have I done. She cannot go to jail because of me! "Thank you, Ernesto. Over and out." Gacha disconnected the line and then did something totally unexpected. He called the F-2 headquarters.

A voice answered on the other end of Gacha's long distance communication. It was a voice that Gacha recognized immediately, it was the voice of General Santander.

"What do you want for her release?" Gacha asked plainly.

The general who had been sitting in his office had been taken by surprise. Suddenly he stood up and began snapping his fingers in all directions and ordering people around the room to intercept the call. Jim Harrison who had been standing beside the general picked up another line to listen in.

"You know what we want, we want you to turn yourself in," said the general.

Gacha chuckled. "You mean kill myself?" The general didn't reply. "You are a shrewd man, General, but I still don't want to die. Why can't we come to an equitable arrangement, let's say a million dollars?"

The general laughed and said, "Don't insult me, Gacha."

"Fifty million?" Gacha came back smoothly.

"No."

"One hundred million?"

"No!"

"One billion dollars that is absolutely clean and untraceable."

"No, not for all the money in the world and especially your money, Gacha."

"Damn it! How can you send her to rot in jail in the United States? What the hell do the *yanquis* have on her?"

"Nothing," said the general, amusement in his voice.

"*Mierda*, you know that every American that comes to Colombia has an angle. So, what is it?" Gacha asked, with a note of desperation in his voice.

"I don't know, I just follow orders Gacha. Here, I'll let you talk to the American in charge."

"Hello, Gacha," said Harrison. There was no response from Gacha. "I'm sorry Gacha, but she was a target and the U.S. capitalized on it. Business, you know? It's just a shame about the kid, but she will be out, oh say, in 2008. Of course she wont be the same, you know what goes on inside women's prisons. She will be a favorite for the dikes with her looks..."

"Can I talk to her?" Gacha asked softly.

"I don't think so; I'm not in charge you know? But I'll see what I can do, hold on?" Harrison put the phone down gently and walked out of the generals office. He walked to the adjacent room where Ana-Alicia was sitting in tears.

"You are on Ana-Alicia, " Harrison said as he entered the room. "Remember, you have to sound desperate. First tell him that your family won't help you and then see what he says. If he won't come in, you know what to do. Good luck."

Ana-Alicia stood up and walked next door. Harrison walked behind her as another man stood up from the corner of the room shaking his head.

"You bastards didn't tell her that you were not going to arrest him, did you?" Ernesto Bosco asked Harrison.

"No," said Harrison, "but we all lose a little more innocence with each passing day, don't we?"

"'The blood-dimmed tide is loosed and everywhere, the ceremony of innocence is drowned.'"

Harrison raised an eyebrow and said, "I would have never believed you read poetry Ernesto, especially William Butler Yeats. I prefer Theodore Roethke, 'I learn by going where I have to go.'"

"Gonzalo?" Ana-Alicia asked, her voice trembling.

"Yes," answered Gacha. "I'm sorry Ana-Alicia, I never thought it would end like this."

"Gonzalo, they want to put me in jail! I'll kill myself first, Gonzalo!"

"Don't worry, you won't see any time in jail, your family will get you great attorneys," Gacha said smoothly.

"Gonzalo!" Ana-Alicia shouted. "They have disowned me. They say I have disgraced the family."

"But you haven't done anything!"

"Gonzalo, it's not that I am involved with...with a drug lord," Ana-Alicia said, knowing the effect the words would have on him.

The words cut through Gacha like an ice-cold knife. Gacha's heart thumped wildly inside his chest, his mouth dry. Did he know what was coming? Gacha asked himself. Yes, he did.

"What is it then?" Gacha asked, his voice cracking.

"My God, Gonzalo, how can you be so blind!" Ana-Alicia shouted. "My son Antonio is your son too!"

"No..."

"Gonzalo, I cannot leave him. He is all that I have left," Ana-Alicia broke down into tears.

"It's okay, put Harrison on the phone."

Ana-Alicia handed the phone over to Harrison.

"Hello?" said Harrison.

"You know what you are asking of me?" Gacha asked.

"Yes, I do," Harrison said his voice as neutral as ever.

"The problem will not end with me, you know that don't you?" Gacha asked, life draining out of him.

"I don't know."

"I was a *gamín* when I first met you, Harrison, remember?"

"I remember, what of it?"

Gacha let out a small laugh. "Why do you think I became King of Bogota? Because I had a thousand opportunities in life? It was the only way to get myself out of the dirt, starving and poor condition I was in." Gacha paused to reflect on what he had just said and then added, "You know, when I made a lot of money people still wouldn't accept me. There is no way to win no matter what people like me try to do unless we play by our own rules or change the ones we are

forced to live under. I don't mean laws of right and wrong but
social laws, you know what I'm saying?"

"Yes," said Harrison. Unfortunately he did.

"The oligarchy, the whole social class structure of it.
When I was a *gamín*, Harrison, there were thirty thousand of
us. Now, Bogota alone must have a half a million. And you
know what, Harrison?"

"What's that?" Harrison asked.

"Each one of those *gamines* is gunning for my job.
They've got nothing to lose by not trying to become the next
King of Bogota." Gacha let a silence fall between them for a
moment then said, "Where do you want me?"

"Fly into the El Dorado International Airport. Before
you land the control tower will tell you where to go from there.
You will have a certain time limit to get there, if you
don't...you know what's waiting for Ana-Alicia."

"I understand," Gacha said and hung up.

The helicopter Gacha travelled in was directed by the
El Dorado Control Tower to the *Autódromo Internacional*
racecar course. The *autódromo* was no longer in use and had
been abandoned several years before. The grandstands for the
viewing public enclosed a vast inner field that was overgrown
with grass. The grass area could accommodate a hundred
helicopters, but for now it only needed to accommodate one.

Gonzalo's helicopter circled the racetrack three times.
It was getting late and the sun was not far off from setting.
From his seat, Gacha could see Harrison, General Santander,
Ernesto Bosco, twelve uniformed police officers, four DEA
agents wearing their dark blue windbreakers with the yellow
DEA logo on the back and a police van was on the race track.

Ana-Alicia stood alone twenty feet in front of them all,
her long hair waving in the wind. She wore a white blouse and
blue jeans, and to Gacha she still looked beautiful.

The helicopter touched the ground. The pilot turned off
the engine and the rotor noise diminished immediately. Gacha
sat in his seat looking at everyone, not only those he could see

with his eyes, but his mind's eye now paraded a number of people he had long since forgotten about. Rodrigo Vargas, Carlos Fuentes, Álvaro Para Reyes, Margarita Coro, Don Emilio Gonzáles, Don Eusebio Corraza, Curtis Mathews, Mario García, Chulo, Francisco Torres, Harry Fosse... How many more had crossed his path during his lifetime?

Gacha's mind suddenly snapped back and he looked outside. He saw Jim Harrison, the man who had inadvertently locked him into the course he had taken at an early age. Ernesto Bosco, was he a friend, enemy or betrayer? And then there was Ana-Alicia. It had always been Ana-Alicia. Did she know what she had asked of him? Maybe; it didn't matter anymore.

Gonzalo opened the helicopter hatch and stepped out and stood on firm ground. He straightened his silk suit and positioned his tie to its correct angle, took a deep breath and walked towards the crowd.

It happened when Gacha was halfway between the helicopter and the lawmen. A single clear rifle shot broke the silence. Gonzalo's legs wobbled and he fell to his knees on the long grass of the park. He looked up to see Harrison, Bosco and Ana-Alicia, and he smiled. It was the smile of the knowing. He always knew that the other members of the Cartel would someday kill him if he ever put them into jeopardy.

Ana-Alicia screamed and ran to him. When she reached Gonzalo, a small trickle of blood was making its way out of his mouth.

"Oh, Gonzalo! My God! I'm sorry...Oh *querido*, forgive me, I did not know," Ana-Alicia cried out, her tears beginning to roll down her cheeks.

"I know," Gonzalo said in a whisper and then chuckled. "Remember what you told me long ago?" Ana-Alicia nodded her head, tears streaming down her face and onto his face as she cradled his head on her lap. "You said that we were doomed and I said... I know, and still I love you..." Gonzalo winced in pain.

"Oh Gonzalo, I love you so. Oh, tell me why should it

324

have been like this?"

"My love..." Gonzalo whispered before he died.

Ana-Alicia cradled Gonzalo's head on her lap, as the sun set leaving a cool wind behind.

THE END

Printed in the United States
99693LV00001B/1/A